DOUBLE
SHARE

ISBN-10: 1-940575-036
ISBN-13: 978-1-940575-03-2

Second Edition: October, 2014

For more information or to leave a comment about this book,
please visit us on the web at:
www.solarclipper.com

Publishers Note:

To my father, Earle P. Lowell

He taught me a lot.
I hope I remember all the lessons when I need them.

Thanks, Dad.

The Golden Age of the Solar Clipper

Quarter Share
Half Share
Full Share
Double Share
Captains Share
Owners Share

South Coast
Cape Grace*

Tanyth Fairport Adventures

Ravenwood
Zypherias Call
The Hermit Of Lammas Wood

* Forthcoming

Table of Contents

DOUBLE SHARE

NATHAN LOWELL

Durandus

Chapter One
Port Newmar: 2358-May-22

Whether I shall turn out to be the hero of my own life, or whether that station will be held by anybody else, these pages must show. Funny the stuff that pops into my head sometimes. I stood on the observation deck of the shuttle port, salt wind in my face, and shiny third mate pips on a uniform so fresh the starch in the label scratched the back of my neck. I still had a bit of a muddled head from the celebration following graduation, and this weird line from some century long past popped into my brain. That's what comes from having an ancient lit professor for a mother.

Nellie, the academy's cruising yawl, swung to her anchor with a flutter of luffing sails and came to rest in the bay on the far side of the tarmac. When I'd first come to Port Newmar, I didn't understand why we had to learn to sail on water. A season or two in the relatively forgiving waters of the outer sound—learning how to take and give orders—had made the reasons abundantly clear. The distance was too great to make out the sound, but I'd been out there often enough to know the routine. My memory heard the commands shouted against the wind and water. I watched the tiny figures of the next crop of cadets man the sheets. They took up the slack on the clews as the great sails dropped to the deck.

High above, a shuttle craft ripped across the pale-gray sky, lining up with the runway, engines shrieking in a dopplered wail as it came in low and fast across the water. While I'd gotten used to the sound of shuttles during my time at the academy, this one was special— the transport which would start the long journey to my first real officer's billet as third mate. I was headed to the home office of Diurnia Salvage and Transport for assignment to one of their fleet. Not a terribly glamorous berth, but it was a start. I knew only

1

too well that some of my classmates were still scrambling to find a posting. The few like me, without family ties in the industry, found the scrambling to be quite difficult. I suspected that without the commandant's intervention, I might well be in a similar position.

"There but for the grace. . ." I mumbled.

As the shuttle made its final bank over the water and began its short run into the landing strip, I turned for one last look at the campus that had been my home for four long years. The manicured lawns looked a bit greener than those I'd grown up with on Neris and the trees still didn't look quite right. They seemed too squat to be called trees. The classroom and office buildings hugged the landscape, most only a single story, as if officers in training to work in the Deep Dark needed a literal grounding to help them remember they came from planets. The exception, Hutchins Gym, loomed on the far side of the campus.

Thinking back over my time there, from those initial tentative days, to the shock of my first set of final exams, and the exuberance of my maiden summer cruise, I smiled. We stood fire watches and did a lot of what looked like just "playing soldier," but it forced us to come to grips with the reality of command. I don't think any of us understood that, even on graduation. I didn't. But the seeds had been sown and under the right conditions they would grow. Between the books, the studying, the physical drills, and the summer cruises, it had been a tornado of experiences.

I'd come to the academy with three of my shipmates from the *Lois McKendrick*—Philip "Pip" Carstairs, Brilliantine Smith, and Beverly Arith.

Of the four of us, only Brill had come to the academy already holding a degree. She had followed a shortened curriculum, more akin to graduate studies than the bachelor's of science that the rest of us pursued. Last I'd heard she was somewhere over in the Gretna quadrant on a Federated Freight clipper and would be sitting for her Engineering Second ticket soon.

Pip was already headed back to Dunsany Roads. His father and uncle had jointly purchased another Damien-class eight metric kiloton ship, similar to the others in their family fleet. Pip had gotten pretty misty when the whole family showed up for his graduation, especially when he heard the news that the new ship would be named *Prodigal Son*. The full details were kinda sketchy, but between all the cousins, siblings, spouses, and assorted others associated with the Carstairs family, it appeared that Pip would be given a free hand to trade cargo on at least one of their ships and that, in the fullness of time, he'd become the skipper of the *Prodigal Son*.

When the shuttle neared the dock, I maneuvered my grav trunk down to the departure gate where Bev waited. We'd take the same shuttle up to the orbital, but we'd separate there. I'd be taking a fast packet to the Diurnia Quadrant, while her family's co-op ship waited for her. We'd have one last trip together.

When I'd first met her, I'd thought she was a lot older than me. Later I learned we were much closer in age. Thinking back to our early relationship—the "boy toy" period—I blushed a bit as the memories came flooding back. Upon leaving the *Lois McKendrick*, strictures against intra-crew fraternization became void, and we took full advantage of that fact for several days with great vigor—much to the amusement of our observers, no doubt.

As with most youthful romances, however, it failed to survive the rigors and demands of academy life. After that first blush of frustrated sexual tension had subsided to a more comfortable level, we had discovered things in common besides the obvious. We liked the same music and food, but her penchant for military action holos left me cold. Similarly, she didn't care much for live theatre, a taste I'd acquired at my mother's knee. The lack of theatre had been one of the things I'd missed in the Deep Dark, but Port Newmar had their own semi-professional company and I had renewed my acquaintance with the venerable masters—Albee and Pinter, Su and Shakespeare. Somewhere around the middle of our first year at the academy, we had stopped sleeping together. Time, energy, and opportunity had been lacking in order for us to maintain the kind of intensity that we had enjoyed. We had found, not surprisingly, that we were just good friends with more than a passing level of intimacy.

She smiled at me when I trundled my grav pallet around the corner and into the waiting area. "You wanna pilot the shuttle to the orbital?"

"Nah, that's okay," I said with a grin.

She was twitting me. While she'd easily picked up her shuttle pilot certification during the course of our studies, I lacked some necessary dimensional sense and had never mastered the mind-body integration required to fly a shuttle "off-the-wire." As long as the computers were in control, I could tell the machine where to go, but I'd never completed the required emergency procedures. As such, I had never earned that qualification.

In a matter of a few ticks, the shuttle had pulled up to the loading dock, and the academy port crew waved us aboard. Regular civilians used the terminal just across the tarmac. We weren't civilians—exactly—and senior cadets, who needed flight time, crewed the academy shuttle. There was a fully licensed pilot in the cockpit,

3

but everybody else was in training.

Bev greeted the grinning cadet who held the cargo tie-downs back for us while we maneuvered our gear into the small craft. "Hey, Martyn."

"Hi, Bev," he said. "Your mom's waiting top side. She's not excited much, is she?"

Bev chuckled that low, dangerous laugh I knew I'd miss. "Not much. I'm surprised she didn't ride down with you."

"She tried, but the skip pulled rank." He nodded toward the bow. "Said the academy insurance wouldn't cover passengers."

"Well, Mom knows insurance." Bev chuckled again. "Probably the only argument that would have worked."

"She's just excited," I said. "You've been away for a long time."

I'd met Bev's mother—an attractive woman with the same deadly grace as her daughter. While she served the family as bursar and chief accountant, I was certain that "bean counter" had never been one of the epithets applied to her.

Bev snorted. "She's just waiting to install me in officer country so she can twist Uncle Jeremy's nose."

The ship's announcer crackled in the overhead, and a laconic voice commented, "Whenever you're ready, Mr. Casserly. Port control has granted clearance and I'd rather like to take advantage of their magnanimous offer."

Bev sniggered. "Spence hasn't mellowed any, has he?"

Martyn grinned, finished latching the tie-downs, and did a final safety check on the gear before ushering us to a pair of seats. "If you'd be so kind as to strap in, sars, we'll be lifting off in the next few ticks."

We took our places, snapped the belts across our bodies, and settled in for liftoff. Casserly made his way forward and disappeared into the cockpit, leaving us alone in the cabin.

Almost immediately the engines started winding up, and the ship slipped down the taxiway. Casserly's crewmate up front must have completed the checklist while we settled in, as there was practically no pause at the final turn. The small shuttle bumbled along the taxiway, swung smoothly into position and exploded exuberantly into the air after a short, but stiff, acceleration.

We banked left off the ground and out over the water. The shuttle tilted its nose and gravity reminded us of its presence. The engines' scream faded as the air pressure outside fell, leaving only the space frame conduction to carry sound into the cabin. Within ten ticks, the sky outside turned black and Newmar's horizon took on a limb-like curve.

I looked over at Bev and opened my mouth to speak, but she

cut me off with a smile and a single word. "Don't."
Her eyes said it all. We'd said our goodbyes. Whatever we'd
had was a long time gone, a long way away. Life in the Deep Dark
was demanding—too demanding for us to carry extra baggage.

I smiled back but didn't speak. I held out the hand that had
been resting on the armrest between us. She took it in hers, smooth
and strong, then squeezed it once. We rode in silence that way, hand
in hand, all the way up to the orbital. When the locking clamps
latched on, she let go. We had our belts unlatched and were waiting
when Martyn came to release the cargo tie-downs.

Command Pilot Mike Spence followed Martyn out of the cockpit
and hunched his lanky frame over to prevent scraping the overhead.
Spence had been one of a long, long string of flight instructors
who'd despaired over my lack of dexterity. While Martyn released
our baggage, Spence held out his hand to me. He smiled with a
sympathetic twist to his mouth.

"If we'd had a few more months to practice, you'd have gotten
it down, I think."

I shook his hand and returned the grin. "I'm not so sure, Mr.
Spence, but thank you for the effort on my behalf."

"Good luck, Mr. Wang. It's been a pleasure."

He extended a hand to Beverly then and his whole face lit up in
a warm smile. "Congratulations, Ms. Arith, you've got the knack
of it, no question."

"Thank you, Mr. Spence," she said, shaking his hand and then
leaning in to give him a brief hug. "Don't let the dolts get to ya."
She winked while pulling away and reached for the tote-handle on
her pallet.

By then, Chris Miller, the other student pilot, had come out
from the cockpit and was helping Martyn clear the docking protocols. When done, they stood away from the hatch to give us
room.

Mr. Spence surprised me by barking, "Hand salute." He snapped
to attention as did Miller and Casserly on either side of the hatch.
They looked for all the world like an honors party, which I suppose
was the point.

Smiling, Bev and I braced and returned the salute crisply.

"Carry on, Mr. Spence," Bev said, as our hands cleared.

"Yes, sar. Thank you, sar," Mr. Spence said and grinned.

Bev led the way out of the lock and onto the orbital, slowing just
a bit as we reached the debarkation lounge. She glanced over her
shoulder once, her eyes shining and a wolfish smile playing across
her lips.

"Take care of yourself, *boy toy*," she said, and then stepped into the lounge to be buried by the avalanche of family, friends, and laughing children, waiting to escort her home.

I smiled to myself, worked my baggage around the boiling, squealing throng, and out into the main docks. The cold stung my face and teared my eyes as I oriented myself. I headed down the docks to starboard in search of my ride—the *SC Christiana Ellis*, a fast packet en route from Newmar to Diurnia, and my first billet as an officer.

CHAPTER TWO
NEWMAR ORBITAL: 2358-MAY-22

The *Ellis* wasn't far from the shuttle bays. The docks had become a second home to me. As part of the academy training, I'd spent a good amount of time working on and around them while learning the ins and outs of ship handling. There had been a lot of grumbling when we'd spent one whole month doing lock maintenance in our second year, but in the end everybody agreed that knowing up close and personal how the docking clamps worked gave us a healthier appreciation for how little it would take to damage one—and the ship attached to it.

Changes from the Joint Planetary Committee on Trade had relaxed some of the standardization rules, thereby permitting the orbital management more leeway in painting the fixtures and dock spaces. They still weren't garish, but regulations allowed for splashes of color, and individualized patterns. Newmar Orbital had adopted a color scheme that displayed the various systems in pastel colors, giving the dock spaces an organic feel. Electrical, air, fuel, water, and data runs, each in different colors, stood out against the pale neutral background of the bulkheads. I had to admit the scheme was pleasing to the eye, although a little disconcerting... like being in the guts of some huge space beast.

Even as I was considering how the docks had changed, superficial though it was, I couldn't help but remember my first tentative steps across the Neris Orbital's threshold after my mother had died, almost six stanyers before. In some ways it felt like a lifetime, and in others only last week. No doubt, the smell of the docks triggered my emotions. The combination of fresh paint, lubricant, hydraulic fluid, and the tang of electrical systems brought it all back. So long ago. So far away.

After two years on the *Lois,* I had been accepted to The Academy at Port Newmar. The four years of physical, mental, and emotional challenges had given me much more than I was able to wrap my head around. Remembering how young and stupid I'd been going in brought a smile to my face. Those first exams had been so easy. . . as long as all that was required had been filling out the forms. My test taking skill had remained strong, but my hubris had gotten me into trouble when it came to the physical tests.

While the book work at the academy was a large part of the effort, occasionally you had to prove you knew something by actually doing it firsthand. The first field trial in engineering maintenance had been a rather messy and embarrassing disaster. Luckily I recovered and learned, much to my chagrin, that my manual dexterity was limited to fine motor control and that my test taking ability only extended to academic work. Nobody could touch me in the "book courses" like Trade Law, Modern History, or Grav Theory, but when it came to the practical stuff—like getting my shuttle certification—I was average at best. My systems marks had stayed high, but being a Third Mate was more than just systems and it showed in my final standing—122 in a class of 438—in the top third, but nothing distinguishing. My academic advisor had been very supportive.

"A good showing for a first generation spacer, Mr. Wang," she'd said with a wink. "Your children will probably do better."

One physical skill that I picked up at the academy came out of my self-defense classes. For stanyers I'd admired Bev's fluid and dangerous grace. I'd seen her practicing with other crew back on the *Lois.* Her skill and training kept her in good standing at the academy. After an introduction to the various schools available, we were required to pick a discipline in our second semester. Beverly, of course, went with her preferred forms of G'wai G'wah—a combination of bare hand and armed combat with lots of kicks, strikes, dodges, and grappling. I, on the other hand, was mainly hopeless in a fight. The training master had taken me aside at the end of the first semester.

"Wang," he had said, "I hope you never get into a fight, because you have the killer instincts of a lawn chair." His words were harsh, but his tone was light and playful. "I could assign you to one of the intro courses in any of the various hard disciplines—G'wai G'wah, tae kwon do, karate, or the like—but you'd be wasting your time."

"Yes, sar," I had replied. All instructors were addressed as "sar" regardless of rank, and he was obviously going somewhere—even if I hadn't known where at the time.

He nodded once, then led me out of his office and onto the

academy grounds. I had followed him, somewhat mystified, as he strode across the manicured lawns to where a small woman with sun burnished skin worked to prune an azalea. I remember thinking, "Oh, great, I'm being demoted to gardener." The training master had stopped about two meters from the woman and bowed deeply. It had been one of those martial arts bows with hand positions and arm movements. I knew right then that this woman was *somebody*.

"Sifu," he had said after she returned his bow, less deeply but still respectfully, "please forgive my interruption but I would like to introduce Cadet Wang to you."

The woman had smiled and turned her gaze on me. She inclined her head gently after a moment.

"Thank you, Mr. Mercer."

It had been all she said, and that's how I found myself studying tai chi with Sifu Margaret Newmar. I had no idea at the time, and it had been stanyers later that I came to understand, that she was, in fact, a direct descendant of the Newmars for whom the system had been named not to mention one of the leading experts in tai chi in the universe.

Her first lesson had been pruning azaleas. The memory of her kind smile and gentle nature warmed me. I had learned so much from her, and I would miss our time together. I had no doubt that I'd be back to see her again. Her students regularly returned to visit and I had met some amazing people that way.

I glanced up out of my reverie and found myself at the lock displaying "CELLIS ETD 2358-May-23" I pressed the call button and turned to look into the video pickup. In less than a tick the lock began cycling, and a rating stepped out, ducking under the door even before it had finished opening.

She greeted me with a smile and said, "Mr. Wang? We've been expecting you. Welcome aboard, sar. I'm Casey and you're the last one to arrive. If you'd come this way, please?"

As easy as that I was ushered aboard, tote and all, and she showed me to a small stateroom. A clever closet allowed me to latch my grav trunk down while still being able to access it easily. A small, fold-down desk, a compact wall screen, and a bulkhead mounted bunk comprised the sum total of the furnishings. I had room to stand, turn around, change clothes, and not much else.

Casey pointed out the controls. They were pretty standard, and she showed me where the san was at the end of the passage. There was a common room and crew quarters farther aft.

"We're pretty informal here, Mr. Wang," Casey said. "Eight passengers and a crew of four, so we can move pretty quickly. You'll meet Bill—Captain Lochlan—tonight, if you care to join us at Freddie's for our send off dinner."

"Thanks, Casey," I said with a nod.

Freddie's was one of the better restaurants on the orbital. Good food and reasonable prices.

She grinned again. "Sure thing! The reservation's for 1900 in the name of Ellis. You'll get a chance to meet the other passengers too. I think most of them will be there."

I nodded again. "Sounds like fun," I said and meant it.

"Oh, the skipper knows how to throw a party. You'll have a ball. Trust me."

With that, she ducked out of the stateroom and closed the door gently behind her.

In the sudden silence, I became aware of the ship sounds around me. When docked there wasn't as much background noise as when underway, but the ever-present environmental blower and the occasional whirr and vibration as pumps or fans started up somewhere in the ship made me feel strangely at home, even though I hadn't been aboard a ship for almost a stanyer. Two years on the *Lois McKendrick* made a lasting impression.

That was when it struck me.

For the first time in a long while, I didn't have anything to do. I sighed and stripped off my uniform jacket, hanging it in the locker. The chrono said 1525 local time, which meant I had a few stans before I needed to head up to Freddie's. I keyed open the grav trunk and started pulling out the clothing I would need for the voyage. It wasn't much, all told—a few personal shipsuits and my comfy boots.

When I finished that small chore, it was only just past 1600, so I took a few minutes to check out the wall screen. I found an extensive library of entertainment programming and some information on the ship itself. If I managed to get through the library I had with me—all the accumulated reading that I had put off during the previous four stanyers—I'd have plenty to occupy myself with.

For fun, I pulled up the ship's specifications. It was a small ship, as clippers go—barely fifty meters. She was rated at six metric kilotons which was more than enough for some small cargo in addition to the bread-and-butter passenger traffic. The ship's amenities included a gym with treadmills and weight machines along with a small hot tub and sauna. I whistled appreciatively when I saw the engine ratings and did some rough calculations. *Christiana* had Tatiana-class Burleson drives which gave her a jump range of six—twice as far as the *Lois* had been capable of. The Pravda fusactors were more than sufficient to the task of powering up the Carillon sail fields and grav keel. I did a double take when I saw the designators on the sails. This ship had about half as much sail area as the *Lois*, but it only massed a small fraction of the larger clipper. *Christiana* was a spritely little boat—according to her specs. She had good reason to be called a "fast packet." We'd make the run to Diurnia in just under six weeks, dock-to-dock.

CHAPTER THREE
NEWMAR SYSTEM: 2358-MAY-30

Eight days out of Newmar I ran out of things to read, or more precisely, I ran out of things I *wanted* to read.

Having grown up with an ancient literature professor, I had been used to being surrounded by books. Mom had made it a habit of discussing them over dinner. My tablet was full of volumes, and the ship's library was available and extensive.

But I wasn't used to inactivity.

Ever since Mom's death, I'd had little more than a few moments of free time. From the planet, to the *Lois*, to the academy—I'd always had things to do, and people to do them with. During my third stanyer at Port Newmar, I had hungered for the opportunity to curl up with a book, a fresh pot of coffee, and bury myself in the story. For three weeks during the spring of that third stanyer, the desire for a fresh book and no demands had been physical—an ache in my stomach. Something bounced me out of it then, so it was with a certain degree of ruefulness that I ran to the end of my "reading binge" within so short a time. Faced with another month in transit, I realized I needed to find something else to do.

The *Ellis's* small workout room—it wasn't big enough to be called a gym—was available around the clock, of course, and the treadmills and sauna saw a lot of me even during the first few days underway. There was a smallish open space where I could run through my tai chi exercises as well. After four years with Sifu Newmar, I had a good grasp of the basics, and felt my energy, strength, and balance develop as I had gotten deeper into the discipline during my time at the academy.

So when I ran out of things I wanted to read, I headed to the gym. During the middle of the morning, I usually had the place to myself. Without distractions I could zone out, my mind not so much disengaged as completely focused. I worked on getting each movement where it needed to be—each finger, each toe, the shifting of weight.

"Your back knee isn't bent far enough."

I blinked out of my focus and saw that one of my fellow passengers— a man I knew only as Kurt—had come into the gym dressed in loose fitting workout clothes. He didn't smile, but then again he never smiled. As near as I could tell, his face never changed from his blank, neutral expression. His eyes were always focused on whatever he looked at, but his expression seemed like he was listening to something I couldn't hear. He traveled with a small man I took to be his employer.

"I said, your back knee isn't bent far enough. It needs just a touch more to free that flow." His voice was a smooth tenor, almost too light for his bull like frame.

I looked down and realized he was right. I was getting sloppy and adjusted my back knee a bit more.

"Thanks," I said with a smile, "that feels better."

"May I join you?"

I shrugged and adjusted my position to make room for him. He stepped into my routine without hesitation and followed along, one step behind and to the left of me, as I completed the Wu Long Form. From the corner of my eye, I saw his large body working smoothly on Wave Hands Like Clouds, but I had a bit of advantage in Snake Creeps Down. His larger frame bent, dipped, and lifted into Golden Cock almost effortlessly, but since I was shorter, I could get lower— although not by much. His movements were smoothly controlled and carried the graceful power I recognized in Sifu Newmar, but tai chi was obviously not his main discipline.

After a few ticks, I put him out of my mind and moved directly into the Yang Short Form, before starting the Wu Long once more. At the end of the Wu, I stopped and let the chi settle, intending to head for a sauna and shower.

"Do you Push Hands?" Kurt asked.

"I have, but I'm not very good," I said with a rueful smile. "The academy master said I have all the fighting instincts of lawn furniture."

Kurt didn't smile, exactly, but I caught a twinkle in his eyes. "You studied with Sifu Newmar at the academy, then?"

I nodded.

He took the beginning pose for the Push Hands technique and waited for me to step in. I did so, and we worked slowly through several cycles of the drill—inside, outside, up, across, swap. We moved faster until I pushed and he wasn't there. I rocked back on my heels from a touch to my shoulder.

He did smile, then, and proceeded to show me a few things.

After two solid stans, the sweat rolled down my legs under my pants and I had that firm, burning glow from a good workout. When we broke, Kurt bowed and I returned it, bowing much lower to him than he did to me.

"Thank you for the workout," he rumbled. "This is the time of day that Mr. Blalock does most of his work, so I'm free if you'd care to meet me tomorrow."

It was less a question than a statement.

"Thank you," I said, and bowed again.

I went to the sauna then while Kurt fired up one of the treadmills and started a run. Half a stan later when I came out of the sauna, he was still running and nodded to me as I headed for the showers.

Afterward, I gravitated to the galley where Paul Mueller held court. I didn't know if it was the same for other people, but my early days on the *Lois* had given me an appreciation for the mess deck and galley as the heart of the ship. The galley on the *Ellis* was no exception.

My first exposure to small ship life had been on the voyage from Dunsany Roads to Newmar on the *Bad Penny* with Pip's Aunt and Uncle. The *Penny* was a family ship with an eat-in galley where we'd spent many an evening gathered around the table, sailing through the Deep Dark. The *Ellis* had a dining room for the passengers and crew. The actual galley itself was tucked away around the corner with a cleverly concealed pass-through and door that connected it to the dining room.

Breakfast and lunch were typically buffet style at the pass-through—always a hot dish or two and plenty of fruits and vegetables. Dinner was something else and served family-style, with platters and bowls on the large table in the dining room. The captain presided at the head of the table with passengers rotated via some formula that I hadn't been able to discern after only a few days underway.

Because of the long work out, I almost missed lunch. The others had come and gone and Paul was already beginning to clear.

"Mr. Wang," he said, "I wondered if you were skipping lunch today."

I snagged a few pieces of fruit, a couple of rolls, and a small block of cheese from the buffet, then stood back to let him work. "Wasn't my intention, Mr. Mueller. I was working out with Kurt and lost track of the time." I waved a hand vaguely at the set up. "Please, don't let me interrupt. I know how hard it is to keep up with the galley."

He smiled and started his clean up routine.

"You've worked the galley, then, Mr. Wang?" he asked as he worked.

"Mess hand on the *Lois McKendrick*. Had some of my happiest times on that mess deck."

I smiled to myself as the warm memories slipped through my mind.

Paul finished clearing the buffet and closed the pass-through after wiping everything down. I finished the fruit, bread, and cheese and noticed the crumbs I'd scattered while I was standing there eating and talking to Paul. While he was clattering in the galley, I grabbed the sweeper from the bracket on the bulkhead and picked up my crumbs and—since I had it out—did the whole floor.

In a few ticks, Paul came into the dining room through the connecting door and caught me with the sweeper in my hand.

"You didn't have to do that, Mr. Wang," he said with a concerned look on his face.

"It was my pleasure, and please, my name is Ishmael. You can call me that. We're gonna be cooped up here for a while yet. Might as well get comfy."

His wrinkled face folded into a lopsided smile and his eyes danced at me as he held out a roughened paw.

"Paul, then, Ishmael, and tell me about working in the galley while I finish cleaning up, if you don't mind."

So I stood in the doorway regaling Paul with stories of the mess deck on the *Lois* as he proceeded to clear and clean everything in the three by five meter galley. The galley itself was a marvel of compact installation. The cook top was a four burner design, but instead of the normal two by two, the four were lined up on a narrow counter. The ovens—there were three of them—were recessed into the bulkhead. Instead of the big steam kettles we'd had on the *Lois*, the *Ellis* had an honest to gods pot rack and I couldn't help but admire the big chillers, larders, and carefully laid out cabinets and counters. It was perfectly designed for a one person operation.

In just a few ticks, Paul finished up his after-lunch routines and shooed me out of the galley. "It's time for my nap, Ishmael," he told me playfully. "Baked chicken for dinner," he said, as he secured the pass-through door, and I heard him clicking off the lights as he exited through the main entry on the other side of the galley.

My brief foray satisfied something I wasn't sure I could name. I found there was another book or two I wanted to read, and I suddenly looked forward to picking up where I'd left off on my reading list. I grinned to myself and headed back to my stateroom.

CHAPTER FOUR
DIURNIA SYSTEM: 2358-JULY-1

After an adjustment period, the days settled into a comfortable pattern. My workouts with Kurt took up the mornings. He helped me focus my discipline from a kind of theoretical exhibition to a more practical mode of self-defense. He was fond of saying, "The most effective defense is avoiding the fight." In spite of that, he had a lot of good tips on how to cope when avoidance wasn't possible. By the time we were preparing to dock at Diurnia, I was not so foolish as to think I'd win against somebody like Kurt, but I was a lot more confident that I could at least survive.

The trip was not without its surprises. The passenger list included Kurt and his boss, Harvey Blalock—who was some kind of wiggity wig on Diurnia who rarely left his stateroom—and an older couple, the Hokensons—who turned out to be rabid bridge players. They soon had a standing foursome comprised of them, a dour sales agent named Philip Jameson, and Georgina Fredericks. Whenever they played, Georgina's husband, William, hung about and behaved like a sulky boy being forced to entertain himself while the adults were occupied. Georgina always exhibited a shy and demure air, even while running a seven no-trump hand. Her jubilation manifested as a smile, which was perhaps just a tiny bit broader than normal.

While the Hokensons and their partners played bridge in the common room most of the afternoon, cinema viewings consumed the after dinner hours. Leslie March, a middle aged woman heading for Diurnia to open a clothing store, turned out to be a very pleasant and knowledgeable film connoisseur. At 2030 each evening the big viewer in the commons became our movie theatre, and regardless of which film we picked, Leslie had a ready stream of information about the story, characters, actors, director, and even producer. She managed to carry on her running commentary without interfering one iota in the viewing experience. She was one of those uncanny people who knew exactly when to speak and—more importantly—when to shut up. As the trip wore on, and we watched more movies, I came to appreciate her ready wit and insightful observations. Leslie would often spend a few ticks before the film talking about it and sometimes we'd sit around for as much as two stans afterward discussing what we had just seen.

The transit from Newmar to Diurnia took forty days. Given the distances involved, that had been pretty darn good. The *Ellis* reached the Burleson limit only sixteen days out of Newmar. Compared to what I had been used to, that was an astonishingly short run out. We had spent six days and three jumps in the between spaces of the Deep Dark running through the un-populated middle of the Western Annex, followed by an eighteen day run into Diurnia Orbital. The published transit time was forty-two days but Captain Lochlan brought the ship in two days early.

One of the differences between being a passenger and being crew was the sense of unreality. I had a feeling of being wrapped in a cocoon—each day largely like the one before. I knew enough not to dwell on the duration of the journey, but my brain went into a kind of contemplative loop that consisted of the daily workouts with Kurt, the quiet afternoons reading in my bunk, and the bridge games providing a homely—and sometimes not so quiet—backdrop. Mr. Hokenson tended toward the boisterous at times, but his wife shushed him with a stern, "Please, William! There are other people on the ship." He would quiet down as the next hand began.

We were a day out of Diurnia when Captain Lochlan put the view from the bridge monitors up on the large screen in the common room. The familiar orbital shape hung like a tin can in space. The light from Diurnia's primary glinted from the sides during its daylight passages, and the station's lights gleamed in the dark whenever it passed into the planet's shadow. The view served as a kind of wake up call for me. Suddenly the end of the voyage was in sight. In a few days I'd be back on ship, trying to be a good third mate.

William Hokenson found me staring into the monitor just before lunch on our last day underway. "Looking forward to a new ship, Mr. Wang?"

I shrugged. "It's going to be different," I said. "I had summer cruises at the academy, so I know every ship is unique, but my first one is still kinda like home to me. I hope the next one will be too."

He chuckled and nodded. "First job out of school?"

"Yes well, intellectually I know this won't be the be-all and end-all, and I'm not anywhere near as good as I think, but part of me hopes that I know at least some of what I'm doing."

He gave me a pat on the shoulder. "You'll be fine, Mr. Wang. You're already ahead of many. The academy is a good school." When I glanced from the screen, his eyes held a twinkle. "Of course, it won't be easy, but in the end? A hundred years from now, who'll know?"

I grinned at that. "Well, I hope I will," I answered.

He chuckled again. "Yes, there is that to consider." His voice stayed playful but his tone shifted as he observed, "Now that school's out, the real lessons begin." His eyes closed and he added, "Learn them early and learn them well. Remediation is painful."

I sighed and nodded my understanding. "I suspect you're correct, sar."

He opened his eyes and refocused with a rueful smile.

"Well, the bitter voice of experience, my boy. Since I crossed the century mark, I find I use it more and more often." He offered an almost apologetic shrug.

"Thanks," I said.

One of the things that the academy had drilled, and practically beaten, into us as cadets on summer cruise was that we weren't qualified to be third mates. The degree only permitted us to have some confidence when taking the Third Mate's exam. The ink was barely dry on my CPJCT license when I had left Newmar. Most of us had sat for the license in a mass examination organized by the academy during the latter half of our senior year. Everybody I knew passed. Or at least said they did. The actual licenses—arcane and freighted with significance—were delivered physically as well as digitally. I had a nicely framed document, complete with scarlet seal, calligraphic embossing, and all the rights and privileges appropriate to my rank—which, from my informal observation, wasn't much. While the instructors at the academy were quick to assure us that we were learning what we needed to know to be good officers in the Deep Dark, the summer cruises tended to disabuse us of any such notions as we mixed it up with "real" officers. I hoped that some amount of that could be chalked up to hazing the next crop of cadets. I knew in my heart of hearts that a large part of it couldn't be. Standing there, staring at the live feed from the bridge, trying to pick out the ships docked around the middle of that gleaming tin can, and listening to Mr. Hokenson, I hoped I wasn't going to be one of those "fresh-out-of-school-know-it-alls." The next couple of stanyers would be fraught with all kinds of peril along those lines, and the last thing I wanted was to add to the stereotype.

As if sensing my thoughts, Mr. Hokenson patted me once more

on the shoulder and nodded. "You'll be fine, my boy. You'll be fine."

Paul Mueller pushed up the door of the pass-through with a loud rattle, announcing the start of lunch. Mr. Hokenson wandered off to get some, leaving me contemplating my future for a moment or two longer before the rest of the passengers trooped in.

That evening's movie was an older one—from around 2290, according to Leslie. The camera work was excellent and the plot revolved around a middle-aged woman rebuilding her life after the tragic death of her husband and children. The lead actress was not the typical media darling sylph but rather a meaty woman made up to look even older than she was. The story revolved around a younger man that she had met on holiday. It was somewhat predictable but poignantly done and—again according to Leslie March—shot largely on location on Fangipani, one of the heavily islanded resort planets in the Chiba quadrant. As the movie ground its way to its telegraphed conclusion—where the woman finally realizes that life is fragile, bittersweet, and worth living brought on by having multiple encounters with the younger man in a variety of settings before being killed herself when a freak ocean storm barrels into their secluded hideaway and blows the small bungalow in on her—Leslie became less and less talkative. Her commentary stopped completely and in the end she sat staring at the closing credits and nursing a gin and tonic while the rest of the passengers called it a night.

She was one of the last to rise. "Ishmael?" she called as I was about to leave the lounge.

I stepped out of the passageway to allow the Hokensons to go by. Mrs. Hokenson smiled at me in a very grandmotherly fashion and murmured, "See you in the morning, Mr. Wang."

Leslie had drained her glass and slipped it onto the rack for Paul to get in the morning.

"What did you think of the film?" she asked, not quite looking in my direction.

"Predictable, but pretty," I said.

"In what way, predictable?" she asked, looking up at me with soft green eyes.

She was very attractive in ways that hadn't been obvious when I first met her.

"Well, women who try to control their own lives—their own destinies—even after all humankind has been and done—those women must die. She was killed by a storm—a wind of fate—because she dared to look for happiness in the arms of a young lover." I shook my head. "My mother, a lit professor, would have had a lot to say about it, I'm sure, but it seems like a recurring theme. Women aren't allowed to be happy, unless their happiness comes from the largess of a man."

As I spoke, Leslie cocked her head slightly to one side. "That's a pretty mature view for a guy who's fresh out of the academy," she said, without making it sound like a left-handed compliment.

"Yeah, well, I learned a lot from my mother. The old stories are full of this stuff. I cut my teeth on it."

She was silent for a few heartbeats, looking at my face, trying to read—something. "You think it's still the case that society believes that men should control their women?" she asked.

I shrugged. "I don't know. My first ship was run by a woman. It was named for her great grandmother." I nodded my head down the passageway. "But we have two examples right here of women who are controlled largely by the men in their lives."

She smiled and asked, "You're including Mrs. Hokenson?"

I grinned ruefully. "Well, that's a good point. She probably let's him think he's in charge."

Leslie chuckled and seemed to make up her mind. Crossing the lounge, she took my hand in hers and started down the passage toward the passenger staterooms. "How do you feel about women who take charge? Do you believe they need to be punished, to be put in their places?" She looked up into my face as she asked.

I smiled, feeling the temperature rising in the ship as we sauntered down the hall. "That depends. Do you like being punished?"

It was her turn for a rueful smile. "No."

I shrugged. "That works for me too."

She led me into her small stateroom and closed the door behind us.

CHAPTER FIVE
DIURNIA ORBITAL: 2358-JULY-2

When we docked at Diurnia Orbital, I got the full treatment of a Confederation customs inspection. It wasn't the first time, but they were much more thorough than on Newmar. Perhaps it was because in the past I'd always traveled on freighters, and this was my first passenger trip. The rest of the passengers didn't seem all that surprised, and Kurt even escorted his very reclusive employer voluntarily into a private inspection room. Or perhaps that was just how the rich people did it. Kurt smiled and nodded once in my direction as he disappeared behind a blank door.

The rest of us presented ourselves and our goods at the lines waiting at the benches behind which stern-faced inspectors in rubber gloves waited. It seemed a waste of time to me. They'd had the ship's manifest for days as we maneuvered into the orbital. Our luggage had been sniffed and scanned when it was taken aboard, but the Diurnian custom officials, men and women alike, had the same no-nonsense expressions. They looked as if they expected to find something, and woe unto the unlucky passenger who neglected an item on the declaration form. All told, though, it didn't take all that long to clear customs. A few questions, such as: "Where are you coming from? Why are you here? Where are you going?" a review of my credentials, a perfunctory examination inside my grav trunk, and a fast body scan were all behind me fairly quickly. I stepped through to the arrivals lounge and caught up with the luggage that had taken an additional pass through some kind of magnetic resonance scanner.

Leslie March was standing there with a pair of grav trunks and thumbing for them as I stepped up. She gave me a warm smile and winked without saying anything, turning to trundle her trunks off toward the exit. We'd exchanged contact information before leaving the ship. I didn't expect she'd call, but one never knows, and she was a very considerate woman.

I thumbed the receipt for my own single trunk and tagged it to trundle along behind me. I had a couple of days before my appointment with Diurnia Salvage and Transport, so I needed to find a room. After cooling my heels aboard the *Ellis* for forty days, the last thing I wanted to do was wait around the orbital, but my appointment was for July 5, 2358, and then I'd find out what ship and when I'd be able to board.

Stepping out of the arrival's lounge into the gently curving promenade of the orbital's One Deck, felt like I was coming home somehow. While I'd spent a lot of time studying cargo and cargo handling on Newmar Orbital, and summer cruises had taken me to several of the orbitals around the Venitz quadrant, those all felt temporary. Diurnia was about to become my new home port. The realization sent a shiver of disbelief through me. I wasn't sure which ship I'd be going on, but Diurnia Salvage and Transport operated among only four other systems in the quadrant. I could expect to see a lot of Diurnia Orbital. As much as a spacer saw any station.

I paused at the observation window and looked out at the *Ellis*, nuzzled up against the small craft lock on the deck below. I marveled again. My next trip would be aboard a freighter and would probably take nearly as long to reach the Burleson limit on its way out as the entire trip from Newmar had taken. I snorted in amusement and pulled my trunk along the corridor in the direction of the lifts. I could find a reasonably priced hotel up on the Seven Deck, and I needed to get settled in for the next few days.

Having all the orbital stations standardized under the rules of the Confederated Planets Joint Commission on Trade made them very easy to navigate for people who saw them a lot. There were always spacers needing rooms as the ships came and went. The rapid turnaround of ships and crews, and predictability of the process, made the operation of the various hotels and hostels run like clockwork. I could have gotten a bunk in a transient hostel at about a quarter of the cost of the hotel room, but knowing I'd be shipping out again soon, and having gotten used to my privacy on the *Ellis*, I decided that I could afford to splurge on a few nights of relative luxury. As a third mate, I was probably going to be sharing a cramped stateroom with another of the junior officers.

Within three stans of docking, I was settled in my room, had my trunk stowed, and my civvies hung in the closet. I'd worn my own shipsuits on the way out, and I was ready to get back into civvies. I took a few moments to double check my accounts and go over my paperwork, just to make sure I hadn't confused any of it in my head.

My tablet linked into the station net without any problems. I could access ship movements, station events, and message traffic. I dropped a quick "I'm on station" message to let Diurnia Salvage and Transport know I'd be keeping my appointment on the fifth.

So I sat there, remembering my first day off the *Lois McKendrick*, sitting in a hotel room paid for by the ship on the Dunsany Roads Orbital. The feeling of "I'm alone now" returned. The memory of it, even so many stanyers later, threatened to overwhelm me. The feeling of rootlessness and unconnectedness was a cold hand in my guts.

I shook myself and muttered, "Get a grip!"

Remembering a small packet in the bottom of my trunk, I went to the closet and pulled it out. The small zippered pouch held all I had kept of my mother's things. When she'd been killed back on Neris, much of her stuff went away—either to charity or trashed. Some small amount of her writing, and her ashes, had gone into storage. The storage agreement had expired while I was at the academy, and the company forwarded her effects to me at Port Newmar. I got rid of most of her books and almost all of her papers. I scattered her ashes at sea off shore at Port Newmar. She'd have liked that, I thought.

I'd kept only a few pages and photos. I didn't look at them often, but I'd riffled through them a few times in the three stanyers since they'd been forwarded to me. The papers contained her marriage license—dated March 3, 2328—and divorce decree—dated May 21, 2335. Both were issued here on Diurnia. My father's name was there on both of them: Franklin Prescott Wang. Talk about non-sequitur monikers. I had only vague recollections of my father from before we'd left Diurnia and went to Neris, but in the papers there was a photo of a young man sitting at what appeared to be a restaurant table, smiling into the lens of the camera. He looked something like me, I suppose, but that young man was my father, apparently when he was courting my mother. The time stamp on the back read "Feb 2327" and had faded almost to illegibility over the years. Mother had never displayed this picture. But she had shown it to me when I was young and asked the "Where's my daddy?" question.

Theoretically, he was here in the Diurnia quadrant. At least that's where Mother had always said we'd left him. Looking at the official Diurnian documentations of marriage and divorce, that seemed the most likely scenario. I wondered if he were still alive. I paged through the thin packet once more, looking for anything that might provide a clue as to his whereabouts. On a whim, I fired up the tablet and looked up Franklin P. Wang in the local data repository.

No hits.

I looked up Franklin Wang and got no hits.

That didn't mean much. He could have changed his name or just removed it from the public directories. After twenty-odd stanyers, the trail was rather cold. I took one more long look and shrugged. Without his ID number, any investigation would hinge on luck, and I'd used a lot of that up in the last few stanyers. I sighed and stuffed everything back into the zippered pouch and stowed it in the bottom of my trunk.

The message icon on my tablet acknowledged the receipt of my note to Diurnia Salvage and Transport, but didn't offer to ship me out any earlier, so I headed for the Oh-two Deck. I was ready for some lunch, a beer, and maybe I could find out something about my new employer.

The main deck of any station is the dock. Decks above the docks have increasing numbers—One Deck, Two Deck, Three Deck, and so on. My hotel was on the Seven Deck. By convention decks below the main deck are prefixed with a zero. Where Deck One is the level above the dock, the Zero-one Deck—or Oh-one Deck—is one deck below. Above the dock are all the retail, administration, and residential areas. Below the dock are all the industrial facilities. Ship chandlers, cargo brokers, and other ship services facilities are on the Oh-one Deck, but below that is the entertainment area. The Oh-two Deck is where ships' crews got together to engage in activities that are not talked about in polite company. Bars, brothels, tattoo parlors, and a variety of entertainments are available for those who have the interest and the credits necessary. One thing I'd found on every Oh-two Deck was a quiet pub where the brew was generally local and good, the food was plentiful and tasty, and neither would leave gaping wounds in my credit balance.

On Diurnia Orbital the place was called *The Miller Moth* and in addition to the obligatory sedate crystal display sign with the name, there was a stylized moth wing painted on the wall. Inside was the laminate and leather I'd been hoping for. Booths lined the walls and tables stood in shoals across the area between bar and wall. I knew that there would be a small dance floor on the side I couldn't see from the door, and that most nights, the place would be full of people who just wanted to sit, chat, and perhaps leave with somebody who might warm them against the cold of the Deep Dark. The big dance club would be almost diametrically across the station from this one, on the other side of the Oh-two Deck. The serious meat market action happened there, but it was probably too early in the station's duty cycle to be busy at the moment.

I glanced around the place as I crossed from door to bar. A few people sat here and there around the room. It was a twenty-four stan business, so somebody was always arriving or leaving on an odd schedule that didn't match the station's. A couple of engineering ratings were holding down one end of the bar muttering quietly to each other over beers and burgers. I slipped onto a stool about mid-bar and the barkeep—a broad-shouldered woman with hands that dwarfed a pint glass—smiled as I settled in.

"Hiya, sailor. New in town?" she asked with a lopsided smile.

I laughed. "Yeah, just made port this morning."

She held out one of those large hands and said, "Welcome to Diurnia Orbital. I'm Jen. What can I get cha?"

"Thanks," I said, shaking the offered hand. "I'm Ishmael. Can I have something light on the beer front and one of those burgers?" I asked, nodding my head in the direction of the engineers at the end of the bar.

She bobbed her head in a small nod of acknowledgment. We dickered over the various conditions, condiments, and accompaniments. In what seemed like just moments, I had a cold beer and a hot burger commanding all my attention.

The barkeep hovered, just out of direct line of sight, and generally kept out of the way. Neither the engineers nor I were terribly demanding. She puttered about—straightening glassware, polishing the gleaming bar. Nothing planet shattering, but all aimed at having the optimal setting for the customers. She moved with the practiced efficiency of a pro.

"So what brings you to our fair orbital?" she asked after my initial engagement with the burger was successfully underway.

"I just graduated from the academy. Diurnia Salvage and Transport offered me a berth."

"You came all the way from Port Newmar?"

"Yup, not a bad trip. Came on a fast-packet."

We passed a pleasant stan of minor chit-chat while I ate and had a second beer. It was early in the day for me, but with nothing to do, and nowhere to go for a couple of days, it seemed a good way to pass the time.

Eventually I thumbed the tab, adding a nice gratuity. I'd be coming back often, so I wanted to leave a good impression. Besides, she was kinda cute.

CHAPTER SIX
DIURNIA ORBITAL: 2358-JULY-5

Other than sleeping, eating, and exploring Diurnia Orbital, I didn't have a lot to do. While I waited I reviewed all the publicly accessible information that I could find on Diurnia Salvage and Transport.

Even before I'd accepted the offer back at the academy, I'd done some homework on them. DST was a smallish concern based on Diurnia. They started out doing salvage work and bulk transport contracts for the Confederated Planets when the CP was developing across the quadrant. The current CEO was the grandson of the founder, a man named Geoffrey Maloney. The database reported a fleet of about a dozen ships, all specializing in bulk freight. A third of them were tankers and the rest were bulk ore and grain haulers.

I took advantage of the station net access to pull up the local broker reports to see what DST was hauling and where. The list wasn't terribly long. Of course, when you're talking about a dozen ships, and transit times are two or three months, there aren't that many trips in a stanyer. The sailing plans were all to or from the same four systems—Dree, Breakall, Welliver, and Jett. Besides Diurnia itself, Dree was the only confederated planet in the bunch. The rest were corporate systems. The Diurnia quadrant was one of the original beads on the string that became the Western Annex. There were a lot of corporate systems out there. It was unusual to have two CP systems adjacent to each other—usually they liked to split up the influence. I dug into a few of the manifests but they were all common cargoes—grain, ores, raw metal, lumber, frozen food, and the occasional load of machine parts or farm equipment.

The 'Net brought up a list of the actual hulls. Only two of those were the newer Unwin Barbell two hundred metric kiloton bulk haulers, but mostly they ran older model Damien tractors and the

29

venerable Manchester one hundred eighty metric kilotons tankers. While the Manchester-built ships would be relatively comfortable, the Damien tractors were built for minimum crews. They were notorious for being long on work, short on crew, and uncomfortable on long trips. The Barbells were relatively modern but definitely built for power and not comfort. Their big drawing card was the single pod cargo container, big enough to hold small ships inside them. They could be loaded in advance, stacked together, and even left in orbit. The containers were particularly valued for security reasons, because they were not accessible from inside the ship. The only way into a bulk container is through the cargo loading ports on either end. When mated with its ship, the ports weren't even available. The end nacelles of the hull blocked access. Loaded, mated, and security bonded, the Unwin Barbells provided as secure a transport medium as possible.

As I finished dressing for my interview with the DST people, I wondered what I'd run into. My appointment was for 0900 in their corporate offices on the Oh-five Deck. Yes, I was nervous. I had to admit that to myself as I collected my tablet, made sure the room key was in my pocket, and snagged my service cap on the way out the door. The butterflies only got worse while I waited for the lift and reached a peak just before I entered the beige and somewhat battered office space with the oval and star logo of Diurnia Salvage and Transport on the door. I took a deep breath, let it out slowly, and entered.

Inside the door was a dingy foyer. A counter ran almost the entire width of the space with a door against the far bulkhead to allow access behind the counter. A couple of chairs—looking plastically forlorn—waited for visitors in one corner, and a plastic tree lurked in the other. It wasn't exactly what I was expecting, in terms of corporate office.

Behind the counter a clerk spoke into a voice headset hanging from his left ear. He looked up when I stepped in and smiled in greeting. He held up his index finger in a "hold on" gesture.

"Yes, sir, the *Geordan VanTassle* is due in later today. That container should be at the terminal in about…"—he consulted the clock on his monitor—"three stans and the ship is scheduled to dock by 1800" He paused then, listening to something on the other end. "Yes, sir, thank you for calling DST. Please let me know if we can be of any further assistance." He disconnected and crossed to the counter.

"Good morning, sar. Welcome to Diurnia Salvage and Transport. How can I help you?" he asked with a pleasant smile.

"Good morning. My name is Wang. I'm here about a third

mate's berth."

"Of course, Mr. Wang, we're expecting you." He stuck his hand across the counter in an offered handshake. "Call me Bitters, with an 's'. While many might think me bitter, that's not my name."

He rattled it off in a well-practiced stream accompanied by a lopsided grin. While I shook the right, his left hand pressed a button under the counter, and the door on the end buzzed.

"Come on back, and we'll get this going."

I walked through the door and Bitters took me into the inner sanctum. He stuck his head into an inner office and said, "Mr. Nelson, Ishmael Wang is here."

"Thank you, Bitters. Please show him in," came a voice from the open door.

Bitters stepped out of the way and swept an open hand palm up toward the door. "Mr. Nelson will see you now."

He had a funny sense of drama about him, and I smiled as I walked through the door to the cluttered cubby. There was barely room for the desk and two chairs in the cramped space. The man behind the narrow desk rose and didn't have to reach far to extend his hand to me.

"Good morning, Mr. Wang," he said warmly.

I shook the hand and murmured some greeting in return.

"Please have a seat." He indicated the only chair on this side of the desk. "Let's get this ship into space."

In surprisingly short order I found myself trotted through the various forms, requirements, orientations, and associated minutiae which I hadn't expected, but in hindsight, should have. He ran through the various contract clauses—all standard, which I recognized from my semester on legal practices—and summarized my pay and benefits—again, all standard. The pay was within norms. It wasn't what anybody would call a "princely sum" but was still about two hundred credits a month above what I knew to be the average. It wasn't a lot more, but certainly a welcome addition. In hindsight, I might have negotiated for more, but I was happy enough with the deal. I remembered that some of my classmates were still looking for berths when I left Port Newmar, so I felt fairly well disposed toward this one.

With the last of the administration work done, and the contracts thumbed and validated, Mr. Nelson rose once more and offered a hand in dismissal.

"You've got an appointment up at medical for your physical, and after that, you're good to go, Mr. Wang. If you have no further questions...?" his voice trailed off.

"No, none," I said, shaking his hand.

"Very well, then, assuming there's nothing odd in the physical—and really—it's just a formality for our insurance records, we'll have you report to Captain Rossett on the *William Tinker* at dock nine in the morning."

I was faintly surprised that a ship was docked and waiting for me but chalked it up to luck. At least I wouldn't be on the hook for an expensive hotel room for an extended period.

The physical wasn't something I had been looking forward to, but it was standard procedure for officers. With a resigned sigh, I headed up to the Two Deck and reported to the medical clinic. Two stans, four jabs, and a body scan later, I was free until morning. Even at that, most of the time consisted of waiting, and the majority of the questions were actually resolved by my academy health dossier. The clinician was pleasant enough but cool and remote. I supposed that "professional" was the proper adjective. She was certainly competent enough.

As I finished buttoning into my shirt once more, she reviewed the records and said, "Congratulations, Mr. Wang. There's nothing in this workup that indicates any problem. I'll forward a copy to DST and you're good to go."

I thanked her and headed out. That was it. I had a moment of jubilation in the passage outside medical, but trepidation seized me almost immediately. Who were these people I'd be serving with? How would I like them? Would they like me?

I squelched the feeling. They'd even warned us about it at the academy. I knew I'd cope, so I put it out of my mind and went looking for some lunch.

Jen was serving again at *The Miller Moth* down on the Oh-two Deck and I shared my good news with her.

"The *Tinker*?" she asked in confirmation. "You're going onto the *Tinker* as third mate?"

"Yeah," I told her around bites of a juicy burger slathered with fried onions.

She frowned in concentration but offered me congratulations on my berth. "I'm sure you'll make a fine third mate," she said but didn't seem very enthusiastic.

"Is there something wrong with the *Tinker*?" I asked.

She shrugged and started polishing the bar. "Not that I *know* of, no," she said with a peculiar emphasis on the "know" part.

"But?" I prompted.

"But ya hear things," she said. "I don't think it's a happy ship, if you know what I mean."

"Um, no. I'm not sure I do."

She looked uncomfortable, chewing on her lower lip as if trying to make up her mind.

I gave her a moment or two to respond.

"The *Tinker* has gone through a lot of crew." She looked up at me. "A lot," she repeated with emphasis. "I don't know how many for sure, but you're the second third mate in less than a stanyer."

I let that sink in for a bit while I considered it. Perhaps they were moving up and out.

"Does it strike you as odd that they imported you weeks ago for a berth that just opened up?" she asked.

"Well, I think it's customary to give some notice," I said. "Perhaps the current third is finishing out his contract?"

She looked dubious but shrugged in acceptance. "Possible, but that's a short contract, less than a stanyer. How long is yours for?"

I considered that. "Two stanyers, but it's a standard contract, and I can get out of it without a major penalty under some pretty normal conditions relating to health, performance, and such."

She nodded, a wry smile turning up the left side of her mouth. "Most of the termination clauses are in the company's favor, though, right?"

She had me there.

"Well, yeah, but even in my limited experience, it seems standard for the company to hold the better cards."

"True," she admitted in return. "Do you have a 'probation' clause?"

I sighed. "Yes, if we don't like each other in the next three months, the contract can be terminated by either side."

"Well, maybe that's it. They're just having trouble finding thirds that fit in."

She didn't sound convinced, but it was rather a dead-end conversation, and it was making me a bit uncomfortable, truth be told.

"How long you worked here?" I asked, steering the conversation onto a new course.

"Oh,"—she stopped wiping the bar and looked up at the overhead, thinking—"it'll be three stanyers in a month."

"You like it?"

She grinned and nodded. "Yeah, I do. Oh, I know it's a bit of a clichÃ© but it's also rather exotic. I mean, I could wait tables planetside, but up here, we get people from all over the Western Annex dropping in."

"Mostly ship people, isn't it?" I asked.

She shrugged a little and said, "Well, yeah. This is the Oh-two Deck after all. Not many tourists come down here."

"So, why don't you work up above?" I asked glancing in the direction of the restaurants higher up on the orbital.

"Well, I used to. I like the clientele down here better. Working people seem to have more respect for working people."

I chuckled a little at that. "Good to know."

I drained my glass, thumbed the tab, and stood up from the bar.

"I'll let ya know what I find out," I said with a smile. "I report aboard tomorrow."

She held out her hand over the bar. "Good luck, Ishmael," she said warmly. "Hope I see you around soon."

I shook her hand and if I held it a little longer than might have been necessary while she smiled at me, well, she didn't pull back quickly either. A hail from the other end of the bar broke the moment and she shot me a shy smile as she turned to deal with her customers and I left *The Miller Moth* for my room.

CHAPTER SEVEN
DIURNIA ORBITAL: 2358-JULY-6

Morning found me on the docks. My grav trunk trundled along behind me, and the receipt for my hotel stay had been stowed in my folio. The familiar bite of cold dock air mixed with the smell of stressed electronics and hydraulic fluid. I was looking for dock nine—the slot my tablet told me held the *William Tinker*, my new home in the Deep Dark.

I passed dock seven. The telltale said, *Jo Alice Long*. It wasn't going to be the *Lois*. I knew that. I'd been on a lot of ships since the *Lois*. They were all different. My summer cruises had given me the opportunity to work on four different vessels and each had seemed okay. Of course, none had ever been more than a temporary billet. There was no real reason to put down roots, to form bonds and connections.

Dock eight stood empty and I saw nine around the curve of the dock's broad passage. I paused and wiped my hands on my pants and took a couple of deep breaths. I used the reflection on the empty lock's view panel to make sure my cap was straight and checked my uniform for unbuttoned buttons and correct gig line on shirt, slacks, and buckle.

"Third mate," I told myself. "You're not the captain and what you don't know about being third mate would fill a seventy-five ton container. You're here to learn, to grow, and to hold up your end. You can do this."

The academy prep was actually reputed to be quite good. I knew I didn't know a lot, but I also knew that third mates were the bottom rung. I expected to get stuck with the same kind of jobs that my old training officer, Leland Von Ickles, did so well. As I gathered my nerve and marched along the dock, I held a picture of him in my mind.

Still, it was with a considerable level of trepidation that I walked up to the gangway and pressed the call button. I looked up at the dock monitor, so the watch stander could get a good look at my face and not just the top of my cap.

After a tick, the speaker beside the lock crackled. "Yeah? Can I help you?" a man's voice asked.

"Third Mate Ishmael Wang, reporting for duty," I said, a little off-balance.

Normal brow procedure would have been to walk out and greet the caller. They couldn't have been surprised. It's not like they wouldn't have known I was coming.

The pause stretched out. I wasn't sure the watch stander had even heard me. I kept my face carefully neutral. I didn't want to start out on the wrong foot with the crew, and I certainly didn't know the ship's conventions. For all I knew, he was following standard procedure. It struck me as rude, but I was the stranger on the dock and needed to keep that in mind.

My hand wrapped around the dolphin shaped whelkie in my jacket pocket, and my thumb stroked the smooth, oiled wood. I found it calming. I'd been carrying the small bit of wood and shell for stanyers, ever since getting it as a gift at St. Cloud. I viewed it as a kind of talisman, a good luck charm. Besides, it felt good in my hand and was pretty. I wasn't sure whether I believed it was imbued with magical powers by a South Coast shaman or not. I just found it soothing to have around.

After nearly three ticks, the small personnel lock began cycling and I stepped back to give it a bit of room. An able spacer in a greasy looking shipsuit with an oily stain across the left arm stood at the head of the brow with his hand on the mechanism. "You the new third?" he asked bluntly and without preamble.

Or salute.

"Yes," I said, eyeing the man and wondering what kind of ship I'd signed up for.

He leaned out and looked up and down the docks—almost suspiciously. It was as if he were looking for any confederates who might jump out and hijack the airlock once it was fully open. Satisfied that I wasn't the leading edge of a takeover force—or whatever it was that he was looking for—he stepped back and nodded his head to invite me aboard.

I stepped into the lock, making sure my grav trunk made it over the threshold, and got my first smell of the ship. To be sure, every ship has its own unique bouquet. My nose wasn't terribly sensitive, and several months working in the damp green dankness of environmental had broken me of any squeamishness. In my summer cruise experiences, I found that each ship's aroma had a specific kind of smell. Some were chemical, as if the crew liked the smell of disinfectants and cleaning solutions. Some were organic—a mixture of cooking, people, and free esters. Some were mechanical and some were electronic. I'd smelled them all and found none of them to be offensive.

Until I smelled the *Tinker*.

It was a meaty kind of scent that I thought the scrubbers should have handled.

The spacer secured the lock. He still hadn't introduced himself although I read his name tag, "Betts" from his shipsuit. He turned to the watch station and settled back down on the stool behind the counter, frowning at the readouts there and ignoring me.

I was about to ask him to notify the officer of the day, when a woman's voice rang out from the passage.

"Welcome aboard, Mr. Wang," she said while looming out of the dimness.

She was a solidly built woman with the typical spacer-cropped hair cut, wearing a shipsuit with DST's star and oval on the left breast and a name—Novea—embroidered above it.

Smiling, she came over and held out a hand. "You're our new third?"

Her hand was smooth, firm, and strong. She didn't try any of the "power move" handshakes on me, but there was little doubt in my mind that this woman could open a jar of pickles without any help or second thoughts. I filed that information away in case I needed a jar of pickles opened. She smiled at me, and I realized that we were probably within two centimeters of the same height. She had a nice smile and clear, brown eyes.

"Yes," I said. "Fresh from the academy, straight to your wardroom."

She smirked and gave a little chuckle. "Sense of humor. Good. That'll come in handy. Arletta Novea, second mate, astrogation."

She let go of my hand then, and I think we were both a bit surprised that she'd still held it.

"Let's get you settled in," she said. "The skipper will wanna meet you as soon as he comes back."

We went through the ritual of establishing my mass lading and crew record. As third mate, I had much more mass allotted than I'd had as a quarter share crewman, but every kilogram needed to be accounted for. I was well under my two hundred kilogram limit.

She led me up to officer country and showed me to a small stateroom. It was almost identical to the one I'd had on the *Ellis* coming in. I was glad to see that I would have the room to myself. On some of the older ships in particular, the junior officers were expected to double up. I was glad to be maintaining my sanctuary.

"Don't look so relieved," Ms. Novea said quietly. "You only think this is a sanctuary."

She caught me flat-footed with that. My snappy rejoinder consisted of, "Wha-?"

She smiled pleasantly. "It was pretty obvious."

I just looked at her and some of the sinking feeling in my stomach must have showed on my face.

She snorted but maintained her smile. "The head is through there, and you do have to share that with me. So, pay attention and knock first, please." She shot me a pointed look.

"Of course."

"You say that now, but let's not have any accidents after we've been underway awhile? Okay?"

I held up my hands palm out. "You got it! I'm not that kinda guy," I said, keeping my tone light while trying not to wonder— again—what kind of ship I'd gotten on.

"Wang? You're a guy. You're all that kind," she muttered, then changed the subject abruptly. "Got your tablet?"

I slipped it from the holster and fired it up. She walked me through the sync up with ShipNet and used her second mate credentials to enable the officer level access.

When it was done she said again, "Welcome aboard. It's all over but meeting everybody. I'm the OD and we're standing twelve-and-twelve in port. David will be relieving me at noon. I suspect he'll want to get you into the rotation as soon as possible so be ready for him to assign you to his watch immediately. You'll probably do two rotations with him and then stand on your own for our last day in port. We're due to leave for Breakall on the eighth—assuming they have a container ready for us."

"When will I meet with the captain?" I asked.

She shrugged. "He's ashore. He'll probably stay there until we get underway. I wouldn't be surprised if you didn't meet him until we're setting out again."

I looked at her dubiously. "Really?"

"Wang, I don't know where you served before this, but DST is a small, locally run company. The captain's wife lives here. When we're in port, he goes down below to visit with her for a few days before we ship out again." She shrugged. "It's up to us to get the ship unloaded, reloaded, and ready to go."

I must have still looked dubious, but she gave me a look that said, "He's the captain. What are ya gonna do?"

I didn't find it terribly reassuring, but I'd been aboard less than half a stan.

"You'll find what you need to know about the ship, including deck plans, on your tablet. T'were me, I'd start exploring to make sure I could find everything." She grinned. "Like the bridge."

With that, she slipped out past my trunk and headed down the passage.

"I'm on until noon," she called back over her shoulder. "Expect a call from David about 1130. If you get lost, bip me. I'll be in the ship's office."

In a tick, I was alone again. I stood there listening to the ship, breathing shallowly through my mouth and trying to ignore the smell. After a moment or two of staring dumbly, I slid the grav trunk into the closet, flipped the lid, and started hanging my uniforms on the rod. A small set of drawers set into the closet provided room for socks, underwear, and other small clothes. I left my generic shipsuits in the bottom of the trunk, along with the folio of my mother's papers, and closed and locked it. I double checked to make sure the grav pallet had engaged to the deck. I wouldn't want that box sailing through the air in the event of a gravity failure.

I sat on my bunk, pulled down the desktop, and started reviewing deck plans on my tablet. I had almost two stans before I could expect to hear from the first mate. I intended to use the time wisely.

The layout seemed pretty straight forward. With a finite number of ways that the massive solar clippers could be configured, the unique cargo container for the Barbell hull class created an interesting collection of ship's spaces. I was anxious to take a look at the environmental controls.

The smell was getting to me.

Chapter Eight
Diurnia Orbital: 2358-July-6

Figuring to beat the summons, I reported to the ship's office at 1130. The door was open and Ms. Novea was there with what looked like an astrogation update running. She glanced up as I tapped on the door frame.

"Well, you found your way here, okay," she said.

"I was looking for the mess deck."

"Oh, that's back down the passage—" She saw the grin on my face and realized it for a joke. "So that's the way you are!" she said with a smirk.

I just shrugged. "I like to try."

"Well, just remember," she scolded. "There's no second chance to make a first impression."

Her mock scowl told me a lot about her. I felt the knot unwinding a little in my gut.

I tried to look contrite. It wasn't my strong suit.

"So, have you managed to find your way around?" she asked.

I stepped into the office and sat at one of the side chairs. "I've been the length of the spine, stuck my head into the mess deck, and found my way to the bridge. The gym doesn't look like it gets much use," I added.

I figured it was too soon for me to say much more about what I thought of those spaces, being the new guy aboard and all.

"Wow! You've had the tour," she said. "See anything interesting?"

The question was light and carefully neutral. Not casually light and neutral, rather a studied tone. She looked at me flat on with one eyebrow arched.

Just as carefully, I answered very lightly, "Oh, a little of this

41

and a little of that. I'll need a bit more time to find the really interesting things, I'm sure."

The corners of her mouth twitched upward just slightly, and the tension in her eyebrows relaxed. Apparently I had passed the test.

A skinny spacer apprentice in a grimy shipsuit exploded into the office and skidded to a halt. Above her pocket was the name Nart. She started to say something to Ms. Novea but caught sight of me sitting there and gawped as if in total surprise.

"You the new third?" she blurted without preamble—or apparent thought, adding "sar" about two beats too late.

"I am. Ishmael Wang," I said and held out my hand.

Nart looked at the hand, glanced at Ms. Novea, and then looked back to me. I'm not sure what she was looking for but she eventually took my offered hand, gave it a single shake, and pulled back quickly.

"Nice to meet you...Nart, is it?" I prompted.

"Oh, yes, sar," she mumbled. "Ulla Nart."

Ms. Novea apparently took a little pity on the girl and informed me, "Ms. Nart is my messenger of the watch." Turning to the spacer she asked, "And do you have a message for me?"

"Oh, yes, sar," she said again, focusing her eyes inward, she struggled to remember. Finally she said, "Mr. Burnside sends his compliments, sar, and will relieve you as soon as he's changed into a shipsuit."

Ms. Novea smiled. "Thank you, Ulla. Would you find Mr. Apones and be ready to relieve the watch, please?"

"Aye, sar," she said and dashed out of the office.

"Comment, Mr. Wang?" Ms. Novea asked.

She must have seen the bemused expression on my face.

I held up my hand to show the streak of—something—that the handshake had left across my palm.

"Hygiene isn't a high priority with the crew?" I asked. "And you can call me Ish."

"Arletta," she said. "It's hard to get them to deal with it," she added with a little shrug. "You'll see."

I nodded slowly and tried to keep my face neutral. Something was definitely rotten in the state of Norway, as my mother might have said. "So, what do I need to look out for?" I asked, lowering my game face a little.

"What do you mean?" she asked innocently.

I glanced out the door once in an exaggerated show of conspiratorial concern. "You know. Every ship has its problems. The troublesome able spacer. The sticky hatch—" I looked at her and my joking statements choked off when I saw the look on her face.

Very precisely and with more heat than I would have expected, she carefully replied, "They're a good crew, Mr. Wang. They deserve—"

"Our respect and support?" her statement was interrupted by a voice from the doorway. I turned to see a broad-shouldered man in a shipsuit looming there. The first mate pips on his collar told me who he was even before I saw the name Burnside on his chest.

Arletta's face turned professionally bland. "Exactly. Respect and support."

She stood from her station and I followed her lead.

"David, this is Ishmael Wang. He's our new third."

I wasn't sure what was happening, but I held out my hand without thinking. "Mr. Burnside." I acknowledged his introduction.

He grimaced at my dirty hand and didn't shake it. "Mr. Wang, welcome aboard."

I remembered the encounter with Nart and pulled my hand back. "Oh, sorry about that. I just met one of the crew and haven't had a chance to deal with this yet."

Arletta reached into a drawer and handed me a box of sani-wipes.

"Sorry," she murmured.

Mr. Burnside merely grunted and turned to Arletta. "Okay, hon, what's the scoop?"

I was glad that Mr. Burnside wasn't paying any attention to me, because the blatant informality of that "hon" took me aback for just a heartbeat. The rituals of watch standing were well documented and engraved on the souls of spacers. Referring to any watch stander as "hon" while in the process of relieving the watch was an appalling breach of etiquette.

"Ship's status nominal. Refueling completed and stores are due for delivery in the morning. Home office reports that the can for Breakall will be ready for us on the eighth and we'll be getting underway on time. Mr. Wang reported for duty at 0900 and his system credentials and mass limits have been established."

"How are the astrogation updates coming?" he asked.

"Almost done. I should have them completed by this time tomorrow," she replied.

I started to say something about automated updates, but thought better of it.

Mr. Burnside nodded. "Okay, clear out. I'll see ya at midnight."

He picked up the ship's phone. "Make the announcement," he said brusquely. "Log it at 1145" He hung up without waiting for a reply.

I blinked at the ships chrono at the numbers 1205 and noticed

Mr. Burnside looking at me with a "do you want to make a comment" expression on his face. I shut my mouth and kept it carefully closed.

The overhead speaker pinged once and crackled a bit. "Now hear this. First section has the watch. First section has the watch."

Arletta logged herself off the work station, grabbed her tablet and coffee cup, and stepped aside so Mr. Burnside could take the chair. She crossed the office and was about to step into the passage when a beefy rating who looked a lot older than the normal spacer apprentice stepped into the door frame and stood there blocking her exit. Arletta stopped and waited, a sardonic grimace on her face while her back was to Mr. Burnside.

"Thank you, Apones," Mr. Burnside said. "Please check the status of the brow watch and bring me a coffee on your way back." His words were—marginally—businesslike but his attitude was slightly dismissive.

The man rumbled a brief, "Aye, sar," and removed himself from the door.

Arletta stepped quickly out of the office and turned in the opposite direction toward officer country.

It took me a tick to process the interaction. From where I was standing it looked like Apones had blocked Arletta's passage out of the office on purpose and then stood there until he was told to move. For her part, she hadn't seemed too surprised by the maneuver.

"So, Ishmael," Mr. Burnside said in a bland tone.

I turned to look at him. "Mr. Burnside," I acknowledged, responding to his informal goad with carefully prescribed formality.

He stared at me for a moment, his expression held a certain amount of pity—or maybe it was resignation. I couldn't be sure.

"You're fresh out of school, wet behind the ears, and way out of your depth. Keep your eyes open, your mouth shut, and try to learn to be an officer. What you learned at the academy is only an introduction, and now it's time for you to get off the playground and into the ring. I don't care what you think. I don't wanna know about your problems. Your job is not to bring me problems but to solve the problems and bring me the solutions. That's going to be a problem for you, because you're too green to know what a problem is, but eventually, given enough time and incentive"—here his eyes took on a menacing gleam—"you'll eventually learn the difference between a solution and a problem. Do I make myself clear, Ishmael?"

"Crystal clear, Mr. Burnside."

He was being deliberately provocative in his manner and attitude. I resolved not to give him an edge to cut me with. I'd seen this "alpha male" attitude before but didn't understand it.

"Do you have any requirements for me during this watch?" I asked.

I hoped that catering to his need for control would defuse his animosity.

"What do you think you should do?" he asked in return.

He was still testing me. I needed to get a collection of shipsuits at the appropriate livery. Until I was actually on the crew, the orbital's chandlery wouldn't issue them. I probably should have attended to that instead of touring the ship, but I was loath to leave so soon after coming aboard. I considered my priorities for about four heartbeats before responding.

"I need to order some shipsuits, get my systems and communications credentials established, familiarize myself with the systems configuration and backup procedures. I need to know more about the ship's layout, and review the standing orders for in port responsibilities for Officer of the Day. I'll need to review the procedures for getting underway, debarkation protocols, and standing orders for bridge watch standers underway." I paused, considered that to be sufficient to the moment and asked, "Do you have any preferences as to which I do first?"

Mr. Burnside targeted me with a baleful stare for about half a tick, then turned to his terminal without responding. A few keystrokes later, my tablet bipped indicating a changed status and I looked to see that he'd given me the system's access I needed to perform my systems manager duties.

"You've inherited training officer so you'll be running the ratings exams and coordinating the ship's drills. Please see the standing orders regarding those drills and don't make the same mistakes your predecessors did. Required drills will be held during day watch on the day before the required ratings exam period. I trust I don't need to tell you what those dates are?"

It was another challenge.

"I know them and I'll be sure to check the relevant ship policies."

Mr. Burnside grunted. "Good. Now get busy and if you have a question, my advice is to try and find the answer yourself before you waste my time with it. If you ask me a question that you could have answered from reading the standing orders, I'm not going to be happy. That would fall under the *not good* heading. Do you copy?"

"Roger that," I said, using the formulaic response almost without thinking.

"Good." He turned to his monitor, dismissing me with his posture.

I settled back to the desk and ordered a set of shipsuits with DST livery at the orbital's chandlery. As I suspected, being the corporate home, the appropriate specifications were on file and the order was completed in less than five ticks. They promised fulfillment by the end of the watch and I paid extra to have them delivered to the ship. I had a feeling I would need those extra minutes and I certainly wanted those shipsuits.

The thing about in-port OD watch is that you're nominally in charge of the ship. Unlike my previous watch standing duties where I'd had specific tasks and assignments to accomplish, the OD was there if something broke or required arbitration.

At 1230 we went to the wardroom—a small dining room off the mess deck—where the officers could eat without mixing with the crew. The noon meal consisted largely of cold cuts and bread on an iced platter. I wasn't sure what the crew was eating, but I suspected not much different. The coffee was predictably horrendous.

Mr. Burnside stood on no ceremony, helping himself from the trays, sitting in what was apparently his accustomed seat—on what would be the right hand of the captain. I took a seat well down the board. It's not like there were a lot of choices, but I didn't need to see the roster to know that I was the junior officer aboard, and I had no desire to attract the attention of the erstwhile alpha male. As I chewed my sandwich of mystery meat and cheese, I idly wondered, how the captain related to the first mate. I suspected that there would be more ceremony when the ship was underway and the captain presided over the mess.

The afternoon passed to evening without incident. I had plenty of time to review the relevant policies and procedures under the careful non-scrutiny of the first mate. Periodically, he'd ask a question about ship's procedures or operations. Most of them were textbook stuff although a couple had hidden teeth relating to local conditions in the Diurnia quadrant. The ship's fittings and fixtures were common enough. I'd not worked with these precise models before, but the manufacturers were certainly familiar.

At 1830, Mr. Burnside stood, stretched, and headed for the

door.

"Come on, Wang," he said. "May as well introduce you to the sewing circle."

When we arrived in the wardroom, he introduced me to the engineering and cargo officers—Amelia Menas and Frederica DeGrut.

Amelia Menas was an older woman, smartly turned out in a shipsuit. The gray hair and crow's feet made her look distinguished. "Welcome aboard, Ishmael." She greeted me warmly with a two-handed handshake. Her dark eyes held a sparkling humor.

Frederica DeGrut, on the other hand, was twitchy. She didn't look me in the eye and only offered the most perfunctory of handshakes. She was birdlike, even frail. She avoided Mr. Burnside as if he carried some plague.

Mr. Burnside led the way to the buffet. He browsed through it like a goat on a junk pile, helping himself with his fingers, pausing to pick up the odd tasty and pop it in his mouth. It was a bit off putting, but he didn't seem overly concerned about making an impression on any of us. Ms. Menas sighed softly and gave me a small shrug when Burnside's back was turned, as if to say, "What can you do?"

I stood back to let the senior officers go ahead of me. Ms. Menas smiled and nodded her thanks, but Ms. DeGrut seemed not to notice until I extended a hand indicating that she should proceed. She almost flinched, but then offered a fleeting smile and a tentative nod, stepping up closely behind Ms. Menas at the steam table.

By this time, Mr. Burnside had seated himself and proceeded to tuck into the piled platter. As he sat, a side door opened and a delicate girl in a white waiter's uniform, complete with side-buttoned tunic and black trousers, stepped into the wardroom with a silver coffee pot. She smiled at Mr. Burnside and placed the pot handy to his setting and slipped quietly out of the room without speaking. She came and went so quickly and quietly, that if I hadn't been watching, I might not have noticed.

Ms. Menas waited while Ms. DeGrut and I finished at the buffet and took our seats, before beginning her meal. I saw Mr. Burnside's sneer at this small courtesy, and I wondered, again, just what I'd gotten myself in to.

"So, Mr. Wang," Ms. Menas started, "this is your first billet as third mate? Are you excited?"

She seemed honestly interested and smiled as she offered the opening volley on the dinner conversation.

"Yes I am, Ms. Menas. I spent two years on a container ship over in the Dunsany Roads Quadrant before I went to Port Newmar.

It seemed a good thing to do at the time."

"You were a crewman?" Mr. Burnside asked with a low chuckle.

"Yes, I was. Two years on the *Lois McKendrick*. It was enlightening for a land rat."

Ms. Menas forestalled further comment from Mr. Burnside by asking, "You don't come from a spacer family? And you went to the academy?"

"Yes, well, my captain rather twisted my arm until I submitted the application. After all she'd done for me, I would have felt ungrateful if I hadn't even tried."

Mr. Burnside barked a laugh. "She? Your captain was a woman?"

Ms. Menas frowned at Mr. Burnside's outburst. "David? Half the captains in space are women. Don't sound so surprised."

"Not in *this* company, they're not," he said with an emphasis on the word "this."

Ms. Menas pursed her lips. "Yes, that's true enough," she said but failed to comment further on that subject.

She turned to me once more to follow up. "Alys Giggone? She was in command of the *Lois McKendrick* last I knew."

I all but gaped.

She smiled. "Don't look so surprised. Alys and I were at the academy together, many moons long past. We keep up."

"Was?" I managed to ask. "She's left the *Lois*?"

"She's still on the *Lois*, as far as I know, Mr. Wang. I think she'll retire from there if Federated Freight can't force her to take the training command at the academy."

I laughed softly at that. "I think her father has to retire first."

"No doubt," Ms. Menas said. "No doubt."

Ms. DeGrut surprised me by speaking with a quick glance from her plate in my direction. "And Alys recommended you to the academy, yes?"

"Yes, she did!" I said with surprise.

Ms. DeGrut smiled into her plate and flickered her eyes in my direction again. "What number were you?"

"Thirty-four," I said.

"Eight," Ms. DeGrut offered with a shy smile, a kind of peace offering to me.

Ms. Menas looked at her companion curiously but didn't ask the obvious question and the conversation died for a moment.

Mr. Burnside had finished his meal and pushed the plate noisily toward the middle of the table.

"So? What was your rating, Ish?" he asked. "Did you make it to half share in your two years as crew?"

It was a curious question. He'd obviously not looked at my hiring jacket or he'd have known. I think Ms. Menas must have realized that, too, because she froze, her fork just lifting from her plate, and stared at him.

"Full share," I said with a glance at Mr. Burnside. "When I left to go to the academy, I was full share."

Mr. Burnside's expression went from bland disinterest to a patronizing smile. "Well, do tell! You made it all the way up to full share in just two years? That's quite an accomplishment for a land rat? What division? Steward?" His tone made it clear what he thought of stewards.

"All four," I answered.

The confusion rolled across his expression and Ms. Menas smirked.

"All four what?" he asked.

"All four divisions."

I focused on my plate. He wasn't going to like that answer and I didn't want to appear confrontational by looking him in the face.

There was a moment of stunned silence before Mr. Burnside barked a harsh laugh and slapped the table. Ms. DeGrut flinched at the sudden sound and movement but Ms. Menas merely looked annoyed.

"Excellent joke, Mr. Wang. All four divisions," Mr. Burnside chortled nastily. "All four divisions, indeed."

Ms. Menas placed her fork gently on her plate and leaned forward to face Mr. Burnside. "David? Perhaps you should review Mr. Wang's jacket one more time. It seems there are some things you've missed."

Ms. DeGrut offered a small, furtive smile in my direction but focused on her meal.

Mr. Burnside's expression went blank. "Indeed?" he asked, rounding on Ms. Menas. "Pray, enlighten me, Amelia? You've obviously seen more in his jacket than I did."

"Our Mr. Wang here did in fact obtain full share ratings in all four divisions, including specialist second in environmental and specialist first in systems. His service record shows commendations from three captains, and his application to the academy was endorsed by ten officers of the line."

Mr. Burnside's expression went even flatter. "This land rat?" he asked finally, looking directly at me as if I were somehow to blame.

"This land rat," I said, hoping against hope to defuse the situation.

Mr. Burnside's eyes shuttered. His expression gave nothing away, but his words were calm and precise. "Well, it seems I owe you an apology, Mr. Wang. Very nice credentials and I look forward to working with you in the Deep Dark."

Ms. DeGrut went stalk still at that last comment. She was pale before, but went positively bloodless at the mention of the Deep Dark.

Her reaction attracted the attention of Ms. Menas who leaned over to her. "Are you all right, Fredi?"

Ms. DeGrut looked like a bird caught indoors. Her eyes darted everywhere but she didn't look up from her plate. "Yes, Amelia, thank you. It's nothing." Her eyes flickered fearfully in my direction, but she kept her head down and made no further comment.

My tablet bipped at just that moment and startled me. It was a message from the lock watch. My shipsuits had arrived.

"Excuse me," I said. "My shipsuits are here. I've got to sign for them and have them added to my mass allotment."

I stood and gathered my dirty dishes, placing them on the sideboard.

"You can just leave those on the table, Mr. Wang," Mr. Burnside said. "The mess crew gets paid to pick this up."

"Old habits die hard," I said.

With a nod to Ms. Menas and Ms. DeGrut, I beat a hasty retreat to the gangway. I stepped off the ship to accept the delivery from the chandlery representative and the smell of clean, fresh dock air washed over me. In a matter of a few ticks, I signed in the bundles and logged them to my mass allotment. I lugged them to my stateroom, and took the tick it needed to shake one out and put it on, hanging my khaki undress uniform in the locker.

I felt a lot less out of place wearing a shipsuit, even a brand new one with the third mate pip on the collar tabs. I brushed my hand across the DST decal on the breast and fingered the black embroidered letters of my name. The suit itself was a neutral tan, not too far from the khaki outfit I'd just taken off. My tablet dropped into the designated pocket, and I felt a bit more settled as I headed back to the ship's office to finish up my first watch.

I felt like I'd been aboard a stanyer, and it hadn't even been a half day.

When I got back to the office, I found Mr. Burnside reviewing my jacket. He looked up as I entered and I expected to get blasted.

He nodded at the screen. "You really do all this stuff?" he asked.

"Yes, I'm afraid so."

"Wang, I owe you an apology. This is an outstanding jacket. I don't usually bother with them—corporate hires and corporate fires. We don't have a lot of say about who comes and who goes."

He sounded sincerely contrite. It didn't make what he was saying any less dangerous, but he did sound like he was sorry. "Looks like we hit the jackpot when we got you, eh?"

I just shook my head. "I'm just a boot third right out of school. I got lucky with the *Lois* and I know perfectly well that I can't expect to stay alive in the Deep Dark by relying on luck. I'm looking forward to what I can learn here, and I'll do my best to cover my mass."

It sounded trite and cheesy even as I said it, but I needed to say something.

"Oh, I think once we get this tub moving toward Breakall, we'll have lessons a plenty, Ishmael. Lessons a plenty."

I didn't like the way he said that, but I kept my face blank and sat back down with my tablet to review the last of the ship's policies and procedures as the watch ticked down to midnight.

CHAPTER TEN
DIURNIA ORBITAL: 2358-JULY-7

I woke with a start, my sweat-soaked ship tee and boxers bound up around me. I heard the blowers moving the air, but my stateroom felt stuffy and damp. I flapped the sheets a little, trying to get some extra air moving and laid back on the pillow for a moment to let the pounding in my chest subside.

The chrono on the bulkhead read 0912 so I only had a couple of stans before I'd have to report for watch. In my belly, I felt a fluttering grumble. The food aboard would take some getting used to, it seemed.

I lay there, weighing the relative merits of putting on some clothes and heading out to one of the diners that catered to dock trade, or toughing it out and waiting for the wardroom lunch. Remembering the coffee onboard, I crawled out of my bunk, knocked on the door—Arletta should have been in the ship's office since she had the watch, but I wanted to get into the habit—and grabbed a quick shower before skinning into my undress uniform for a trip to find some breakfast.

At 0940, I stopped by the office and stuck my head in. Ulla Nart sat in one of the chairs, reading something on a tablet, and Arletta worked on one of the stations. They both looked up when I stopped at the door.

"Good morning, Mr. Wang," Arletta said with a smile. "You survived your first day aboard?"

"Good morning, Ms. Novea, Ms. Nart." I smiled back. "Yes, it was an interesting first watch."

Her mouth twitched in a near smirk, but with a glance at Ulla she managed to control it. "I dare say, Mr. Wang."

"I'm going to go grab a bite ashore, if that's okay?" I said.

"Get it now, because we'll probably be underway before you get another chance," she said in return.

"Any favored places for breakfast?" I asked.

"*Over Easy*," she answered immediately. "Looks like a pit, but the coffee is wonderful and he does bacon perfectly."

"Sounds ideal. Where abouts?" I asked.

"Oh-two Deck, two doors to starboard of the lift. Follow your nose. You'll find it."

"Thanks," I said with a smile. "I'll be back soon."

It only took a tick to get to the lock and Betts had the watch. It looked like he wore the same shipsuit with the stained left sleeve as from the previous day.

Only a day... it seemed much, much longer.

"Good morning, Mr. Betts. How's the watch going?" I asked by way of greeting.

"Fine, sar," he replied without standing up.

That was it. Just the flat statement. I let it sit there on the deck for a heartbeat or two before saying, "I hated brow watch. Long, boring, and the only amusement was watching drunk crew try to get back aboard in the middle of the night."

He looked at me, a flicker of curiosity behind his eyes. He didn't follow up, though, and I left it.

"I'm going to go grab a bite to eat. I've checked out with the OD. If you'd be so good as to log me ashore, Mr. Betts, I'll be back in about a stan."

The able spacer reached for the keyboard and made an entry in the log. "Aye, sar. Mr. Wang is ashore for approximately one stan."

"Thank you, Mr. Betts," I said and slipped out onto the docks.

The bite of the dock air was like ambrosia. I found myself breathing deeply, pressing the exhalations as if trying to empty my lungs of the residual smell of the ship. The mechanical and electronic aromas that permeated every dock I'd ever visited seemed somehow sweet and familiar and I drank deep.

The Oh-two Deck was always redolent with the smells of brew, booze, wine, and food. Throngs of spacers were almost always here, although midmorning wasn't a peak time. In spite of that, the nature of the spacer's life meant that somebody was always on liberty. Someone was always looking for something, and almost always that search lead to the Oh-two Deck.

I turned to starboard and found a hole in the bulkhead place with a smeared plexidoor lettered with "Over Easy" and a stylized picture of a cartoon woman holding a plate with a pair of fried eggs in a strategic position over her chest. Arletta was right. It looked like a pit.

I pressed through the door and inhaled the aroma of fresh coffee, layered with the scent of fried potatoes, onions, and bacon. My mouth exploded in saliva as I stood there blocking the door and bathing in the fragrance.

The place wasn't full, but it was far from empty. One long counter stretched almost all the way across the back. A pass-through window opened to what looked like the kitchen. I saw someone moving back there, head down and back to the opening. A couple of wait staff covered the busy counter and another pair circulated around the herd of square tables between the counter and the door. It was a small place. It felt like a closet, but nobody seemed to mind. A guy in civvies carrying a rack with six cups of coffee elbowed me out of the way with a venomous look as he left, and I stepped out of the traffic pattern and found myself a seat at the counter.

A young man wearing a spotless white tee shirt, white apron, and denim pants came over immediately. He slapped a coffee cup and napkin wrapped silver onto the counter in front of me.

"Ya know what ya want?" he asked with a slight tilt of his chin. His name tag read, "Seth."

"Coffee. Eggs. Bacon. Toast. Home fries," I answered.

With each word, Seth nodded. He reached under the counter and pulled out the pot, pouring before I even finished ordering.

"How? How many? What kind?" he asked when I finished.

"Over easy. Three. Wheat," I answered.

He grinned at me then. "You've never been here before?" he asked as he scribbled something on a lined slip of paper and ripped it from the tablet.

"First time," I said. "New to the quadrant."

"Welcome." He turned and slipped the paper into a spinning contraption of clips and metal, then shouted, "Order, Frank."

He moved down the counter, filling cups as he went.

I picked up the crisply clean, heavy china mug and looked into it. Coffee. Real, rich, dark coffee. No swirl of oil on the surface. I stuck my nose into the mug and took a deep breath. I put the cup down, added a dollop of milk from the pitcher on the counter and threw a couple of sugars into it. A swirl with the spoon and the coffee was heavenly. Dark, rich. It tasted like one of the Arabastis. Not Djartmo, but it had the signature after taste of a perfectly brewed Arabasti. Perhaps it was one of the local variants—Djartmo beans grown in a local setting.

As I sat there savoring the coffee, plates clattered onto the pass-through every few ticks, and a man's voice shouted a name and the phrase "Order up!" In a surprisingly short time the call, "Seth! Order Up!" came and my breakfast slipped onto the counter in front of me.

Seth called back, "Thanks, Frank."

The eggs steamed. The bacon glistened. The aroma of potato fried with onions and bacon drippings wafted up and grabbed me. The toast was perfect, crisp, buttered, with just the right texture for sopping up the loose egg yolk from the plate. From first fork to last swallow, I never looked up. It was delicious.

With a slightly regretful sigh, I realized that I'd inhaled my breakfast, leaving only the china, the silver, and the odd crumb of toast. Sitting up, I noticed Seth grinning and watching out of the corner of his eye as he took care of the people on either side of me. He worked his way down the counter with the coffee pot once more and pulled the dirty dishes off the counter and into a tray with smooth, practiced movements.

"You want anything else? Another one, just like the other one, maybe?"

I chuckled. "Yeah, but I need to get back to work. That was great."

"Glad you liked it."

Suddenly remembering the man with the carrier full of coffee, I asked, "Can I get some coffees to go?"

"Sure. How many? How big?"

"Large, two... no, three... cream and sugar on the side," I answered.

"Comin' right up," he said and in just about two ticks he filled three cups, locked lids on them, and put them in a carrier. A fourth cup got a handful of creamer and sugar packets. He slid it onto the counter along with the tab, to which I added a generous tip and my thumbprint.

I scooped up the carrier, nodded my thanks, and headed back to the ship.

It is amazing what a good breakfast can do for your outlook. At the lock, I took a few deep breaths of the cold dock air, then keyed the entry sequence. Stepping aboard, Betts glanced up at me and frowned at the coffee carrier.

I slipped one of the cups out and stood it on the station. "Cream? Sugar?" I asked.

"Black," he said.

I grinned in reply and headed down the passage. Even the smell of the ship didn't dampen my enthusiasm.

From behind me I heard a belated, "Thanks."

At the office, I found Arletta alone again when I breezed through the door. Her eyes targeted the coffee carrier as I stepped into the ship's office.

I held it out as if it was a silver salver and she looked up at my face like it was some kind of joke.

"You brought back coffee?"

"Well, they were just sitting there looking forlorn and they followed me back to the lock. I thought we might give them a good home," I said.

I put the carrier down and took a cup, grabbed a few sugars and a creamer from the stash, and popped the lid off long enough to add the requisite modification. I sipped appreciatively and settled onto a side chair while Arletta was still eagerly adding sugar to the remaining cup.

She lifted it and took a tentative sip of the hot drink, eyes closing in happiness and a beatific smile stretching across her cheeks. "Oh, my"—she sighed—"that's so good."

"Thanks for the tip about Over Easy."

We sat there sipping in silence for a few ticks while I considered my next move. I needed to get into a shipsuit and get ready to take the watch. Glancing at the chrono, I realized I had about a stan before I needed to be back in the office for my watch. I also needed to get a handle on the training dates and the ship's status. We'd be getting underway in a day or so and I needed to have a firm grip on the ship's systems before that happened. Green third mate or not, I knew my way around systems. I wondered about the forerunner, and what had been left undone.

"How long since my predecessor left?" I asked.

Arletta looked at me strangely. "What?"

"Oh, sorry," I said. "I'm having this conversation in my head and I forgot you're not listening in."

"Ah. And do you do this often?" she asked with an amused look on her face.

"Too often. But I was just thinking that the last update was probably before the last guy left, unless you or Mr. Burnside have done one lately. I just wondered how long ago."

"She left when we docked on the fourth," Arletta said.

I blinked. "She?"

Arletta looked at me with one arched eyebrow, "You have a problem with women in systems? Or as third mates?"

I shook my head. "Not at all. But two things hit me at the same time. One, except for the captain and first mate, all the officers are women."

Arletta's mouth twitched. I couldn't tell if she was suppressing a smile or a curse. "Yes. Curious that," she said. "And second?"

"I had lunch at The Miller Moth and news of her leaving had already been common knowledge."

"When was that?" she asked, a strange look on her face.

"Day before yesterday. The fifth, I think."

"My, my, news does travel fast," she said, her brows meeting in a frown. "How'd it come up?"

"I was having lunch and talking about getting the berth, and the waitress made some comment about the ship going through a lot of turn over—something about two third mates in less than a stanyer."

Arletta's eyebrows twitched in surprise. "Interesting. We're the talk of the dock now, huh?"

"Well, DST is a local company and this is its hub. It would make sense that the people around the docks would pay attention more to DST vessels than to some of the larger more transient players."

She nodded, a thoughtful expression on her face. "Did she say anything else?"

I shrugged. "Not really. Can I ask—"

"Why'd she leave?" Arletta interrupted.

"Yeah."

"It was personal."

It was my turn to raise eyebrows in question.

"Personal," she repeated. "Not my story to tell."

"Anything I should be aware of? Just...shipmate to shipmate?"

She glanced at the open door and said very softly, "You've already noted the distribution of males in the chain of command." She closed her mouth very carefully and looked me straight in the eye. "That's all I'm sayin'"

"My appointment must have come as something of a surprise to Mr. Burnside, then," I commented lightly.

"Indeed it was."

Glancing at the door myself, to let her know I'd gotten the message, I asked softly, "Should I be concerned?"

At that moment, Ulla Nart burst into the office and whatever Arletta was about to say got side tracked.

"Beggin' the OD's pardon, sar, but Spec One Otsuka requests your presence in Engineering to co-sign for the refueling."

"Thank you, Ulla," Arletta said and stood, grabbing her tablet from the table she headed for the door while Ulla glanced shyly in my direction.

Arletta stopped at the door and looked back at me. "Yes," she said, and left, heading aft toward the spine and Engineering.

CHAPTER ELEVEN
DIURNIA ORBITAL: 2358-JULY-7

"So, Ishmael," Mr. Burnside asked as we settled at the wardroom table, "what do you think you should do for the next twelve stans?"

We had just relieved the OD watch and adjourned to the wardroom to grab some lunch. Arletta was undoubtedly heading for a shower and civvies. It was our last night in port. I knew what I'd be doing in her place and wished her luck.

I sipped some of the execrable coffee to buy some time to consider. I made quite a production of it, but I already knew what I needed to do. I just didn't want Mr. Burnside to think I did.

"Well, Mr. Burnside—"

"David, please."

"Well, David, I need to get up on the bridge and look over the ship's systems. I've been reviewing them on my tablet, but the larger displays and computing power up there should let me get in and give them a good shake down. We're undoubtedly due for a system back up and I'd like to double check the spares."

He nodded, a smile of approval pasted on his face. "Good ideas. I'm not certified in systems myself, but you're right about the backups. We'll leave a set here in the corporate office just before getting underway."

I kept my expression attentive. I wasn't sure what the point of an off-ship backup might have served in this situation. If anybody needed that data after we got underway, it would undoubtedly not be anybody aboard the ship. A failure of that magnitude would most likely be fatal. It was a common practice throughout the fleet, so I didn't question it.

After a moment of shared silence while we ate, he said, "You've reviewed the standing orders for OD, I assume."

"Yes, David, I have."

"Excellent. Then, why don't you relieve me and take over the watch when we get done with lunch. It'll be good for you to have the watch once before we get underway." He paused. "You've stood bridge watch, I assume?"

"Oh, yes, many times. Summer cruises are mostly bridge watch."

"Well, yes, but if they were anything like my summer cruises, you had an experienced officer on hand so you weren't actually on your own while on the bridge."

"True enough."

I didn't contradict him in anything. He was going to have to put me on bridge watch and the only question was who and how much babysitting I'd get before they trusted me with the ship by myself. In a lot of ways, being underway was a lot less demanding than being in port. He knew that, of course, but it wasn't my place to point it out.

"Anything else you think we should do in this last watch before getting underway, Ishmael?"

I thought for a moment before replying, "There wasn't anything in the standing orders. I'm assuming that the various ship's stores and services need to be checked and verified...?"

He nodded. "Excellent," he said again with a broad—and patently false—smile. "Let's get on with the watch then, shall we?"

"Certainly." I stood, collected my dirty dishes, and placed them in the tray at the sideboard.

"I told you that you didn't need to do that, Ishmael," David said. "You're going to make the messmates think you're taking their jobs."

"Old habits die hard," I said as off-handedly as I could.

He just tsked and shook his head. "A good officer knows when to delegate."

"A sound lesson, David. Shall we get the watch swapped over, and I'll go up to the bridge?"

It was funny, really. I felt so off balance until Burnside signed me onto the OD watch. I'd had my share of them at the academy and in-port duty held no terrors. Once the mantle of watch stander fell on my shoulders, I suddenly felt centered. I ran through a series of system queries to check basic ship status from the office while Burnside looked on. He soon grew bored watching me flick through screens.

With an off-hand, "I'll be in my stateroom if you need me, Ishmael," he left me to my own devices.

As soon as he left, I shut down the terminal, used my tablet to bip the messenger of the watch, Mr. Apones, and asked him to meet me at the brow. Apones and the gangway watch stander, Steven Mallory if the watch roster was correct, were waiting for me. They stopped talking as I approached, and Apones looked as if he'd swallowed something sour.

There wasn't a hands breadth between them in terms of physical build—both squat, bull necked, and broad shouldered. Apones looked older than Mallory, although Mallory carried the rank. I wondered if Apones had lost his stripes somewhere along the line. In my brief time aboard, I hadn't had time to review the full jackets of everybody on the ship, but I made a mental note that I should do so as soon as I could.

"Gentlemen," I said, smiling as I approached the station. "Mr. Burnside has signed the watch over to me, and I just wanted to check in with you both. I'll be working on the bridge getting the system backups going. Is there anything going on in the ship that I should know about?"

Apones and Mallory glanced at each other in confusion.

"Sar?" Mallory asked.

"I've got the watch. I'd like to know if either of you two have seen or heard anything that's going on in the ship that would preclude my going to the bridge."

Apones actually sniggered. "You're the officer, sar. Ain't that your job to know?"

I dredged up my best Alys Giggone stare and leveled it at him.

"Yes, Mr. Apones, it is. So I've asked the two crewmen aboard who are tasked with having that information—your report, Mr. Apones?"

"My report?" he looked confused and a little off-balance.

Again he and Mallory exchanged glances.

"Thank you, Mr. Apones, that tells me what I needed to know."

I turned to Mallory who was not trying to hide his amusement over his shipmate's discomfort. "Mr. Mallory? Your report please?"

"No unauthorized entry or attempts since I took the watch, sar. The captain and second mate are ashore. First mate, chief engineer and cargo boss are all aboard. Crew is at liberty until 0900 tomorrow."

"Thank you, Mr. Mallory," I said. "I'll be on the bridge running system checks and backups, probably until chow time. Mr. Burnside has retired to his stateroom. If you'd be so kind as to notify me of anything requiring the OD's attention?"

"You have the watch. Mr. Burnside is in his stateroom. Aye, sar," Mallory said.

"Thank you, gentlemen. I appreciate your time."

I turned to head up to the bridge.

As I walked away, I noticed Apones and Mallory carefully not saying anything. When I got to the first dogleg and disappeared from view, I heard Apones start to laugh. It wasn't a happy sound.

I sighed and kept going for the bridge.

The bridge wasn't deserted when I got there. I half expected it to be. According to the ship's standing orders, the engineering watch was held in the after engineering space. There was no need to keep a bridge watch with the ship moored. So it was with some surprise that I found Ms. Menas, the engineering chief, and an astrogation spec two with the name De Silva on her suit. They were each sitting at separate stations. Ms. Menas had a schematic of the ship up on her screens while I recognized the standard astrogation update screen running on De Silva's.

Ms. Menas smiled when she saw me step onto the bridge and De Silva looked up from her screen with a fearful look on her face. She seemed confused for a moment and looked over her shoulder to Ms. Menas.

"Mr. Wang, what brings you to the bridge," the engineer asked. "I figured that Mr. Burnside would have you reviewing standing orders until we got underway."

The grin on her face indicated that she was amused rather than being critical.

"After last night, he's behaving like I'm his best friend. He signed over the OD watch to me and went to his stateroom."

I turned to De Silva and held out my hand. "I don't believe we've met. I'm Ishmael Wang, the new third."

She stood at her station and took my hand briefly, looking at me with something akin to astonishment.

"Binaca Consuela Garcia De Silva, specialist second, astrogation."

I smiled. "Nice to meet you, Ms. De Silva. Some of my best friends have been astrogators." I nodded at her screen. "Running updates?"

Her eyes widened in surprise. "Yes, sar, tedious work but it needs to be done."

"You're still copy and pasting?"

She frowned. "I don't understand."

"You've grabbed the downloads and now you're copying and pasting the changes into the database?"

"Oh, yes, sar."

"Let me get myself settled, Ms. De Silva, and I think we can lighten your load on that score. In the meantime, I need to get backups running. Don't let me interrupt."

She turned back to her station and settled into the chair.

Ms. Menas watched the exchange and winked at me as she went back to studying the screen in front of her.

I looked around and identified the main systems console through the expedience of a large label reading "Main Systems Console" on the cabinet. In a matter of ten ticks, I had the system backups cycling and went down to the systems vaults under the bridge to load a rack of removable media. Some ships just replicated the system onto a "hot backup," that is, a separate computer that could be swapped quickly in case of data problems. The *Tinker* didn't have that kind of system redundancy so it relied on backup drives and removable storage.

When I was satisfied that the backups were spooling properly to the removable drives, I went back to the bridge to check on other systems. They all looked nominal. Communications channels seemed to be performing properly. The major electronic systems were largely off-line at the dock, but from what I saw, looked fine. I ran a quick scan of the environmental systems, propulsion systems, and on-board network status. By the time I finished with those, the backups had still only run about a third of the way. I sighed and went back to my system's survey.

After another half a stan, my console beeped to let me know the first set of backups were done, so I set about securing the logs and checking my own system updates. With less than a day before we headed out into the Deep Dark, I wanted to be sure I had all my chips in a row.

CHAPTER TWELVE
DIURNIA ORBITAL: 2358-JULY-7

The afternoon sped by. Between the system checks and updates, brainstorming with Ms. "Call me Mel" Menas, and all the associated running up and down ladders from the bridge, to storage lockers, to data closets, I felt like I'd earned my pay. It felt good.

At 1730 I secured my station on the bridge and made a tour of the ship. I pulled up the ship's environmental sensor net and made the rounds as if I were on a sensor watch tour. The sensor net is uniformly distributed bow to stern. Only the inside of the big cargo pod lacked sensors. It was my first real opportunity to go from bow to stern and examine every area in the ship. There was almost nobody aboard. It was the last night in port on a four-day stay, and everybody who could go ashore had gone ashore.

As I strolled through the various passageways and clambered up and down ladders, I found the same level of crud. It wasn't that the ship was filled with trash or anything, but there were little things, like smudged light switches and built up dirt in the corners and crevices. Almost every hand rail on every ladder had some kind of deposit on it—oil, dirt, paint. It was disconcerting.

The exception to the rule was Engineering, where the spaces appeared to be maintained at a higher level. The fusactors, sail generators, and associated equipment were clean, and appeared to be in good order. I was no expert but it sure felt better in those areas.

I ended my tour on the mess deck. Dinner had started at 1800, and I found a couple of ratings dining aboard. The mess deck was a bit worse for wear. There were sticky spots and deposits on most of the tables. It looked like a lot more than just the normal build up from an afternoon's in port activity. The deck was just short of gritty, and I saw dirt ground into the tiles. The tarnished coffee urns looked like they hadn't been wiped down for a month and that was just the outside. I had a feeling I knew where the coffee problems started.

Getting them solved might be harder.

As on every other ship I'd ever been on, the in-port dinner mess consisted of a buffet with a hot dish, a soup, a salad, and lots of bread and cold cuts. The two ratings looked up—scowling at me— as I walked along the buffet. I smiled and nodded, ignoring the surly stares while becoming more and more disconsolate at the state of the ship. The food on the buffet was adequate. If the bread looked a little dried out, it was because it had been there for a while. The cheese didn't look a lot better, and I didn't want to think about the cold cuts. I refrained from lifting the lid on the soup or hot dish. The warmers didn't appear to be all that warm, and I didn't want to let any of the heat out.

On my way back through the mess deck, I stopped at the table. The two ratings—an able spacer and a spec three from gravitation, both wore the signature dirty shipsuit. They stopped talking and looked up at me. "Hiya. I'm Ishmael Wang, the new third mate," I said and held out my hand to the one with the deepest scowl.

She eyed my hand dubiously. "Able Spacer Juliett Jaxton," she said, taking the offered hand briefly and then added, "Sar."

I turned to her companion, an olive skinned man who looked like he'd been beaten recently. He didn't quite flinch when I turned to him, but he didn't look away either. "Xin Xhang," he said, "And yes, I know I don't look Chinese."

I kept my hand outstretched and, eventually, he shook it, although just briefly.

"Nice to meet you both. You been aboard long?" I turned from one to the other waiting to see who'd respond first.

Xin answered, but spoke into the tabletop. "Stanyer," was all he said.

"It's in my jacket," Jaxton said, with a confrontational tone.

I nodded as if we were, indeed, having a polite conversation. "Thank you, I'll be sure to look it up."

If anything, her scowl deepened, but before she could reply, I breezed on. "Well, sorry to interrupt your dinner. Just wanted to say hi. It should be an interesting time in the Deep Dark."

I nodded in what I hoped was a genial manner and left the mess deck.

As I rounded the corner into the passage and headed for the adjacent wardroom, I heard Xin say, "From Sissy to Isshy."

His chuckle sounded grim.

Jaxton replied with a growled, "Gods, save me from boot thirds."

I kept on going. Either I had really good hearing, or these people wanted me to overhear. I was pretty sure my hearing wasn't all that good.

My timing was perfect, though, and I stepped into the wardroom at precisely 1830. Mel Menas was there and smiled at me from the side board where she was pouring a glass of water. She raised it in a toast to my arrival and I smiled back.

"Ms. DeGrut not joining us tonight?" I asked.

She shook her head. "No, she's gone ashore for one more port side meal before we get underway."

David stepped into the wardroom at that point and added, "Can't blame her for that. Hope she finds something with some substance to it. Put some meat on those bones."

He smiled but I got the sense that he wasn't concerned with Ms. DeGrut's frailness.

Mel drank from her glass and frowned slightly rather than respond.

"So, I guess we're it for dinner tonight," David continued. "May as well get going."

He took a plate, rummaged through the buffet, plunked himself down, and began eating. Mel and I exchanged a glance and took our own turns at the buffet. As senior officer, she went before me, but waited until I joined the table before beginning her meal. David, for his part, just smirked and continued to eat.

The hot dish was some kind of pork and noodles in what should have been a savory sauce. Even with my limited exposure to the culinary arts, I could tell this was a simple dish. The flavor in the sauce owed itself more to the pork and a heavy grind of black pepper than any subtlety of the chef's skill. At the end of my second day aboard, I couldn't decide if the food was just bad or if my sensitivity to the ship's odor has caused my taste buds to rebel. Whichever it was, I thought I saw a contributing factor for the turnover rate.

"So how was the afternoon's watch, Ishmael?" David asked. "Run into anything unusual?"

"Operations normal," I replied, keeping my tone carefully neutral.

Mel shot me a glance across the table but didn't say anything.

"How did you spend the time?" he asked.

"I went up to the bridge to run the backups and install the system and comm updates. After that, I took a tour of the ship and met some more of the crew just before dinner."

He made an exaggerated "I'm very impressed" face which did little to actually convey the idea that he might have been impressed.

"And did you find anything interesting?" he asked.

I considered my answer carefully. "I'm new here," I finally said. "It's not my place to judge. I can't tell what might be interesting or not. I'm still working on the context."

"Context?" he asked. "You're working on the context?"

Mel looked interested but didn't give me any hint that I'd overstepped my bounds.

"Yes," I said. "Every ship has a context. The ship, the crew, the officers, the cargo, the way it's run. All of those things combine to create a unique context—almost a culture—wherein everybody understands their roles and positions—their responsibilities and benefits."

David's eyes had glazed over, but I saw Mel trying not to grin.

"And your assessment of our... context... so far?" David asked.

"I'm still working that out. I'm in no position to make any real summary assessment yet. I'm a boot third mate in his second day aboard. What I know about this context wouldn't fill a teaspoon."

Mel arched an eyebrow in my direction and a small smile hid behind her glass.

I shrugged very slightly and turned my attention to the pork and noodles.

David looked truly amused at my turn of phrase and finished clearing his plate, chuckling periodically, and wiping the china clear with a bit of bread which he tucked neatly into his mouth. Chewing thoughtfully, he pulled his coffee cup nearer and scanned the table looking for the absent coffee.

"Davies!" he called. "Coffee is customary with the evening meal!"

In less than a tick, a young woman burst through the door with the silver coffee pot in hand. "Sorry, Mr. Burnside," she said.

He scowled at her and pushed his cup to where she could fill it.

She had to step up close to him to reach it, but she took the hint and leaned over to pour. She frowned a little in concentration, making sure not to spill it.

As she was pouring I saw Mel stiffen in her chair. I glanced over at her and she was studying her plate as if looking for a new subatomic particle. Her neck had reddened up behind her ears but she sat very still. If I'd had to guess, I'd have said she was angry.

I found that curious and I glanced back to the steward pouring the coffee. Yes, she poured from the wrong side, but what caught my eye was a flicker of movement lower down. From my angle, I saw David Burnside's hand caressing the back of Davies' thigh all the way up to her butt. He wasn't looking at Davies or even me. He was staring at Mel while he did it, and it was obvious from the angles that he'd intended for her to see.

Davies, for her part, didn't react at all. She finished pouring the cup, placed the pot on the table, and stepped back.

"Sorry to be late, Mr. Burnside," she said, and turned to leave.

David picked up the coffee and took a sip. "So what else did you do this afternoon, Ishmael?" he asked.

"I spoke to a number of the crew. Apones finds me humorous, and doesn't seem to have a firm grasp on the duties as a messenger," I said lightly.

Mel looked at me sharply but David just stared blandly.

"Really? I've had no problems with his performance. Could you be more specific?" he said.

Mel shook her head just slightly.

I took the hint.

"I asked him if there were any issues I needed to be aware of before I went to the bridge to work. He didn't seem to understand the question. Mr. Mallory provided an excellent synopsis of the situation, however, so it was fine."

David nodded as if he actually had heard and understood what I'd just said.

"Excellent," he said. "Well, I'll leave you to get on with the watch. I'll be in my stateroom if you need anything," he said with a smile.

With that, he pushed his plate back from the edge of the table, took another sip of coffee, and stood to leave.

"Amelia," he nodded his farewell and she nodded back without speaking.

We ate in silence for a tick or two after he left. Then Mel shot me a glance out of the corner of her eye.

"Context?" she asked.

"Yes," I replied. "Context. It's important to understand the context if one wants to effect a change."

"And you want to effect a change in the *William Tinker*?" she asked, her voice barely audible across the room.

"Don't you?" I asked back with a pointed look at David's empty chair.

She shrugged a reluctant agreement before looking back at me. "What do you want to change?" she asked, a speculative gleam in her eye.

"Well, as I said before, I'm new. At the moment there's a lot I don't understand."

"Such as?"

"Why the duty crew is almost universally in dirty shipsuits, for example. Why almost every deck on the ship is cruddy, for another.

Your engineering spaces are not that way, by the way. I noticed."

She smiled. "They better not be." After a few heartbeats, she asked, "What else?"

"Why the food is so bad. I understand cooking on a budget, and I sure know that in-port meals aren't generally high on the list, but this stuff is only marginally edible. And the coffee, gods, the coffee is disgusting."

A short laugh exploded from her in a gust of breath. "Well, you don't pull any punches. How do you intend to deal with these issues?" she asked after a few moments.

"I don't know," I confessed. "I haven't even met the captain yet. It may be that he likes it this way, and I'd be an idiot to go against the captain."

"As long as you recognize that much, you should be okay," she said with another smile.

"I'm green, Mel," I said with an answering grin of my own. "But I'm not totally stupid."

She chuckled. "I'm glad to hear it, Ishmael. Very glad to hear it."

CHAPTER THIRTEEN
DIURNIA ORBITAL: 2358-JULY-8

We were scheduled to go to navigation detail at 1330, which would give us all a chance to get a meal before the long process of undocking and pull back began. Accordingly, Captain Rossett called an officer's meeting at 1000 in the wardroom. I needed to start the required backups four stans prior to undocking, according to the standing orders, so I was in the main systems closet loading removable media when the captain returned to the ship. I kicked the backup at exactly 0930 and figured there would be time to get it to DST's home office after the meeting and before we went to navigation detail. I skinned into the wardroom at 0950 while everybody stood around waiting for the captain to be seated, which would call the meeting to order.

He didn't seem to be in any hurry.

When I slipped into the wardroom, he was standing at the far end of the room, a mug of coffee in one hand and a big smile pasted on his face. He was chatting with the first mate, and I had to look twice to make sure it was the captain.

One of the things that I'd always maintained was that I could tell a clipper captain just by their bearing and attitude. It's not the uniform that makes a person a captain. I always thought a clipper captain would be recognizable as such if wearing a towel. Crossing to the side board to collect my own cup of bad coffee, I thought I might need to reconsider that assessment. He wasn't short, tall, thin, or fat. He didn't look particularly young or old. He had all the aura of an accountant, which probably did a disservice to accountants. I had to admit, that if he hadn't been wearing the uniform, I probably would not have pegged him as the captain of a solar clipper.

That didn't make me feel any better about getting underway, but I was too far down the rabbit hole to back out.

As I finished getting my coffee, I saw Mr. Burnside lean over to the captain and say something. His eyes flickered in my direction. The captain turned his head and stared straight at me, his brow wrinkling in a full on scowl. I kept my face down, pretending not to notice that I was the subject of his scrutiny, then slowly worked my way toward my place at the table.

I hadn't made it all the way before the captain spoke loudly. He didn't need to. The wardroom was small, and there were only the six of us in it.

"Well, now that our junior man has seen fit to join us, I think we can begin," he announced and took his seat at the head of the table.

Mr. Burnside sat on the captain's right while Ms. Menas sat on his left. Beside her, Ms. DeGrut took her seat and beside her, a slender man with cook's insignia took the third chair on that side. Ms. Novea flashed me a quick smile as she sat next to Mr. Burnside, making sure to leave him plenty of room by sliding the chair ever so subtly away from him. I took the last seat, across from the cook.

"Right then," the captain said. "You know the drill, let's get this over with. Menas?"

"All tanks are full. Batteries are charged. Fusactors are hot and the sail and keel generators are on safety standby. Surplus waste has been removed according to standing orders and the regulations of the base. The ship's Engineering Division is ready to get underway, Captain," she replied without looking at him or varying her inflection one iota. She sounded a bit like a robot.

"DeGrut?" the captain asked.

"Cargo pod locked and checked. The embargo seals were verified at 0900 according to port regulations and standing orders. Cargo manifest and mass ratings are on file in ship's systems, correlated against station records and tested using the required metrics for accuracy. The ship's Cargo Division is ready to get underway, Captain," she said, just as flatly as Ms. Menas.

"Vorhees?" the captain barked again.

"Ship's stores of fresh, frozen, and packaged food stuffs have been inventoried and cross checked. Expiration dates on all food stuffs have been checked and are within the parameters established by rule, regulation, and common practice. The ship's Steward Division is ready to get underway, Captain," the man across from me reported crisply.

"Wang?" the captain said. He pronounced it with an "a" sound rhyming with pang instead of the correct "o" sound, rhyming with gong.

"Ship's systems have been checked, updated, patched and validated according to CPJCT regulations and local station rules. Communications queues have been flushed in preparation for getting underway and last-port-backup is running according to established custom and standing order. Systems Section of the Deck Division is ready to get underway, Captain," I rattled off.

The captain stared at me for a moment. He glanced at Mr. Burnside with a small frown before barking, "Novea?"

"Ship's astrogation sensors have been collimated and resolution is within CPJCT tolerances. Databases are up to date and verified against station reference. Chart corrections completed. Standard course for Breakall has been plotted, verified for ship's mass, and filed with Port Authority according to established rules and customs. There are no ATON warnings outstanding for our projected course. We are cleared to undock at ship's discretion at or about 1330 hours this date. Astrogation Section of the Deck Division is ready to get underway, Captain."

"Mr. Burnside?" the captain said.

"All hands present or accounted for. All ship's systems are reported space worthy and the required forms and procedures have been filed and followed. We have cargo and are cleared for Breakall according to CPJCT rules and regulations governing ships of our class and size. The ship is ready to get underway, Captain."

"Thank you, everyone," the captain said. With the formalities over he looked around the table. "Mr. Vorhees? Can you do anything about the coffee?" he asked with a grin on his face.

Vorhees smiled at what was, apparently, a long standing point of contention.

"There's naught wrong with the coffee, Captain. It's dark. It's strong. It's bitter. It's plentiful. What more could you ask?" he said.

The captain turned his gaze to me, then and said, "We have a new member in our merry band. Welcome, Mr. Wang. Would you be so kind as to report to my cabin after we secure from navigation detail?"

"Aye, aye, Captain," I replied.

While it's common for a captain to talk about "my ship," even when the hull belongs to somebody else, it's verbal shorthand for "my command" and nobody thinks too much about it. But when Rossett referred to "my cabin," it jarred me. Every ship I'd ever been on had only one compartment designated as "the cabin." The captain used it as a combination living quarters, office, meeting room, and—sometimes—courtroom, but it belonged to the ship much the same way as "the main lock" or "the ship's office." Hearing Rossett take such a proprietary view spoke volumes, and I knew right then that Captain Leon Rossett was not the kind of person I had been used to sailing with.

The captain turned to Mr. Burnside and said, "My goodness, he's a nautical little devil, isn't he, David."

"Mr. Wang is full of surprises, Captain," Mr. Burnside replied.

"I'm sure he is," the captain said, his eyes tracking back to me. His lips curled into a frightening approximation of a smile. "I'm sure he is."

The silence lasted for about three very long heartbeats before the captain slapped the table with his right hand as if bringing down a gavel. "Good! Company dismissed to final preparations for navigation detail at 1330"

The chairs all scraped as everybody stood. The captain said, "David? A moment, please." The rest of us filed out of the wardroom without another word.

I dropped my used cup in the tray on the sideboard as I walked out, and Arletta Novea caught up with me on the way to the bridge to check my backups.

"Nice job on the report," she said. "They expected to trip you up."

"I figured as much."

"How did you know?"

"It's standard procedure. It's written up in the standing orders. They just didn't think I'd had time to read them."

"When did you?" she asked.

"I haven't yet."

"Then—?" she stopped in mid sentence, confused.

We'd reached the ladder up to the bridge. "Easy, I had three reports to go by before he got to me. Each was logical, succinct, and all used the same formulaic language. All I did was walk through the various items I know I'm responsible for, threw in some of the boilerplate verbiage, and said we were ready to go. They have no idea what I'm supposed to report and I'll bet that when I do get to the standing orders they only say something about getting underway after the appropriate section and division reports have been made."

"You bluffed?" she asked with a laugh almost bubbling up.

"Well, not really bluffed. I just figured I stood a better chance by giving a complete report than by sitting there and saying I didn't know what they wanted."

She laughed then, the first laugh I'd heard aboard. "This is gonna be an interesting trip. A very interesting trip."

She turned and scampered up the ladder ahead of me and I couldn't help but notice certain aspects of her personality that I found quite appealing.

She had a very nice laugh.

CHAPTER FOURTEEN
DIURNIA ORBITAL: 2358-JULY-8

Lunch in the wardroom was strained. The captain presided from the head of the table. Mr. Burnside had taken the first section OD watch at noon and left me at loose ends. All through the meal, whenever the captain would look at my end of the table, he had a frown. I remembered Captain Giggone's unhappiness when the company put a new crewman on her ship when she wasn't expecting it. The situations weren't identical. I wasn't replacing an existing third mate but filling an empty berth.

The whole thing made my head hurt. What should it matter?

Mercifully, the lunch was brief. Davies served very competently. She was one of the few crew members I had ever seen who wasn't wearing a dirty shipsuit. With six of us at the table, she moved sharply to get everyone served and then circulated around, keeping coffee and water topped off. Mr. Burnside did not repeat his inappropriate behavior, and I began to wonder if I'd imagined it. Perhaps I'd seen something that my eyes misinterpreted because of the angle. Davies hadn't reacted at the time and she looked no more concerned now.

At 1315 the captain dismissed the mess, and we all trooped up to the bridge. I was last out of the room, of course, and took a moment to put my dishes in the tray. Davies, who was already starting to clear the board looked startled, but said a demure, "Thank you, sar. That's not necessary."

I smiled and shrugged.

"Old habits, Ms. Davies. I used to be a messman apprentice myself," I said and followed the other officers to the bridge.

There was, I confess, a certain frisson of excitement in getting underway as a real third mate. It's not like I hadn't done it a dozen times already as a cadet, but this time I was getting paid for it. That shouldn't have made a difference, but it did. This wasn't a station on loan to me for the purposes of the exercise. This was my station, my ship. For perhaps the first time since coming aboard, that idea had begun to sink in.

The captain took his seat in the command chair and nodded to Mr. Burnside.

Mr. Burnside said, "Call navigation stations, Mr. Mallory."

Mallory spoke softly into the ship's intercom and I knew speakers around the ship would be calling crew to quarters. The bridge crew looked to be in place already. Ms. Novea sat at astrogation with Ms. De Silva. Ms. Menas had the main engineering station and my systems console showed another station slaved to hers which was probably in the after engine room.

"Take us out, Mr. Burnside," the captain said.

"Aye, Captain," Mr. Burnside replied. "Astrogation, clear us with the orbital. Mr. Mallory, signal the tugs, if you would?"

Mallory spoke into his mic and I saw the tugs lashing onto our systems in a coordinated maneuver. The familiar schematic of ship and systems expanded to include the two tugs outboard from the orbital.

Mr. Burnside waited for a tick and added, "Prepare for pullout, Mr. Mallory."

Mallory spoke into his headset again, but loudly enough for the bridge to hear. "Secure forward locks. Make ready for pull out. Disable docking clamp interlocks."

I saw the repeater on my console as the docking clamps went from the red indicating locked to green showing that they were ready to release.

Mallory's voice came almost immediately, "Locks secure. Docking clamps are green. The ship's board is green once, sar."

Mr. Burnside asked, "Astrogation?"

Ms. Novea answered, "Astrogation online and running. Ship's board is green twice."

I scanned my boards one last time as Mr. Burnside said, "Systems?"

"Systems are online and running. Ship's board is green thrice," I completed the formula.

Mr. Burnside turned to the captain and said formally, "All boards are green and the ship reports ready for departure at 1330, Captain."

The captain said, "Log it, Mr. Burnside."

Mallory's voice came back with, "Logged, sar."

"Make the announcement, Mr. Mallory," Mr. Burnside said

crisply. "Stand by for pullout in ten."

As Mallory gave his announcement and the countdown, I could sense the others around me, getting ready for what should be an anticlimax but which sometimes was a bit more exciting. The tugs took up the strain on the ship as the countdown got to "three"—not pulling but keeping the ship steady. At "zero" the clamps went from green to red again as they released and I felt, as much as heard, the familiar clunk from the bow as the ship came loose from the station.

"Clamps released," Mallory confirmed.

"Back dead slow," Mr. Burnside ordered.

"Back dead slow, aye," Mallory confirmed and the tugs increased their pull ever so gently as the side of the orbital slipped away from the forward ports. I felt the ship move under me for just a moment before the inertial dampeners kicked in.

The tugs did their job, helping to maneuver the heavy vessel back from the fragile orbital. Carrying as much mass as we did, it would not have taken much to damage the station fatally. While we drifted backward, I watched the systems data flows. The *Tinker* was considerably shorter than the *Lois McKendrick* at only a hundred and forty meters. The barbell design made up for the difference in length by making the ship twice as wide. The ship had a roughly hexagonal cross-section which made for short, but wide decks in the fore and aft sections. In spite of the difference in length, the ship was rated at two hundred metric kilotons, or nearly five times the cargo capacity of the *McKendrick*. The huge Victor-class Burleson drives gave the ship a jump range of four BUs fully loaded. The ship was basically one big cargo hold with engineering and crew spaces strapped to each end. From a design standpoint, it was as subtle as a brick.

The systems data flows stayed nominal and the pullback went without incident. As we came up on the departure position, Mr. Burnside announced, "On station for getting underway, Captain."

"Log it," the captain said. "Bring us about and let's get this show on the road."

"Aye, Captain. Log departure at 2358-July-8, 1405," Mr. Burnside ordered.

Mallory confirmed with a brisk, "Aye, aye. Departure logged at 2358-July-8, 1405, sar."

"Release tugs with our respects. Engines all stop. Prepare to come about."

Mallory signaled the tugs and I saw them release us smoothly and the systems readouts confirmed the engines had stopped.

"Tugs released. Engines are stopped, sar. Ready to come

about," Mallory announced.

"Astrogation, bring us around. Engines ahead one quarter."

Ms. Novea replied, "Thrusters maneuvering to bring us onto departure vector."

The station swung out of our forward view and I saw the two tugs heading back into dock as they slid by.

"Engines ahead one quarter, aye, sar," Mallory confirmed.

We began the long climb up out of Diurnia's gravity well. In another stan, Ms. Menas started winding up the sail and keel generators and by 1530, the ship was clear of local traffic.

"Shake out the reefs," Mr. Burnside ordered and I watched the huge sails billow on my systems display.

Nothing actually showed in visible light. It was one of my great disappointments. The sails and keel were insubstantial force fields, driven by sail and keel generators in the fore and aft sections. They were invisible to the naked eye, but to the various field sensors, they showed as huge panels against the background radiation of the universe. The main sail extended some twenty kilometers and was configured to catch the solar wind from almost directly astern as we pulled up and away from Diurnia's primary. We were climbing up, perpendicular to the plane of the ecliptic to carve the shortest possible path to the Burleson limit. Even so, it would be five weeks before we'd be far enough out to fire up the drives and bend space-time. Once the Burleson drives had given us our little hole in space, we'd be another five weeks clawing our way back down into the Breakall System.

Ten weeks in space, more or less, then we'd get four days in port. On the *Lois*, that hadn't seemed like such a big deal. I had an uneasy feeling as I watched Diurnia Orbital fall away that ten weeks on the *William Tinker* might be a life time.

"We're underway, Captain," Mr. Burnside announced.

"Very well. Secure from navigation detail. Set the watch."

"Please make the announcement, Mr. Mallory," Mr. Burnside said. "First section has the watch."

"Aye, sar, first section has the watch."

As Mallory made the announcement a few people swapped places on the bridge, and I watched the ship's status monitors shift.

The captain stood then and headed for the ladder. "Mr. Wang, at your convenience," he reminded me before descending from the bridge.

"Aye, Captain," I replied to the empty spot where he wasn't waiting for my acknowledgment.

I secured my console after one more—very fast—review of ship's systems. As I crossed the bridge, I checked my tablet to verify that it was slaved to the console so I'd be notified where ever I was on the ship if anything threw an alarm.

Arletta gave me a smile as I walked past her station, but Mel looked grim as she watched me drop down off the bridge and head for the cabin.

As in most ships, the cabin was just down the passage from the bridge. The rest of officer country was only slightly farther. In the crowded confines of the *Tinker*, that distance wasn't far at all.

I knocked on the door and heard, "Come in, Mr. Wang," from the other side.

I entered and stopped just inside the door. "Third Mate Ishmael Wang, reporting as ordered, Captain," I said bracing to attention.

It wasn't the first time I'd been called to the cabin by a captain. It was one drill I knew pretty well.

"Come in, Mr. Wang. Have a seat," the captain replied, releasing me from formality with a wave of his hand to a side chair. He still mispronounced my name, in spite of having heard me say it.

"Thank you, Captain," I said and took the offered chair.

He stared at me with something like a smile on his face. It wasn't a smile. It was too threatening to be that. It was more like an expression he'd learned in front of the mirror when somebody told him he needed to look pleasant when dealing with subordinates. It wasn't working for him.

"I must say, Mr. Wang, you're not what we expected."

I wasn't sure how to respond.

"In what way, Captain? Is there something wrong?"

He stared at me for a moment.

"We don't usually get people right out of the academy," he said. "It's a long way for a boot third."

"You got the offer from DST when?" he asked.

"The beginning of May, Captain. Just before graduation."

A snowball started to build in my stomach.

"And did they offer you the *Tinker* at that time?"

"No, Captain. It was just a pro forma offer for third mate on a vessel to be determined at such time as I was able to present myself to the corporate offices at Diurnia. I booked passage on a fast packet and arrived just three days before reporting aboard."

He stared for several long moments, then leaned over his desk with a frown.

"Who do you work for?" he asked, his voice almost a whisper.

That question came out of the port side airlock for all I could tell and I blinked stupidly for a couple of heartbeats trying to figure out what the answer might be.

"Technically, I suppose it's Mr. Maloney, since he owns the

company, Captain, but I report to you."

"No," he said. "Who do you *really* work for?" His expression had taken on a dangerously flat look.

"I don't know what you mean, Captain. I work for DST."

He sat back in his chair, bracing himself against the side of the desk. He seemed to be trying to weigh me or something.

"You expect me to believe that you've come all the way from Newmar to take a berth on my ship that didn't even exist when the company sent you the contract?" he asked.

"I didn't know it would be this ship, Captain," I pointed out in what I hoped was a reasonable voice. "Lots of my classmates got offers from companies in other systems."

"Federated, Saltzman, Coopers, Western Annex..." the captain flicked off the names of some of the largest companies in the business.

"Yes, Captain," I agreed.

"Diurnia Salvage and Transport isn't exactly in their league, now is it, Mr. Wang? Don't you think it's a bit unusual to have a two-bit operation like DST recruiting months in advance directly from the academy?"

"I don't know, Captain. This is my first experience in being hired out of the academy. I never gave it a second thought. The opening was on the boards so I applied. DST sent me an offer and a transport voucher. Here I am."

"How many third mates do you think are employed by DST, Mr. Wang?"

"I don't know, Captain. Twelve ships so, probably not more than twelve."

"Exactly four, Mr. Wang," he replied.

Reviewing what I remembered about DST's fleet I realized his point. The Damien tractors were notorious for being short handed. They reputedly got underway with barely enough crew to mount two watch sections. The other Unwin Barbell and the two Manchester tankers were probably the only ships in the DST fleet that carried third mates.

"So, why did Maloney offer you a job and fly you all the way out here from Port Newmar, Mr. Wang?" the captain persisted.

I opened and closed my mouth a couple of times before I finally managed to put together any kind of response. "I really don't know, Captain. You'd have to ask Mr. Maloney about that." I put every ounce of credibility that I had into it. It helped that I didn't have any idea. "It never even struck me as unusual, Captain."

We sat there without speaking for a couple of ticks. I didn't dare move, and he kept examining me as if he could somehow read the answer on my forehead.

"Very well, Mr. Wang," he said at last. "I'll take your word for it...for the moment...but let us be perfectly clear on one thing, shall we?"

"Certainly, Captain. What's that?"

"Out here I am the captain. I am the law. What I say is the answer. As far as you and the rest of the crew is concerned, out here in the Deep Dark, I am God." He paused to let that sink in. "I do not like smart asses, troublemakers, or surprises. I like my universe orderly and predictable. If you have a problem with me, then *you* have a serious problem." He placed a heavy emphasis on the "you" part of that.

"In the Deep Dark, Mr. Wang, what I say will be the final word, and I never have any problems. Am I making myself clear, Mr. Wang?"

"Yes, Captain, crystal clear," I said, my voice surprising me by staying relatively even.

"We will be watching you, Mr. Wang. Please do not give me cause to take any unfortunate action," he said.

"I will do my best, Captain." I tried to sound reassuring.

"You are dismissed, Mr. Wang."

CHAPTER FIFTEEN
DIURNIA SYSTEM: 2358-JULY-8

Luckily my stateroom wasn't far from the cabin. I managed to get back there before my legs gave out, and I flopped on my bunk. I was on the third watch section, so I didn't have anywhere to be before midnight, which was a good thing. I didn't know how to react, and my body was doing it all by itself.

Only a couple of ticks went by and I heard a tap on the door to the head. "Ishmael? You okay?" Arletta asked softly.

I sat up, reached over, and slid the door open. She stood there with her hand upraised as if to knock again.

"You okay?" she repeated, looking at me closely.

"Yeah, I think so. But the captain seems to think I'm a spy."

Her expression went from concern to incredulity in an instant. "A spy? For whom?"

I shrugged. "I don't know. He was mostly concerned that DST hired me before there was an opening, and he wanted to know who I was working for."

She blinked slowly at that. "What? Back up... they hired you before there was an opening?"

"Yeah," I said, nodding. "You wanna sit?"

I pointed to the only chair in the room.

She slipped in and perched on the chair. "What do you mean they hired you before there was an opening?"

"I just graduated from the academy."

"Yeah, I heard that part. What were you doing on Diurnia? Is that where your family is from?"

I shook my head. "DST brought me here. They had an opening posted at the academy. The commandant gave me a recommendation for it and DST made an offer. I accepted and they sent me a travel voucher."

"But...?" she started to say. "You weren't here already? They brought you here from Port Newmar?"

I shrugged again. "Yeah, I didn't think anything of it. At least four or five of my classmates got offers like that."

She was blinking owlishly at nothing in particular as she considered. "But they were all from big companies, right? Not mom and pop outfits like DST?"

"I guess, but there wasn't any reason for me to take note of that. I just assumed they had a projected need for a third mate when they made the offer—somebody due for a promotion or something like that. Honestly, I never thought twice about it."

"Holy Hannah, I can see why he's more paranoid than usual."

"Is he always like that?"

She shrugged. "Hard to say. He's a bit of a martinet and very reclusive. When we get to Breakall, he'll disappear again, and he'll not come back until we need to get underway. Visiting family. Apparently he has family every place we go."

"Every place?"

"Well, we only go to four ports—mostly Breakall and Jett—but he pulls the same thing when we go to Welliver and Dree."

"Woman in every port?" I asked.

"I assume so, but he might just like getting out of the smell for a few days." She wrinkled her nose.

"I hardly notice it when I'm aboard now. My nostrils must have burnt out."

"Yeah, you notice it most when you go out and come back. It'll still catch you when you get a stronger whiff every once in a while, but after a few days aboard, you hardly notice it again."

I looked at her for a moment and then asked, "So, what did happen to my predecessor? I'm not likely to find out anything out here in the Deep Dark. What am I up against?"

"She wouldn't sleep with Burnside or his bully boys," she said.

I gaped. I know I gaped.

"I didn't realize that was a job requirement," I said.

I must have also looked worried, because she said with a little smirk, "You won't be required to. It's only the women they're interested in."

She looked at me sharply. "Get it out of your head. I won't sleep with them either."

"But...they tried?"

She sighed and shook her head, looking at the deck some more. "I was gonna say it's none of your business, but that's hardly fair if the captain has it in his head that you're some kinda threat."

She grew silent and I watched her shrinking into herself. "Yes, they tried. I said no and made it stick."

"But Sissy couldn't?" I asked.

Her head snapped up and she scowled at me. "Where'd you hear that name?"

"Couple of the crew said the ship had changed Sissy for Isshy. I presumed that was her name."

"Burnside called her that. It was his little slap. She wouldn't give in. Locked herself in here between watches, and only left to go to the bridge and the wardroom for meals."

She sighed and scrubbed her face in her palms. "There was an incident with a couple of Burnside's bully boys. It wasn't pretty. After that she was afraid to go anywhere on the ship alone. So, Burnside started calling her 'Sissy' for being so afraid all the time."

"That's crap!" I exploded. "They can't do that. It's harassment!"

"Yeah, but who ya gonna complain to?" she asked with a serious look. "The captain?"

She had a point.

"How'd she get out of her contract?" I asked.

"I don't know. Maybe she didn't and just took the penalty clause."

"She didn't talk to you?" I asked, looking at the connecting doorway. "I'd have thought you two would have..."

"Discussed it? Banded together against the common foe?" she asked with a fair amount of bitterness in her voice.

I gave a small shrug. "Something like that."

"She didn't trust me either."

"She thought you were in on it?"

"I was already aboard. She thought I was a bunk bunny already, I guess."

"Bunk bunny?"

"You've been through the academy and never heard the term?" she asked sardonically.

"Oh, no, I've heard it. I just never knew it applied to officers."

"Well, typically there aren't enough officers for it to be an issue," she said wryly. "Here? Why do you think the captain and Burnside are so upset that you're here? You're not exactly their cuppa tea."

"They prefer their bunnies with a little more padding?"

"Something like that."

"How have you escaped? Or have you?" I asked suddenly very concerned.

"I let them know I don't like guys. When they tried to change my mind, I broke Apones's arm and kicked Mosler so hard in the jewels that he sang soprano for a month. I got Mel and Fredi to back me with the captain. After that, they left me alone. As far as they're concerned, I'm just another filthy lesbo."

"Why didn't you press charges?" I asked.

She shrugged. "They made me a deal. If I didn't pursue it, they wouldn't charge me with aggravated assault. They had more proof than I did."

"Kinda hard to hide a broken arm?"

"Something like that," she screwed up her face and said in an almost dead on impersonation of the captain. "'Now, Ms. Novea. You know boys will be boys. And after all, they've taken more damage than you have.'"

"Was that before or after the 'my word is law' speech?" I asked.

"Oh, that was the first day. Just like you got," she assured me. "I didn't get the spy routine, though. I was already on station when the job opened up. He spent a lot of time hinting that I should sleep in the cabin, but he didn't come out and do anything I could haul him up on charges over."

I nodded my understanding. As second mate, if she had a problem with the skipper, she could file a grievance with the company, but problems with the crew got stonewalled without the captain's support. Even with the support of the chief engineering and cargo officers, she'd have had a hard time making anything stick. I was no lawyer, but I'd sat through enough Legal Implications of Space Command lectures to have a pretty good guess of what the problem was.

"Why do you stay?" I asked.

"The hard part's over," she said with a shrug. "They leave me alone. I don't break any more arms. Mel and Fredi are good people and there are some of the crew who appreciate having somebody besides the Testosterone Gang to talk to."

"And you can't get out of your contract," I finished.

She shrugged. "That too. A few more months and it'll be over. Two stanyers goes by quickly. I'll be eligible to sit for first mate before we get to Breakall."

"Not soon enough for some people," I pointed out.

"Roger that," she said ruefully.

We sat there thinking our own thoughts for a bit.

"So, what's with Mel and Fredi?" I asked. "Fredi seems afraid of her own shadow."

"I don't honestly know," she admitted. "And before you ask, I have no idea if they're a couple or not. I don't care. Mel is a great person and Fredi, if you can get her away from these goons, is one of the sharpest minds in the Western Annex."

She grinned. "Personally, I think the 'frail bird' thing is an act, but whatever it is, it keeps them out of harm's way."

"So, who're the troublemakers in the crew?"

"I already told you about Apones and Mosler. Mallory is okay, but he won't buck the flow. He'll walk away rather than put his butt on the line. Xhang likes a bit of fun now and again, but I think they just take advantage of the general chaos. I don't think they're really bad."

"Who're the victims?"

"Davies in the wardroom. She's bearing up under the strain pretty well, but she's a very unhappy camper. Ulla Nart, I'm keeping her under my wing as best I can. Some of the boys think she's my bunk warmer, and I let them think that, for obvious reasons. Vicki VanDalon and Osmia Lignaria in Engineering were both getting a lot of the captain's attention, but he's having to be careful when poaching from Mel's group. Below decks, I don't know how well that's working out. The official policy is, 'No blood, no problem.'"

"Could this group be any more dysfunctional?"

"Yeah, it could. They still speak wistfully of the BDSM parties on the mess deck and there's reputed to be one body still missing back from the 'good old days' before there were so many uppity women in the ranks."

I blinked in disbelief a couple of times. "You don't suppose the smell..." I started to say but couldn't finish.

Arletta shook her head. "No, that was too long ago. The smell would have dissipated by now. It was before I came, and I think they just tell that story to terrorize the new hands."

"This is so wrong. It doesn't have to be like this."

She sighed. "We can only do so much, Ishmael. Even though he's a megalomaniac, the captain is correct about being the law out here. He's got the mechanics of it down. In port, he's never on the ship. Underway, his word is gospel. You go against him at your peril. Put in your time, keep an eye on your back, and get out when you can."

She was right, of course.

"Okay," I said. "So what can we make better? Why is everybody always in a dirty shipsuit? Why is there crud on the decks?"

She snorted. "I think that goes hand-in-hand—dirty ship, dirty crew. If we could get one cleaned up, then the other would probably follow."

"Okay, well, other than brow beating the watch section to put on clean clothes, what else?"

She shrugged. "The coffee sucks. I don't remember the last

time I had coffee this bad."

I grinned. "Coffee, I can fix. How do we get to it?"

"Prove that you can make better coffee and I think you'll have Vorhees eating out of your hand. That 'joke' that the captain used on Vorhees this morning? That wasn't a joke. The captain wants better coffee, but Vorhees doesn't have a clue what to try."

I looked at her skeptically. "Isn't he a spec one chef?"

"Indeed he is, but he took a lateral over as spec one from Environmental to Steward."

"He's an engineman?" I asked.

"Well, not now, but he was, yeah."

"No wonder the coffee tastes like burned engine oil. I think we can do something about that much. Give me a couple days to work on it."

She looked at me with a dubious expression. "*You're* going to make the coffee better?"

"Nope," I said with a grin. "I'm going to help Vorhees make coffee to die for."

The worst of the shakes had run their course by the time Arletta went back to her stateroom to get ready for watch. Having that back door felt a little like sneaking around, but it also felt more like normal. Everything was going to be okay. The captain was a loon. The first mate was a sadist. The engineering and cargo firsts were probably sleeping together. But it was going to be okay, because at least I could talk to Arletta.

"You're a sick man," I told myself with some degree of satisfaction as I made my way down to the mess deck.

As I expected, the place was largely deserted. The chrono said 1700 and we'd been underway for only a couple of stans. Those who had day work were undoubtedly doing it, and those who had watch standing duties were either on, or preparing to go on, watch. The galley proper was just beyond the mess deck. The door was open and I heard voices. They'd be getting ready for the dinner mess which meant making sure the coffee was made.

I stepped up to the galley door and stuck my head in.

Mr. Vorhees spotted me right away and smiled. "Mr. Wang, can I help you?"

The two messmates looked up from their work—Davies, whom I recognized from wardroom service and another woman whom I'd never met. I read, "Cramer," on her shipsuit.

"Actually, Chief, I think I can help you. I know you're getting ready for the evening mess, but I wonder if I could borrow whichever of your mates usually makes the coffee?"

He frowned slightly at that and crossed the galley to where I was standing, and I backed out of the doorway so we could step onto the mess deck for a modicum of privacy.

"Something wrong with the coffee, Mr. Wang?" he asked with a guarded expression.

"No offense, Mr. Vorhees, but my sense from the wardroom meeting this morning was that the captain has been raggin' your coffee for a while now? Correct me if I'm wrong."

He looked at me hard. "You got that just from one question and my answer?" he asked.

"No, I've had the coffee."

He barked a laugh in surprise. "Well, Mr. Wang, you shoot from the hip, but you got the right of it. What's on your mind?"

"I know a bit about making coffee. Long story, but I was a messmate before an officer. I know what you're up against."

"I'm still listening, but the clock's tickin', sar," he said.

"You buy beans or ground?" I asked.

"Beans, we grind it by the bucket load."

"Okay, who does the coffee? Cramer?"

"How'd you know?"

"Because Davies has wardroom duty and you strike me as a fair man."

"Fair? How's that, sar?" he asked, curiosity getting the better of him.

"You'd not give all the crap duty to one messmate."

He barked another laugh. "Guilty as charged, sar."

"Could you send Ms. Cramer out, and we'll see if we can do a little good here. Which one's the next urn to go?" I asked.

"Number two," he said, pointing at one of the chrome monsters mounted on the bulkhead.

I rolled up my sleeves and nodded. "Excellent. If you'd have Ms. Cramer bring out a step stool, a scrub brush, and a couple of liters of white vinegar, we'll get on this."

He didn't stand there looking for more than a heartbeat before he went back into the galley and started giving orders.

Ms. Cramer came out looking scared and confused but lugging the supplies I'd asked for.

"You wanted to see me, sar?" she asked.

"Yes, Ms. Cramer. How would you like to make coffee to die for?" I said with a smile.

"Oh, sar, if we could get people to stop complaining about the coffee, sar..." she said wistfully.

"I think your next problem will be keeping the urn full, Ms. Cramer. Now look sharp because we don't have a lot of time."

We got to work and between the two of us, managed to overhaul the number two urn. There was a fair amount of sludge built up in it, but the vinegar and hot water made short work of it. The mess deck smelled like a pickle vat for a while, but that was actually an improvement.

I explained the ratios of water to coffee, and we went back to the pantry where the requisite equipment was stored. I tossed the bucket of stale ground coffee and had her break out a fresh one. We ground enough for three urns, which would take the ship through dinner, evening, and the following morning. I had her write down the amounts and the grinder settings. It was a standard twenty liter model. It was so much like the *Lois's* that I felt a little homesick. We loaded a basket and filter and I had her check the water temperature to make sure we were brewing with cold water. She looked at me one last time and I nodded encouragingly. She opened the valve and began the brew cycle.

While the urn brewed, I stuck my head into the galley.

"Thank you, Mr. Vorhees," I called. "I'll get out of your hair, but I think you'll find Ms. Cramer has a most astonishing talent for making coffee."

He didn't look like he believed me, but as I left the mess deck, the smell of fresh coffee was beginning to overwhelm the pickley smell of the vinegar. I smiled in satisfaction and headed for the bridge to check on the ship's systems before I needed to report to the wardroom for dinner.

I got to the bridge just as the watch was changing at 1745. I still wasn't used to so few people on the bridge. The only two underway watch standers consisted of the bridge officer and helm watch. The engineering watch standers sat in the aft section's engineering control room. Because the ship was under one hundred fifty meters, it didn't require an astrogation watch even though the mass of the ship was considerable. It was part of what made this Barbell class so popular. Fewer hands required meant greater profits.

Mr. Burnside left the bridge, followed by his helm watch stander, Mallory. Neither of them looked back as they left. Arletta checked the instrumentation and chatted for a moment with her helm—Arnold Betts—before crossing to my station.

"Everything okay?" she asked.

"Oh, yeah." I replied with a grin at my screen. "Should be interesting."

"You got to Vorhees?" she murmured.

"Keep your fingers crossed, but I worked with Cramer for about a half a stan and showed her a few tricks about making a big pot of coffee." I glanced up at her. "You were right about Vorhees. He was skeptical, but willing to give me a shot."

"Can you make the coffee better?" she asked with more than a little skepticism of her own.

I snorted. "Well, I would be hard pressed to make it worse. There were some relatively minor adjustments which taken as a whole should yield coffee the likes of which this ship has apparently not seen in a long, long time."

"Humble, too, I see," she said with a grin.

"Well, don't look at me. Ms. Cramer did all the work. Any improvements are the direct result of her diligence and hard work."

Arletta looked at me for a long moment in the glow of the screen.

"Ishmael Wang, you are a strange man," she said softly, but with humor in her voice. She patted me on the shoulder and went back to her duty station.

I satisfied myself with the status of the ship's systems and secured the station. It was time to see if this first small effort would pay dividends.

It was all I could do not to go directly to the mess deck and check on the coffee, and the suspense nearly killed me. I'd left before the urn had finished brewing, so I wasn't sure if the changes had made that much difference.

Sure, we'd washed out a lot of sludge, and used fresh grounds which was always better than trying to coax flavor out of week old—or month old—grinds. But I didn't know if the problem was related to the beans, the urn, or even the water supply.

In due course, Ms. Davies served the wardroom meal. It was some kind of bland chicken dish with a light sauce and some rather badly overcooked green vegetables. I sighed, wondering whatever made a lube jockey take the lateral move to steward. The food wasn't bad, just not good. I vowed to count my blessings should I ever get to a ship with a decent cook again. Finally, Davies came in with the coffee carafe, and she gave me a little wink behind Mr. Burnside's back. She poured around the table, leaving the pot between the captain and first mate before leaving the way she'd come.

I took a sip and suppressed a smile of satisfaction. Whatever the other problems, the coffee would not be one of them for the remainder of the voyage. The brew was rich, flavorful, and completely devoid of the burnt, oily aftertaste. Mel must have seen something in my expression because she frowned just slightly in curiosity before trying her own coffee. I saw the surprise in her face, and she looked at me sharply but didn't say anything. I tried to look innocent and paid close attention to not tasting my dinner.

Fredi was the next to sip her coffee, her head bowed over her plate, not looking at anybody directly, but casting the small glances out and around as required. I saw her stiffen as she raised the cup to her mouth. She straightened slightly and took a tentative sniff. I could practically see the gears turning in her head as she processed the reality that the coffee was very good. Finally, whatever calculus of logic swirled through her brain reached a solution, and she looked at me directly for the very first time with a shock of recognition. She didn't ask how, but she knew that I'd had something to do with the change.

Mel murmured something to Fredi and Fredi lowered her head once more into her normal posture but a gentle smile curved the edges of her mouth.

The captain and Mr. Burnside paid no attention to the table. They were busy regaling each other with commentary on various issues of mutual interest and general jocularity. The captain actually sipped from his cup and put it back down without noticing any change. Mr. Burnside took a sip, and he looked confused for a moment. As he started to put the cup back onto its saucer, he stopped and raised it again to take another careful sip. He put the cup down and sat there looking at it in consternation for a moment before looking around at us. Mel sat with the smug look of a canary-filled-cat, cradling her cup in her fingers and inhaling the aroma. Fredi hunched in her usual position, head bowed, but smiling a slight smile. I pretended not to notice, eating my dinner methodically.

Eventually the captain noticed the shift in dynamic, proving that even the most self absorbed individual will pay attention when enough people are not looking at them.

"Is something going on, David?" he asked.

"Try the coffee, Captain," Mr. Burnside suggested.

The captain frowned, but took a careful sip and then another before placing the cup back on its saucer with a thoughtful expression.

"Well," he said, looking up. "It seems Mr. Vorhees has resolved the coffee issue."

As if surprised, I lifted my cup for a sip, once more savoring the smoothly flavorful brew and nodding in appreciation.

Mel watched me through slightly narrowed eyes, but the captain and Mr. Burnside engaged themselves in discussing how lovely, marvelous, and unexpected the change in the coffee was.

After dinner, I retired to my stateroom, making sure to secure the door behind me. I crawled into my bunk for a nap before watch. I had, at least for the moment, a feeling of profound satisfaction and I drifted off to sleep secure in the knowledge that I'd managed to do a little good.

My tablet bipped me awake in time to take a shower and change into a fresh shipsuit. It was the roundabout route, but on my way to the bridge, I stopped into the galley and was pleased to see that Ms. Cramer had gotten to the number three urn and the coffee in it was as good as I'd hoped. I filled a mug and headed for the bridge.

Arletta smiled as I climbed the ladder balancing my coffee cup carefully. Betts eyed me curiously from the helm but offered no comment.

"You about ready to get off watch?" I asked, eyeing the chrono on the watch station—2340. I was still a little early.

"How in the world did you fix the coffee?" she asked in a lowered voice.

"Me? I didn't *do* a thing," I said. "It was all Ms. Cramer's work."

She fixed me with a look. "Yes, but you told her what needed doing, right?"

I shrugged. "Guilty as charged, but that's just between us."

"And the mess crew," she said.

I nodded a reluctant agreement.

"How long do you think that'll stay under wraps?" she asked.

"Probably not long, but it needed doing."

It was her turn to nod in agreement.

"Still. Burnside isn't going to like it," she said. "You're hob-nobbin' with the enlisted and givin' advice to other divisions."

"Hobnobbing?" I asked with a chuckle. "I haven't heard that word in ages."

She frowned at me.

"Yeah, I suspect I'm painting a target on my forehead, but gods,

I couldn't drink too much more of that mud without doing *something*."

"I wish I'd known how to deal with it," she said ruefully. "I've been drinkin' that crap for months."

I gave a little one shouldered shrug. "See me between watches and I'll explain it."

The chrono clicked over to 2345 and I heard footsteps on the ladder. Jaxton, my helm watch, was dragging onto the bridge, wearing the predictably grubby shipsuit.

"Well, I think I can relieve the watch now, Ms. Novea," I said.

"Ship is on course and on target," she replied formally. "No incidents or actions. Standing orders are unchanged. You may relieve the watch, Mr. Wang."

"I have the watch, Ms. Novea, logged on 2358, July 8 at 2345 per standing orders."

She stood.

I sat.

Jaxton and Betts changed positions with a few murmured words which included the current course and speed. I watched as Jaxton logged the watch change on the console and then looked on line to see the watch change in Engineering and Environmental as the names of the watch standers flickered and changed to the third section.

"Well, good luck, Ishmael," Arletta said. "I'm off on my twenty-four so I'll be sleeping in tomorrow."

"I'm sure we'll be fine. Sleep well."

She headed down the ladder ahead of Betts and I felt the ship settle into the only quiet time it had while underway—midnight to about 0400. That's when the cycle would start again—when the galley started baking and getting ready for the morning meal. I sipped my coffee and looked out of the ports at the points of light out there in the Deep Dark. Aft, I saw the glowing Diurnian primary. The planet Diurnia itself fell away, almost visibly and the limb of the planet obscured the orbital station we'd so recently left.

"Well, good morning, Ms. Jaxton," I said. "Looks like we'll be spending some time together."

"Yes, sar." It wasn't quite a sulky response, but one that spoke volumes about her outlook.

I sighed and stood up from my station. Jaxton flinched at the movement as if expecting that I was going to come at her. She glanced quickly in my direction but glanced away when it became clear that I was just crossing from one station to another.

At the system's console, I fired up a schematic showing the data and electrical flows in the ship. Each switch, node, and interlock glowed in high-resolution detail. The consoles, while far from new, had been upgraded recently and were considerably better than what I'd grown used to at the academy. I watched as the automated backups kicked in, rotating the logs and spooling the copies out to the removables in the closet under my feet.

Straightening from the console, I stretched and began wondering what I could do to stay awake. I crossed to the after observation port and looked out at the wide bodied ship. I found myself shifting back and forth to see around the smudges on the armor glass. I saw only the glass rather than the scene beyond it and snorted. It was covered in a layer of finger prints, smudges, and what looked like a series of evenly placed nose prints that ran from one side of the two meter window all the way across to the other in an unbroken line.

"Somebody had too much time on their hands," I said aloud.

Ms. Jaxton asked, "Sar?"

"Oh nothing, Ms. Jaxton."

I looked around and noted for the first time just how cruddy the bridge actually was. I had been so focused on the systems and backups during my previous trips that I hadn't noticed that the bridge was as bad off as the rest of the ship.

"Ms. Jaxton, what's the common practice on bridge watch?" I asked.

"Depends on the watch, sar," she replied warily, "and who's on it."

"I see. Thank you, Ms. Jaxton. What do you think we should do for the next few stans?"

"Me, sar?" she asked apparently shocked by the question.

"Yes, you. What do you think the two of us should do?"

She looked at me hard, square in the eye. It was an assessing look that I couldn't quite fathom, but I kept my features very still while she made up her mind. She sighed.

"Well, sar, you're the officer here," she said in a sort of resigned voice. "What did you have in mind?"

"Well, I can think of a lot of things that need doing, but I suggest we get Ms. D'Heng up here, since she's part of this section."

I saw the confusion crossing her face. I wasn't sure what she might have been thinking, but given what little I knew about the culture of this particular ship, I was pretty sure she had no real clue about where I was headed. I just smiled a little and pulled out my tablet to call the messenger of the watch to the bridge.

Charlotte D'Heng was one of the crew I hadn't met yet. Small, fine boned, and quite pretty, she had a ready smile but a guarded expression as she climbed the ladder to the bridge.

She shot Ms. Jaxton an apprehensive look, before saying, "You called, sar?"

"Yes, Ms. D'Heng. I hadn't had a chance to meet you yet and since you're in my watch section, I wanted to get to know you a bit."

"Oh, I see, sar," she said, and started to unzip her shipsuit. "And you wanted Ms. Jaxton to watch?"

"Um, no!" I said.

"Understood, sar," she purred and crossed to the helm. "We're used to working together aren't we, dear," she said to Ms. Jaxton with a gentle hand on her arm.

"Oh, yes," she replied and started to reach for her own zipper.

"Ladies!" I barked, in a desperate attempt to get the watch back under control.

"Sar?" Ms. D'Heng asked, looking at me curiously.

She turned to rest her rump on the helm console beside Ms. Jaxton. Her shipsuit was already unzipped to the waist and too much of her torso was exposed for my comfort. She didn't appear to be wearing a ship tee under her suit.

"That's quite lovely, I'm sure," I said, more than a bit flustered by the unexpected turn of events, "but that wasn't precisely what I had in mind."

"Oh, you can join us, sar," Ms. D'Heng said.

"No!" I snapped too quickly.

I took a deep breath while they looked at me with confused expressions that were beginning to make me very, very angry—and not at them. I took a deep breath and started over. "I'm sorry I wasn't very clear, and it's obvious that common practice aboard is not what I'm used to. Please zip up and we'll start over."

Ms. D'Heng looked confused while Ms. Jaxton gave me a considered frown. Obviously this wasn't going anywhere they were used to, either. Ms. D'Heng zipped her shipsuit—not all the way—but at least far enough to be just a moderate distraction.

"Thank you. Now. Let me start again."

I took a deep breath and began outlining what I wanted to accomplish during the watch. It wasn't a long list, and when I was done, the two of them looked at each other and then at me.

"You're serious, sar?" Ms. D'Heng asked with what might have been a pout.

"Yes, Ms. D'Heng. I'm getting a little tired of this. I'm going to do something about it, with your help."

They exchanged another look.

"It doesn't sound like as much fun as I was thinking about," Ms. D'Heng said with a twinkle in her eye, "but it'll certainly be a change of pace."

With a small giggle, she headed for the ladder. "I'll be right back, sar. Three ticks."

"Thank you, Ms. D'Heng," I told her.

She slipped quietly down the ladder. It was just past midnight and we had almost six stans to make a difference. I intended to use every tick.

Underway bridge watch tends to be really, really boring. During the night watches, crew are encouraged to study for ranking exams or just read. What they're not allowed to do is sleep. The reality is that as long as you're anywhere on the bridge, you can pretty much do what you like. Apparently that practice had gotten a little out of hand, and it bothered me a bit that these two spacers were quite so ready to engage in fraternization. It spoke volumes about the other male officers on the ship. I had a pang wondering if I was being sexist in that regard, but I had a hard time imagining Arletta ordering Betts out of his shipsuit on watch, and there was something about Mel and Fredi that made me think that we shared more commonality in outlook than I shared with, say, Mr. Burnside. Obviously D'Heng and Jaxton were used to behavior that I wasn't.

But then again this was the first ship I'd been on that had bunk bunnies.

I started rolling up my sleeves and Ms. D'Heng returned from the janitor closet with the cleaning supplies we'd need. I set Jaxton, the tallest of the three of us, to work on the ports. The armor glass was smeared and, in some places, practically obscured by greasy hand, head, and even—in one case—what looked like a butt print. I wondered how that fundamental part of the anatomy could have been elevated high enough to be placed there, but decided that was something I didn't want to know. D'Heng and I split the consoles and did a first level wipe down of the screens and horizontal surfaces. I got the broom out of the locker in the back of the bridge and proceeded to sweep the loose dirt from the deck corners into a pile.

"I didn't even know that locker existed," Ms. D'Heng said.

I chuckled. "Every ship's bridge has one. You just need to know it's there to look for it."

Jaxton finished the last of the glass about the time D'Heng and I finished the consoles and deck. There was a lot of armor glass and it took close to four stans to get through it all. We were all three filthy and tired from the effort, but the bridge looked more like the bridge of a real ship and not like some abandoned crap trap. Freed of their loads of static charged dust, the screens and repeaters glowed with new vibrancy. The light glinted off the desk tops and the Deep Dark was revealed in all its majesty through armor glass that was once again transparent.

We all just stood there in the middle of the bridge admiring our handy work.

"There now, isn't that better?" I finally asked.

"Well, Mr. Wang, I have to say, you give new meaning to the phrase getting down and dirty," Ms. Jaxton said in a flat, deadpan voice.

A huge yawn seized Ms. D'Heng but she laughed afterward and said, "I think I liked my idea better, but this is certainly a change."

I checked the chrono and saw that we still had a couple of stans to run on the watch.

"Okay," I said. "Ms. D'Heng, if you'd be so kind as to run down to the mess deck and grab us some coffee. Make sure to get it from the urn closest to the galley. I take mine with a bit of milk and two sugars."

"Aye, sar!" she said and scampered down the ladder.

After she left, Ms. Jaxton resumed her seat at the helm and glanced shyly at me. "I'm—ah—sorry, sar. For before."

I wasn't sure which before she was talking about. "Before, Ms. Jaxton?"

"Yes, sar, on the mess deck the other day."

"Space beneath the keel, Ms. Jaxton. You didn't know me. I didn't know you. Chalk it up to lack of experience and move on, shall we?"

"Yes, sar," she said, sounding a little relieved. "Thank you, sar."

"One other thing, Ms. Jaxton?"

"Yes, sar?" she asked curiously.

"Call me old fashioned, but I don't screw with crew. Ever. It's nothing personal. It's just the way I work."

"Yes, sar," she said.

Ms. D'Heng returned with three steaming cups of coffee and we settled down to sip and admire the Deep Dark.

CHAPTER EIGHTEEN
DIURNIA SYSTEM: 2358-JULY-9

Mr. Burnside and Mallory relieved third section right on time at 0545. Burnside all but stumbled onto the bridge, and I wondered if he were even awake. As he crossed to the station to relieve me, he reeked of sweat and sex. He blinked blearily at me. He must have known I could smell him because he just gave me a sardonic grin and a wink.

"Short night," he said. "Anything new up here?"

"Ship is on course and on target, No incidents or actions. Standing orders are unchanged. You may relieve the watch, Mr. Burnside."

"Yeah, whatever," he mumbled.

I stood up and he sat down, somewhat heavily, stretching his legs out with a sigh.

Mallory on the other hand eyed Jaxton as if trying to figure out what was different. She was filthy, of course, from the night of cleaning. Not the normal, low grade grubbiness that the majority of the crew exhibited, but really dirty. The sleeves of her jumpsuit were still pushed up and her face had a smudge of something across the left cheek.

"Rough night?" I heard him ask her with a laugh in his voice.

He flashed a furtive glance in my direction.

Jaxton smiled a lazy satisfied smile.

"I've never felt so dirty or so alive in my life," she cooed with a sigh.

It was all I could do to keep from bursting out laughing at the confused look on Mallory's face.

"Mr. Wang?" he hissed in disbelief.

Jaxton nodded languorously with half lidded eyes.

"Charlotte helped. He showed us things we'd never seen before," she said before rising to let a very disconcerted Mallory take the helm.

I glanced down at Burnside. They'd been talking too softly for him to hear, apparently, because he never even twitched. His eyes were closed and I wondered, briefly, if he'd already fallen asleep on watch. I decided that I didn't want to be on the bridge if he had.

"Have a good watch," I said.

Without looking at him or Mallory I smiled warmly at Ms. Jaxton and watched Mallory's eyes narrow suspiciously.

We got to the bottom of the ladder and I asked, "Weren't you laying it on a bit thick?"

She snickered. "Mallory doesn't do subtle very well. He's not as stupid as Apones, but he's a long way from the sharpest tack in the box."

"Well, don't press it too far. You have a reputation to protect."

"True," she said, "Maybe now it'll be more positive."

"This is a sick ship, isn't it?" I asked, only half joking.

"You have no idea, Mr. Wang," she said. "Well, I've got time for a quick shower before breakfast so if you'll excuse me, sar?"

"Of course, Ms. Jaxton, thanks for your help tonight."

"You're welcome, sar. You know we'll probably have to do it again tonight?"

I sighed. "I suspect you're right, but at least we should be able to clean up the worst of it relatively quickly. We've a good foundation to start from."

"True," she agreed, and with a little wave that wasn't quite a salute she headed on down the ladder to crew quarters.

I shuffled down the passage to my stateroom and carefully locked the door behind me. I stripped off my filthy suit and pulled a fresh one out of the closet. The dirty one went into the hamper, and I knocked gently on the door to the head. There was no answer, and I didn't hear the shower running, so I stepped in and started getting cleaned up for breakfast. There were a few things I wanted to do before I went back on watch at noon, and chief among them were getting a good meal and finding the workout room.

Breakfast was served in the wardroom at 0630. When I arrived at 0625, I found Mel and Fredi there with their heads together over coffee.

"Good morning, Ishmael," Mel said as I entered. "How did you do this?" She held up the coffee cup.

"Do what?"

"We've been complaining about the muck that's been served here for a stanyer," Fredi said. "You're on board a few days and it improves as if by magic?"

I shrugged and crossed to the sideboard to pour myself a cup. "Maybe Mr. Vorhees changed suppliers. Perhaps he got a better blend."

"Or maybe you got them to scrape down the pot and change their procedure so they actually made good coffee with what they have," Mel said.

"Maybe, but I have it on good authority that credit for any work should go to Apprentice Messmate Cramer, and any contributions that I may have made were strictly limited to offering suggestions as to how to get the most out of the beans with the least amount of effort."

I took my seat and folded my hands on the table in front of me. Fredi snorted in amusement and Mel only shook her head and smiled.

"What? I'm a boot third mate. What do I know about coffee?" I asked with as much wounded innocence as I could muster.

"Watch your back, Ishmael," Mel murmured with a sharp look in my direction. "Change is not welcome here, generally. You can probably get away with this but...just...be careful, all right?"

Davies came through the door to the galley, bearing a large platter of scrambled eggs in one hand and another with bacon and potatoes in the other. She smiled and placed them on the table for us to serve ourselves and walked back out of the wardroom without a word.

I gaped after her. She had circles under her eyes and walked as if each footfall pained her.

"Close your mouth, Ishmael," Mel said. "And don't be so surprised. First night underway is always like this the next morning. I suspect half the crew is walking funny today for one reason or another."

Fredi added, "It'll calm down in a few days. They know it's a long trip. They'll settle in."

It was one thing to know that some ships had *bunk bunnies*. It was another thing to actually serve on one. If my introduction from the previous watch had left any doubt in my mind, the breakfast encounter had rubbed my face in it.

Arletta came in, grabbed a coffee, and slid into her seat beside me. "Good morning, everybody. How was your first watch underway, Ishmael? Any problems?"

I shook my head. "It was pretty quiet after I convinced my watch section that I wasn't interested in an orgy on the bridge."

Mel and Fredi looked at me strangely. Arletta was getting to know me well enough that she didn't blink.

"And you were shocked that Davies is walking a little funny this morning?" Fredi asked after a moment.

"Well, I'm not surprised," Arletta said. "They were being rather loud when I got back from watch." She shook her head. "You'd think they'd be a little more discrete."

Fredi surprised me by snickering and Mel just winked at me. It took me a tick to realize that Arletta was pulling my leg. Maybe.

"Well? Shall we eat?" Arletta asked. "I can't imagine the captain will break with his long standing tradition of skipping breakfast, do you?"

Mel shrugged and helped herself to the eggs, passing the dish along. In a matter of a tick or two, we all had eggs, bacon, and potatoes. A covered basket held buttered toast, and we passed that around as well. The whole experience struck me as a bit surreal and I didn't say much over breakfast.

Mel and Fredi left just before 0700, leaving Arletta and me with the leftovers.

"Welcome to the love boat," she quipped. "Where you don't need love, just lube."

"I didn't really believe it... or maybe just didn't understand. Even last night on the bridge, when D'Heng started to strip down for a three way with Jaxton, it was unreal."

"She what?"

"Long story, but the short version is I asked her to come to the bridge so she could help us clean. She thought I wanted something else. She didn't seem to be too surprised with it all until I asked her to go to the janitor's closet and get the cleaning gear."

"You didn't!" She gave me a wide-eyed stare.

"Why not? It needed cleaning and we needed something to do for six stans."

"And they went along with it?"

"Sure. Why wouldn't they?"

"Lemme get this straight. You sat and watched your helm and messenger clean the bridge for the whole night?" She was turned halfway around toward me in her chair as she spoke.

"No. Of course not. I helped, and we were pretty much done by 0330. I sent D'Heng down for coffee around 0400 and we all sat around and admired our work until David relieved the watch at 0545"

She sighed and turned back to her plate. "I hope you know what you're doing."

"How much trouble can I get in for cleaning the bridge?" I

asked.

"That's not the point, Ishmael. You're changing things and people who try to change things sometimes get their heads handed to them."

"What? Just for cleaning the bridge? Or by not screwing my watch standers while on duty?" I asked, a bit exasperated myself.

"Both." She stood and stormed out of the wardroom.

I blew out a long breath and shook my head. I hoped I knew what I was doing, but there seemed to be a lot of people who thought I didn't. I picked up my dishes and stacked them in the tray before snagging one last piece of bacon and heading back to my stateroom to change for a workout. I hadn't had a good run in days and the treadmills in the gym were calling my name.

When I got there, I found Betts running alongside a tallish woman I didn't recognize. There were so many people aboard that I didn't know. It was strange to think that the crew knew everybody because they saw them all, eventually, either on the mess deck or on duty. The wardroom kept the officers isolated. There were people in my crew that I'd never seen. That set me thinking, again, about what I'd let myself in for.

With the two treadmills in use, I stepped into the workout area and began a tai chi set. I started with some warm ups and stretching, then moved into a Wu Long Form. I worked slowly and deliberately through the form, focusing on breathing and hand tension. I felt myself relaxing into it as the pressures of the previous few days slipped away. About the time I finished the first set, the woman pulled up and stepped off the treadmill, leaving it empty as she headed for the showers.

I took advantage of it, stepping onto the machine and punching in a brisk pace. I lost myself in the pad-pad-pad of my feet on the fabric. Or tried to.

"Sar? What was that dance you were doing?" Betts asked from the other treadmill, his words coming in short pants between breaths.

"It's tai chi, Mr. Betts."

"You do that often, sar?"

"As often as I can."

His treadmill beeped and slowed so he stepped down from the track, shutting it off as he went.

"That's my ten klicks," he said with a grin. "See ya round, sar."

I watched him head for the showers and went back to my running. It felt good to be moving, and if it wasn't exactly on a track, at least I was running.

When I'm running, I can think. Tai chi stops thinking. You

have to focus too much on the now. Hands, feet, weight, balance, tension or release. It's just not possible to think while you're doing tai chi. At least not if you want to do it well. Running, on the other hand, got my brain into full motion. I wondered how much trouble I was going to be in by cleaning the bridge. If I'd thought about it before I did it, I might not have, but it just seemed like the logical thing to do. It had certainly been more pleasant afterward, and the displays did look crisper.

Thinking on it, my action could be construed as a criticism. I wasn't sure how involved the captain or first mate was, but I knew that Arletta was trying to keep a low profile to stay out of trouble. Mel seemed concerned for me, too, and Fredi just seemed scared. She was one of Alys Giggone's officer recruits, so I suspected she'd spent at least some time as crew as well. I tried to imagine what a woman of her obvious experience and skill would be scared about in the wardroom. The captain was a bit of a pain, and the first mate was a dangerous man in his own way, but I had a hard time coping with the notion that he might actually harm—physically, at any rate—a member of the crew—his crew.

It just didn't make sense.

CHAPTER NINETEEN
DIURNIA SYSTEM: 2358-JULY-9

After the run, I went back to my stateroom to shower. I knocked carefully and listened before going into the head. It was my second shower of the morning and I wondered if Arletta was going to think I was some kind of weirdo with all the bathing. Still, after a workout, it felt good. Even with all that, it was barely 0930 when I was finished so I set my tablet to wake me at 1100 and lay down on my bunk for a quick nap.

Sleep was elusive, though. I generally didn't have much difficulty falling asleep. I was usually so exhausted that the opportunity for a few stans sack time resulted in instant slumber. Something about being on that ship had my mind going, and it wouldn't shut down. Maybe it was the tension. Maybe it was the smell. Maybe it was just that I was a boot third mate and in over my head.

Maybe the captain had a point, and I was working for somebody without even knowing it. The whole idea was preposterous, but the captain had raised a lot of valid questions. Why me?

I must have nodded off because my tablet bipped me out of a sound sleep. I zipped back into my shipsuit and, after splashing a little water on my face, went to the mess deck for a cup of coffee. As I was filling the cup, Chief Vorhees came out of the galley with a grin on his face.

"Well, the coffee is a hit. Thanks for your help." He said, studying his boots.

"It was my pleasure, Mr. Vorhees. I didn't do much, though, just offered some suggestions to your excellent Ms. Cramer."

"Uh huh," he said with a wry grin. "That's the way you wanna play it, that's fine with me, sar. You're making me look better and I appreciate it. Anything you need, lemme know, okay? I owe ya one."

"Thanks, but I have to drink the coffee, too, and I'm just glad Ms. Cramer is such a quick learner."

"I'm serious, sar. You need anything, just call. Okay?"

"Thanks, Mr. Vorhees. I appreciate the offer." I raised my cup in a toast and headed for the bridge. It wasn't time for my watch yet, but I needed to change out the removables to get ready for the next backup cycle before I relieved Mr. Burnside.

I cleared all my backups and made it to the bridge by 1140. Mr. Burnside looked a tad more awake, but he didn't smell any better. Stewing in a dirty shipsuit for six stans when you weren't too clean to begin with wasn't a good idea. He looked at me with one eyebrow raised as I crossed the bridge to the duty station.

"You're early," he said.

"I was in the neighborhood. Had to clear my backups."

"You had a busy night, looks like," he said, waving his hand around to indicate the bridge.

"Not so much, really. The three of us made pretty short work of it."

He frowned at that. "The three of you?"

"Yeah, I had helm and the messenger up here working with me to get it shipshape and Bristol fashion."

"You cleaned alongside the crew?" His voice sounded flat.

"Well, yeah," I said, not picking up the tone until it was too late.

He nodded toward the wing away from the helm, and we stepped over to the side of the bridge. He lowered his voice and said very precisely, "Mr. Wang, you are now an officer. You are expected to comport yourself like an officer. I know you're fresh out of the academy, and that you've actually been a crewman and all, but you must learn to keep a professional distance from the crew at all times."

He could have hit me with a stick, and I'd have been less surprised.

"I need to keep a 'professional distance' you say?" I tried to keep the disbelief out of my voice.

"Yes, Mr. Wang—Ishmael. I've seen it before in new, young officers. These people are not your friends. They are your employees. You are in charge, and it weakens your position... and the position of every officer on the ship... when you stoop to doing menial tasks like cleaning the bridge."

He looked at me so earnestly that I realized he actually believed what he was saying. He stood there, smelling of sex and sweat and dirty uniform, and had the stones to admonish me about keeping a "professional distance" from the crew, and he was serious.

"Thank you, David. That's valued advice, and I appreciate your taking the time to point out the problem," I said with as much sincerity as I could muster through my anger.

He seemed a bit nonplused in return. "That's a very encouraging response, Ishmael. Most new officers don't take that kindly to being corrected." He smiled. "You're going to go far on this ship, if you can keep that kind of attitude."

"Thank you, David. I appreciate your candor."

I really did appreciate the candor. One of the important lessons was to know your enemy. He was giving me a lot of good information.

Ms. Jaxton clambered up the ladder to the bridge then and interrupted our little conference.

"Shall we relieve the watch and get on with the afternoon's festivities?" I asked.

Mr. Burnside nodded with a small smile. "Yes, excellent. Nothing new and we're on course. You can have it," he said with a wave.

I replied formally with, "I have the watch, Mr. Burnside. Logged at 2358-July-9 at"—I had to check the chrono—"1143 per standing order."

Jaxton and Mallory swapped places and the two men vacated the bridge without another word.

"So? Any the worse for wear after your hot night on the bridge, Ms. Jaxton?" I asked her as I settled into the watch station.

She chuckled. "None in the least, sar, although Charlotte is suddenly very popular below decks."

"I would have thought she was already quite popular," I replied dryly.

"Well, news of the three way on the bridge during the midwatch appears to have spread, sar," she said with a lot more humor than I found in the situation.

"How in the world has that story managed to spread so quickly? I mean I know the ship is small, and gossip spreads fast, but you were just teasing Mr. Mallory about it six stans ago."

"I told you he wasn't the sharpest tack in the box, sar. Apparently he and Mr. Apones had their heads together over breakfast and they've come to the conclusion that we made such a mess of things up here that we had to clean the bridge entirely to hide the evidence."

I almost choked on my coffee. "They what?"

"I confess," she said with a satisfied grin. "I told them I had to clean butt prints off the glass, sar. That probably fueled the frenzy."

"But those prints were already there!"

"Well yes, sar, they were. You know that. I know that. Ms. D'Heng knows that. But I think we neglected to mention that to the rest of the crew."

I didn't know whether to laugh or scream. "Let me get this straight. The crew thinks that you and I and Ms. D'Heng had an orgy on watch last night? And that we spread—evidence—all over the bridge to the point where we had to clean it to hide what we'd done?"

"Well, not all the crew, sar. Just a few of the more gullible."

I buried my face in my hands right there at the watch station.

"Ms. Jaxton, did it occur to you that this little story might be giving me a reputation that I don't deserve?"

"Oh, yes, sar. And you're welcome. And may I say, sar, that I'm grateful for your gentle consideration. Thanks to being under your protection, I think I slept peacefully for the first time since I came aboard."

"Being under my protection?"

"Yes, sar. The crew wouldn't expect you to share, now would they? That puts Charlotte and me out of reach, at least until you tire of us."

The smugness of her tone got to me.

"You're enjoying this aren't you, Ms. Jaxton?"

"Yes, sar."

"You realize this whole thing is impossible?"

"Of course, sar, but if I'd known that screwing an officer would keep the filthy fingers out of my bunk at night, I'd have found one long ago."

The smugness in her tone had been replaced by something just a bit darker, a tad more bitter. At no point had she ever turned to look at me. I sat just behind her right shoulder while she stared straight ahead.

I just stared at her back. What could she be thinking? Was she mad?

Then I noticed that she wore a clean shipsuit. It was the first time I'd seen any member of the crew in a fresh one since I'd been aboard. I sighed, shook my head, and checked the systems logs to make sure the Environmental and Engineering watches had changed on time. I did my best to focus on the task at hand. There wasn't much I could do about the crew. I had to just focus on my job.

At just past 1200, Charlotte D'Heng climbed up to the bridge and relieved Ms. Jaxton for lunch. They had a murmured conversation and I pretended not to notice the rapid glances in my direction. Ms. D'Heng wore a clean shipsuit as well.

After a few ticks, Ms. D'Heng said, "Thank you, sar, and I'm sorry if we caused you any problems."

I looked up and saw her looking at me over her shoulder. "Ms. D'Heng?"

"The story, most people know it's a joke. Only the most obnoxious believe it, sar." She bit her lower lip uncertainly. "It just kinda got out of hand."

"I see," I said, although I really didn't.

Or maybe I did. I tried to imagine what it would be like in the berthing area for these two women. The hands in the dark. The unwelcome attention. The pressure to go along to get along. I found myself frowning in Ms. D'Heng's direction, but not at her. I relaxed my expression and offered a smile.

"Well, what's done is done, eh? We'll just have to see how it all shakes out over time. Maybe it'll serve to smarten up a few people," I said with as friendly a smile as I could muster.

"Thanks, sar," she said with obvious relief. "But I wouldn't count on it adding any IQ points to the crew's total."

"You're probably right there."

Ms. Cramer appeared at the ladder then, carrying a covered tray. "Your lunch, sar."

I'd forgotten about that. Officers of the watch didn't get relieved for meals. Their food was delivered to them. I indicated a corner of the console and she put the tray carefully on the desk. There was plenty of everything, even a small carafe of coffee and a pitcher of milk. It looked wonderful and I was hungry.

"Thank you, Ms. Cramer."

"You're very welcome, sar. You'll need to keep your strength up," she said with a giggle and scampered off the bridge.

"Ms. D'Heng?"

"She knows the truth, sar. I swear she does."

"I see, Ms. D'Heng."

I came to the full realization of just how much of a problem the whole situation was going to be.

Within a few ticks Ms. Jaxton returned to the bridge, and took the helm watch back. I ate my lunch, keeping an eye on the displays. I tried not to get caught up in the gossip I couldn't control. I finished my coffee and put the dishes back on the tray. It had been a good lunch, and I still had a ways to go on the watch. There wasn't anything I needed to do, except stay on the bridge, so I brought up the educational oversight system to check the dates. The next scheduled testing period was the end of September. I checked the ship's calendar and realized that we'd be on our way back from Breakall before that. I flagged it on my tablet so I would be reminded before the date got too close.

On a whim, I scrolled back through the last few test sessions to see who'd taken exams. Only one person aboard had taken an exam in June. I supposed I wasn't surprised. Philippa Ballantine, a specialist three in power, took and passed her spec two test. I wondered how long she'd be aboard if a ship needing a spec two in power posted an opening. The test was certified by the training officer, Third Mate Theresa Jaffee.

"So, that was your name. Where did you get off to, Ms. Jaffee?" I muttered under my breath.

"Excuse me, sar?"

I shook my head. "Nothing, Ms. Jaxton, just talking to myself again. Sometimes I do it out loud."

"They tell me that's not a symptom of insanity unless you're surprised by your answers, sar."

"You're a comfort to me, Ms. Jaxton. A real comfort."

"I try, sar," she said with a smirk of her own. "I try."

CHAPTER TWENTY
DIURNIA SYSTEM: 2358-JULY-18

We were ten days out of Diurnia before I realized that the captain never came out of the cabin. To be precise, I hadn't seen him since we'd secured from navigation detail, and he'd taken me down for his "welcome" speech. He had never showed up in the wardroom for meals, or turned up on the bridge while I was there. I suppose he could have been out when I was asleep but somehow I doubted that.

By comparison, I saw a lot of Mel and Fredi. They were at every meal. Mel was often on the bridge during the day, working on the engineering station there, reviewing logs, watching ship's grav and power status, and running her own environmental checks. My favorite times were the meals where Mr. Burnside had the watch, sparing us his boorish table manners. These were the times where I could enjoy the company of Mel, Fredi, and Arletta.

Fredi came out of her shell at those meals, looking less frail, speaking up more. She was never the center of attention, or the life of the party, but she was guilty of a wonderfully wicked sense of humor.

"So, the captain doesn't come out at all?" I asked over breakfast.

Fredi made a face. "He has everything he needs delivered to the cabin."

"He'll come out for the jump," Mel commented.

"And then scurry back into his hole when we're on the other side," Fredi added.

Arletta shot me a look from the corner of her eye. "You looking for more quality time with him?"

I chuckled and shook my head. "No, Captain Rossett made

enough of an impression on me that one time."

"He's not so bad," Mel said. "At least he stays out of the way of ships operations."

Fredi nodded her agreement. "True. Be grateful he's not one of those micromanaging captains," she said. She turned to Mel and asked, "Remember... oh, what was his name? On the old *Geordie*?"

Mel sat still, thinking for a heartbeat, and then said, "Oh, yes. What was his name? On the *Geordan VanTassle*..." She thought for a moment longer. "James..."

"Jankowitz," Fredi finished. "Captain Jimmy Jankowitz. That was it. The man would drive ya crazy. I swear he wanted to help the crew pick out which shipsuit to wear."

"As long as it's a clean one," I muttered.

Arletta heard me and chuckled. "What? You think the hygiene of our crew is being compromised?"

"Is it just me, or does anybody else find the ship to be just a bit on the whiffy side?"

"Depends on who's in the room with you," Arletta said. She leaned over to sniff me. "You don't smell too bad. Today."

Fredi grinned. "I'm glad I don't have any staff to deal with. All I have to do is make sure the can is tied on securely and stays there for the whole trip."

Mel shook her head. "Honestly, I don't know what the problem is. Getting them to do anything—from keeping the workspaces clean to putting on clean clothes. It's ridiculous."

Arletta gave a sly smile in my direction and said ever so sweetly, "I notice you've got your girls in clean ship suits, Ishmael. Your first midwatch certainly made an impression with the crew."

I sighed and speared another slice of bacon from the platter.

"They're not my girls. They're my watch section and I didn't do anything. We cleaned the bridge. That's all."

They all laughed.

"I know," Arletta said, "and they know"—she nodded at Mel and Fredi—"but Mr. Burnside is still trying to figure out how to get only women in his watch section."

"He'll need to find some pretty beefy girls if he's gonna replace his bully boys with women," Mel said with a scowl.

Fredi snorted but didn't say anything.

"Thanks, by the way," I said to Arletta. "I notice that when we follow your section onto the bridge, there's a lot less mess to clean up."

"Every other ship I've ever been on has a regular cleaning schedule," Fredi said. "I don't understand how this one has gone so long."

"It's not in the standing orders," Arletta pointed out. "I looked."

"Okay, how do we change that?" I asked.

"What? Add it to the standing orders?" Arletta replied.

"Well, that or just get the ship clean? I got the bridge taken care of in a single watch. If we do a quick wipe down every time we go on, and then a full sweep and swab during the mid, that would probably take care of it."

"So, that's why the bridge has been so clean?" Mel said.

"Well, after that first night, it only takes us a few ticks. One stan out of the watch and we have the rest of the time to study and read."

"Study?" Arletta asked. "You've got someone studying?"

"Um, both of them, actually," I admitted. "D'Heng is preparing for able spacer and Jaxton is working on ship handler."

Mel blinked. "You've been aboard ten days and you've got your section cleaning the bridge and studying for their ratings?"

"Yeah, Is that bad?"

"No! It's excellent. But how did you do it?"

"You didn't hear about the orgy?" Arletta asked.

We all laughed; I'd grown used to the twitting I was getting over that one. Arletta knew full well what happened, and that I was still a bit shocked and appalled over the whole situation. What truly disconcerted me were the requests from other women in the crew who wanted to be like my watch standers. Arletta knew about those—that shared door had gotten a lot of use—but she didn't tease me about it. The fact that there were crew who felt like they needed that kind of protection was disconcerting enough for both of us.

"Seriously, how did you do it?" Mel asked when we stopped laughing at me. "I've been an officer for thirty stanyers, and I've never had as much trouble with any crew as I've had with this bunch."

I shrugged. "I don't know. Cleaning the bridge was actually easy. Jaxton was actively hostile. I think she thought I was gonna make a pass at her or something. She definitely didn't trust me. When I called Charlotte up to the bridge that night I had to practically wrestle her shipsuit back on her."

"Back on her? You didn't mention that before," Arletta said archly.

"You know what I mean," I said. "She was ready to go and I had to convince the pair of them that I wasn't planning on playing with them."

Arletta grinned. "Yeah, so you say."

"Go on, Ishmael, I want to hear this," Mel said.

"So I outlined what I wanted to do, sent D'Heng down to the

janitor locker for supplies, and we cleaned the bridge. Jaxton is the tallest so she did the ports. D'Heng and I did the consoles and screens. I showed them the broom locker on the bridge and it didn't take that long to do a first sweep and swab of the deck. We've done a couple of them now and we're making headway."

"There's a broom locker on the bridge?" Arletta asked.

"Yeah, just to the port of the—" I saw the wide-eyed, innocently fascinated stare coming from her direction and stuck my tongue out at her.

"You said, 'We cleaned...'" Mel pointed out. "You rolled up your sleeves and cleaned consoles?"

"Well, sure. I work there too. Mr. Burnside gave me some management advice about what a bad idea that was for earning and keeping the respect of the crew when he found out about it."

Mel leveled a stare at me.

"And what do you think of that advice?" she asked after a heartbeat.

"I was crew once myself. The officers I respected, respected me. They earned my respect by working hard and making sure I was able to do my job in a safe, secure, and efficient manner. Now that I'm an officer, I want to be like them. We're all in the same tin can and it's a long way to anywhere."

I sipped my coffee, hoping I hadn't just gotten into trouble, again. The academy offered a series of courses on the officer-crew dynamic. It was deemed particularly important since so many officers came from families who were crew. They'd grown up on ships where gramps or grammy were the captains and cousin Flo ran the galley. I'd had a lot of time to think about the relationship between officer and crew while at the academy, but the only role models I had to draw from had been the *Lois McKendrick* until I started shipping out on the summer cruises, and I began to see different perspectives.

"So, how did you get them to study?" Fredi asked after a tick had gone by in relative silence.

"I just asked them what their next rating was and how far along they were. Our normal routine is to get the watch relieved, let things settle in for the first stan, deal with meals, and such, then clean the bridge up, and settle down to study. Charlotte usually fetches the coffee and joins us on the bridge. It's a pleasant way to spend a watch."

"But how did you get them to study?" Mel asked again.

"I didn't do anything. Jaxton has to be there. She can sit and stare at the helm and watch the stars go by or she can study. D'Heng can sit on the mess deck or she can sit on the bridge. The bridge is clean and comfortable."

"And safe," Arletta added.

"Well yes, of course, safe. So she joins us on the bridge. We're studying. She studies. We have coffee. Sometimes we talk about ship's operations. Why some things get done a particular way, that sort of thing. Sometimes they trade practice test questions."

"What are you studying, Ishmael?" Mel asked.

"The ship. I need to know a lot more about the ship if I'm going to be an effective officer when things go bad."

"You think things will go bad?" Fredi asked with a small smile.

"Let's just say, I've been on a ship where everybody worked together and everybody watched each other's back, and yet we still almost died, taking half a planet with us. I hope things will never get that way again, but I'm not going to bet that they won't, so I want to be prepared. When it comes right down to it, I wanna know a lot more about what I can do to keep breathing, and I'm perfectly willing to work very hard for that knowledge even if I'll never use it."

They all nodded and we turned to finishing off breakfast.

"You know, we never did settle how to get the ship clean." I said, finishing off the last of my toast. "I mean, the bridge is small enough to keep up with. How do we deal with the passageways? I don't even want to think about the berthing areas."

"Well, the captain has to change the standing orders," Mel pointed out. "But those are only the minimum requirements. We've gotten to the state aboard where the minimum has become the maximum."

Arletta said, "The bridge is clean and we didn't have to change the orders for that."

Mel sipped her coffee, looking at me over the rim. "I'll see what I can do about the engineering spaces. We have a regular field day there, but if the mids are the 'cleaning' watches, then everybody gets one, and as Ishmael has found out after the first one, the maintenance is pretty easy."

"Frankly, if we could get everybody to wear a fresh shipsuit every day and keep the common areas cleaned, I think we'd all be a lot more comfortable, and probably happier and safer," Fredi said.

"I think we can deal with the watch spaces—Bridge, Engineering, Environmental—but that leaves berthing, mess deck, and passageways," Arletta added.

I turned and looked at the corners of the wardroom. "This place probably could use a thorough swab too," I said.

A voice spoke up from the doorway. "I'd be happy to do it, if you'd talk to Mr. Vorhees for me, sar," Davies said.

We all looked up in surprise. "Why would we need to talk to Mr. Vorhees, Ms. Davies?" Mel asked. "Isn't this your normal duty?"

"Well, yes, but he doesn't want me in here except to serve and clear, sar. He says that it's for officers and I need to steer clear."

"Does anyone use the wardroom between meals?" I asked, confused.

Fredi said, "I come in once in a while to get a cup of coffee and read."

Mel nodded. "I do too. It's a quiet place to review logs, although lately, I've enjoyed the view from the bridge while I'm working."

Fredi added, "The staterooms seem so small after a while."

Davies made a little "that's what I mean" face.

"Thank you, Ms. Davies," I said. "I'd be happy to visit with Mr. Vorhees, and you and Ms. Cramer too, to talk about the wardroom and the mess deck."

"Thank you, sar. May I clear now?" she asked with a glance at the chrono.

I saw with a shock that it was nearly 0800.

Mel stood and said, "Yes, thank you, Ms. Davies, We're just leaving."

I stood too, and was pleased to note that everybody picked up their dirty dishes and put them in the tray as we headed out to deal with the day.

"Mr. Vorhees?" I stuck my head into the galley. "A moment, if I may?"

I'd timed it just about right. Mr. Vorhees was just finishing his breakfast routine. Davies was still in the wardroom, and Cramer smiled at me from the griddle where she was running a cleaning stone over the surface. The place smelled faintly of soap and bacon. Not one of my favorite aromas but it meant things were getting clean.

Mr. Vorhees smiled and followed me out onto the mess deck, and I went to the coffee urns to get a cup. I was a bit uneasy and wanted something to do with my hands. I didn't want to mess with another division's workings, but I also needed the chief's help. I tried to think of what Mr. Maxwell would have done on the *Lois* if he had Mr. Vorhees instead of Cookie.

"How can I help you, sar?" he asked with a smile.

"Is the coffee getting a good response?" I asked in reply. "It's been over a week now. I know I certainly appreciate the change."

He snorted a small laugh. "Yes, sar. You were right. The biggest problem now is keeping the urn full."

"Yes, I remember that problem on my old ship. It's actually a good problem to have."

"Yes, it is, sar," he said. "Now if I could just get them to return the cups."

"Return the cups?"

"Yes, sar. They come down, get coffee, take the mugs and leave them everywhere: berthing, engineering, even the passageways."

"Oh, I see," I said with a nod. "In that case, I think I have another solution for you." I dangled the bait out there to see if he'd bite.

He grinned and gave me one of those senior-hand-to-junior officer looks but only said, "Well, sar, I'd love to hear it."

"On the *Lois*, the mess deck was like the ship's living room. When we were underway, it's where everybody went to get a cuppa, grab a cookie, sit, and visit. You know what I mean?"

"Oh, yes, sar," he replied with a knowing nod. "Same on practically every ship I've ever been on. On the *Billy*, it seems like the crew has other things to do than sit around the mess deck." His comment was freighted with an odd collection of baggage, but I let that go for the moment.

"Well..." I started, drawing the word out a bit, "if it were you, would you want to spend time here?" I looked pointedly at the stained tables and littered deck. "I know it's just after breakfast and the morning cleanup hasn't had a chance here yet, but—and pardon me for saying it..." I let my voice trail off before I actually did say it.

He sighed. "Oh, I agree, sar. Some days I think that if I'd let my engine room get to the state that this mess deck gets sometimes, my old chief would have snatched me bald."

"How can I help, John?" I asked gently, deliberately using his first name to step outside the formal relationship of crew and officer. After a couple of heartbeats, I added, "It occurs to me that if they're sitting here drinking coffee, then there's that many fewer cups for you to collect from around the ship."

He pursed his lips and eyed the room for a moment before looking back at me. "How'd you get your watch section to clean the bridge? I can't believe it was...you know...like the stories."

I almost burst out laughing. He was so earnest. I had a hard time controlling my face. At the same time I had a hard time believing this guy had been an engineering spec one. Spec one's are the backbone of the fleet. They're what keep the ships going. They keep junior third mates from walking out airlocks and sticking their heads into fusactors. Then again, maybe his lateral to Steward Division actually made a little more sense than it had seemed at first.

"I just laid out what I wanted done, and the three of us got it taken care of," I told him. "Simple enough."

His brow furrowed in a thoughtful expression as he looked around the mess deck. "Yes," he said slowly, "of course." He paused for a moment and I let his train of thought pull fully into the station while I sipped my coffee. "So? Is there something you needed from me, sar?" he asked, finally remembering that I wanted to talk to him.

"Yes, actually there is. While we're on the subject of cleaning, would you ask Ms. Davies to give the wardroom a good swab? It's beginning to build up a little in there. I know Ms. Menas and Ms. DeGrut use the space between meals sometimes, but we had a discussion about it over breakfast and they'd rather be interrupted once in a while than have the place get all grubby, if you know what I mean?"

"Is she not doing a good enough job, sar? Ms. Davies?" the chief asked.

"Oh, that's not the issue, chief," I said and waved my coffee cup at the mess deck by way of illustration. "Every so often you need to catch up with it, you know?"

He frowned and nodded. "Yes, sir. I do know."

"When I was on the mess deck of the *Lois*, Cookie, he was my chief, always had us do the major cleaning right after evening meal: top to bottom in both the mess deck and galley. Pip and I got so we could do it in half a stan, and it sure made life easier in the morning."

"Half a stan?" his eyebrows rose in surprise. "That's all?"

I shrugged. "I suspect it'd take more than half a stan the first time around," I said, pointedly looking at what looked like coffee stains on the overhead, "but once you got it done once, it'd be pretty easy. All that's needed is the old sweep-n-swab after breakfast and lunch and then a full swab down after dinner. We got so fast that we had a couple stans in the afternoon off between lunch clean up and dinner prep."

His gaze tracked across the mess deck, and I saw him pause here and there, cataloging things that needed doing. "I see what you mean, sar."

"I really do think that would help your stray coffee mug problem." I reinforced the idea one last time as I turned back to the urn to top off my mug again.

"Yes, sar, I do, too. And I'll have Penny—uh, Ms. Davies—give the wardroom a good cleaning today."

"Thanks, John," I told him with a warm smile, "I appreciate it and I know Ms. Menas and Ms. DeGrut will as well."

Mission accomplished, I strolled off the mess deck as nonchalantly as I could. According to the chrono, I had two stans before I had to take over the bridge watch, so I headed for my stateroom to change into my workout clothes. I had time for a good run before watch.

I rounded the corner and headed down the passage past the cabin when the door opened and one of the engineering crew—Bayless, according to his shipsuit—slipped out, closing it behind him. He started when he saw me coming, and I gave him what I hoped was a reassuring smile. He ducked his head as we passed, but neither of us said anything. Poor guy looked embarrassed and I wondered what he'd done to earn the captain's wrath so early in the voyage. I snorted to myself as I started changing into my sweats, wondering how the captain even knew of any infractions, considering he never left the cabin.

The gym had a modest collection of equipment. There were two stationary bikes, two treadmills, and a rowing machine. The space wasn't big enough for a track, but there was an open area for those who practiced various versions of the martial arts, or just wanted deck space to do a few push-ups. It even had one of those spring driven weight machines. Free weights might have been dangerous if we lost gravity and they started flying around. What it lacked, and what I missed, was the steam room from the *Lois*, or even a hot tub like the *Bad Penny*.

On the other hand, considering the crew, I wasn't sure either of those things was all that desirable. I could envision the kinds of activities that an uninhibited crew might engage in while underway, and I didn't want to consider stumbling onto that.

When I got there the place was deserted, so I started on the treadmill first thing. It wasn't as good as a track, but it let me move. It was one of the better units, too. I punched in a pre-programmed routine and started a slow jog to warm up. I was about half a stan into the program when I heard somebody else come in. Looking over my shoulder, I saw Nart limbering up on the rowing machine. She smiled and gave a little wave when she saw me look and I nodded back. I was beginning to work up a good sweat and the program changed to an incline so I buckled down and gave it my attention.

Only a few ticks later, I heard voices behind me and glanced over to see Apones and a beefy engineman standing, one on either side of the rowing machine. Nart was flushed but staring straight ahead and rowing steadily. Apones was saying something over her head to the engineman on the other side. I couldn't hear what over the sound of the equipment, but the tone was obvious. His buddy laughed nastily and Nart's jaw clenched.

Sighing, I punched the reset on my treadmill, picked up my towel, and scrubbed it across my face to dry the sweat from my eyes. I stepped off the machine while the tread slowed, and the two chuckle wits glanced in my direction as I crossed to them.

"Good morning, Ms. Nart," I greeted her with a smile. I looked at Apones and then at his buddy, noting the stenciled "Mosler" on his chest. "Gentlemen," I said, "are you here for a workout?"

Apones grinned in a way that I found not terribly endearing. "Well that depends on Ulla here," he said with a leer.

Nart shot him an angry glance but kept rowing.

Mosler nudged the rowing machine with the toe of his ship boot. "How about it, sweet thing? Feel like a little workout?" he asked in a tone that left no doubt about what he had in mind.

"Buzz off," she growled. "I'm busy." She didn't look up, not at them, not at me.

"Aw come on, honey," Apones wheedled. "We can go a lot farther than that rowing machine can."

"Hell yeah," Mosler added. "How about around the world?" He leaned down with his hands on his knees.

She didn't respond, other than to ignore them and continue rowing.

"Gentlemen," I said softly. "I think Ms. Nart is occupied at the moment." It was a warning. I wanted to smash their smug faces in, but that would have been a dangerous thing to do.

"Aw, Mr. Wang," Apones said—purposefully mispronouncing my name—"we're just having a little fun. You know about having fun, I hear." He shot a knowing smirk at Mosler.

"You may be, Mr. Apones, but Ms. Nart is not." I looked from him to Mosler and back. "Don't you two have something else you should be doing? If not, I can find plenty for a pair of big strong guys like you to do."

They looked at me for a long moment as I wiped the sweat from my neck and face with the now slightly soggy towel. I thought, for just a heartbeat, that they were going to push it, but they backed down. Apones stepped away, and when he did, Mosler went with him.

"Come on, Herm," Apones said, and they headed for the door.

"Yeah," Mosler said in a too loud voice, "he's probably got plans himself. Don't wanna get in an *officer's* way, now do we?" The way he said officer made it clear that it wasn't a term of respect or endearment.

I let it go and focused on the trembling woman on the rowing machine. "Are you all right, Ms. Nart?"

She looked up at me with an expression that clearly said, "Are you insane?"

"I'm sorry," I said. "Of course, you're not okay. Is there anything I can do to help? Anything you need?"

She shook her head silently, and I saw tears start to well in her eyes before she ducked her head so I couldn't see them slide down her face. All through it, she kept rowing.

"Do you want to press charges?" I asked.

She let out a single wretched, "Hah!" She didn't look up. After a moment she added bitterly, "No, Mr. Wang, I think I'd prefer to live, thank you."

"Very well, Ms. Nart. Please let me know if I can help," I said, cursing myself for offering platitude in the face of pain, but I had no idea what else to do. I crossed the room and positioned myself to begin the Wu Long Form.

"Thank you, sar," she called after me in a small voice.

"You're welcome, Ms. Nart," I replied and let the ship disappear for a time as I focused on my chi.

CHAPTER TWENTY-TWO
DIURNIA SYSTEM: 2358-JULY-18

The afternoon watch was uneventful when I finally got there. I wanted to mention something to Mr. Burnside about the incident with Apones, but in the end, I didn't know what to say. In theory he wasn't supposed to allow harassment of crew at all, let alone when ostensibly on his watch. Asking Mr. Burnside to keep a shorter leash on his watch standers would be an exercise in aggravation for both of us, so in the end, I didn't say anything. It ate at me, but I just didn't know what else to do.

I realized it upset me more than I had thought when Ms. Cramer brought my lunch before I'd even gotten through the change of watch reports. Nothing outstanding had happened, but I found myself reading the same thing over and over.

"Thank you, Ms. Cramer," I told her when I realized she was standing at my elbow.

"Where would you like me to put this, sar?" she asked.

I started to point to the side of the desk when I noticed some kind of spill there. It looked like about a half a cup of coffee that had almost dried. Frowning, I realized that the entire desk had something or other smeared on all the available surfaces. The fact that I'd been sitting there for almost half a stan and hadn't even noticed it underscored my mood.

"Oh I'm sorry, Ms. Cramer," I said totally disconcerted by the situation but not wanting her to put the tray down in the mess. I pointed to the systems console, and said, "Over there if you would please. I'll need to get this mess cleaned up."

"Of course, sar," she said with a smile and a pleasant wink to Ms. D'Heng, who'd relieved Ms. Jaxton for lunch already. "Penny—that's Ms. Davies—asked me to thank you for speaking to the chief, sar," she said over her shoulder.

"It was my pleasure," I told her as I rummaged in the broom locker for some of the cleaning supplies we kept there.

She smiled again, watching me spray off the desk and wipe it down, then she nodded once more to Ms. D'Heng and retreated down the ladder.

"You've another fan, Mr. Wang," Ms. D'Heng said from the helm, a cheerful smirk plastered on her face.

Distracted by Burnside's apparent willingness to make a mess on purpose, I looked up blinking and replaying the last few ticks in my brain. "Oh, Ms. Cramer? She's a very capable messmate." I replied a bit fatuously.

"Yes, she is, sar."

I finished wiping down the console and stowed the cleaning gear back in the locker. Ms. D'Heng's tone registered then and I found myself wondering what, exactly, she'd meant.

"Is there something I'm missing, Ms. D'Heng?" I asked.

"Oh, I'm sure I couldn't say, sar." The smirk never flickered.

I crossed to the systems console and sat down to eat. Ms. D'Heng watched me with *that look* so I bowed to the inevitable. "And you have a secret bit of knowledge that you'd like to share with me, Ms. D'Heng?" I asked, taking a sip of the coffee while it was still mostly warm.

"She wants to join your harem, sar," she said with almost a straight face.

It was only with a great deal of control, and no small amount of practice, that I managed not to spray coffee across the console. "My *harem*?" I finally asked when the liquid was more or less under control.

"Juliett and I, sar," she said with a small, amused twitch of her lips while staring straight ahead at the helm console.

"You two are my..." I paused, not wanting to actually use the word. "...harem?"

"Some of the less well-informed believe so, sar," she replied smoothly.

"You know, Ms. D'Heng, when I was at the academy, they tried their best to prepare us for what we'd be facing when we got out into the field."

"Yes, sar?"

"I don't think they ever had this situation in mind."

"No, sar, I'm sure they didn't. But if I may say so, sar, you're handling it very well."

I sighed and ran a hand through my hair, forcing myself not to grab a handful and pull. With as much calmness as I could muster

I said, "Thank you, Ms. D'Heng."

"You're welcome, sar," she replied as if we'd been discussing the weather.

I turned to my lunch and tried to sort out the horror and dread. Somewhere, people on this ship thought I had turned my watch section into a harem. On this ship, it seemed that was a very real and literal interpretation. As I worked my way through a rather bland bowl of noodle soup and a crusty roll, I remembered the morning's incident with Apones and Mosler. The implications made me very uneasy. Was it actually necessary for women on this ship to need protection from the males? And if they did, what harm was it for me to provide said protection with this fiction? The people who knew it wasn't true weren't the problem.

That was the rub. The ones who believed it were the people from whom the crew needed protection, and they were stupid enough, and likely strong enough, to take exception to my getting in the way of their fun. People like Apones and Mosler—the "boys will be boys brigade" and their ringleader, David Burnside.

Ms. Jaxton returned from her lunch and took the watch back from Ms. D'Heng while I stayed lost in the horrible realization of just how nasty the whole situation had gotten.

With a sigh I tossed the crust of a roll onto the tray, salvaged the last cup of coffee from the carafe, and covered the remains with my napkin. Ms. D'Heng took the tray with a smile and headed back down the ladder.

"Back in a flash," she said as her head disappeared.

I took my coffee and went back to the bridge console to finish checking reports.

"Something wrong, sar?" Ms. Jaxton asked.

"I'm fairly certain there is, Ms. Jaxton, but it's not going to get solved on this watch." I settled into the console and she took the hint.

Around 1300 Ms. D'Heng came back and the two of them busied themselves doing the wipe down and quick sweep we did during day watches. More and more, the only time we had any serious amount of cleaning to do was when we followed first section. I sighed as I considered the implications of that. I needed to have a heart to heart talk with Arletta.

In the background I heard Juliett and Charlotte chatting. They really were funny together—Charlotte the vamp and Juliett the humorist. Except sometimes they forgot their roles and Juliett vamped while Charlotte loosed a wickedly dry sense of humor.

It wasn't long before they finished the afternoon clean up and settled in to study.

"Sar?" Ms. D'Heng asked. "Do you think it would be out of place for us to help Penny and Karen clean up the mess deck this evening?"

I must have looked very blank.

"Sar?"

"Yes, Ms. D'Heng, I'm just trying to switch mental gears. Penny and Karen? Ms. Davies and Ms. Cramer? Are they soliciting for help to clean the mess deck?"

"Oh no, sar," Juliett said. "Charlotte heard them talking about it and offered to help, but they were concerned with whether or not it would be proper to have people who weren't, you know, messmates working on the mess deck."

I closed my eyes and pinched the bridge of my nose. Every time I thought I'd plumbed the depths of this benighted ship, something new and troubling came to the fore.

"Why would it not be proper, Ms. Jaxton?" I asked, trying to see a course through the asteroids.

"Well, you know. It's not my job, really, sar."

"Is it your ship, Ms. Jaxton?" I asked.

"Well no, sar, it belongs to the company."

The answer was breathtaking. Literally. I had trouble breathing for a couple of ticks after she said it. Everything was so obvious.

"How about you, Ms. D'Heng? Is it your ship?"

She wrinkled her forehead in confusion. "No, sar," she said with a little shrug. "Juliett just told you. It's the company's ship."

I smiled.

Juliett and Charlotte exchanged glances.

"No, ladies, it would not be improper for you to help your shipmates," I said. "That's what crew does. They help each other."

"Like you helped Ulla this morning?" Charlotte asked.

"If need be, yes," I said. "But I'm thinking more like your helping Juliett and I keep the bridge clean and sitting with us up here on watch."

They looked at each other again.

"You two never worked on another ship?" I asked.

"I'm on my second contract on the *Billy*," Juliett said a little sheepishly.

"The *Billy*'s my first ship," Charlotte admitted.

"Why did you stay, Juliett?" I asked.

She shrugged. "I'm not pretty or popular. I don't get the attention that some others do." She was carefully not looking at Charlotte. "I know there are problems aboard, but so far nobody's pressed me."

Charlotte flushed, but didn't say anything.

"I take it things are different for you, Charlotte," I asked. I felt brutal asking, but I tried to keep my voice soft.

"This trip's been much better," she said, not looking at me or Juliett.

"You had trouble—unwanted attention—before this trip?" I pressed.

"Yes, sar, and no. I'm not gonna tell. I have to live with these people," she was quite vehement but still didn't look me in the eye.

"And you'll be leaving the *Billy* as soon as your contract is up?" I asked.

"The very first chance I get, sar," she said, and at that she did look at me. "Unless things get a whole lot better, I'm out of here the day my contract expires."

"Well, we'll have to make sure you make able spacer before then, won't we?" I said softly. "We've got plenty of time between now and testing."

"Sar? I'm only a spacer *apprentice*," she pointed out, speaking slowly for the benefit of the officer in the room.

"Yes, Charlotte, I know." I smiled at her. "But I'm the training officer and I know what you need to do to make able spacer and it doesn't involve taking the ordinary spacer exam first."

"You don't have to take them in order, sar?" she asked, her curiosity fighting with her disbelief.

I shook my head. "Nope. If you can pass it, it's yours. Half a brain and a decent study regimen makes able spacer pretty easy."

Juliett frowned. "I didn't think it was that easy."

"Ah, but you didn't have me to help you, now did you?" I asked with what I hoped was an endearing grin.

"No, sar, that's true. I didn't."

I shook my head again, to try to clear out the bees. "Okay then, we'll just have to do what we can and tough out the stuff we can't. You have any problems with that?"

They exchanged another glance and shrugged. "No, sar," they said almost in unison.

"Okay, then. Back to the question that started this. Yes, it's entirely proper for you to help clean the mess deck. You use the mess deck. It's one of the common areas of the ship, and while it's attached to the galley and the messmates have some responsibility of keeping the space up to snuff, there's nothing in any rule, order, or custom that says you can't help them. Anything from stacking your dishes, to running a wipe across a dirty table, to picking up stuff that's been dropped on the deck. It's all good."

They both nodded and shrugged a little. "That makes perfect sense, sar," Juliett said, "but what if some people won't help?"

"What about them?" I asked.

"We'll be doing things for their benefit, sar," she said.

"Ah, that's actually not true. As long as you're getting the benefit, say from a clean place to sit and study with your friends, then what do you care what's going on with this hypothetical freeloader?"

Charlotte piped up with, "But he's getting something for nothing! That's not fair." She added, "Sar"—as a kind of afterthought.

"What's your point, Ms. D'Heng?" I asked. "If the incremental cost to you is nil, and you're willing to work for what you want, what's the problem with a freeloader as a byproduct?"

"It's not fair," she said again.

"Not fair to whom?" I asked her.

"Well, to the people who did the work, sar. To have somebody just come in and take advantage of that work without...I don't know...paying..." she said, petering out a bit at the end.

"Okay, try this on. Juliett, let's say you have planetside liberty and want to go to the beach, but you need to rent a ground car to get there. What does it cost you?"

Juliett nodded. "Well, sar, I guess that depends on the system, but probably somewhere between twenty and thirty creds."

"Exactly, and what would you get in return?"

She didn't think very long before saying, "Use of the vehicle and a day at the beach."

"So far, this is fair?" I asked Charlotte.

"Yes, sar," she agreed.

"Okay, so, Ms. D'Heng wants to go to the beach, too, and your car can carry the extra load without any problems. How do you handle that?" I asked.

Juliett spoke first. "Well of course she can come with me."

"I'd offer to pay for fuel or split the cost of the rental or something, though," Charlotte added.

"Okay and we're still fair?" I asked. "If she splits the cost of the car, she has some interest in what you do with that car, Juliett. Are you going to accept her payment?"

"I don't know, sar," she said, thoughtfully. "I never thought about it."

"Fair enough, but now that I've raised the issue, what do you think?"

"I'd probably be grateful for a contribution to the fuel fund, sar," she said at last. "But I'm not sure I'd be willing to give up control of the car by accepting a shared payment for the rental."

Charlotte was thinking very hard about this idea. I saw the intensity in her face.

"Okay, so the two of you work out a deal. Whatever it is. Now suppose Ms. Nart wants a ride. She just wants to go out to the beach and doesn't even want a ride back. You going to make her pay, too?"

"Sar, I'm already tired of these negotiations, and we aren't getting any closer to the beach," Juliett said as understanding began to dawn. "I'd probably just tell her to get in and we'll drop her off. We're going that way anyway."

"But it's not fair, if I had to pay, sar," Charlotte said.

"But you didn't have to pay," Juliett said. "You just offered to chip in some gas money, and maybe Ulla would to, but the point is that I rented the ground car because I wanted to go to the beach. I was going to pay the whole cost until you came along and wanted a ride, and I would have taken you just for askin'," she said with a grin.

"Yes, but that wouldn't be fair, so I offered to pay something to help out," Charlotte insisted.

"Okay, and what if I refused?" Juliett followed the logic without needing my prompting. "What if I said, 'Don't be silly! Get aboard. I'm going anyway'?"

"That would be very generous of you," Charlotte said.

"Not really," I pointed out. "Just pragmatic. The value of her investment was not changed by your being there. For her the point is to get to the beach. If she decides to let you chum along, what's the cost to her?"

"Nothing," Juliett said, "and I might actually enjoy the ride more if you came with me because I enjoy your company."

"So is it fair?" I asked again.

Juliett was smiling now, but Charlotte was still frowning and trying to process. Finally, Charlotte said, "Under those conditions, I can't say if it's fair or not, sar." She had a kind of helpless expression on her face.

Juliett turned to Charlotte and said, "It's not a question of fairness. That's the point. If you pay or not—it just doesn't matter if I've rented the vehicle to get my butt to the beach. My willingness to let you ride with me has nothing to do with whether or not you're helping to pay. The point is whether or not I want to sit in the car with you during the trip."

I waited for Charlotte to catch up with that logic.

"So, what has this got to do with cleaning the mess deck?" she finally asked.

"Cleaning the mess deck is the trip to the beach," Juliett said. "The question isn't who gets to use the beach. It's who do we want in the car with us. Just between you and me? Anybody who doesn't want to help, probably isn't going to be that much help to begin with so who cares?"

I finally saw Charlotte get it. "Because when it's over, we'll be at the beach and we can do whatever we want."

"Exactly," I said. "And just like it would be easier if everybody chipped in on the fuel for the ground car, it'll be easier to clean the mess deck with more people who'll chip in on the cleaning. Everybody will get the benefit of the clean mess deck, but the more people who help, the smaller the cost for any person."

"So we should find some more people who'd be willing to help," Charlotte said almost instantly looking at Juliett.

"Well, I've got the watch," she pointed out, making an ostentatious show of examining the helm console.

"I'll go check with Penny and Karen and find out when they're gonna work on it," Charlotte said. "Then we can ask around and see if anybody else wants to help."

"Ulla will, I bet," Juliett said. "First section has evening watch tonight, so that means second will be off. I don't know about Betts, but I bet Ulla will."

"Ask him anyway," I suggested. "He may surprise you."

Chapter Twenty-three
Diurnia System: 2358-July-18

"So you found my little present?" Mr. Burnside asked when he relieved me at 1745.

"Sorry?" I had no idea what he was talking about.

He pointed to the console. "I left you a little something, since you were having so much fun cleaning."

"Oh, that?" I shrugged. "Forgot all about it, but thanks for your consideration." I tried to keep my voice carefully neutral.

He just snickered, but then his expression changed as if he'd suddenly remembered something. He motioned me over to the bridge wing where we could have a bit of privacy. "I talked to Apones this afternoon," he began.

"Really? Something I should be aware of?" I asked.

"Yes, actually." He paused. "You were out of line," he said seriously.

"I was out of line?" I repeated it back trying to figure out if I'd seen Apones some time during the day other than when he and Mosler were assaulting Nart. "What exactly did you talk to Mr. Apones about?"

"The little incident in the gym," he was giving me the stern, superior to junior officer look.

I glanced over to where Mallory was relieving Jaxton and Burnside stepped into my line of sight, backing me up into the bridge wing a little farther and blocking my view.

"I'm talking to you, Wang," he said sharply but softly. "You are not to interfere with my watch standers. Ever. Are we clear?" He bit each word off.

"Interfere with your watch standers?" It shouldn't have surprised me, but the sheer stupidity of it took me off balance. "Apones and Mosler were assaulting Nart!" I said trying to keep my voice down. "What was I supposed to do?"

"Walk away," he said. "Apones is on my watch. If there is a problem, you come to me."

I stared at him.

"Did you hear me, Wang?" His fetid breath rattled across my face.

"You must be joking! You think I'm going to walk away—"

He cut me off with a fast, hard right, once, up under my ribcage which drove me back into the bulkhead and left me trying to suck air back into my lungs. The pain was amazing. I thought I was going to keel over right there.

"Be quiet, Wang. Listen and listen good. You do not *ever* interfere."

I sagged against the cold metal. If he hadn't been standing so close, my feet would have probably slid out from under me. My world was narrowed to a gray tunnel and aching gut-punch.

After one last glower, he turned and stepped over to the console.

"I have the watch, Mr. Wang. Logged on 2358-July-18, at 1745 per standing order," he said.

Juliett knew something was wrong. Something about the way I was leaning against the bulkhead—or perhaps it was the redness in my face or the way I was trying to wheeze air back into my lungs. She started to say something but I caught her eye and shook my head once, nodding toward the ladder.

I managed to stand upright and cross the bridge without staggering. I did stumble a little at the bottom, where she was waiting and caught me by the arm.

"Are you all right, sar?"

I managed a weak chuckle as her question echoed mine from earlier in the day. It was rather an inane question when viewed from this side. The movement eased the cramp though, and I was able to get almost a full breath again. "A little disagreement with the first mate. Nothing to be concerned about."

She eyed me dubiously. "Anybody ever tell you you're a terrible liar, sar?" she asked after a moment.

"Yes, Ms. Jaxton, they have—on numerous occasions. I practice in hopes that some day I'll get better."

"Keep practicing, sar." She glared up the ladder and then looked back at me.

"Ms. Jaxton?" I said gathering her attention. "It's almost time for dinner mess. Shouldn't you be heading in that direction?"

"Yes, sar, I was just waiting to see if you'd fall down when you let go of the ladder rail, sar. It's not often you get to see an officer fall over from 'a little disagreement' and I thought it might be instructive, sar."

I snorted a soft laugh. The sudden contraction stabbed at me, but at least my sense of humor wasn't permanently damaged. "Have you ever considered the academy, Ms. Jaxton?"

"Me? No. What would make you say something like that?"

I shook my head and felt the crooked grin on my face. "No particular reason, Ms. Jaxton." I let go of the ladder and walked with as much dignity as I could down the passage.

Behind me I heard her snort, but she headed in the direction of the mess deck and not back up the ladder.

I let myself into my stateroom without falling down or throwing up. I heard the shower running in the head, so I sat on my bunk and curled up around the pain, letting myself deal with it for the first time, now that I had a little privacy.

In a few ticks the shower cut off and, after a few more, I heard a soft tap. I straightened up from the near fetal curl and tried to compose myself a bit before I reached up and released the latch.

Arletta was in her terry robe and still rubbing her hair with a towel. "How was—my gods! What happened to you?" she said.

"Oh, hiya, neighbor."

"'Hiya, neighbor'? That's your answer?" She scowled at me, but looked more concerned than angry.

"What makes you think anything happened?" I asked trying to sit up straight, but still feeling my shoulders curling inward.

"Hmm," she said with a considering tone. "Might have something to do with the fact that you're sitting there hunched over like somebody kicked you in the jewels and your face looks like you been punched in the gut."

I nodded appreciatively. "One out of two. Not a bad average."

She blinked at me as she processed what I was saying. "Somebody kicked you in the jewels?" she asked incredulously.

"No, punched in the gut," I said and stopped trying to pretend it didn't hurt.

"Who? Why?" she asked. When I didn't answer right away, she said, "Burnside." She made the name a curse.

I sighed and nodded. "I *interfered* with his watch stander."

"You what? This is about Nart, isn't it?"

"Yeah, how do you know about it?"

"Ulla came to me this afternoon. Thanks for standing up for her, but you have to be more careful. Those two are bad news."

"They're crew," I said.

"They're mean, vicious, and stupid," she spat. "Being an officer won't protect you from that."

"Nor from Burnside, either, apparently," I said.

"What happened?" she stepped into my stateroom and took the guest chair. She smelled wonderful. Warm, clean, soapy. I tried not to think too much about her bare knees poking out from the bottom of her robe.

"When he came to relieve the watch," I said, focusing on her eyes, "he took me over to the bridge wing and we had a little discussion over my interference with his guys. He backed me into the corner, and while Mallory was relieving the watch, he snuck one up under my ribcage."

"What were you supposed to do? Those thugs were assaulting a crewman!" She was getting angrier by the tick.

"His words? 'Walk away.'"

"You can't do that! It's illegal."

"What? Like punching an officer?"

"That's illegal too, but if you'd walked away and something happened? If it came out that you'd been there and done nothing, then they'd take your ticket."

"At least."

"At least," she said scowling at me as if her fierce expression could make the reality any plainer to me.

"But you're forgetting one thing," I said.

"What?"

"Who's the law here?"

"We're governed by the rules and regulations set forth by the Confederated Planets Joint Committee on Trade. This is illegal!" she sputtered.

"But who's the law *here*?" I asked again.

"Rossett," she said, her indignation collapsing as the reality hit her.

"It's only illegal if you can make a case to the authorities," I pointed out. "We can't do anything in space, and we'll have no standing once we make port if the captain won't back us."

We sat there, silently contemplating the situation.

"He's going to be even more insufferable, you know," she said.

"Which one?" I asked. "Burnside? Or Apones?"

She closed her eyes in resignation. "I was thinking Burnside, but you're right."

My tablet pinged to remind me that it was almost time for dinner in the wardroom. Arletta stood and slipped back through the door to the head. "I better get dressed. You grab a quick shower and I'll walk down with you."

I nodded and she closed the door on her side as I slipped gingerly out of my clothes and into the shower. The hot water felt good.

CHAPTER TWENTY-FOUR
DIURNIA SYSTEM: 2358-JULY-18

By the time Arletta and I got to the wardroom, Mel and Fredi were already there and waiting. Arletta did the "sorry we're late" routine and I got into my chair without incident.

"We were just admiring the handiwork," Mel said with a wave around the room.

It registered then. The room was immaculate. The table cloth was white. So white I hadn't realized that it wasn't before. The cutlery and glassware gleamed, and the room itself was perfect. I glanced down at the deck, around at the bulkheads, and even up at the overhead.

"Did she do all this in one afternoon?" I asked.

Fredi smiled and nodded. "Well, she had some help. I came down to read, and they were going to town. It was quite a party. When I saw them in here I backed out, but Ms. Davies brought me a carafe of coffee to take back to my stateroom."

Ms. Davies stepped through the door with a serving tray just at that moment and she smiled at us. "It was my pleasure, sar. I know you like a little coffee in the afternoon so I was ready."

"It was most considerate, Penny, thank you. And you and your colleagues did a wonderful job here."

"We had fun, actually, sar," she said with a pretty smile. She served us with her usual competence while she talked. "Karen, Ulla, and Vicki were great to help."

"Vicki?" Arletta asked. "VanDalon from Power?"

"Yes, sar," Penny said. "We had more people who were willing, but that's all we could fit in here and still have room to move."

"That's amazing," I said. "Thank you for your hard work."

She smiled, pleased by the praise. "You're welcome, sars. Thank you for speaking to Mr. Vorhees, Mr. Wang. We're going to have a field day on the mess deck tonight, and he's made one of his cakes for dessert afterward. It should be fun."

"A field day?" Mel asked.

"Yes, sar. Mr. Wang suggested that perhaps if we got the mess deck cleaned up a little more, the crew would sit there and drink coffee. That way we wouldn't have to pick up cups from all over the ship so often. A bunch of the crew has offered to help."

"And Mr. Vorhees is making a cake?" Fredi asked.

"Yes, sar." She nodded. "He makes the most amazing cakes, but only for special occasions."

Mel and Fredi shared a look.

"Mr. Vorhees is a man of hidden talents, it seems," Mel commented dryly.

"What time's the party?" I asked.

"2000, after we've had a chance to get the dinner mess cleaned up."

"Did you have much trouble rounding up people to help?" Arletta asked.

Penny shook her head. "No, sar. After people saw this place, and how nice it looks now, everybody wanted to help fix up the mess deck too." By then she'd finished serving and stood back with her tray. "Is there anything else I can get you, sars?"

"No, thank you, Ms. Davies," Mel said. "You've been very helpful."

She ducked her head almost shyly and left through the pantry.

"Will wonders never cease?" I said as I tucked into dinner.

"Ishmael?" Mel asked. "Was this what you expected when you brought this up over breakfast today?"

I shook my head. "No, I just thought maybe we could get the wardroom looking a bit better. Mr. Vorhees mentioned his problem with cups, so it seemed like a good way to ease into bringing up the state of the mess." I shrugged, gingerly. "The rest is history."

"How'd it spread?" Fredi asked.

"Ulla and Penny are bunkies," Arletta said. "Ishmael is taking on a certain romantic flavor with some of our younger and more impressionable female crew."

"Oh, not just the younger ones," Fredi said with a wink in my direction.

I sighed. "This is getting out of hand."

Mel grinned. "Ishmael, we're only ten days into a ten week trip. If you think it's bad now, wait until we get to Breakall."

"I was hoping things would calm down as the novelty wore off."

"It better or you may not live to see Breakall," Arletta said.

Mel and Fredi thought she was kidding and chuckled. I knew she wasn't.

Knowing that there was a party planned, we didn't dawdle over dinner. Ms. Davies seemed pleased when she came back with the desserts at 1915 and we were ready for them. I just took coffee, and Arletta excused herself entirely. "Midwatch and I'll need a nap," she said with a smile.

Fredi and Mel each had pie with their coffee, and I sat with them while they ate.

I wanted to ask Mel about Burnside but I didn't know how to broach the subject. It's not like a junior officer can actually complain about a senior officer to another senior officer without repercussions.

"I discovered something today that I hadn't expected," I announced to the table at large.

Mel looked up thoughtfully. "I suspect you did, Ishmael," she said with a careful expression on her face. "Care to share?"

"It's not our ship," I said.

Fredi and Mel both stared at me like I'd grown a second—or possibly third—head. Fredi spoke first. "Meaning what?" she asked.

"I had a discussion with my watch on the bridge this afternoon. They were concerned that it might not be appropriate for them to assist with the mess deck cleanup this evening."

"That must have been early in the watch, because that movement was gaining momentum by 1500," Mel said.

"It was," I agreed. "But I was pole axed when they questioned me whether or not it would be proper to offer to help. It's not their job, not their duty station, so they were concerned that somebody might think—I'm not sure what. That somehow it would be inappropriate for a non-mess hand to work on cleaning up the mess deck."

"I can't say I'm surprised," Fredi chipped in. "The emphasis here is do your job and mind your business. I don't think I've ever been on a ship this dysfunctional."

"It's because they don't think it's their ship," I said. "They don't clean it. They don't care for it. They don't care for each other. It's not their ship."

"Well, it's not their ship," Mel said. "It belongs to the company."

"Yes, but that's the point. All the ships everywhere belong to somebody, and it's almost never the crew. Only the family co-ops are the exceptions."

They nodded in agreement before Mel asked, "So what's the

point, Ishmael?"

"The point is that every other ship I've ever been on, from the *Lois McKendrick* to the *Bad Penny*, and through all the summer cruises, every other crew saw the ship as *theirs*. My ship. My crew. My duty. My responsibility. My family, even." I looked at them to see if they understood what I was saying.

Mel looked skeptical. "Isn't that a bit metaphysical for this bunch?"

I shook my head. "It's not a conscious decision, or I'd agree with you. I think there's something that makes most people identify with their ship. Before the *Billy*, I would have said everybody, but it was clear that my bridge crew has no connection to the ship—other than a place to move from A to B while being sexually assaulted and harassed."

Fredi stiffened at that but Mel said, "That's a little harsh, isn't it, Ishmael?"

"Not to Ms. D'Heng," I said. "Not to Ulla Nart. Not to Theresa Jaffee."

"Harassed, maybe... but sexual assault?" she pressed.

"Yes," Fredi said softly. "That's the correct term."

Mel looked at Fredi curiously but didn't press the matter, instead she turned back to me. "So, what's your conclusion, Ishmael?"

"If it's not their ship then they're not really crew. Just a bunch of people who happen to work in the same place. No unity. No interdependence. It becomes easy to beat up on each other. Easy to have a 'what's in it for me' attitude."

Mel said, "Well, it's my ship."

"Mine, too," I said. "But you said yourself that it's difficult getting them to wear clean shipsuits. I think that's why. They're all just drifting through. Until somebody gets hurt and then that person leaves."

"What about the mess deck cleanup party?" Mel asked. "How does that fit your theory?"

"I think it's a simple affiliation thing. They *want* to belong. Until now, there wasn't anything to belong to. The captain doesn't even belong. That sends a huge message. As far as I can tell, the only communication he has with the crew is through disciplinary actions."

"And they're all coming together now because we have a wonder boy third mate?" Mel asked with a grin, which took the sting out of what might have been a full hand slap. "What are we? Chopped liver?"

"I'm not saying that. You've had some luck with your crew. Just judging from the engineering spaces, which are head and shoulders above the regular deck areas. I'm not hearing about rampant abuse in the Engineering Department."

"Mosler," Fredi said. "He's a bad egg."

Mel sighed. "Yes, Mosler. I've tried to get rid of him more than once. Burnside always overrides me with the captain."

"Mosler and Apones, Apones and Mosler. How have those two managed to stay employed here?"

"They're David's stooges," Fredi said. Mel frowned at her but Fredi turned to her friend. "No, Mel, you have to admit it. David uses them to find female crew members that he can use and abuse. They get his cast offs and his protection. There's nothing we can prove, but you and I both know that's going on."

Mel sighed. "Yes, probably."

"Not probably. Remember that SA? Three trips ago? We were inbound from Dree? Alice something?"

"Oh..." Mel looked at the tablecloth as if trying to read the name there. "Stewart, Alice Stewart."

"Yes. Thank you. That would have kept me awake trying to remember," Fredi said with a smile. "Remember her? She actually recorded her own rape!"

Mel sighed. "Yeah, brave girl."

Fredi turned to look at me. "She saved the recordings and took them to the authorities when we got to port. Bypassed the first mate. Bypassed the captain. Straight to orbital security. For all the good it did."

"What happened?" I asked, although I knew I wasn't going to like the answer.

"She recanted after we'd been docked for two days. Refused to press charges," Fredi said. "Captain released her from her contract and left her there when we shipped out."

"Why did she do that? I'd have thought she wanted to nail them."

Mel spoke up then. "Dunno, Ishmael. Mighta had something to do with falling down the bridge ladder and breaking her arm."

"They broke her arm?!" I was aghast. I couldn't believe it.

Fredi shrugged. "Mosler and Apones were ashore at the time. Couldn't have been them."

A suspicion sprouted in the back of my mind. "Lemme guess. David was OD?"

Mel nodded and said, "On her way back from medical on the orbital, she stopped at security and withdrew her complaint. The next day she was gone."

Fredi finished her coffee and put the empty down on the table—

hard enough to bang. She closed her eyes and took a deep breath. "I think I'll go to my stateroom for a while," she said softly. She rose and left.

I looked at Mel who stared after her friend with a troubled look on her face.

Outside in the passage I heard the party starting up on the mess deck. Mel heard it too and turned to me. "Well, I suppose I should go help," I said.

Mel shook her head. "This is their party. Visit tomorrow and admire, but tonight leave them alone."

She stared into my face for a few heartbeats.

"You're right," I said.

"You can't turn them into a crew. It's something they'll have to do for themselves. All we can do is provide some protection while they work on it."

I sighed, figuring what that protection might cost me, and what it might gain.

"You'll earn no brownie points with the captain," she pointed out.

"I'm mostly just worried about surviving," I admitted. "I'm counting on self-interest and cowardice to prevent outright murder."

"What if they make a mistake and do it anyway?"

"That's the part that scares me," I said.

Chapter Twenty-five
Diurnia System: 2358-July-19

Underway watches sound like they should be easy. And they are, taken a few at a time, but when they go day after day, week after week, they get a little numbing. The routine takes some getting used to, and I was out of practice. When my tablet bipped me awake at 0500, I was disoriented. It was dark, except for the light my tablet gave off, and I had a pain in my lower ribs.

"Oh yeah, watch," I grumbled to myself. At least I didn't have to worry about falling on the deck from an upper bunk or scraping my knee from a lower. It was almost civilized to sit up in a normal height bunk and place my feet on the floor. Of course, when I stood, I banged my knee on the visitor's chair, and when I recoiled from that, I managed to bash my hip on the corner of the pull down desk, which I'd neglected to stow.

Still, having a twelve stan period off watch had let me get a good meal and gave my stomach a chance to recover. I went into the head and checked for bruises in the mirror. Nothing showed, but the lower rib was still pretty tender. Sighing, I got into the shower and let the water sluice the sleepy slime away. I was looking at six on, six off, six on, and then Burnside would relieve me. I hoped I wouldn't be as easy a mark again.

It only took a tick or two to dry off, skinny into a fresh shipsuit, and head for the mess deck. I was anxious to see what they'd done. I noticed the changes well before I got that far. The ladder rails gleamed and the passageways from crew quarters all the way to the mess deck had been freshly cleaned and the metal work polished. The deck had a few worn spots, and the paint looked scuffed in places, but all in all, *Billy* looked as good as I'd ever seen. It felt good just walking along and not grinding grit under the soles of my ship boots.

The mess deck was pristine. Every table and chair shined. Every surface and every bit of metal gleamed in the subdued nighttime lighting cycle. I could still smell the tang of cleanser and polish in the air. I went to the big coffee urns and admired the effort that had gone into burnishing every bit of filigree and angle of stainless steel on the counter. I pulled a fresh cup and stuck my head into the galley where the chief was working with the two messmates.

"My congratulations, Mr. Vorhees. Looks like things went well last night. The mess deck looks amazing."

Penny and Karen smiled and blushed as the chief answered, "These two organized it all. It was a wonder to behold. I bet we had a dozen people helping out, sar."

He picked up a side towel and carried it with him, wiping the flour from his hands as he stepped out into the mess deck to talk. "We had a little bit of a problem," he said softly once he was clear of the galley. "Nothing serious—just the normal troublemakers trying to disrupt. It didn't get beyond some catcalling and the odd soggy sponge, sar. But I thought you'd like to know."

"Thanks, John. On balance, was it worth the effort?" I asked.

He eyed the mess deck scanning around from table to table and across the coffee urns and steam tables. "Yes, sar. Yes, it was. I don't think I've seen the place look this good in the stanyer and a half I've been aboard." He looked at me and nodded. "I'll tell ya something else, sar. They"—he nodded back toward the galley—"and their friends did darn well with the hazing and such. I don't think it took us more than a stan to pull it all together. The biggest problem was not enough cleaning gear to go around. We had Engineering, Deck, and Steward Division people all pulling together."

"The operative phrase there being 'pulling together' I take it?"

"Yes, sar. I've been around a lot of ships. This is the only one that's scared me, but I'm beginnin' to think it's gonna be okay, sar." He looked a little abashed and I realized that this spec one was probably old enough to be my father. "Pardon my sayin' so, sar."

"Thanks for letting me know, John," I told him. "Keep an eye on it, but I think we may be turning a corner."

"Aye, sar," he said with a smile, "and thanks again."

I toasted him with my coffee mug and headed up to the bridge.

Betts had the helm and Ulla Nart was curled up at the auxiliary console reading something on her tablet. Arletta gave me a warm smile as I clambered up the ladder.

"How was it?" I asked.

"It was a blast."

"Any problems?"

"Nothing outrageous. Quiet night after the party in the mess deck wound down. For a while I thought we might have to send for the shore patrol."

I looked at her hard to see if she was kidding me. She was and snickered a little.

"I slipped in around 2130 on my way to work out," she said. "Apones and Mosler were standing in the passageway outside the mess deck doing their best to sneer at anybody who came by." She grinned. "Do you know how hard it is to sneer at somebody that's ignoring you?"

I chuckled. "I can only imagine."

"Is it still looking good down there?" she asked.

"Yeah, I stopped by to congratulate Mr. Vorhees and his crew on a job well done. I was hoping I wouldn't find it trashed."

"Ulla made a few passes through, but I suggested she study up here with us instead of down there alone in the dark."

Ms. Jaxton climbed up onto the bridge at that point, putting an end to the conversation, and we all proceeded to get the watch changed over.

When we had the bridge to ourselves she asked me, "Are you okay, sar?"

"Oh, yes, thank you for asking, Ms. Jaxton. I had dinner in the wardroom, then called it an early night and got a good night's sleep." I paused to kick the system backups on and then asked, "So, did you have fun at the party last night?"

She grinned a little and a yawn took her. "Sorry, sar," she said, covering her mouth, "but, yes. We got almost everybody who wasn't on watch to help. We had people working in the passageways, scraping off the tables, and polishing the metalwork. They piped in music and we were dancing in the aisles. It really was a party. I don't remember ever having that much fun with this group."

"Where's Ms. D'Heng this morning?" I asked.

"Oh, she's gonna eat before she relieves me, sar. More efficient," she said.

I nodded and finished my watch checklists as Ms. Cramer brought up my breakfast tray. "Thank you, Ms. Cramer," I told her with a smile.

She blushed, nodded, and then scampered off the bridge.

Ms. Jaxton snickered but I pretended not to hear as I settled into my breakfast. It was good and the portions were a bit larger than normal. Before I'd finished, Charlotte clambered up to relieve

Juliett.

After Juliett went down for breakfast, Charlotte turned to me with big eyes and asked, "So what do you think of the mess deck, sar?"

"It's amazing! Really," I assured her as I finished off my toast, washing it down with coffee.

"We had such fun," she gushed.

She proceeded to give me a very complete recap of the evening's festivities and I wasn't listening to it all, I confess, until she got to the part where she said, "... and so I expect we'll have a few more people join us on the bridge to study."

"Excuse me, Ms. D'Heng?" I interrupted.

"Yes, sar?"

"Join us on the bridge to study?" I asked.

"Oh, yes, sar. We all got to talking last night about trying to make ratings and finding time to study and all. Juliett and I mentioned what a great help you were. So a few more people will probably come up..." her voice tapered off. "That's not a good idea, is it, sar?"

"No, Ms. D'Heng, it's not. Part of the reason that you cleaned up the mess deck was so you'd be able to sit down there when you're not on watch."

"Yes, but you're up here, sar."

"And what has any of this to do with me, Ms. D'Heng?" I asked—almost afraid of the answer.

"Well, you're the training officer, sar. And you have a way of explaining things that really helps," she said, playing the flattery card without any self-consciousness or hesitation.

I thought about it for a while and then sighed. "I'm sorry, Charlotte, but we can't have a lot of extra people here on the bridge. It's a working space, not a study hall."

She looked disappointed.

"If you have people meet in the mess deck, I'll come down and answer questions for a stan or so in the afternoons when we're not on watch. How's that?"

The expression on her face said "knight in shining armor," but my gut was saying, "Don't get me hit again."

"Besides," I pointed out, "with enough people studying in the same place, you can get help from each other."

This was apparently not an idea she'd actually had before and I saw her working with it in her head. She eventually shrugged and that seemed to be that.

Ms. Jaxton returned from breakfast with three fresh coffees, and we settled in for another watch.

Chapter Twenty-six
Diurnia System: 2358-July-19

When Burnside came to relieve the watch at midnight, he was coming off his twenty-four. He hadn't been on watch since Arletta had relieved him the previous night. I eyed him warily as he climbed the ladder to the bridge and he actually had the nerve to smile at my wariness.

"Come, come, Mr. Wang," he said. "Discipline administered and over. Lessons learned need no repetition, right?"

I forced myself not to glare at him as he approached to take the watch. He'd have to work much harder to get in striking range. He wouldn't be taking me unaware again.

"Ship is on course and on target," I told him, standing up from the watch stander's chair. "No incidents or actions. Standing orders are unchanged. You may relieve the watch, Mr. Burnside."

He flopped bonelessly into the console's chair. "Yeah, fine, whatever. You need to loosen up a little, Ishmael. With all the hunnies you've got hangin' around, I'm surprised you haven't started a rotation for your stateroom."

Ms. Jaxton was just leaving the bridge, and I saw her color rise. I just shrugged. "I don't screw with crew," I told him and walked across the bridge to the ladder.

"That's a shame," he shouted so that I heard him as I descended the ladder. "That D'Heng is one hot little hoochie." I was glad that Juliett was ahead of me on the ladder, and I could keep her moving downward.

Her face and neck, already red, went to scarlet as her temper rose. She turned to start back up the ladder, but I had my hands on both rails. She would need to go through me.

"Words, Juliett, just words. Hateful, ignorant, and spiteful though they may be. Just words," I told her.

"He can't say that stuff!"

"He can and he did, but we don't need to sink to his level. He's trying to goad me into fighting, so he has an excuse to haul me up on charges. If he can't get me, he'd be happy to have you."

"He's—" she started to say.

"He's the first mate," I said. "It behooves us to remember that and treat the office with respect."

She looked at me as if I'd stabbed her.

"I know," I said. "But I'm not that kind of person, and I don't think you are, either."

She stared at me for another few heartbeats and the tension slumped out of her.

"This isn't fair, sar."

"Fair is a weak term. There's a better construct for this situation, I think."

I waited for her to bite.

Finally she asked, "Which is?"

I continued down the ladder, forcing her to step off the bottom step. She turned and frowned at me.

"On my old ship, the *Lois McKendrick*, we had a saying. 'Trust Lois.'"

"Sar, you did pass your psych eval, right?"

"Barely. They were concerned that I might be too sane to be an officer at first, but I convinced them I was psychotic enough."

"But trust the ship?" she asked.

"Well, not exactly, the ship. See, everybody on the *Lois* had a kind of belief in the ship's spirit, its pooka. So we believed in the spirit of the ship, which taken as an abstract is like saying you believe in fairies, I realize. In reality, we believed in each other. We always knew that somebody on the ship would have whatever would be needed to take care of whatever problem we faced, and that when the time came, that person would do whatever was needed."

"The pooka?" She had an incredulous look on her face, like she'd just heard the most fantastical story ever and wanted it to be real. "Wasn't that risky, sar?"

I shrugged one shoulder. "Maybe, but the key element was that while we all trusted *Lois*, we kept in mind that when the time came, we each needed to do our part. And often, that meant getting off your butt and making something happen."

"Like cleaning the mess deck?" she asked.

"Precisely. I changed algae matrices in the environmental section in my off watches and helped make sludge cakes."

"Eeeww. Wasn't that nasty?"

"Not really. Smelly at times, sure, but it needed doing. . . besides with the right company, even dirty work—like cleaning the mess deck—can be fun."

"You're not saying 'Trust Billy' are you, sar?"

That stopped me cold. *Could I trust Billy?*

She saw the indecision in my eyes, and I had to be honest. "I don't know, Juliett. My training and experience says yes, but given what I know about what's happening on this ship, I have to confess, the idea never entered my mind until you just suggested it."

"Sar, are you sure you passed your psych eval?"

"Yes," I said with a smile. "Lemme think about that trusting Billy part. There's a terrible power in belief." I looked at her for a moment, thinking hard. "Have you ever heard of South Coast shamans?"

"I don't get out much, sar," she said, shaking her head.

"Never mind."

"Sar, you're a little bit spooky at times."

"I'm improving then, Ms. Jaxton. I used to be really spooky *all* the time."

"I haven't known you that long, sar. May I reserve judgment?"

"Yes, Ms. Jaxton, you may." I chuckled, then turned and headed down the passage. "Good night, Ms. Jaxton."

"Good night, sar, and watch out for Billy."

I was still chuckling as I let myself into my stateroom. On a whim, I dug into the bottom of my grav trunk and pulled out a small cloth bag. I tossed it onto my bunk while I stripped down to ship tee and boxers. I was starting my twenty-four stans off and that meant I could sleep in if I wanted. After the last watch cycle, I was ready for a good sleep and crawled gratefully into my bunk to start the first stages of what felt like might turn into a real long nap. But before I settled, I opened the bag and pulled out seven individual bundles of cloth tied off with string. I unwrapped and examined each, weighing them in my hand for a moment before carefully re-wrapping and re-tying the strings. I put them all back in the bag, and slipped the bundle under my pillow rather than get up again.

It was one of those perfect times. The temperature was just right. The sheets were cool and crisp on my skin but warmed as I felt the tension drain from my body. I rolled onto my side, glanced at the chrono glowing on the bulkhead: 0042, and let my eyes close. The darkness flowed up around me and pulled me down.

When the darkness finally receded, the chrono read 1154. I blinked at it. In the dimness of my stateroom it was the only focus. The numbers flipped to 1155 and a couple of heartbeats later I heard Arletta close the door to her stateroom. I heard her rummaging around. The numbers flipped to 1156 and I heard her go into the head and run water in the sink.

It was the running water that did it. I could have lain there, maybe drifted off again, but she ran the water and I knew that I needed to get up—traitorous bladder. Still it wasn't urgent. Yet.

Yawning and scratching, I rounded up fresh boxers and tee shirt, retrieved the bag of whelkies from under my pillow, and put them carefully back in the bottom of my grav trunk. I did the tug-pull-pull-tug-flip to my bunk. It wouldn't have passed muster at the academy, but it was good enough for shipboard.

I heard the water turn off and then a tap-tap on my door. Releasing the latch I swung it open, just as another yawn grabbed me. "Sorry, I haven't quite woken up yet."

She looked at me with a quizzical expression. "You're just getting up?"

I nodded and blinked. My eyes were still a little bleary and I needed to use the head. "It's my twenty four," I said in mild protest. "I needed some beauty sleep."

"I can understand that. Mine's tomorrow and I'm so ready you can't imagine."

"Oh, I can imagine, and we aren't even half way there yet."

"Don't start counting now," she told me with a bitter chuckle.

"I know. I know. We still have a long way to go."

The trip was scheduled for sixty-two standard days. We'd been under way a little more than ten, so we had barely begun, and it was too soon to start thinking about how much was left.

"And speaking of long way to go..." I said.

She took the hint with a slightly embarrassed little smile and backed out into her own stateroom. "Walk me to lunch, spacer?" she asked with a mock vamp expression on her face.

"Sure, lemme just get a shower and some clothes on," I said with a smile of my own.

She grinned, spoiling the vamp-look she had working, and closed the door to the head on her side.

It didn't take long for me to do the needful, including a fast shower and shave. I slipped into my room and closed the head door behind me, latching it while I tossed on the fresh clothing.

Fredi was just finishing up something on her tablet when we stepped into the wardroom. She was already halfway through a cup of coffee and smiled a welcome as we stepped in.

"Hello, Fredi, what's new in cargo?" I asked.

She never talked about her work. Not surprising, I supposed, but if she were one of Captain Giggone's cadets then there had to be a story hiding somewhere.

She shrugged. "It's all in the can."

It was a cargo joke. All cargo jokes were like that.

"Doesn't this get boring, for you?" Arletta asked. "I mean, there's not a lot to do once we get that can strapped on, and even before. You don't get to pick the cargoes. You don't get to do anything fun, do you?"

"Oh, I don't know. Being cargo chief on a bulk hauler isn't all that taxing, no. These barbell designs, like the *Billy,* are made to take advantage of the regulation loophole on ship length. I'm surprised they haven't made spherical ships, frankly," she added with a soft chuckle.

"Loophole?" I asked.

"Normally, any ship carrying over a hundred and fifty metric kilotons needs both a cargo chief and a first. About twenty stanyers ago, they put a loophole in the regulations to allow bulk haulers under a hundred and fifty meters in length to get by with just a chief. *Billy's* only one forty so, I'm the only member of the Cargo Division."

"Yes, but do you have any fun?" Arletta asked again.

"Not as much as I used to," she said with a little sigh. "But then, a few more trips and I can retire. I'm young yet, and I think I'd like to take up being a cargo broker."

I tried to control the expression on my face. I don't know how well I did with it. Fredi looked like the oldest spacer I'd ever seen. As I looked at her, though, I realized that she wasn't all that old, just frail. I couldn't imagine her horsing an anti-grav pallet full of canned goods around, but then again, I couldn't remember the last time I'd seen a cargo officer horse a pallet full of anything around. That's why they had crew.

"What do you need to be a broker?" I asked.

"Contacts, mostly, and a sharp eye."

Mel came in just then and smiled fondly at Fredi. "Talking about being a broker?"

"Yes, and don't be an old poop," she shot back with a fond smile of her own. "They asked. I'm answering. That's all."

Mel winked at Arletta and me as she passed behind Fredi on the way to her chair.

"Do you need a license or something?" I asked in order to keep Fredi talking. It was the most animated I'd seen her since coming aboard.

She shook her head. "No. You need to register and get bonded with the CPJCT but that's only to get your name on the broker registry. After that, you have to cultivate your contacts on the planet and with the shippers, then trade and keep trading."

Penny Davies came in with the lunches then, and we all tucked in. It still wasn't as good as Cookie used to make, but as baked mouta went, it wasn't bad.

Over coffee Mel said, "So, I understand you're holding classes on the mess deck this afternoon, Ishmael?"

I looked up at her and the surprise must have been on my face because she grinned. "I am?"

Arletta said, "That's what Ulla told me too." She said it with a lilt in her voice that made me suspect that she hid a smirk behind her coffee cup.

I sighed and asked, "Did she say what time I'm supposed to be holding these classes?"

Mel answered, "1400"

I looked back and forth between them. "How is it you both happen to know this?"

Arletta shrugged. "When Charlotte D'Heng told Ulla that you'd be willing to hold classes on the mess deck—"

"Wait, she said what?"

"Charlotte said that you had problems with people cluttering up the bridge while you were on watch so you'd hold classes in the mess deck instead."

"Oh," I said.

Fredi and Mel were doing the "I'm so innocent" face across the table at me. Fredi's reaction didn't concern me, but Mel was the officer in charge of the largest division on the ship. With Propulsion, Power, Grav, and Environmental, her division made up more than half the ship's crew.

"What I said was that the bridge was a work space, and when we were on watch we shouldn't have the area filled up with people who weren't required to be there." I pointed out in what I hoped was a reasonable voice.

"Yes," Arletta agreed, "and then you said you'd be willing to hold classes on the mess deck in the afternoons instead."

I closed my eyes, trying to remember what I'd said, exactly. "I'm pretty sure I only agreed to answer questions for a little while. That's hardly what I'd call *holding classes*."

Fredi and Mel looked at each other and shrugged. "I don't know..." Fredi said.

"Sounds kinda like it to me," Mel finished.

"And how many people know about this little party?" I asked, becoming concerned.

Well, to be honest I'd been concerned all along. It was just rising to the level of near-panic by then.

Arletta said, "All of them, I think." She looked to Mel.

Mel looked at the overhead as if considering a careful response.

"Yes," she agreed after a couple of heartbeats. "I think all of them."

"Well, only people on the ship," Fredi pointed out. "Not everybody everywhere. We're just talking locally."

"Thank you, Ms. DeGrut for that clarification." I raised my cup in mock toast.

She returned the toast with her own mug and said, "Most welcome, Ishmael. Feel free to come to me any time."

"Well," I said. "Maybe nobody will show up."

The three of them laughed. Loudly. It wasn't an encouraging sound.

After lunch, I went back to my stateroom for a few minutes. I wasn't sure what I was going to face so hiding seemed like a reasonable response. I told myself it was so I could look up the dates for the next testing, but it was really to make myself scarce. It was one thing to talk with Ms. Jaxton and Ms. D'Heng about their rating exams, and another to stand up in front of a mess deck full of people.

As it turns out, I needn't to have worried.

At 1400, fortified with the date of the next testing period displayed prominently on my tablet—and after about twenty ticks of ponderation about what they might want to know—I headed down to the mess deck to brave the crowd.

All four of them.

Well, five actually, but I didn't think Apones was there to study. He sat sprawled on a chair in a corner. His scowling face tracked me across the room to the coffee pot and back to the table where Juliett, Charlotte, Ulla, and a wiper named Raymond sat.

"Can I sit here?" I asked, indicating an empty seat at the table.

"Of course, sar," Ulla said. "We were waiting for you."

I smiled and settled with my coffee. "How can I help?" I asked, and that was all it took.

For the next stan and a half, they peppered me with questions. Not one of the questions had to do with the next testing date.

We talked about the sequencing of ratings.

It was Raymond who asked, "Why don't I have to take them all in order, sar?"

"That surprised me, when I heard it, too," I said. "But the tests are set up so that if you haven't mastered the previous material, you can't pass the higher test. It becomes an exercise in how far you can reach."

"How so, sar?"

"If you sat for spec one power right now, what would the likely outcome be?"

"I probably wouldn't get it, sar," he said with a self-conscious grin.

"Okay, why not?"

He shrugged. "Well, because I don't know anything about power, sar."

"So, you're studying for, what? Engineman?"

"Yes, sar, I just started."

"Just started what? Studying for Engineman or being aboard the ship?"

"Oh, studying, sar, I'm on my second contract. I did my first two stanyers on a UFH tanker. When my contract was up, I decided not to renew and got off in Diurnia. I discovered I had missed being underway, so I signed back on with DST, but didn't have much in the way of ratings—so here I am. Thought it was about time to move up a bit, sar, just in case I have to find another job. I'll be ready."

"So, you probably know your way around the engine room pretty well already," I pointed out. "Why don't you try for Machinist and skip Engineman?"

"Oh, I couldn't, sar!"

"Why not? All you have to do is try for it. Worst case you miss. Best case, you skip a rank."

He looked dubious, but Charlotte D'Heng asked, "Could I do that, sar?"

"What? Test for machinist?" I asked. "Do you know anything about engineering?"

I liked the way she giggled—very bubbly. "No, sar, able spacer? Can I skip ordinary and go for the able spacer test?"

"Of course. If you take the test and pass, you're automatically granted the subordinate rates."

"But the tests only come around every ninety days, sar," Juliett pointed out. "If you miss it, you have to wait another ninety days to try again for the lower rank. Wouldn't it make more sense to take them in order to make sure you have the building blocks firmly in place?"

"That's why I say it's an exercise in how far you can reach. Yes, it's a risk and a lot of people just build the ratings in order."

The four of them looked at each other and then back at me. They weren't convinced. I could see it in their faces.

"It's not a complete shot in the dark, you know," I said.

"How so, sar?" Juliett asked.

"The study materials have practice tests included. If you get in the top five percent, you can probably pass the exam. If you don't score more than half, you're probably over your head. If you're somewhere in between, then there's a pretty good chance you can pass if you study."

Raymond looked thoughtful for about five heartbeats and then said, "So I can use the practice tests to see where I should be studying, sar?"

"Precisely, Mr. Raymond. Humor me, whatever you're thinking of studying, go to the next higher rating and try that practice test. See what you find out."

"But I haven't studied that material yet, sar!" Ulla said in dismay.

"Yes, Ms. Nart. That's the idea. If you can get half the answers on the practice test before you even study, the probabilities are good that you could learn the other half with some judicious application of study time."

Juliett, ever the practical one, asked, "If this is so easy, why don't more people do it, sar?"

"I don't know, Ms. Jaxton," I admitted. "It seems the most sensible way to approach it to me, but then I'm not a spacer. My mom was an ancient lit professor."

At that, they all looked around the table at each other as if that explained everything. Perhaps it did.

"Somebody said you were rated before you went to the academy, sar," Raymond said. "Is that true?"

"Yes, Mr. Raymond, I was rated. I took my share of the exams."

"How many did you take, sar?" Charlotte asked.

I had to count on my fingers, and did so out loud. "Four half share, two full share, plus Spec two environmental and Spec one systems. Eight, I think. There was a test for Spec two systems, but it wasn't a written one. Yes, I think that's all. After four years at the academy it's hard to remember."

When I looked up, there were four pairs of eyes bugging out at me.

"What?" I asked.

"You're rated in all four divisions, sar?" Mr. Raymond finally managed to ask.

"Well, I was, yes, but now I'm third mate."

Juliett slapped her hand on the table then and said, "Well!" She looked around at her cohorts and added, "I don't know about you, but I think I'm gonna take a practice exam or two."

They all fumbled for tablets and started punching up content.

"Any advice on the specialist rates, sar?" Juliett asked after working for a tick or two.

"Spec three is easy. It's only a little more difficult than the divisional full share but it has the bare minimum additional information for that specialty. If you know anything about the specialty field, look at spec two," I told her. "Drop back to spec three if you score below a fifty. Spec one is not impossible but they tend to cover nuts and bolts in spec two and teach theory in spec one."

"Thank you, sar. Very helpful," she said without looking up.

I picked up my cup and walked over to the urn for a refill. It hadn't been that long, but I'd gone through a lot. I watched Apones watching me out of the corner of my eye. He was not a happy spacer. I crossed to him with my full cup and nodded a greeting without attempting to sit.

"Do you have any questions about testing, Mr. Apones? You looking to pick up another pay grade?"

He snorted. "Yeah. I'm going for king of the world. I'll be sure to check with ya if I decide to take the test for it."

"Excellent, Mr. Apones. I'm sure we'll all be watching for that day."

He smirked, as if he'd somehow been funny or something, and I returned to the group.

It took them a while to get through the practice tests. I knew from experience they could take up to a full stan but I waited.

Ulla Nart finished first with a bright grin. She turned her tablet around to show the 74% score. I checked and she really had done the able spacer test.

I gave her thumbs up and a smile.

Eventually everybody finished. Charlotte D'Heng got the lowest score with a 60% against the able spacer exam.

"Okay, everybody," I said when the initial jubilation had run its course. "You got a boost, but now you need to buckle down. If you go through the lessons, do the exercises as you go, and pay attention to what you're doing, you'll be fine. There's still a few weeks left to study and not a lot else going on here, so you should have plenty of time to learn enough to jump a rank."

They all looked so jubilant, I felt like I needed to temper their expectations.

"Remember that if you pass you only earn the rating, which only means you can apply for a better position. The ship's not obligated to hire you for one, nor pay you at the higher rating for your current post," I said as sternly as I could, looking around the table.

Juliett said, "Are you kidding, sar? With the turnover we have, jobs get refilled at almost every port."

"Still," I said, "don't get too excited. It will qualify you for more positions, but you're still going to have to convince the people who hire spacers that you're a good shipmate."

The smiles around the table still blinded me, but I was cautiously optimistic that the message had gotten through.

"Okay, I've got the watch tomorrow afternoon, but why don't we plan to meet again the day after?" I said. "If you have any questions, need any advice, or would like some feedback other than what the tablets give you, see me then, okay?"

Nods bobbed around the table and I headed back to my stateroom to get changed. It was almost 1530 and that gave me enough time for a good workout before dinner. As I left the mess deck, I noticed that Apones had disappeared as well. Perhaps he got bored, but I thought it more likely that he'd gone to report to David Burnside.

CHAPTER TWENTY-EIGHT
DIURNIA SYSTEM: 2358-AUGUST-10

Once you get into the routine of being underway, the ticktock of the watch cycle, wake—work—sleep—repeat, makes it hard to have awareness. Usually this shift to grayness, the brain blur, is disconcerting. I had always felt it was a kind of mixed blessing. On the one hand, if you were aware of every day as it crawled past—every one identical—nothing changing except the meal on your plate: same people, same clothes, same activities, day after day after day—you'd probably just step out an airlock from the boredom. On the other hand, there was a kind of mental buffering that protected you from realizing just how many days had passed, and how many were left. The internal buffer just refreshes without a lot of effort or thought.

Wake—work—sleep—repeat.

As a crewman, I'd thought of this as the merry-go-round of watch standing. Your world shrinks to the people who are in your watch section—awake when you are, eating when you do, going to the gym when you are. The rest of the crew is on the other side of the carousel and, while you can catch glimpses of them between the horses, you don't get much chance to do more than wave. People who were day workers, like the mess deck crew, were like the people watching the merry-go-round spin. You'd see everyone, but never stop to talk as they swung by, once per revolution.

On the *Tinker*, as an officer isolated in the wardroom and stateroom, my world shrank even more. Say what you will about the lack of privacy in the berthing areas, at least there were people around. Mel and Fredi were constants at meal times, when I could get to the wardroom to eat. Arletta and I became good friends. Something about sharing a head, I think. It's hard to maintain romantic illusions when digestion and its by-products get involved.

It was just as well. I certainly didn't want to open that door with all the rest of the bunk jumping that appeared to be going on in the ship. Without the mental blur, I might have found it depressing.

Juliett and Charlotte were the only people I saw regularly for any amount of time. I have to give them a lot of credit for keeping me amused. Juliett had a dry quick-wittedness about her that could find something bitingly humorous in the darkest situation. Charlotte was one of those unnaturally upbeat people who seemed to smile all the time and who could find the joy in the most mundane of activities. They helped make the blur tolerable. I'd like to think I held up my end as well.

The thing about the blur is that it doesn't take a lot to break it.

Something will happen and it's like a sudden noise in the night. You go from asleep to awake all at once. Sometimes you're aware of what it was that you heard, and sometimes you wake to only the memory of noise with no conscious awareness of what it might have been. About thirty-two days out of Diurnia and only a couple away from transition, I woke up from the blur when I stepped onto the mess deck for our afternoon tutorial session and I realized that almost every table had somebody at it.

Granted, Apones monopolized one of the tables in his usual position against the far bulkhead. It was his unofficial watch station when first section had the duty. He never said anything, just glowered at me and the group. For our part, we ignored him.

Still, looking around the mess deck, I realized that this wasn't something new. The numbers had been growing for weeks. From that first four, we picked up a lot of crew from the engineering staff. That wasn't surprising, given how many of them were aboard. The only people from the Deck Division who weren't involved were the astrogation spec two's—De Silva—and Apones, who may as well have been participating, given the amount of time he spent glaring. Even Mallory, the first section's helm watch, participated on days when he wasn't on duty. He worked on his spec one in ship handling.

I drew a mug of fresh coffee and started circulating. My fear that I'd wind up as some kind of teacher standing up in front of the group never materialized. When we'd out grown one table— which we did by the second meeting—we split up by division and then by level. Ulla and Charlotte had their heads together over the able spacer test. Betts and Jaxton worked on spec two in ship handling. Three enginemen, Lignaria and VanDalon from Power, and Cottonwood from Environmental, studied spec three power. Xhang worked on his spec two in grav.

The stan from 1400 to 1500 was designated study period on the mess deck, and it was the only time I saw a group of the crew in one place. I confess it felt good to be wandering from table to table and visiting with them. They seemed so—I don't know—grateful. It never ceased to amaze me.

During that period, I visited with everybody. Most had things under control, but there were a couple of issues I was able to help with. I couldn't necessarily answer questions directly, but was able to find somebody who could. A lot of times, that was better anyway.

As usual, Apones wasn't at his table any longer. I don't know if it was a function of his watch standing, bad timing on my part, or perhaps he was reporting to Burnside about the training. Whatever it was, I found it odd that he was always gone before I left.

I shrugged it off. At least he wasn't bothering the people who were trying to study.

I refilled my coffee cup and headed back to my stateroom to change into workout clothes. There was just enough time for a good run, a little tai chi, and a hot shower before dinner. After dinner, I'd be ready for a nap before going on watch.

I had just passed the cabin when I heard the door open behind me and saw Bayless slipping out again. He saw me looking, ducked his head, and walked quickly away. I shrugged and kept going myself, but as I changed clothes it occurred to me that I'd seen Bayless, or one of the other engineering crew, coming out of the cabin or walking along that passageway a lot. By a lot, I don't mean every day. One of them—Bayless or this other guy—I couldn't think of his name, but my mind provided the face—would be in the passage maybe a couple of times a week.

It's not unusual to see crew in officer country, but to see the same two engineering crewmen near the cabin and not down the passage near Mel's stateroom, that was curious. I wondered if these two were Mel's problem children.

I shrugged it off. Not my division, not my problem, and I had a few kilometers to run before dinner.

When I got to the gym, the tall Power Section engineman, Lignaria, was just getting off the treadmill. She nodded at me with a friendly smile as we traded places.

"Watch out for the pothole around twenty klicks, sar," she said.

It was a standing joke with us, since I'd caught my shoe on the tread one day when we'd been running together. I'd been horribly embarrassed, and made an offhand joke about finding the pothole. She thought it was much funnier than it actually was, and it had become a kind of ritual with us.

"Yeah, thanks," I said with a grin as I finished my stretches. As the treadmill started to spin up, I let the endorphins take me and zoned into the running. A full stan passed before I was even aware of it, and the machine's program slowed to a cool down cycle. It felt great.

I toweled off some of the excess sweat, got a drink of water to replace some of what I'd lost, and stepped onto the floor for some tai chi. I had found that the combination of a long run, followed by a good session of tai chi, to be the best response to the day-to-day grind. It bled off excess stress and re-centered me. Burnside's petty abuses—leaving puddles of coffee, smearing the armor glass ports with granapple jam, and once even leaving something that looked and smelled too fecal for comfort in the watch stander's chair—didn't matter. Apones' constant potential for mayhem melted away.

I focused on my hand position.

I paid attention to my weight distribution.

I sighed as Mosler and Apones entered the gym.

"Well, look at the purdy dance," Apones said to Mosler. "Don't he dance good, Herm?"

"Real nice," Mosler answered. "Kinda girly, but some guys like that, don't they?"

"Oh yeah, they do," Apones said.

They closed the distance and stood just off the cleared exercise floor. I ignored them.

"You like dancing purdy, Isshy?" Apones said.

I kept my form moving smoothly.

"I think he likes it, Rick," Mosler said.

"Yeah, maybe we just traded Sissy's," he said with a low chuckle.

"Maybe he's a girly man," Mosler replied.

"You gentleman crossed the line of insubordination some time ago," I said.

I hoped I said it calmly, because I didn't feel terribly calm. I did manage to keep the Wu Long Form going, but regulations required me to warn them before I did anything rash.

"And what are you going to do about that, girly man?" Apones asked.

"Probably nothing," I said, feeling the calming chi moving through me.

My body remembered the push-hands exercises I'd done with Kurt on the trip from Newmar. He'd worked with me for stan after stan. While his skills were somewhat rougher than Sifu Newmar's polished grace, they were also more appropriate to what I knew was inevitably coming.

"At least nothing at the moment," I told them.

"Aw, girly man afraid?" Mosler said with a sing songy babytalk inflection.

I let the chi take me. The movements smooth, deliberate, balanced. I was suspended from the top of my head and a spike of chi ran through my center. I closed my eyes.

Apones laugh, a deep ha-ha kind of sound, was almost a chortle. "Look, Herm, he's closed his eyes, so he can pretend we're not here. Peek-a-boo, Isshy!"

I heard Apones step closer to me.

I slipped sideways and felt the wind of his hand slide past my face, and I actually heard him grunt from surprise. I slipped sideways again, spinning into a Slant Single Whip as he stepped again. I knew he was going to put his weight into this one, so I moved to Step Back and Ride the Tiger as his body filled the space I'd just left. A quick Turn Body Slap Face Palm pushed him off balance and he sprawled onto the deck taking Mosler down with him.

It happened quickly. People always underestimate the speed and power of tai chi. I centered myself and stopped the form. Only then did I open my eyes. Mosler was still trying to get out from under Apones, and Apones was looking at me when my eyes opened.

"If you gentlemen would kindly take yourselves out of my sight, I won't have to close my eyes again," I told them.

Yes, it was cheap theatrics.

Almost.

Kurt had taught me the trick of listening with almost closed eyes. It was nothing mystical. I just saw a bit of shape and movement, and in the quiet of the exercise room, every motion of their bodies made sounds that I could hear: cloth on cloth, foot on deck. Even breathing—since neither of them was trying to control it. They huffed like steam engines.

I stood there waiting while they untangled themselves and stood up. I saw Apones wasn't done, but Mosler seemed more hesitant. My performance had unnerved him. I don't think he would have prevented Apones from trying again, but he was already taking a step backward when Cottonwood and VanDalon came into the gym, joking and horsing around. They looked curiously at the three of us standing at the end of the room but stepped up onto the treadmills and began a workout.

I smiled at Apones. "Tsk, tsk, witnesses, now scat before they see you get beaten up by a girly man."

Mosler had seen the two enter and was already pulling Apones back. "Come on, Rick, let's go."

Apones let himself be tugged back a step or two, turning as if it were his own idea and striding out of the gym. The two engineering crew ignored him, but cast sidelong glances at me as I limbered up for one Yang Short Form to steady myself before I would have to

follow them out into the passageway. By the time I was done, I felt almost okay again.

I made it back to my stateroom and into the head before throwing up.

168

CHAPTER TWENTY-NINE
DIURNIA SYSTEM: 2358-AUGUST-10

"You okay in there?" Arletta called from her stateroom.

I ran some water and rinsed my mouth and washed my face before answering.

"Yeah," I said.

There was a pause. "Are you sure?"

I released the handle so she could open the door on her side. "Yeah. Just a little more exercise than I expected."

She was obviously getting ready to go on watch. Her hair was still wet and she sat on her bunk, slipping into her ship boots. When she got a look at my face, she frowned.

"Really?"

I shrugged and swiped a towel across my mouth.

"Mosler and Apones tried to jump me in the gym," I told her and ran through the basic outline of events.

She sat there through the whole thing without saying a word.

"You don't seem surprised," I said when finished.

"I guess the surprising part is that it took so long. I'm certainly not surprised at the stupidity of it," she said with a kind of bitter edge to her voice. She glanced up. "Mosler actually said, 'Girly man'?" she asked.

I chuckled. "Yeah, if I hadn't been so intent on the situation, I probably would have burst out laughing."

"Why didn't you put them on report?" she asked.

"Two against one. No witnesses. They were stupid, but they were careful. I still expect to hear from Burnside about how I roughed up his watch stander."

"That's ridiculous!" she spat. Continuing in a more resigned tone she said, "Typical of Burnside, though."

"Yeah. He'll use the fact that I didn't put them up on charges as evidence that I'm in the wrong."

"And you can't put them on report because there's no corroborating evidence," she finished for me.

"You got it. As soon as witnesses showed up, they beat it."

She sighed in return. "Well, just a few more weeks for me." She looked up at me apologetically. "Sorry."

"Don't blame ya," I told her.

She glanced at the chrono and then slumped back on her bunk. "Not yet," she said, as much to herself as to me.

"So you're the second mate. Any advice from your vast store of experience and exalted rank?" I asked only half joking.

She pondered it for only a moment.

"Why yes, young sar. I have learned one important lesson when dealing with these kinds of situations," she answered in a somber and serious tone.

I waited expectantly.

In her most ostentatious voice she pronounced. "Ask Mel."

It caught me by surprise, although it shouldn't have. I guffawed.

She lost it herself and giggled a little. It was a musical sound and she folded her shoulders forward a bit when she did it. All told, it was a delightful three heartbeats.

"That's the best advice I've heard all day," I admitted after half a tick. I leaned in to look at her chrono. "I wonder if she's in."

"Bip her," Arletta said with a one shouldered shrug. "There's over a stan before you have to face Burnside in the wardroom. You might wanna line up a few ducks before you get there."

"Good point."

I slipped back into my stateroom to sit on my bunk and compose the message: *Gotta few ticks to advise a junior officer? Before dinner if we can?*

The answer came back almost instantly: *Right now in my office?*

On my way. I sent back.

And in just that much time it was done. I looked up to see Arletta standing in the door to the head.

"She has time right now, so have a good watch, and I'll see you at midnight."

"Thanks, Ish. Be careful, huh? I'd hate to have to break in another new third."

"Am I broken in already?" I asked.

She shook her head. "No, but I don't want to start over fresh. Again."

She grinned and waved as she closed my door from the other side.

I beat feet to engineering. Mel's office was just off the spine at the top of the aft section of the ship, and while it wasn't the same distance as on the *Lois*, it was still a rather long trundle.

The whole engineering deck was packed with control monitors and I looked into the bay and saw grav, power, and engine consoles. It reminded me a lot of the bridge, except it lacked the armor glass ports. Mel waved me into her office as I crossed in front of the open door.

"Mr. Wang," she said loudly, "how can I help you?"

I stepped in and motioned to close the door. She looked intrigued but signaled her agreement with a shrug and a nod.

"Thanks for seeing me," I said and took the offered chair.

"Problem, Ishmael?"

"Yes, and I'm leery about taking it to the first until I can get some insight from you," I said. "You're the senior officer aboard— barring the captain and the first—and I need some advice on how to stay out of trouble."

She snorted. "On this boat, the only way to stay out of trouble is to sleep with the captain. What's on your mind?"

Having been through the story once already, it didn't take long to spin the yarn again.

Mel nodded when I had finished.

"Those two are not the only problems on this ship, but they're the dumbest," she said with a sigh. "It's not like I can tell Mosler to not play with Apones in his off stans. I'm not his mother, and there just aren't that many people he relates to."

"I understand," I said. "The question is more about how I can keep from getting into a position where Burnside can reprimand me?"

"Leave the ship," she said. "If he wants to find an excuse, trust me, he will."

"It's rather a long walk back to Diurnia."

The left side of her mouth curled up in a lopsided grin. "You may find that preferable, if they've decided to target you."

"Suggestions? Anything?"

She crossed her arms in front of her and leaned on her desk, eyes focused inward and face tilted down in consideration.

"The problem is evidence. You need to be with somebody who can corroborate what you're saying or you need a record of it somehow."

"Recording didn't help what's her name," I said.

"Alice Stewart?" Mel asked. "Yeah, but she was trying to use it to convince the authorities, for all the good that did her. You need to record it to show you have evidence against the bully boys.

Not that it'll ever see the light of a courtroom, but you might be able to convince David not to beat you up himself."

My hand went to my stomach almost reflexively. I still remembered my last blatantly hostile interlude with the first mate.

I saw in her eyes that Mel caught the movement, but she didn't say anything.

"So, any suggestions?" I asked.

"You're the systems guy. If I wanted to set up any kind of surveillance on the ship, you'd be the one I'd ask for help."

There haven't been many times in my life when somebody hit me with the "obvious stick" so hard it left me sitting there staring blankly.

"Ishmael?" she said.

I shook my head. "I'm okay. I was just thinking about how I might do it."

"You'll want remote recording or at least storage."

She nodded at my tablet.

"You can use that to record sounds, but you'll want to offload the audio to something less obvious as soon as possible."

She was way ahead of me in the problem solving curve. I struggled to keep up.

"If they're close enough to hurt you, they're close enough to break your tablet," she said. "Poof." She sketched an explosion in the air with her fingers. "No more evidence."

"Oh," I said as the stick whacked me once more in the head.

My brain finally started ticking under its own power then. I began to trace various possibilities in my mind.

"Hey! Ishmael!" Mel spoke sharply and regained my attention. "If you're gonna do that, go do it in your own place. I know how you system's people work," she said it sternly, but she had a smile on her face. "Next thing you know I'll need a sweeper to get the bits out of my office. They'll be piled up in the corners for weeks."

"Thanks, Mel. I appreciate the insight. If they find my body somewhere, you'll know who did it," I joked as I rose and headed for the door.

"If they do it, we won't find the body," she said.

I looked back at her but she wasn't smiling. She wasn't even holding a smile back. She just looked at me and then looked up at the overhead—that thin metal shield between us and the Deep Dark.

"Yeah. Well, there is that." I sighed and headed out the door. "Thanks again," I said over my shoulder as I stepped into the passage and ran into a spacer walking by outside.

"Oh, sorry!" I said and I recognized him as that other engineman I'd seen outside the cabin. I looked at his name badge. "Mr. Simon, I should pay more attention to where I'm walking. Sorry about that."

"No problem, sar," he said with a smile.

He nodded through the open door at Mel and kept going. A pleasant enough guy, but I wondered why he spent so much time in officer country.

I stood there for a moment, until he'd cleared the ladder heading down into the Engineering section, before turning back to Mel who watched me with a curious look on her face.

"One of your problems?" I asked, nodding in the direction he'd gone.

She frowned in curiosity at that. "No, Ed Simon is as nice a guy as you could ask for. Why?"

"I've seen him over in officer country coming out of the cabin. More than once. I thought he was up for an infraction."

She looked thoughtful but shook her head. "He's never gotten even a reprimand as far as I know."

I shrugged. "Dunno. The only people I've seen over there on a regular basis are him and Bayless."

"Bayless?" Mel asked sharply. "You're sure it was Bayless? For that matter, are you sure it was Simon?"

"Well, there aren't that many people aboard. Unless it was somebody wearing Bayless's suit, it was him. This is the first time I've seen Simon's nametag, but yeah I'm pretty sure it was him."

Her face clouded. "Coming out of the cabin?"

"Well, not always. Sometimes just in the passageway in officer country. It struck me as odd because they're both in engineering. Not like deck crew on the way to the bridge or something."

"Thanks for letting me know, Ishmael," she said.

She looked angry but not at me.

"Is there a problem?" I asked.

"I'm afraid so, but I don't know what and I'm gonna pull rank on you and tell you to shut up about it."

"I have no idea what you're talking about, Ms. Menas."

"Thank you, Mr. Wang," she said with more gratitude than I felt was warranted. "See you at dinner."

I considered that all the way back to my stateroom. She was more grateful than she should be, which could only mean it was a bigger deal than I thought it was.

Terrific.

CHAPTER THIRTY
DIURNIA SYSTEM: 2358-AUGUST-10

Dinner was another of those painful episodes with David Burnside being obnoxious, Mel not responding to him, and Fredi hunched over her plate. Burnside's contribution to the dinner conversation consisted largely of chewing with his mouth open, belching loudly, and calling for Davies to bring more coffee. I wondered what David would have been like had the captain been at the table. In the end I figured it probably wouldn't have mattered.

I expected him to comment about Apones and Mosler, but either the boys hadn't reported anything, or he was waiting for a time without witnesses. I smiled inwardly thinking that he'd have a much more difficult time backing me into a bridge wing than he might expect.

Fool me once, shame on you. Fool me twice...

Burnside burped once more and slid his dish back from the edge of the table, plowing silver and salvers alike, he stood and without looking at anybody headed for the door.

"Later, ladies," he said. "Long watch. I need some sleep."

And he was gone.

Mel sighed. "He's such a charmer. I can't understand why he's not married."

She shook her head in wonderment.

Fredi snickered into her plate, but with Burnside gone, began to resume a more normal posture, as if his leaving took a weight off her back.

"Any ideas yet, Ishmael?" Mel asked.

I was in the middle of a sip of coffee, and I finished it before speaking.

"Yes indeed, but I want to check out some things on watch

tonight from the big console on the bridge."

She smiled. "That didn't take long."

"All I needed was a little incentive and a kick in the butt, I guess."

Fredi looked back and forth, and I could tell she was dying to know what we were talking about, but before she could ask, Penny Davies came in to start cleaning up the wardroom.

"You sars just sit there and enjoy your coffee if you want. I'll just get some of these bigger pieces out of the way for you," she said.

"You go right ahead, Ms. Davies," Mel said. "We're done here and there's no good reason for us to slow you down."

Mel drained her cup, stood, picked up a load of dirty dishes and placed them in the tray while Fredi and I followed suit. I let the senior officers precede me out the door and then started to follow suit.

I heard a tablet bip and looked down to see if it was mine, but then I realized the sound had come from behind me. When I looked over my shoulder, I saw Ms. Davies reading a message on hers and frowning.

"Something wrong, Ms. Davies?" I asked.

She looked up quickly as if surprised that I was still there. "Oh! No, sar, just a little extra duty."

I didn't like the way she said "extra duty" but I didn't press it. I just closed the door, leaving her frowning into her tablet.

When I got back to my stateroom, I stripped down to boxers and tee before crawling into bed. At the last tick I remembered to set my tablet to wake me at 2300. I had the mid-watch, but I knew I needed sleep before I tackled the job of figuring out how to spy on myself.

The midnight watch change with Arletta went smoothly. While Juliett relieved Betts, Arletta took me aside.

"What did Mel say?" she asked.

"She gave me some good advice, I need to make sure I'm never alone or that I collect some evidence."

"How are you going to do that?"

"I hope to have an answer to that before Burnside relieves me in the morning."

Betts stepped back and Juliett stepped up to the console.

"I have the watch, Ms. Novea. Logged on 2358-August-10, at 2345 per standing order," I said.

"Good luck," she said.

When they'd left the bridge Juliett asked, "So, what was it I wasn't supposed to hear, sar? Mr. Burnside punch you again? Or was it about you facing down Apones and Mosler in the gym?"

She had a very straight face, but a twinkle in her eye.

"Why, Ms. Jaxton, I can hardly believe you'd stoop to such gossip mongering!"

"Why, sar? Is that Ms. D'Heng's job?" she asked in return.

The apprentice in question came up the ladder bearing the customary three cups of coffee, "Is what my job, Juliett? What are you sticking me with this time?"

"Gossip mongering," Juliett replied.

"Oh, yes. Actually I monger with the best," she said with a little giggle and distributed the coffee. "Was there any gossip in particular you need? Or something you require spread around, Juliett?"

"Apparently Mr. Wang thought I was trying to take your job by commenting on the altercation in the gym yesterday."

After long exposure to this pair's repartee I was used to it. I wondered how much they knew, and how accurate the ship's rumor net was.

"Which altercation were you commenting on?" Charlotte asked. "The one between Mr. Wang and the Bumble Brothers? Or the lovers' spat between Bayless and Simon?"

Juliett grinned. "Well I was actually talking about the Bumble Brothers, but is there anything new on the triangle?"

"Nope. Nobody seems to know who the new boy is. They're keeping it pretty hush-hush. But Bayless and Simon were spitting and clawing in the gym. There's trouble in paradise, I think."

Charlotte looked over her shoulder at me and Juliett followed her glance.

"What, sar?" Charlotte asked. "You look startled."

Juliett added, "Yes, was there some other gossip you were interested in?"

"What happened with Mr. Apones and Mr. Mosler after they left the gym?" I asked.

"Mosler convinced Apones that he shouldn't say anything to Mr. Burnside so they went down to engineering berthing and harassed Ballantine until she kicked Mosler in the jewels and threw him off her bunk." Belatedly she added, "Sar."

"How do you know this?" I asked.

"Mr. Wang, there are twenty eight people on this ship. At any given point in time, a third of them are trying to sleep, a third of them are working, and the other third is just trying to amuse themselves until we get to port. How in the world can you expect to hide anything?"

"But who told you? How do you know?" I asked.

I was familiar with rumor nets, but Charlotte D'Heng was obviously rated spec one in rumors.

"I would have expected with only twenty-eight on board, it would be easier to slip into corners and hide."

"Well, obviously some stuff gets away, sar. But the big things sorta fall out pretty easily. Somebody sees something and tells somebody else, who adds it to what they know and passes it on. At the end of the day, we have a good idea of what happened. The details might be a bit sketchy but we know, for example, that Apones and Mosler attacked you in the gym—or tried to. You did something to stop it and they got out when VanDalon and Cottonwood came in."

I sat back in my chair, trying to get a grip on what had just happened. I couldn't count on this level of surveillance, but my preconceived notions about how much anybody in the crew was aware of were being challenged.

"What makes you think they attacked me? Or tried to?" I asked after a couple of heartbeats.

Charlotte gave me a look that was straight out of Pul-Lease 101.

"Sar? We're pretty sure you wouldn't have attacked them," she said slowly and succinctly. "Ispo Factoid, they must have attacked you."

"Ipso facto," I corrected automatically, while thinking.

"You sure, sar?" she asked.

"Yeah. Ipso facto. That's right, but I think you actually meant prima facie, but never mind the Latin."

I took a deep breath and started over. "What makes you think anybody was attacked?"

Juliett and Charlotte shared a look containing the despair that all crew feel when faced with the absolute denseness of officers.

D'Heng turned back to me and said, with no small degree of derision, "Sar? It was Apones and Mosler. The three of you were in the gym... alone... without any witnesses. Are we supposed to believe that you played parchesi?"

This little spitfire was so unexpected, she just tickled me to no end.

"Do you know what parchesi is, Ms. D'Heng?" I asked.

"Well, sure!" She was quite positive about it.

"What is it then?" I asked.

"Well, it's a kind of a game that you play on a board... with dice... " her voice petered off a bit and then she finally added, "Okay, so no I don't."

"You're pretty close. Only thing you're missing is that it's a long, boring game where you try to move little pieces around the edges of the board and then be the first one to get all your pieces all the way around and into the middle. A very tedious, frustrating game."

"So, it's a lot like being a spacer, sar?" Juliett said with her tongue so far into her cheek it was in danger of becoming disjointed.

"Quite, Ms. Jaxton, quite. They assigned it to us at the academy to teach patience, but back to Mr. Apones and Mr. Mosler. Why do you call them the Bumble Brothers?" I asked Charlotte.

"Because when they're together, they're so busy trying to impress each other, they bumble around and bump into walls. There's a certain faction of the crew that thinks that when they get together, the sum of their IQs is actually less than each taken separately."

"They seemed to be doing a good job of harassing Ulla Nart—" I began.

"Yes, they're not exactly friendly puppies, sar," Juliett said.

D'Heng said, "They're stupid animals. Even stupid animals are dangerous. They raped that one girl—Stewart—and they did a number on your predecessor, Ms. Jaffee. We call them the Bumble Brothers, but we don't take them lightly."

"Anything else I should know about them?" I asked.

The two women traded glances again. Juliett nodded slightly and Charlotte turned back to me.

"Sometimes they do things for Mr. Burnside," she said.

"What kinds of things?" I asked.

"He calls them his enforcers, and when they get into that enforcer thing, they leave the Bumble Brothers behind and become laser focused, sar."

Juliett added, "They stop thinking for themselves and just follow the first mate's instructions. That's when they get really dangerous."

I thought about what they'd said for a good two ticks, letting it filter through.

"Thank you, both," I said. "Let's get this place cleared away. You two have studying, and I've got some tinkering to do."

In less than half a stan we'd finished the midwatch clean up and swab down, and the two women pulled out tablets and began studying. I sat down at the systems console and pulled up an overlay of the ship's intercom and loudspeaker system.

One of the things that got my attention when talking with Mel was that I couldn't be sure that my tablet wouldn't be broken in any scuffle. Therefore, using the tablet was too risky. I needed some other way to record. The tablet had a microphone, but if the device got broken before the incriminating activities happened, then I'd be out of luck.

The tablet was also tied to ShipNet and could triangulate its position within the ship. Every place in the ship had an intercom for safety purposes. If I could get the tablet to track me as I moved around and trigger the intercom's microphone. That might allow me to capture the audio into a file on a system drive, that way I'd have a full-time watch dog listening around me where ever I was.

I dug into the intercom controls and started looking for a way to remotely control a particular microphone. I flipped through several sub programs looking for the specific coding structures and data identification fields for the bridge microphone. I thought that if I could figure out how the bridge microphone worked, and if I could figure out how to control it, I could just copy that to any other intercom on the ship. As I zeroed in on the bridge controls, I spotted exactly where I would need to modify the control code to use it as a bug.

The modification had already been made.

Once I knew what I was looking for, locating the network of inter-com connections became easy. There were the typical redundancies built into any ship's system, but over and above that, it was a clean machine. The industrial strength code looked like production grade. There were signatures and sign-offs noted in the appropriate places on the system maintenance logs.

People call the device I looked at a microphone, but techni-cally it was a digital audio transducer. It grabbed the sound waves from the air using a standard mechanical diaphragm, but instead of turning those vibrations into variations in electrical energy like a classic microphone, it used a small sensor in the intercom unit to measure and encode those variations digitally. The system then routed the signals to several data hubs around the ship. Those hubs existed in key places like nerve ganglia around the body. Each had a redundant connection path and could be reached in at least two ways. Even the main data paths between the fore and aft nacelles had a parallel redundancy built into the keel of the cargo container. When the can locked in, it closed the loop on a secondary path, which permitted data to flow from bow to stern even if the main data backbone was cut.

Each intercom had a button for the bridge and a button for en-gineering central. In case of emergency, which was all the devices were intended for, pressing the button would cause a buzzer on the bridge or engineering to go off. The bridge unit and the engineer-ing units were more complicated and had the ability to buzz any intercom on the ship using a number pad. The main issue was that you needed to know the number. Tablets provided much faster and more reliable communications from individual to individual, but the

CPJCT safety regulations required these intercom systems, and so they were on every ship.

I turned my head from the console and looked at the bridge intercom on the aft bulkhead. I wondered if anybody else was listening. Turning back to the system's display, I began teasing out the codes that linked the speakers with the system. These were supposed to be very simple systems and reliable even during significant shipboard failures. Press to talk, release to listen, digital routing independent of other data sensor streams. I'd actually been in a situation where they had failed but only once. Of course, on that occasion practically everything else had failed as well and we almost died, but almost doesn't count.

Just before the change of watch, I found what I had been looking for. The sound system spooled into a data array. Any or all of the intercoms could be triggered to record. When turned on, they'd record into a time stamped storage device which would identify the location of the audio transducer and the time the recording was made.

Somebody had already wired the entire ship for sound.

There was a lot I didn't know, and I didn't know who to ask. From the records in the system, the function had been installed when the ship had been built, or at least during one of the authorized maintenance periods. The file names, dates, and provenance traces were all correct. They certainly were a lot better looking than what I was planning to do, and appeared to be a planned function in the ship's infrastructure.

I wondered if it was just the *Billy* or whether every ship had built-in bugs and only the captain knew about them or something.

The chrono display on the bottom of my terminal clicked over to 0530 and I realized I'd been sitting there focused on the systems display for almost five solid stans. I noticed Juliett and Charlotte behind me, and they were being much quieter than normal. I cleared the display, kicked my daily backups, and then stood up as nonchalantly as I could.

"Anything wrong, sar?" Juliett asked.

Charlotte sat at the spare console looking at her tablet, but apparently not actually reading anything. They both held themselves very still.

"Not that I know of, Ms. D'Heng. Why do you ask?"

"Oh, I don't know, sar," she said with a drawl that meant I was about to get zinged. "You've been sitting at that console without looking up since about double-naught thirty. When Charlotte brought up fresh cups of coffee after her rounds at 0300, she handed one to you, and your reply was—and I quote—'Thanks, hon.' You then put the coffee on the desk and haven't touched it since. I suspect it's quite cold now." She paused deliberately before adding, "Sar."

While Juliett rattled off her little speech, Charlotte looked up as if to see what I would say.

"I must have been really distracted. My apologies, Ms. D'Heng, I meant no disrespect."

"Disrespect, sar?" she seemed confused.

"For calling you 'hon,'" I said.

"Oh, not to worry, sar. It's much better than what I get called by some others," she said with a grin. "You *were* distracted."

They both just sat at their stations, staring at me.

"What is it?" I asked.

"That's all, sar?" Juliett asked. "Just 'I mean no disrespect'? Nothing is wrong with the ship? You're okay, aren't you?"

"As nearly as I can tell, the ship is fine," I said. "I am too. I'm not sure what I'm supposed to say."

The two of them shared that long-suffering look that I was getting used to seeing between them.

Juliett said, "Well, pardon my saying so, sar, but in the thirty odd standard days we've been underway and we've been standing watch, I've never seen you not finish a cup of coffee. You've also never zoned out so completely that you would have failed to notice Ms. D'Heng strip out of her ship suit, turn it wrong side out, and put it back on."

Startled, I looked back at Charlotte's suit. "Her suit isn't wrong side out," I said, confused.

Juliett grinned. "No, but you had to look to make sure, didn't you, sar?"

"Ms. Jaxton, I think he's busted."

"I think so too, Ms. D'Heng."

I couldn't help it. I snorted in laughter.

"Okay, you got me. I was playing in the ship's systems and got sucked in. Nothing's wrong with the ship. It's for a little project I'm working on for Mel—er—Ms. Menas."

They shared that look again, but Mallory clomped up over the ladder followed closely by Mr. Burnside and they didn't pursue it. We got the watch changed over without casualty. Burnside made no reference to the incident with the Bumble Brothers and I certainly wasn't going to bring it up. In typical Burnside fashion he flopped into the console chair, looking like he'd had about three stans sleep and smelling of sex.

"Ship is on course and on target," I told him, standing well back in case he was just trying to lure me into reach. "No incidents or actions. Standing orders are unchanged. You may relieve the watch, Mr. Burnside."

"Yeah, great. See you in six stans," he mumbled through a yawn.

Charlotte had scooted as soon as Mallory and Burnside came onto the bridge, taking our coffee cups with her. When Juliett had been relieved, I headed down the ladder with her at my heels. At the foot of the ladder I headed to my stateroom for a quick face wash before breakfast and Juliett headed down to the mess deck. Crew's mess would start serving soon.

As we split to go our separate ways, she said, "Keep practicing, sar."

I nodded and went to my stateroom. It was barely 0600 and I felt sticky and sweaty. Spending the whole watch with my head in the console like that probably dehydrated me, and I felt simultaneously wrung out and wired up. I tapped on the door to the head.

"Occupied," Arletta said.

"Okay, no rush."

I sat down, trying to determine how to tell her what I'd found.

I couldn't talk freely until I could figure out who, if anybody, was listening. I couldn't send her a message via tablets unless we could encrypt it. I might be able to write on my tablet, and as long as I didn't save it, or send it, I'd be safe. Of course, that had always been true. Only an idiot thought that their tablet messages were secure from the company. I guess I felt a bit like a fool for thinking that the ship wasn't wired for sound as well. I wondered if it were recording video as I heard the shower start. That disturbed me until I realized that it took a huge amount of storage and I had a very accurate picture of how much memory was aboard and how much of it was used by the ship's operations. I made a mental note to look into that when I went back on watch. The problem was that it might not be recorded in the ship's schematics and the required storage might not be in the ship's data array.

The shower cut off and after a couple of ticks, I heard a soft tap on the door to the head. I released the handle and smiled at Arletta.

"Good morning," she said. "How was watch?"

"Hey," I greeted her. "It was a midwatch. What can I say? How about you?"

I held up my tablet, slipped the stylus out of its slot, and wrote a sentence: *No problems with Burnside... but discovered the ship is bugged.* I held up the tablet so she could read it.

Her eyes widened in surprise and she pointed to the deck and mouthed the word, "Here?" without making any noise.

I nodded broadly.

"He left a little mess for me to clean up," she said, "but I think he had a hot date because he was out of there like a shot."

I erased the tablet and wrote: *Next watch will know more.*

"Woulda been nice if he's showered before he came up," I said.

"Yeah, well, I'm starved. You wanna shower before we head over to eat?"

"I was going to, but I'm hungry."

She backed out of the doorway and I walked into the head. There wasn't much to say but I ran the water in the sink and washed my face off. It felt good, like peeling a layer of grime from my skin. The coolness of it refreshed me and my eyes stopped burning, mostly.

It struck me then. The intercoms were in the staterooms. I scanned the bulkheads in the head and realized that there was no place to put one in there.

"Ya know, I think I'll take a shower after all," I said, but motioned her to step in with me.

I pulled the door to my stateroom closed and turned on the water.

Arletta looked at me curiously, but pulled the door to her room closed too, and we stood practically nose to nose in the small room with the shower running. Being that close to her was a bit distracting, but it gave me a chance to whisper in her ear.

"Any intercom in the ship can be triggered from some system utility that I haven't found yet. The audio gets recorded. I don't know if anybody is listening, or if I'm just being paranoid, but it's there."

She leaned and whispered back, "You got any idea what to do about it?"

"Yes, but I need to get some sleep and get back onto the bridge for the afternoon watch to do it."

"This is the strangest thing yet," she whispered.

"It may be nothing. The installation looks like it's original to the ship. It's possible that nobody knows it's there."

"Okay," she said and shocked me by giving me a quick hug, "thanks for letting me know."

I nodded and she slipped out of the head and into her room, closing the door carefully behind her.

Once she was gone I waited a couple of ticks, shut off the water, and then went out into my own stateroom. After a few more ticks, I stepped out into the passageway, stopping at Arletta's door. "Come on, slow poke. I'm starving."

She chuckled as she came out of her stateroom, and we headed for breakfast.

Chapter Thirty-two
Diurnia System: 2358-August-11

Breakfast was a bit strained. I was conscious of the transducer on the bulkhead and wary of the potential listeners. Mostly it was quiet anyway. Mel seemed distracted by something. I think Arletta was having the same kind of paranoid reaction to the bugging as I was. Fredi was the only one who seemed to be having a normal morning, and Fredi was never a morning person. Even Penny Davies seemed a little worse for wear. Poor kid looked like she hadn't slept in a week. She gave me a worn smile and made sure my coffee cup was full.

About halfway through breakfast, I found myself caught by the yawns. I finished my eggs and excused myself.

"I think I should lie down now. Longer midwatch than I thought."

They all smiled sympathetically, and I half stumbled back to my stateroom. I passed Ed Simon on my way into officer country and nodded a good morning as we passed.

When I got into my stateroom, I stripped down to boxers and tee and fell onto my bunk. I didn't bother to get in. I just pulled the coverlet around me and rolled into it like a rug. The last thing I remember thinking was that I must have burned a lot of energy studying the ship.

When I relieved Burnside at 1145 it looked like he'd barely moved. He hadn't even bothered to leave me a mess to clean up. I wondered if he'd slept through the whole watch. Mallory was, as ever, blandly non-communicative, but Juliett relieved him smartly enough.

"You may relieve the watch. Nothing happened," Burnside said. "It never does."

He stood from the console and stumbled off the bridge almost before I had a chance to say, "I have the watch."

Mallory followed him down the ladder.

Juliett looked at me with a little shrug and said, "You look livelier than the last time I saw you, sar. Feeling a little better?"

"Yes, thank you, Ms. Jaxton." I managed a small smile. "I got a nap and a shower in. I'm feeling almost human again."

I checked the logs and standing orders and discovered that we needed to do a minor course correction to line up with the jump point for the next day. She and I laid in and locked down the change before Ms. Cramer brought my lunch. I made myself take slow and deliberate bites to mask my absolute screaming need to get into that audio system again and find out who, if anybody, was listening.

Charlotte came to relieve Juliett for lunch and she started the sweep down while I finished eating. I helped clean up so the bridge was shipshape by the time Juliett made it back from the mess deck.

The two of them settled down to watch and study, and I fired up the systems console. My first concern was who had been listening, and how would I know if they were. I wasted a full stan looking for the utilities that would enable the listening capabilities, and I never found anything. I made a point to stand up, walk around the bridge, and drink some coffee.

When Charlotte went on her afternoon rounds, Juliett looked at me as if to say, "You're not fooling me."

I grinned at her and sat back down.

When you're dealing with complex systems—especially large complex systems—forget the forest and trees thing. Sometimes you get lost in the weeds. That's where I was. I'd been so derailed by finding the software tap already in place that I forgot that I'd gone there to put my own in. I'd traced it through to the recording logs and apparently that was when my brain took a holiday.

The logs kept track of date, time, and transducer number along with the audio. I'd seen that. Even wondered how I could use that information. I wanted to bang my head on the screen, but I was relatively sure that Ms. Jaxton might notice that kind of behavior. I was so hung up on the who, that I'd completely lost track of the what.

I sighed at my own stupidity and opened the log to see when the last entry had been made.

When I saw it, I just sat back in my chair. I didn't know whether I could even believe what I saw. It was dated 2358-July-06 at 1453, and lasted only two seconds. I looked back a bit farther and realized that the record had come from docking at Diurnia Orbital. There

were three records on that date. Taken in correct sequence I saw
from the time stamps that these were routine checks. Bridge called
engineering central, central replied, and the bridge acknowledged. I
didn't even need to listen to them, but I plugged in a head set just
to confirm. While I listened to what they contained, I extended the
log window and found that all the logs had routine maintenance
tests.

I set up a query to look for other instances of the log elsewhere
on the system. If somebody were clandestinely monitoring the ship,
there was a good possibility that they wouldn't store that data in
the main storage. While that was running, I wrote a little routine
that would periodically poll every intercom in the ship to see if it
was listening. It might not tell me why, or who, but it would at least
tell me if and when. I set my routine running in the background of
the main systems array and routed the output to my tablet. I tested
it by crossing to the bulkhead and pressing the "talk" button on
the intercom. My tablet popped open a window with the message
indicating that the bridge transducer was active. I let go of the
button and the message went off.

I knew Juliett and Charlotte were watching me so I crossed to
the watch stander's console and checked the logs. I was careful not
to look at either of them. In theory my tablet would tell me when
somebody monitored any of the intercoms. I had established the
first beach head.

The next order of business was to find out if anybody else was
monitoring the ship. Frankly, I suspected Mr. Burnside, but anybody with access to the interface could be doing it.

And I still hadn't found the interface program.

My systems console gave a soft bip and a window popped open.
I crossed over to read: File not Found. I stood there staring at it.
I tried to imagine how anybody could be using the system without
routing through the logs. I finally came to the conclusion that it
was possible that somebody might route the intercom's transducer
directly to a tablet without passing the data through the logs. It
would require a lot of specialized knowledge about the data stream
in order to strip out the time track. In theory an instance of the
audio log files could be on a tablet. If that were the case, I might
never find it. There were just too many variables.

I flopped back into the systems console chair and started bringing up all the information I could find about the intercom system
and interface. I tracked back through all the console code and into
the archives. I almost laughed out loud when I went all the way
back to the installation record, and there, in an associated file, was
a promotional broadsheet describing the features of this particular

model. There, bulleted out for the world to see, was, "Security mode allows for remote triggering and logging of incoming audio during emergency response and damage control operations."

"So, you finally found what you were looking for, sar?" Juliett asked.

I turned to look at her, but she was carefully studying her helm display. Out of the corner of my eye, I saw Charlotte industriously reading her tablet.

"Yes, Ms. Jaxton. Thank you. I have," I said.

I felt a combination of relief and embarrassment wash over me as I realized that I was jumping at shadows. The oh so sinister tap on the audio transducers was a public feature of the equipment.

Now all I needed to find was how to use it.

On a hunch, I went to the installation record and found the software control program that had been installed at the same time as the hardware. The control shell name was listed there and I checked the file logs to check for the last execution of the code. It didn't surprise me to find a date that corresponded to the equipment installations. Nobody had run that software in twenty-five stanyers. I wondered if anybody else even knew it was aboard.

I stood up from my console and walked to the front of the bridge, staring out at the Deep Dark to gather my wits. The records solved the mystery of the pre-installed taps, but I was left with my original problem. How could I gather evidence to protect myself if Apones and Mosler got out of hand again? If? When was more like it. Having another run-in with those two was inevitable.

A quick glance at the chrono showed that I had about a stan left to find a solution. In my mind I ticked off the possibilities. One, the brute force approach: turn 'em all on and record everything. Two, the subtle approach: get my tablet to ping its location all the time and record what happens around me. Three, short term approach: use my tablet to manually turn on the closest transducer.

The first was fast. I could do it instantly, but the data storage requirements would be large. The second was subtle and right on target, but it would take a while to get the code together. A few watches at least. The third would work if I grabbed the control shell and ported it to my tablet. Then I could run it from where ever I needed to. It wouldn't be perfect but it would buy me time.

And my tripwire program would tell me if anybody else was using the transducers besides me in the mean time so I'd know what was going on.

By the time Burnside reported for duty, I had my plan under control, and I'd earned the concerned stares of my watch section.

The bridge seemed crowded after weeks of having just the duty watch section up there. The captain emerged from the cabin and joined us on the bridge just moments before the countdown clicked into the imminent area. Per standing order, the jump team convened on the bridge at jump minus fifteen.

"Set jump stations, Mr. Burnside," the captain said.

"Jump stations, aye, Captain," Mr. Burnside answered. "Make the announcement, Mr. Mallory."

Still, it was routine. Mostly.

Mallory finished making the announcement, and I moved from the deck watch to the systems console. Burnside took the deck watch for the transition and Arletta already had the astrogation console running. She'd been monitoring our position for half a stan.

The sail and grav keel generators had already been shut down and the *Billy* was coasting along on a pure ballistic trajectory toward a precise spot in space.

Mr. Burnside started the jump checklist. "Engineering?"

Mel was at the engineering console and said, "Sail and keel secured. Burleson drive is charged and ready to engage."

"Astrogation?"

Arletta answered, "Course plot locked. Ship is dead on plot. Jump is locked for transition."

I didn't have anything to add to this checklist. For transitions, the systems console was only manned in case of an emergency.

Mr. Burnside reported, "Ship is ready for transition, Captain."

"Jump when ready, Mr. Burnside," the captain gave the authorization.

"Jump when ready, aye, Captain," he replied formally. "Authorization for jump has been given. Remove safety interlocks. Prepare to jump on astrogator's mark."

Mel said, "Safety locks are disengaged. Burleson drive is released to fire. Astrogation has authority and control."

"Astrogation has authority and control," Arletta said. "Stand by for my mark in four ticks."

Out of the corner of my eye I saw the ship plot on her screen and the counter ticking down.

"Stand by for mark—transition in ten... mark," she said.

Mallory started the countdown announcement and I think I held my breath. Transitions always seemed a little magical to me. I understood that the Burlesons created a worm hole by bending space/time in such a way that two areas of space separated by a very large distance became contiguous. It was like drawing a small circle on the top and bottom of a piece of paper and bending the paper so those two circles were flat against each other. That was our worm hole and we just moved from one side of the paper to the other by dropping through that hole.

Mallory finished his countdown just as the Burlesons discharged and folded the universe. I saw the discharge represented on my console but felt nothing at all from the energy crackling through the systems and into space around us. The view out the forward port simply changed from being a panoramic view of the Deep Dark to being a slightly different panoramic view of the Deep Dark with one bright star practically dead ahead.

"Jump completed," Arletta announced, "position is within parameters. Transition logged at 2358-August-12 time 1014"

"Thank you, Ms. Novea," Mr. Burnside said. "Plot and lock for Breakall Orbital."

"Plot and lock, aye, sar," she repeated.

"Engineering, secure Burlesons. Put up the sails, if you please."

"Burlesons are secure. Grav keel and sail generators spooling up," she acknowledged.

"Course plot to Breakall is locked," Arletta announced.

"Helm, come to new heading," Mr. Burnside ordered.

"Aye, aye, sar. Helm locked to new course, sar," Ms. Jaxton confirmed.

"Transition complete. Drives are secured and the ship is under sail, Captain."

"Thank you, Mr. Burnside. Secure from jump stations. Resume normal watch."

"Secure from jump stations, aye, Captain," Mr. Burnside replied. "Resuming normal watch. Make the announcement, Mr. Mallory."

I secured the systems console and went back to the deck watch. The captain had already disappeared down the ladder, and in a matter of three ticks, Juliett and I were alone on the bridge again. The chrono showed 1043.

"Well, Ms. Jaxton," I said. "What'll we do for a stan until Ms. Novea gets back?"

"Parchesi, sar?" she asked, staring straight ahead.

"I don't think we have time. It's a long game."

Charlotte came up from the mess deck with coffee, and we settled in for the last stan of the watch. I made sure my logs were up to date.

At 1140 when Arletta came up to relieve me she leaned over my shoulder and asked, "You ever hear of Groundhog Day?"

I looked at her curiously. "Yeah. Old Earth tradition. Something about an animal predicting spring?"

"I can't remember where I ran across it, but this big rodent would allegedly come up from his hibernation, and if his shadow scared him, he'd duck down into his hole. That was supposed to mean something like another month and a half of winter or something."

There must have been a quizzical expression on my face.

She flicked her eyes at the captain's chair, and it was all I could do not to snort out loud.

"Captain Groundhog?" I asked.

She grinned a lopsided smile. "Well, we don't have quite a month and a half left, but..." she left the rest unsaid and I had to chuckle softly.

"I haven't had a chance to tell you but I got a break on the intercom thing. I'll know if there's somebody listening, but the logs all show that the intercoms haven't been used since they were installed."

She blinked and I saw her mind ticking over behind her eyes. "That seems very strange."

I shrugged. "Yeah, but the only records in the log are from the installation when the ship was built and some routine mechanical tests."

"Could somebody erase the logs?"

"Anything's possible, but they'd have to be really good to do it without leaving a trace."

She looked at me then with an expectant expression.

"What?"

"You wanna stand my watch, too? Or would you prefer that I relieve you?" she asked with a grin.

I chuckled as I said, "Ship is on course and on target. Transition successfully accomplished. Standing orders are unchanged. You may relieve the watch, Ms. Novea."

"I have the watch, Mr. Wang. Logged on 2358-August-12, at 1145 per standing order. See ya in a few stans."

I headed down the ladder just as my tablet bipped. I almost slipped on the step when I saw it was from the captain.

My cabin at your earliest convenience.

I confess that I was more than a bit frightened by that short message. The timing and wording were the equivalent of "You better be in the cabin before you do anything else." Thinking over the last few days, I was a bit concerned that maybe I would be getting out to walk the rest of the way to Breakall.

I took a tick to use my tablet controls to trigger the intercom in the cabin and then took the few steps down the passage to knock on his door.

One word, "Enter," came from the other side.

I opened the door, stepped in, closed the door behind me, and braced to attention.

"Third Mate Ishmael Wang reporting as ordered, Captain."

Yes, it was a bit of overkill. But no junior officer ever got cashiered for showing too much respect to a captain. It went with the turf. With the audio pick up live on the wall above his desk, I was going to make as good an impression as I could, in case it ever needed to be listened to. Something told me I'd need it because Mr. Burnside was there as well.

"Mr. Wang, I told you when we first met, I don't like smart asses, troublemakers, or surprises. I like my universe orderly and predictable. You, Mr. Wang, are disrupting my orderly and predictable universe," he said without preamble.

Somehow he still didn't seem to understand that my name rhymed with gong, not gang. I didn't plan to correct him.

He didn't ask me a question, and I was at attention. The fact that I had no idea which particular thing he might have perceived as disruptive just encouraged me not to admit to anything he didn't know about.

He and Burnside glared at me for a long tick.

"You have nothing to say in response, Mr. Wang?" the captain asked.

"I'm sorry, Captain, but I do not know how to respond. If the captain could enlighten me on the actions which he finds distressing, I'd be happy to modify my behavior to be more in keeping with the captain's wishes."

"Are you being a wise ass, Wang?" he asked.

"Not intentionally, Captain. I don't know what incident, activity, or behavior the Captain finds problematic."

"Well, shall we start with interfering with a watch stander on duty?" he said.

Burnside smirked.

"I'm sorry, Captain, but I don't know of any instance where I interfered with a watch stander's duty. Could you be more specific?"

"Mr. Burnside tells me that he had to reprimand you for interfering with Mr. Apones while he was on duty," the captain said.

"Oh yes, Captain. He did reprimand me."

"And do you have anything to say about that?" he asked.

"Why, yes, Captain. I was not aware that sexual assault was considered part of a messenger-of-the-watch's duty. It's not listed in any of the standing orders and I've received no instructions that require or authorize watch standers to abuse other members of the off duty crew," I said with a straight face. "Since Mr. Burnside's reprimand was the first, and last, I've heard of it, I assumed that all other physical and sexual assaults that Mr. Apones may have engaged in have gone without incident."

Burnside's face turned an exquisite shade of red.

The captain stared at me for a long, cold tick.

"Do you presume to make fun of me, Mr. Wang?" he asked finally.

"No, Captain, it is not my intention. The only reprimand I received from Mr. Burnside was for preventing Mr. Apones and Mr. Mosler from sexually assaulting a junior member of the crew who was trying to work out in the gym. The situation has not come up again. I haven't had any call to interact with Mr. Apones while he was on duty." I hoped that little fib would fly. "At least, I'm not aware of any additional infractions that Mr. Burnside may have noted but has not yet shared with me."

A blatant hedge, but maybe I could get away with it. Cold sweat ran down the back of my legs. I was afraid of what Burnside was going to do, but he wasn't saying anything.

The captain stared at me, and I was suddenly unsure whether he was angry or merely pausing for effect. I could almost see him counting to ten before speaking, as if somebody had given him a formula for dressing down a junior officer. Over the stanyers, I'd had my share of hide stripped—often for good and sometimes sundry reasons. As I stood there, I began to think Captain Rossett was following a memorized script.

"Very well, Mr. Wang," he slapped his desk with an open hand. "How do you respond to the charges that you're inciting the crew to flout authority?"

"By asking who's making such charges and on what evidence, Captain," I answered.

I didn't know which possibility was scarier at that point—that the captain was a vicious psychopath with delusions of grandeur and a side order of megalomania or that he was an incompetent actor following a poorly written script in a play that somebody else directed.

"Come now, Mr. Wang. You've told the crew that they can skip ranks in the ratings exams. Do you deny this?" he asked sharply.

"No, Captain, that's true. I have told crew that they can skip ranks. The current CPJCT regulations for ratings exams specifically permit the practice of taking a higher rating exam in order for those individuals who have the demonstrated skill and knowledge to leapfrog the lower level ratings." I took a breath. "That's not flouting authority, Captain. It's following the rules set forth by the Confederated Planets Joint Committee on Trade. The crew still has to study for the exams, take the exams, and pass them."

"And then what happens, Mr. Wang? Have you thought farther than the end of your nose?" he snapped.

"I'm not sure I follow, Captain. Then what happens, when?"

"When we have a ship full of crew who have ratings above their station, Mr. Wang. I realize you're a junior officer, but don't tell me the academy has started graduating fools!"

By this point, the scene was lacking only a small white rabbit, and I was pretty sure the Red Queen was sitting at the captain's desk. I took a breath before answering.

"Then we proceed to port, Captain, and some of them will, undoubtedly, find other berths and move on."

"Exactly!" he said with great vigor and another slap on his desk for emphasis.

He held up his forefinger pointed at me in what appeared to be a very well practiced gesture of threat.

"Mister, this is your only warning. I brook no interference in the smooth operation of my ship. You will toe the line from this point forward or, by the gods, I'll have you thrown off the ship at the next port. Do I make myself clear, Mr. Wang?"

"Crystal, Captain," I said as confidently as I could. I was having a very difficult time keeping a straight face.

"This reprimand will go in your personnel jacket, Mr. Wang. This is hardly an auspicious start to your career in the Deep Dark. You may go."

"Yes, Captain, thank you, Captain."

I turned and left the cabin as smoothly as possible, closing the door as gently as I could and still be certain that it latched.

The chrono said I had time to wash the sweat off my face before lunch in the wardroom. I made sure the door to my stateroom was secured before I went into the head. I didn't think it would help much if Burnside wanted to come in, but it was psychological distance as much as anything. I kept trying to make sense of what had just happened, and I wondered where and how Burnside was going to exact his retribution. One thing was certain, I needed to finish the coding so my tablet would turn on the microphone for whatever room I was in. I had a very bad feeling that I'd need it.

At 1230 I made my way to the wardroom and slipped in. Burnside was there, but so was Mel. Fredi came in right behind me, and after a couple of heartbeats of uncomfortable silence, Ms. Davies entered with the first of the servings, and we took our seats. The meal was typical midday fare with some kind of noodle in a sauce. There were some green vegetables that looked like banapods—but a bit chewier—and an isolated bit of white mystery, which could have been meat or possibly bean curd. In my month or so aboard, I'd come to miss good food.

It was odd, really, that the food on the summer cruises wasn't all that memorable. Some of the ships had good food, some were mediocre, but none of them stayed with me as much as Cookie's spiced beefalo casserole. I was half inclined to pay the galley a little visit and talk about recipes, but given the session in the cabin, I thought that keeping my head down, and my nose pointing straight ahead, might be a better idea. After all, the food wasn't bad—just not good.

Conversation offered little refuge to the meal. Burnside's concept of polite table manners was difficult to talk over, and his contributions to the discourse usually consisted of inarticulate grunts and the odd belch. Fredi, as was her habit, sat hunched over her plate while Burnside was in the room, and Mel just occasionally smiled sadly in my direction.

Still, on the bright side, he had been on watch as often as Arletta and I, so we managed to have some lively and enjoyable meals when he had the duty. Even Ms. Davies seemed more relaxed.

Through the course of the meal, he never referred to the interview with the captain or indicated that anything at all had happened between my leaving the bridge and appearing in the wardroom. Yet, I knew that he was upset, and I couldn't help but fret over all the ways he could attack me.

Luncheon ended in good time, and Burnside left the wardroom with his usual lack of grace. When he'd left, Fredi said, "There are few things so constant in this universe." Then she snorted a small laugh through her nose.

"More's the pity," Mel agreed and turned to me. "So, did the captain call you down to the cabin?"

I blinked at her a bit stupidly before finally saying, "Yes. Why?"

She smiled. "You had that look when you came in."

Fredi, who was already sitting up straighter, added, "And it's his pattern."

She turned to look at me carefully.

"Are you all right, Ishmael?" she asked after a moment.

"I think so. At least for the moment, but I didn't make any friends in the exchange."

Fredi gave a little shrug at that. "Nobody does."

"Any insights into that subject we talked about in my office, Ishmael?" Mel asked.

"Some significant progress, in fact. I just need a few more stans to finish up, but I'm feeling pretty confident that the next time the Bumble Brothers bother me, I'll be ready."

Fredi smiled a crooked grin. "You heard that name, huh?"

"Yeah, my watch section is a wealth of information."

Mel and Fredi both chuckled.

Penny Davies came in to clear, and we all stood and helped her load up the first tray before getting out of her way. As we stepped out into the passageway, Fredi stopped me with a friendly hand on my forearm.

"Be careful. Now that the captain has had a chance to reprimand you on the record, David has fewer constraints," she said softly.

She looked up into my eyes and I realized just how short she was.

"Not that he had all that many before," she said with a trace of bitterness.

"Thanks, Fredi, I'll be as careful as I can." I shrugged. "But if he wants me badly enough, he'll do it when I'm asleep in my bunk—with no witnesses."

She nodded, just a little rocking of her head up and down. "Yes," she said and turned down the passage toward her stateroom.

I checked the chrono and I had about four stans before watch: time for a short nap followed by a long run. I headed back for my stateroom and pulled out my tablet to set an alarm. That was when I noticed that the intercom in the cabin was still open. I triggered the microphone off and wondered what I'd recorded.

On the one hand, I was horrified that I'd left it that long. It was one thing to record my conversations with the captain. I had a feeling I might need them. The ethics of self-defense had priority, but it was another to record conversations that I had no part in.

I could easily find part of my brain that said, "Just because you're not in the room, doesn't mean they're not plotting against you." There was another part that recoiled from the idea that I might be a person who bugged the ship. A few stans before I had been paranoid over who was listening.

Would anybody be happy to find out that it was me?

There was also the issue of legality. Was it illegal for me to record people without their knowledge? In a corporately owned vessel in the Deep Dark was there any real expectation of privacy?

A cold chill raced down the small of my back. Would I be in more trouble if I produced the recordings than not? Considering what I thought the group might be capable of, I wasn't sure.

I stumbled back to my stateroom, peeled off my shipsuit, and crawled into my bunk, pulling the covers over me. The conflicting demands of self-defense and ethical behavior warred with each other. I didn't know if I could sleep, but the narrow circle of concern ended with a dark curtain of exhaustion.

Say what you will about the watch stander merry-go-round. After over a month in the Deep Dark, your body will sleep if it can. Minor concerns like ethical conflicts will not stand in its way.

A small sudden sound woke me with a start. I lay there blinking and listening, trying to make out where the noise had come from, when my tablet bee-bee-beeped again. I punched the alarm off and let my breath out. The chrono read 1600 and I wanted to run before I got ready for watch. That much stress was a heavy load to carry, and I knew from extended experience how to bleed that off.

I was glad to see Lignaria stretching when I got to the gym. The lanky engineman had been my running companion on more than one occasion. She was in the third watch as well, but as Power Section watch stander, her duty station was in engineering central.

"Ah, somebody to run with!" I said.

"Sure, sar. These six-on-six-off-six-on days are a killer, aren't they?"

"Oh, yeah. Intellectually, I know that it's only eighteen stans from start to finish and with a little nap in the middle, it's not that bad, but some days it sure seems like a long day, doesn't it?"

"Yes, sar," she agreed. "Very long."

She finished her warm up and started up a treadmill. While she was occupied with that, I triggered the local intercom to record anything that might happen in the room. I did a few stretches of my own, then stepped on the machine and fired up my favorite program. Out of the corner of my eye, I saw Lignaria casting little glances my way and grinning.

I smiled and asked, "Is there something funny, Ms. Lignaria? Do I have my shorts on backward?"

"No, sar, although your shirt is wrong-side out," she answered.

I glanced down at the sleeve and saw she was right.

"So much for the dignity of officers."

"Sar? I don't think you ever need to worry about that," she said.

"What are you trying to tell me, Ms. Lignaria?" I asked with a mock frown. "I have no dignity to begin with?"

She blushed a little, or maybe it was the running that was coloring the back of her neck.

"No, sar, that's not what I meant. I was just thinking of Mosler calling you a 'girly man' and—" She stopped then, and a look of panic skittered across her face.

I recognized the look. It's the one I probably got when I discovered I was about two-thirds of the way across a conversational minefield, and I didn't want to take that next step. The look that I probably got when I realized that the only thing keeping me from stepping on the mine was the fact that my foot was firmly planted in my mouth.

She cleared her throat and looked straight ahead.

"That is, sar, I can't believe he'd think you were a girly man."

"I can't believe he'd pull up such a stupid phrase and think it was in any way insulting," I answered, trying to put her at ease. "I mean how do you follow that? 'Doo-doo head'?"

The ludicrousness caught her by surprise and she barked a single laugh.

We slapped along awhile in silence before she glanced at me again.

"Can I ask a personal question, sar?"

"I reserve the right not to answer," I told her with a smile, "but sure."

"You really had ratings in all divisions?"

"Yup, when I started out, circumstances forced me into taking a job on the mess deck of the *Lois McKendrick* over in the Dunsany Roads quadrant. I didn't like being helpless—being in a position where I had to take whatever job was available."

I glanced at her and she nodded her understanding.

"I liked being aboard ship, and I figured the best way to make sure I could stay there was to become qualified so I could work as many different jobs as I could."

"Makes sense, sar, but why not just climb the one division's ladder?"

"It was a trade off. I'm a land rat. No background in space at all. Being a spacer was almost totally incomprehensible to me. I reasoned, for whatever it's worth, that it would be faster to get two or three half share ratings than a half and a full. I learned a lot about ship's operations that way."

"You don't come from a spacer family, sar?" she asked, genuine curiosity obvious on her face.

I shook my head.

"No. My mother taught ancient literature at the University of Neris before she died."

"Oh, I'm sorry," she said.

I nodded to acknowledge her response, but continued my train of thought.

"I had to learn everything the hard way—as an outsider."

"I'm surprised you got on a ship at all, sar. There aren't that many people who can get through the Union Hall. You almost always have to know somebody or have some experience."

"I didn't know that at the time. Nobody told me I couldn't, so I just went ahead and applied anyway."

She chuckled at that and we lapsed into a friendly silence. Soon, the hum of the treadmill's motor and the slap-slap-slap of my feet on the spinning tread took me into that quiet place in my mind and I just ran.

CHAPTER THIRTY-FIVE
BREAKALL SYSTEM: 2358-AUGUST-26

We were only two weeks out of Breakall before I completed the software hack that automatically turned on the intercoms when I moved from one space to another within the ship. I'd discovered some dead spots in the process and even—out of boredom more than anything—added a patch to turn on the lights when I entered my stateroom. In all that time, nobody else had ever turned on a microphone.

The study sessions continued to meet on the mess deck every day. A couple of the crew had to step back and re-evaluate their progress toward skipping a rating. I thought it was interesting that they did it among themselves and then told me about it after they had decided.

A few people—mostly Mosler and Apones—still glowered. They didn't like it that their ability to intimidate their shipmates was so severely curtailed. It was good to see the crew becoming more cohesive, more supportive of each other. I smiled thinking that perhaps it was going to work out after all.

"Something funny, sar?" Juliett asked, breaking into my reverie.

"Yes, Ms. Jaxton. I was just thinking about being a 'girly man' and how much things have changed in the last few weeks."

"You're considering a change, then, sar?" she asked with that twinkle in her smile. "Gonna jump the fence?"

Charlotte snorted from the other side of the bridge.

"You have some contribution, Ms. D'Heng?" I asked.

"No, sar. Not me, sar," she looked up from her tablet grinning.

"So, tell me." I said. "What's the news below decks?"

The two women exchanged glances and Juliett shrugged.

"News, sar?" Charlotte asked. "Is there anything in particular you're interested in?"

I looked back and forth between them, not sure how far I could push. "How's life aboard?" I asked. "Has it gotten any better?"

It was apparently Juliett's turn to snort. "I don't think it could have gotten much worse, sar."

Running some of the more egregious possibilities through my mind, I wondered if she was being a bit naive.

Charlotte picked up from Juliett's lead. "We haven't had anybody seriously injured or killed this trip."

"Yet," Juliett added.

"True," Charlotte responded with a small nod, "but except for a couple of the stupider members of the crew, I think there's a lot less tension. Getting people together on the mess deck in the afternoon has done a lot for morale." She shrugged.

Juliett added, "It's made a difference in the berthing areas." She looked at me with a kind of apologetic half smile. "There's a lot less bunk jumping. People seem to be pairing up..."

Charlotte coughed.

"Well, that's probably not the right word...forming groups?" she looked at Charlotte who shrugged agreement. "At any rate there's less random carnality, with the accompanying bad feelings and black eyes."

I blinked and decided I did not need to know what kind of circumstance led to "random carnality" in the first place. I couldn't decide if it was something specific to the *Billy* or if bunk bunny culture was inherently askew.

"It's harder to get into a bunk where you're not wanted these days, that's for sure," Charlotte said. "Especially if it's already full," she added with a wink.

I couldn't be sure if Juliett blushed or not. She was paying very close attention to her helm.

"I see," I said, although I didn't. "Thank you for that insight."

"You're welcome, sar," Charlotte said. "Any time."

I settled back down to my watch logs while Juliett and Charlotte returned to their studies.

When 1745 rolled up, Burnside and Mallory clambered onto the bridge. Perhaps I was just being paranoid, but I couldn't help but brace myself. He just walked over to the watch stander position and flopped into the chair. For once he didn't stink of sex, but he didn't look all that lively either.

"Ship is on course and on tar—," I started to say.

"I relieve you," he interrupted, and then he put his head back and closed his eyes.

I shrugged and followed Juliett down the ladder. We separated at the passageway. She headed to the mess deck and I made a beeline for my stateroom. We had twelve stans off and I didn't need to be back on duty until 0600 the next morning. I looked forward to cleaning up, having a good meal, and then a solid night's sleep. I was firmly into a routine, and even passing Simon in the passageway outside the cabin no longer seemed strange to me.

Dinner in the wardroom was a convivial affair to begin with. Arletta and I arrived a bit early and Fredi was already there with her tablet open and reading. She put it away when we breezed in the door.

"How are you, Fredi?" I asked.

"Fine." She smiled. "Just catching up on the sector's trading situation. Hasn't changed much since the last time we were here."

Mel joined us with a warm smile and a hearty, "Good evening! How is every one?" she asked while walking around to her place, patting Fredi on the shoulder as she passed.

Arletta looked alert and rested, as well she might. She was on her day off and hadn't had to deal with the ship that much. She returned Mel's smile with a grin and said, "A few more days and we can get off this tub for a while."

"Aw," Mel said with mock sadness. "You don't like *Billy*?"

"It's not that," Arletta said with a wicked grin. "I just think we should see other people."

Penny Davies brought in the trays and we set to. There wasn't a lot of gusto but it was filling and warm. That counted. I also think I was finally getting to the point where the food was the food, and my mind wasn't looking for more than minimum requirements. Whatever else one might find fault with, the food was always filling and warm.

It was a typical Burnside-free meal with fun companions and pleasant banter. For all my dark trepidations about the ship, I felt a little foolish about my concerns. Afterward I headed back to my stateroom, and began taking advantage of the long break between watches by stripping down to my skivvies and crawling into my bunk. I must have been tired because I don't remember actually lying down.

When the tap-tap-tap on my stateroom door woke me, I immediately thought I'd overslept and missed relieving the watch. It's one of those recurring nightmares that plague watch standers, like missing the final exam haunts students. The little spike of adrenalin left me confused but I managed to say, "Yeah?" loudly enough to be heard on the other side, while I was still blinking my eyes into focus.

I heard a woman's voice say, "Mr. Wang? It's Davies."

Double Share

"One tick," I told her and scrambled out of my bunk and into a shipsuit. The chrono said 2250.

When I opened the door, Penny Davies was standing there nervously looking both ways up and down the passageway. She glanced at my face but said, "Sorry, to bother you, sar, but may I come in?"

I backed into my stateroom to give her a chance to enter.

She slipped in with another glance at my face and a grateful smile. She closed the door behind her and I had a moment of doubt. She didn't come any farther into the room than was absolutely necessary, but stood there just inside the door playing with her fingers, her gaze fixed on the deck.

"Okay, Ms. Davies," I prompted softly, "I'm almost awake. What's up?" I backed up a little farther, but didn't sit. I didn't want to sit on the bunk and the side chair was the only other seat.

"I'm sorry, sar," she said again.

I saw her working up her nerve for something and I was pretty sure I did not want to know what it was.

"I want to be in your harem, sar," she said without looking up.

I scrubbed my face with my hands and sighed. It was not an auspicious start to the conversation.

"I don't have a *harem*, Ms. Davies."

"Oh, yes, sar," she said softly with little glances flicking up from the deck to my face and back. "I know you don't have a harem like that, but there are some that think you do, and I'd like them to think that I'm part of it so they'll leave me alone."

"Just say no, Ms. Davies," I said naively. "It's not like they can force you or anything."

She did look up at me then, a stricken look on her face.

"Well that's just the thing. Yes, sar, they can," she said matter-of-factly. "You're in a private stateroom by yourself, but I sleep in deck berthing. They most certainly can."

She lowered her eyes to the deck again.

I blinked stupidly. Of course, they could. I was being dense.

"I suppose I can't ask who—"

"I'd rather not say, sar. I have to live there."

"Of course," I said, scrubbing the back of my neck with one hand trying to force a stream of logic through my sleep-bogged brain.

"Sar?" she pleaded after half a tick. "I don't know where else to go."

"Why me? Why not go to Ms. Menas?"

"Because you keep your people safe, sar," she said. I barely heard her over the low hum of the blowers.

Her response surprised me.

"What makes you think Ms. Menas doesn't?" I asked.

206

She snorted and gave me the "you've got to be kidding" look.

"Because she can't, sar," she said.

"And you think I can?" I asked, trying to find some kind of footing in the conversational bog.

"You do, sar, yes," she replied instantly.

I sighed again. "How do you propose to join my so-called *harem*?" I asked after a few heartbeats.

"Well, sar, if I spent the night here a few times..." she started to say.

"Whoa," I said.

She stopped and flickered a few of those furtive glances up toward my face.

"You know I don't sleep with crew?" I said.

She gave a small nod.

"And that includes my watch section," I added.

She gave another small nod.

"But that's why I need to stay the night. I'm not on your watch section, sar. I'm not even in your division. We wouldn't have to do anything, sar. I'll sleep on the deck, if that's what you want." There was a note in her voice now that had gone over the edge into pleading.

"Do you think people will believe we're sleeping together?"

"I suspect they will, sar. That's the whole idea."

"But I don't have a harem."

I kept trying to get back to the logic, but I wasn't having any luck.

"Maybe you could start one, sar," she said, a small smile curling her lips. "I know others who'd like to join."

I did sit on the edge of my bunk then. It occurred to me that this might be a nightmare, that I might be still asleep.

"Why?" I asked.

"So you'll protect them, sar. Like you protect Ulla and Charlotte and Juliett."

"Ulla?" I asked. "Ulla Nart?"

"Yes, sar," she said with another of her little nods. "They stopped bothering her after you stood up to Mosler and Apones in the gym. Everybody thinks she's with you now and they leave her alone."

With that we'd moved out of nightmare country and into surreal. I didn't even know where to go from that point.

"Sar? Please?" The desperation in her voice kept me off balance. "I need you to look, just look. Look at me."

She reached up and unzipped her suit, stripping it back to show she wasn't wearing a ship tee under it. It was too fast for me to protest and what I saw stopped me cold. She had a patchwork of bruises—some fresh and dark, some yellow, and others long healed discolorations. Mixed in were what looked like bites and scratches.

"I can't keep going on like this, sar. This is what you get if you try to say no... it just makes it more painful."

I had a hard time catching my breath. Behind me I heard Arletta moving around in the head. I glanced at the chrono—2315. She'd be getting ready to go on watch. She tapped on the door and I reached over to release the latch without thinking.

She opened the door and stuck her head in. "You okay, Ish? I thought I heard—"

In such a small, confined space she couldn't help but notice the figure trying to get her shipsuit back up over her shoulders.

"I know you're on your way to watch, Ms. Novea, but if you could spare a few ticks, I think you could be of some assistance. You see, Ms. Davies wants to join my harem."

Davies finally got her shipsuit back on and zipped, but not before Arletta had seen.

"I can see that. What do you want me to do?" Arletta asked.

"I was hoping you'd have some ideas," I said.

Chapter Thirty-six
Breakall System: 2358-August-26

"Burnside," Arletta hissed as she stepped out of the head and into my stateroom.

Davies gave a little panicky intake of breath, and all the loose pieces clicked into place.

"Well?" I asked. "You're senior to me. What do we do about this?"

I watched Arletta's brain engaging as she stood there staring at Davies. "Fredi," she said almost instantly. "Get Fredi. I have the watch in less than half a stan."

"Fredi?" I asked, more as a way to get my brain moving down the path. "Not Mel?"

"Mel's too obvious," Arletta said, shaking her head. "We need Fredi."

I reached for my tablet intending to bip her, but Arletta said, "Go in person, right now. Ask her to come to my stateroom."

Davies looked back and forth between us trying to figure out where this was going. I understood her confusion. I wasn't sure myself, but I trusted Arletta on this.

"Penny, come into my stateroom while I get ready for watch, and we'll get you some help."

Davies looked at me and I nodded encouragingly. "We'll get you some help," I repeated, pulling back my legs so she could slip past me. Arletta flattened against the bulkhead and Davies disappeared through the bright light of the head and into the dimness of Arletta's stateroom beyond.

Arletta and I traded a glance and I headed for the passageway.

It was only three long steps to Fredi's door, and an alert, fully dressed Fredi answered my tap almost instantly. "Ishmael?" she said when she saw me standing there. "What's wrong?"

"There's a problem. Arletta's stateroom," I said softly and stepped back out of the way as Fredi practically exploded out of her door and headed down the passage. The hunched over, frail woman was gone, and some new Fredi closed the distance before I even had time to be surprised.

She tapped on Arletta's door and slipped in when it opened, leaving me standing alone in the passage.

I wondered if I should go to Arletta's room or my own. In the interest of sanity, I went to my own. Fredi and Arletta were much better equipped to deal with this than I was, and if they needed me, they knew where to find me.

The door to the head was closed and I heard voices on the other side. I couldn't hear what they were saying but it was only a tick or two before there was a tap on the head door again. I slid the door and Fredi stuck her head in.

"Ishmael, please scout for me. We need to get Penny to sickbay and into the auto-doc before the watch changes," she said.

"Aye, aye," was out of my mouth and I was halfway to the mess deck before I had realized it. I didn't see anybody in the passageway and slowed my pace when I got outside the mess deck. I sauntered as nonchalantly as I could over to the big urns. Taking a cup from the rack, I started filling it while glancing out of the corner of my eye at Apones, who sat with his head down on the table. He looked asleep, and I left without disturbing him.

The sickbay was just across the passage from the wardroom. It wasn't much more than a walk-in closet with the auto-doc pod inside. Regulations required every ship above fifty metric kilotons to carry an auto-doc pod and any passenger ship with more than ten passengers had to have someone with a medic certification aboard. The pods weren't a replacement for a fully qualified doctor, but with weeks between ports, they provided a critical safety margin for the odd broken bone or laceration. In the case of severe injuries, the pod could seal around the patient, providing a full range of diagnosis and treatment.

I scurried back to Arletta's stateroom and tapped on the door. She stuck her head out to make sure it was me.

"Apones is asleep on the mess deck. I didn't see anybody else in the passages. It's quiet."

She nodded and opened the door wider, stepping out into the passageway to make room for Fredi and Penny.

"I need to relieve the watch," Arletta whispered.

Fredi nodded and told her, "Go, but do it slowly. I need a couple of ticks to get this poor dear settled."

I handed Arletta the coffee cup and headed back toward the sick bay, Fredi and Penny trailing me by a few meters. I went past sick bay, blocking the passage that led toward the mess deck. Behind me I heard Fredi opening the sick bay doors and then the hum of the auto-doc. In a bit the sound subsided and all I heard was the normal underway sounds of the blowers.

Fredi came out with a glance in my direction. I turned to follow her back to officer country.

"She's getting treatment and a mild sedative," Fredi said quietly as we reached my door. "Nobody can get to her there. She'll be safe until morning."

"Thanks for your help, Fredi."

"You're welcome, Ishmael. I wish this would be the end of it, but I think..." her voice trailed off.

"Yeah," I agreed, "but let's take one step at a time."

"Sleep well," she said and headed back to her stateroom as I slipped into my own.

It seemed like I had just dropped off to sleep when a loud banging on my door woke me again. "Open up, Wang," Burnside said from the other side. The chrono read 0035. He'd been off watch for less than a stan.

When I opened the door, I found him glaring at me from the passage.

"What do you think you're doing, Wang?" he spat.

"Trying to get some sleep before I have to take the morning watch," I said, then yawned in his face. "What's the matter?"

I didn't have to stretch it too much to play the muzzy-headed, half-awake junior officer.

"You know perfectly well!"

Down the passage Fredi's door opened, and she stepped into the opening, clutching her robe at the neck. She didn't say anything, just stood there watching. Burnside gave her a sneer, and then turned back to me. He reached to push me out of the way, but I stepped sideways leaving him pawing at empty air and he almost fell. He covered his stumble by stalking into my stateroom, crossing to the head, and jerking open the door—as if he was expecting to find somebody.

I stepped out of the room and into the passageway where Fredi winked at me with a little smile.

Burnside threw back the covers on my bunk, looked in the closet, and even used his pass key to open the door to Arletta's side, flooding the empty stateroom with light.

When it was obvious there wasn't anybody hiding, he closed Arletta's door with a slam and stalked back out into the passage where he seemed to realize that Fredi was giving him a colder than normal look.

"What are you looking at?" he snapped at her.

"Why, David?" she asked in her bird like way, cocking her head a little to the side, "Have you been drinking?"

I thought for just a heartbeat that he was going to attack her, but instead he turned to me and put a finger under my nose in warning.

"This was a mistake, Wang. A serious mistake."

For once I kept my mouth shut and let him think it was from fear.

With a glance over his shoulder at Fredi, he turned and stomped back down the passageway heading toward the mess deck.

Behind me I heard Fredi sigh. "Get some sleep, Ishmael. It's going to be a long day."

"Going to be?" I asked, covering a yawn with my forearm.

She snorted a little laugh and said, "Good night, Ish."

I went back into my stateroom, locking the door behind me. It wouldn't be much deterrence if Burnside wanted in, but maybe it would slow him enough that I could at least get on my feet.

I crawled back into my bunk and grabbed another short nap before my tablet beeped me awake at 0500. The shower revived me, and with fresh clothes I felt human again. Walking by the sickbay, I thought perhaps I didn't feel that bad after all. I went into the mess, grabbed coffee from the urn, and stuck my head into the galley.

Mr. Vorhees looked up when he saw me and came out onto the mess deck. "I heard. Ms. Novea let me know what happened last night." He looked a little embarrassed. "Is she okay?"

I shrugged. "You know where she is now?" I asked.

"Yes, I didn't know she was that bad, sar, I swear," he added, twisting his hands together.

I patted him on the shoulder.

"I don't think any of us did. I'd guess she'll be out this morning, but you may want to have Ms. Cramer cover the wardroom duties for a while," I said.

"Already arranged for that, sar. We'll do a buffet here this morning and see where we are at lunch time."

"I've got to go relieve the watch. If you need me, you can find me on the bridge. And just ask Ms. D'Heng to bring up my tray. There's no need for somebody to make a special trip."

"Thanks, Mr. Wang," he said a little bit gruffly. "That's two I owe ya."

"Bah, we have to watch out for each other." I smiled at him

and took my coffee up to the bridge.

I knew it was going to be a long watch.

Arletta and I changed the watch with as little fanfare as possible. She asked, "Is everything okay?"

I shrugged. "As near as I can tell, but. . . "

She nodded and left Juliett and me on the bridge.

Juliett gave me a serious look when we were alone.

"Something on your mind, Ms. Jaxton?" I asked, not looking up from the overnight logs.

"At the risk of mongering without a license, the rumor is we have a new member of the harem this morning, sar. Is that true?"

"You're aware that there is no *harem*, aren't you, Ms. Jaxton?"

"Oh yes, sar, or at least there wasn't one until last night."

"There still isn't, Ms. Jaxton," I assured her.

"If you say so, sar," she answered after a moment, not sounding convinced.

I managed to get through the overnight logs and check the status of the systems backups before Charlotte brought up my tray.

She placed it gently on the console and then took the helm from Juliett.

"Where's Karen?" Juliett asked her.

"Serving in the wardroom this morning," Charlotte told her. "Mr. Vorhees asked if I wouldn't mind bringing the tray since he's short one attendant this morning."

Juliett blinked. "What happened to Penny?"

With as evil a grin as I have ever seen on the fair face of woman-hood Charlotte said, "Well, apparently she had such a rough night last night, she was totally exhausted and needed medical attention to recover her strength."

I almost choked on my coffee.

"Ms. D'Heng?" I asked.

"You have quite the reputation, Mr. Wang. Ooo la la, sar. The rumor is that you quite wore the poor girl out."

Juliett looked at me with a muttered, "Lucky girl," before heading for the ladder and her own breakfast.

Charlotte waited until the footfalls faded away before muttering, "Amateurs."

"Ms. D'Heng? How is Ms. Davies this morning?"

"She just got out of the auto-doc a few ticks ago, sar. She's still a little woozy but she's heading for her bunk. Ms. DeGrut said she'll be ready for duty by lunch."

"Will she be safe in her bunk?" I asked.

"As safe as any of us harem girls, sar," she said with a straight face.

I closed my eyes and sighed. "I was afraid you were going to say that, Ms. D'Heng."

"You're welcome, sar," she replied in a jaunty voice. "I do try."

After the insanity of the trip, it was rather peaceful to be docked again. Third Watch got the duty, which was fine by me. Burnside hadn't said more than absolutely required to change watches. He glared at me but hadn't attempted another "reprimand." According to my rumor monger, he'd been totally unsuccessful in convincing Davies to take up where they'd left off.

There was an odd feeling having him come to the wardroom to eat meals. Everybody pretended that nothing had changed, that nothing was wrong, yet we all knew he had this skeleton in the closet. As time wore on, I finally realized that everybody else had already known what a miserable excuse for a human being he was. I was just late catching up to the rest.

One thing that changed was Fredi. After that night with Penny Davies, she didn't sit hunched over when Burnside was in the room. Whatever burden she'd been carrying had been lifted. I was glad to see it, because she was a pretty amazing individual.

Liberty was delayed while the customs officials certified the embargo locker, of course, but once that was over, the parade off the ship started with the captain, and David Burnside. As the afternoon wore on, almost everybody who wasn't on duty left the ship, and it seemed almost like old times.

I still remembered my first impressions when I had come through the lock, and I didn't want to be embarrassed that way again. Anybody could come to call and I was afraid what that would say about us. So for a couple of stans that first afternoon, Juliett, Charlotte, and I got busy with the sweepers and swabs. We cleaned from the lock back through the main passageway to the ship's office—deck to dock, bulkheads around. After the first rush of liberty goers, there wasn't anybody to get in the way or leave foot prints in the freshly swabbed deck. When we had finished, I took a moment to step off the ship and get a good snoot-full of cold dock air, then stepped back aboard. The sour smell that I had associated with the lock and the *William Tinker* was gone. A faint chemical smell from the cleaners replaced it, but we left the big lock open for half a stan to let it air out. It chilled the main corridor down, but it was much fresher after that.

About 1630 Mel stopped by the office. "Nice job on the lock and passageways," she said.

"Thanks," I told her. "I think that's the last bit of the ship that needed to be brought up to snuff, except maybe here in the office."

I looked around embarrassed because I hadn't thought of it even after sitting in there for over a stan.

She chuckled. "Don't sweat it. We'll only be in port a couple of days, and just so the OD knows, I'm going ashore to get dinner at a real restaurant. I'll have my tablet. Bip if you need me."

"Okay, that leaves just me aboard as officer?" I asked.

"I think so. Try not to break the ship, okay?"

I laughed and agreed.

When she'd gone, I headed to the galley. Mel had reminded me of something. I found Mr. Vorhees with his head in an oven looking over a tray of cookies. The smell was wonderful, and the cookies looked absolutely gorgeous.

"Mr. Vorhees?" I called from the galley door.

"Yes, sar?" he said, pulling the sheet out and shutting the oven off.

"I'm going to be the only officer aboard for dinner tonight. Is there any reason why we have to use the wardroom?" I asked.

"Sar? You don't fancy dining alone, then?" he asked.

"No, Mr. Vorhees, I don't," I said with a grin. "Is there any reason why I can't take my chances on the buffet here on the mess deck with the other six people aboard?"

"No, sar, if you don't mind eatin' with the common people," he said with a grin.

I laughed. "Well, I don't know about the common people, Mr. Vorhees, but I'd be honored to dine with the crew. I'm guessing that would save you and the duty messmate a bit of work?"

"Yes, sar, it would indeed, and you're welcome on the mess deck any time."

"Thank you, Mr. Vorhees. I'll take you up on that while we're in port." I made a mental note to see about getting the wardroom secured. We were eating the same food, so it just made extra work for the galley to serve an individual plate in another room just for me.

"Thank you, sar," he said and went back to getting the evening meal ready.

I prowled the ship looking for anything amiss or out of the ordinary until 1800 and then headed back to the mess deck for a bite to eat. As I worked through the buffet, I found a small pebble of envy for those who were eating ashore. Still, it seemed like old times to have a mess deck tray in my hands again, and I took a seat at one of the tables. It didn't matter which. I was the only one there.

Charlotte D'Heng came in shortly after I sat, and she did a double take when she saw me on the mess deck. "Sar?"

"I couldn't see having the wardroom set up when I'm the only officer aboard. Join me if you'd like, Ms. D'Heng."

She got a tray and did just that.

"Pardon if me I nibble and go, sar," she said. "I want to give Juliett as much of a break as I can."

"I've stood my share of brow watches, Ms. D'Heng. No need to apologize."

The pleasant company made the bland food more enjoyable, and she soon traded places with Juliett who came to join me for her dinner as well. By then I was down to coffee and some of Mr. Vorhees's cookies. There was no question that the man could make great ones. Apparently he was more baker than chef, and I wondered if he'd mind a few pointers.

While Juliett and I were eating, the engineering crew came in— the elegantly tall Lignaria from power, Ari Baronofski from Environmental, and Mosler from Grav. When they entered, all in a bunch as they did, they looked like any group of crew I'd seen anywhere. Seeing me sitting at the back of the mess deck with Juliett brought some confused looks, but they collected their food and took a table near the buffet.

Juliett finished her dinner and headed back to the lock, and the engineering crew left shortly after. With nobody else around, I figured I might get away with talking to Mr. Vorhees. Since the coast was clear, I took the chance.

"Mr. Vorhees?" I called when he came out of the galley to check the buffet, which was another adequate but largely monotonous collection of soup, sandwich, and casserole.

He smiled and came over.

"This isn't quite the same ambiance as the wardroom, is it?" he asked.

I chuckled. "No, but there are times when I think this might actually be better." After a couple of heartbeats I added, "If you've got a few ticks before you have to pick up here, I'd like to talk about... menus."

He shrugged and settled across from me. "Sure thing. You've helped me out a lot in the last few weeks, Mr. Wang. How can I help you?"

I leaned forward and cradled my coffee cup between my hands.

"This is awkward, John. I don't want to stick my nose in where it's not wanted but as I've been watching you and your crew over the last few weeks, a couple of things seem pretty obvious." I looked him in the eye then and said, "This is just me talking here, John. If you think I'm out of line, I'm out of line. Just let me know, okay?"

"Okay, sar, I think I can do that."

He looked a little apprehensive, and I knew full well I was pushing my luck.

"First, let me just say you're an excellent baker. Your cookies and cakes are marvelous."

His smile lit up the mess deck. "Thanks, Mr. Wang. I love to bake. It's the reason I took the lateral into the Steward Division."

"I thought as much. You're also good with your staff. Penny and Karen are both hard workers and very personable, at least from the 'customer' side of the house. They take good care of us. You may have issues I don't know of, but if you do, they're sure not obvious from my seat."

"Thank you, Mr. Wang. That's very nice of you to say. They're both great people to work with. To be honest, they treat me like a rather dim uncle at times, but we get along I think."

"I have a watch section like that myself. Just between you and me... I'm not entirely sure they're not right some days."

We shared a chuckle over that.

"So? What's the *but*, Mr. Wang?" he asked as the chuckles petered out.

I didn't even try to pretend. "My sense is that you're having problems with the everyday meals. You're great with the baking, but when it comes to the rest, you're following a recipe, but it's not working out a well as you'd like."

He sat very still for a few ticks.

"Am I wrong, John?" I asked. "Tell me to butt out, and I'll say no more."

He thought about it for a few heartbeats then shrugged. "No, if I'm gonna be honest with myself, these aren't meals to remember."

"You're a good man in a tough job, John, and I didn't want to joggle your elbow, but I didn't want to leave you floundering if I can give you a hand."

I watched him considering the idea and I left him to his thoughts.

"Well, you were right about the coffee and cleaning up the mess deck," he said at last. "What's your idea this time?"

"What's in your spice pantry?" I asked.

He shrugged. "Normal stuff. Salt, pepper..."

"Parsley, garlic, basil, oregano?" I asked.

"Yeah, I guess. Come on. I'll show ya."

He stood up and I followed him into the galley.

He walked to the back of the prep area and pulled open a locker door. There was a canister of salt and a large can of ground black pepper on the handiest shelf. Under that was a collection of dusty cans, jars, and bottles. The oregano didn't look like it had been opened in a month. Tins of onion and garlic powder were so covered with galley grime that I would've been afraid to hold them over a steam kettle for fear the crud might melt off, drip into the pot, and poison the crew.

He looked into the locker with me and said, "Doesn't look very good does it, sar."

"Well, John, let's just say, I think I can help if you're willing and interested."

He stood there for a couple of ticks looking into the crufty locker. "I don't have anything to lose, do I, sar?"

"You're a good cook, John, and a great baker. I think you could be a great cook as well with a little help and some honest feedback."

"Where do we start, sar?"

I grimaced at the mess in the locker. "Make some room here. Toss anything you haven't used this trip. We need to make some room."

"Okay." He shrugged. "Then what?"

"Then tomorrow morning we'll go shopping."

He began to grin. "You're having fun, aren't you, sar!"

I shrugged. "What can I say? I started on the mess deck, and I've got a soft spot in my heart for it."

He chuckled.

"Oh, hi, Mr. Wang," Penny Davies said from the galley door. "More big plans?"

"Shh," I said. "It's a secret."

She smiled and turned to Vorhees. "Are we ready to break down the buffet and do the clean up, Mr. V?"

"Yes please, Penny. When I've cleared out this mess, I'll give you a hand," he said with a glance at me.

I headed back to the office by way of the brow. I found Juliett working on her ship handling course.

She grinned at me when I came up to the watch station.

"You planning more changes, sar?" she asked.

"Changes, Ms. Jaxton?" I asked.

"Yes, changes, Mr. Wang. You know? When what we do today isn't the same thing as yesterday? Those kinds of things, sar."

"What makes you think I'm responsible for any changes, Ms. Jaxton?" I asked innocently.

"Sar," she said patiently, "please don't play innocent. Charlotte saw you in the galley with your head together with Mr. Vorhees. Are we going to be getting something good for dinner any time soon?"

"I think so, Ms. Jaxton."

"If you can do for the menu what you did for the coffee, Mr. Wang, the crew will be in your eternal debt."

I chuckled as I made my way to the office.

Chapter Thirty-seven
Breakall Orbital: 2358-September-09

After weeks of standing bridge watch together, standing watch in the ship's office felt a little lonely. I think Charlotte missed my company, because she soon camped out in the office too. She had only a couple of weeks to get ready for her test and was fretting over it. Personally, I thought she was ready, but I couldn't say anything. I spent some time drilling her on her able spacer practice tests anyway. There wasn't a lot else to do.

At around 2030, Arletta came into the office. "Hey, there!" she said. She looked like she was up to something.

"Hi, yourself," I replied.

Charlotte added a polite, "Good evening, sar."

"Ishmael, I need a favor. . . " she said.

"Do you want me to leave, sar?" Charlotte asked.

"That depends on how badly you want to see an officer beg, Ms. D'Heng," Arletta said with a grin.

"What do you need, Arletta?" I asked.

"I need you to trade watch with me. If you'll take my watch tomorrow afternoon, I'll take yours the following morning."

"The whole section or just us two?" I asked her.

"Just you and me. I've got an appointment that will pretty much take all day. I tried to change it to the day after, but I can't."

I looked at Charlotte. "You have any problems with that?" I asked.

"Standing watch with, Ms. Novea?" Charlotte asked. "No, why would I?"

"Just checking. Nope that's no problem for me either," I told Arletta.

"Thanks, both of you," she said with a grin in Charlotte's direction, then headed off into the ship.

"What do you think?" I asked Charlotte. "You going to be okay with Ms. Novea?"

"That depends, sar. She's not going to try to form her own harem, is she?"

"You're an evil, wicked woman, Ms. D'Heng," I told her with a laugh.

"You're quite welcome, sar," she said and went back to her studies.

At 2330 Charlotte got up and stretched. "Well, sar, I'm gonna head to the mess deck now. Apones will be dragging in soon."

The fact that she didn't want to be alone in the same small room with Burnside was left unsaid.

"Okay, Ms. D'Heng. Have a good day off tomorrow and have fun with Ms. Novea."

"Thanks, sar. We'll have a right cheery hen party, we will. Ms. Novea, Juliett, and I. Guess who we'll all talk about?"

She didn't wait for an answer, just sailed out of the office and headed into the ship.

David Burnside came into the office on the stroke of 2345. He reeked of beer and was still in his civvies. He'd obviously had just come from the lock. "I relieve you, Mr. Wang," he said very precisely. "Sign off the watch, and I'll change my clothes."

If he was slurring just a little bit, it was hard to tell. He looked steady enough. He didn't wait for me to even acknowledge his order, but turned and stalked heavily toward his stateroom in officer country.

That was beyond acceptable, but I didn't have any options. I followed his command, and put him on watch. I also stopped by the lock before going back to my stateroom, passing Juliett on the way.

"A heads up about tomorrow, Ms. Jaxton. I'm swapping watch with Ms. Novea. She'll be your OD for the next watch."

"Anything serious, sar?" she asked.

"I don't know. She asked for a favor and I said yes. We didn't get into the particulars."

"Very good, sar. I'll find out from Charlotte. Good night, sar."

She smiled brightly and headed off toward deck berthing.

I just sighed. She probably would find out from Charlotte and long before I'd find out anything from Arletta. Shaking my head, I continued to the watch station at the lock. "Mr. Mallory," I called, as I came down the passageway.

"Good evening, Mr. Wang, can I help you, sar?"

I walked up to the watch station and leaned on it, trying to think of how I wanted to phrase the question. I looked up and saw the intercom grill on the bulkhead and decided to go for the direct approach.

"Is Mr. Burnside drunk, Mr. Mallory?"

"I'm sure I don't know, sar. I've been asleep for the last four stans and just now got up to relieve the watch. Is he even aboard?"

"Yes, Mr. Mallory, he is. If you run into any problems, please bip me?" I asked.

"Of course, sar." He shrugged.

"Thank you, Mr. Mallory. See you tomorrow."

That was about all I could do. I contemplated calling Mel or Fredi, but under the circumstances, there was little they could do, either. I shrugged it off and went to my bunk. I just hoped he didn't do anything to kill us all before he sobered up.

When I went back past the office, he wasn't there, but I heard voices on the mess deck when I turned off to go to officer country. It sounded like Apones and Burnside, so I didn't fret it. He was at least up and moving around.

My tablet bipped me awake at 0800. It wasn't a lot of sleep, but it was some. I'd missed breakfast, but I knew the morning cleanup would be getting done soon and I wanted to take Mr. Vorhees down to the Oh-one Deck for some shopping before he started working on lunch.

There was no sign of Arletta, and I wondered what she was up to that would take all day. I brushed that thought out of my mind and focused on getting myself clean, awake, and into an undress uniform for a short trip ashore. By 0830 I was on the mess deck and made a cup of coffee serve as breakfast.

Penny Davies was swabbing down the mess deck as I came in, keeping a careful eye on Apones who sat—nose down—at his usual table in the back. She smiled when she saw me. I waved and she knew enough not to get between me and the coffee. She finished sweeping while I applied caffeine to my blood stream through oral ingestion, then came over and stood shyly.

"Good morning, Ms. Davies," I said softly to keep from waking the watch stander.

"Mr. Wang," she started, "I just wanted to say thanks."

"Don't mention it, Ms. Davies. I didn't do anything except call for help."

"You didn't take advantage of... um... the situation. You could have... others would have."

"No, Ms. Davies," I told her with a smile. "I couldn't."

"Well, thanks, anyway. It's better. He keeps pestering, but

I keep saying no, and his trained gorilla over there has kept his distance, so... thanks."

"You're welcome, for whatever it's worth, you're welcome."

She took her sweeper and headed back into the galley just as Mr. Vorhees came out.

"Ah, Mr. Wang," he grinned when he saw me.

"Just getting a little liquid breakfast," I said raising the cup. "You about ready to go shopping?"

"Oh, aye, sar, I got that locker cleaned out, so it's right spiffy. Now you're gonna tell me what I should put back into it, right?"

"I'm ready now, Mr. Vorhees. If morning clean up is done and you can accompany me?"

"Of course, sar. Penny's just going to finish up, and I have one small little task to do before I leave."

I drained the cup and put it on the tray in the sideboard. Mr. Vorhees walked over to the pile of clean trays that were waiting for lunch service and picked the top one off the stack, turning it this way and that in his hands. I watched curiously for a while before he noticed me looking.

"Does this tray look clean to you, Mr. Wang?" he asked, holding the tray up for me to see.

He had an odd look on his face but before I could answer, he flung it down on the tiled decking. The metal rang like a bell, bouncing and clattering from the momentum of his throw. Apones sat bolt upright in his chair. He looked much more awake. Not happy, but awake.

"I think it's dirty now, Mr. Vorhees," I said when the clangor died down enough to speak over.

He picked it up and considered. "I think you're correct, Mr. Wang."

He crossed to the galley door and put the tray on the counter just inside. "Penny, would you put that into the washer for me?"

I heard her laughing in the empty galley.

"Of course, Mr. V," she said with a giggle.

"I think I'm ready now, Mr. Wang. Shall we go?"

I led the way off the mess deck, and I stuck my head in the office door on the way out, but Burnside wasn't there. I suspected he was in his bunk sleeping, but I didn't say anything to Mr. Vorhees about it. At the lock, Mallory was alert, more or less, and nodded politely when we came up.

"The OD isn't in the office, so if you'd be so kind as to note that? I'll be down on the Oh-one with Mr. Vorhees for a stan or so."

"Of course, sar," he said and did so as the lock was opening.

"All quiet overnight?" I asked him by way of idle chitchat.
"Very, sar," he said, but winked.

John Vorhees may have been an engineman, but he had the makings of a great chef. What he lacked in experience, he made up for in enthusiasm. I have to give him credit. When we went to the chandlery on the Oh-one Deck, I led him back to the galley supplies. There, in the back corner of the complex, we found just about everything from soup spoons to nut crackers. The bigger items like ranges and refrigeration units were represented by catalog but there was a fully stocked spice locker.

For the better part of a stan, I went through the basics with him. He knew the difference between spices and herbs, and the advantages of whole over ground, but what he lacked was an understanding of how to use them. As we went through bales of herbs and tubs of spice, the scents and textures took me back to the *Lois McKendrick* and I couldn't help but think of Cookie. He collected his spices from all over the quadrant and some of them were his own secrets. I knew I couldn't hope to match his level of expertise, but I could at least get John Vorhees started with a few basics.

We each carried a pair of bags when we left. It wasn't a lot and it was nothing spectacular, but it was the basics—all the things he'd need to get started with learning how they all worked with foods and in enough quantity to make it back to Diurnia. His grin lit up the lift.

It was no big deal to get the bundles back aboard and checked in. There were special mass allotment accounts for food stuffs, and these definitely qualified. We went back to the galley and I helped him set up his pantry—scooping some of the contents of larger containers into smaller canisters for use while cooking, lining up the herbs and spices in groups and families so the cinnamon and nutmeg weren't mixed with the peppercorns.

When we got done he started putting together a fish stock for the lunch buffet and browning some meat for a pasta dish. His initial instinct was to try them all, and I had to convince him to master a few first. I reminded him that we'd have ten and a half weeks to play with the rest on the way back to Diurnia.

I steered him toward a bit of tarragon and a few bay leaves for the soup stock and had him lace the meat with basil and oregano. A quick dusting of garlic powder brought out the aroma of the meat just that little bit more.

"When we get back to Diurnia, we'll look for some whole garlic," I told him. "The flavor adds so much more when it's freshly diced."

I left him chortling to himself in the galley and the smell of the browning meat wafted throughout the passageways. I had time for a little run before I needed to relieve Mr. Burnside. So I headed for my workout clothes and the gym.

I wanted to work up a good appetite.

Chapter Thirty-eight
Breakall Orbital: 2358-September-10

At 1140 I reported to the office to take the watch. Burnside just grunted when I relieved him. I don't think he even realized I wasn't Arletta. He just walked out of the office and headed into the ship. Ulla must have been watching the passageway because she came in as soon as he was gone.

"This is going to be different," she said with a smile. "It's been so long since I stood watch with anybody but Ms. Novea."

"Well, I hope it won't be too different. It's still port side OD watch, and if we're lucky, nothing will happen."

She laughed. "Well, I can study then. Is it okay if I study in here?"

"Sure. I'm not very good company, but you're welcome to stay, if you like. I should go see how Mr. Betts is doing before I get too settled, but be my guest."

She settled into a side chair and pulled out her tablet.

I went to check on the brow watch and found him going over the logs from last night. "Any problems, Mr. Betts?"

He smiled when he looked up. "No, sar. Just looking to see who came in really late."

I chuckled. "One must find one's amusement wherever possible on the brow watch, eh, Mr. Betts."

"Yes, sar," he agreed. After a moment he added, "Sar? Can I ask? Did we get a new cook?"

"Not that I know of. Why?"

He lifted his nose and sniffed delicately. "Whenever I open the lock, I get this scent of food that wafts out. Do you smell it, sar?"

I focused, and sure enough, the delicate fish and the robust oregano and basil aromas floated at just the edges of my awareness.

"Oh yes, that would be Mr. Vorhees. He picked up some fresh herbs and spices this morning after breakfast."

"I hope it's almost time for lunch," he said with feeling. "That smells wonderful."

We shared a laugh and a knowing grimace over the quality of the fare aboard the *Billy*.

"Well, I just wanted to stop by. Ms. Nart is in the office, but I suspect she'll be relieving you for lunch soon."

"Thanks for checking on me, sar," he said with a grin, then added, "You're not going to try to add me to your harem are you, sar?"

"I have no plans in that regard, Mr. Betts," I told him seriously. "You'll be the first to know if I change my mind."

"I appreciate your consideration, sar. Ms. Jaxton speaks highly of you."

"That woman is dangerous, Mr. Betts. You mark my words."

"She likes you, too, sar," he said, and I headed back into the ship.

Twelve on, twelve off for an in-port watch schedule is hard. Logically, I knew I was trading days off and in reality I'd be getting a thirty-six stan break back from it and I probably wouldn't be standing another OD watch until we got back to Diurnia. The small stub of watch just before we got underway hardly counted. Still, the ship's office felt pretty small by the time I got back to it.

On the other hand, I got a new group of people to work with, and I already knew Ms. Nart was a lively companion, and Mr. Betts certainly seemed to be cut from the same cloth. Moreover, we were about to try Mr. Vorhees's newest culinary masterpieces.

I stopped at the office and stuck my head in.

"Ms. Nart? I believe it's time for lunch," I said.

She smiled and closed her tablet. "I hope so, sar, that smell has had me drooling for the last stan."

Apparently we weren't the only ones who'd noticed, because there was a larger than normal crowd waiting for the buffet to be set up. The obligatory cold meats and cheese platter was already in place along with a basket of breads and rolls. When the clock struck noon, Ms. Davies brought out the fish soup and slipped the large serving dish into a warmer. Mr. Vorhees brought out a large baking dish of meat and pasta and put that in a chafing dish with a rollback cover. They added a platter of cookies on the end of the buffet and signaled us to begin. I waited for the watch standers to fill their trays and then got in line with the rest of the crew.

The soup was a lovely, clear broth with some flakes of white fish and small cubes of potato. Green onions floated on the surface and the tarragon added a delicate anise flavor to the bouquet coming off the top of the pot. The pasta was baked with a meat and tomato sauce that, when seasoned with basil, oregano, and garlic, became something close to ambrosia. I noticed that nobody was eating the cold meats and cheeses, but several added crusty rolls to their trays.

I didn't linger in the line, just took a portion and moved on. Taking a seat at a table to the side, I invited Ms. Nart to join me. Her eyes gleamed as she placed the tray on the table and leaned over to savor the aroma of the food. I looked up in time to see Fredi come into the mess deck, assess the situation, and get into line herself. She saw me looking and waved while she waited for her turn at the soup. I nodded to the seat beside me, and she smiled broadly. It wasn't a crowd, as mess deck meals go, but with almost fifteen people eating lunch, it might have been a record for in-port meals on the *Billy*.

Fredi came over and sat with Ulla and me.

"Ishmael, this is a marvelous idea. I meant to tell you before. With so few people aboard, it's absurd for us to eat in the wardroom. This is so much more festive," she said with a smile.

Ms. Nart was working methodically through her soup and seemed to be enjoying it greatly. "How did he do this, sar? This is wonderful."

I took a sip and tested the flavors.

"If I had to guess, Ms. Nart, I'd say he used a normal fish stock, added a bit of poached mouta and some diced potatoes, and seasoned it with salt, pepper, and a hint of tarragon, to give it a little bite."

She blinked at me. "That was a guess, sar?"

I shrugged. "I've some knowledge in the culinary arts."

"I'll bet you can cook, too," she said, returning to her tray and moving on to the pasta bake.

Fredi leaned in on the other side.

"You need to tell me how you did this?" she said.

"Did what?" I asked back, just as quietly.

"This," she nodded at the tray.

"I didn't *do* anything," I said. "I just helped Mr. Vorhees realize that being a baker is one thing, and being a chef is another, but they have a lot of things in common."

"And you took him out to buy the spices," she said with a shrewd look.

"Well, yes, I had a few minutes this morning."

She chuckled. "A few minutes before you had to cover Arletta's watch?"

Ulla finished her tray and had tomato sauce on her nose. She giggled and wiped it off. "I have to go relieve Arnie, sars. He's not going to believe it."

With that she scooted off, taking her dirty tray with her and leaving us alone at the table.

"You know that David is going to punish you for this, don't you?" Fredi asked as she broke open one of the crusty rolls.

"Yes, I suspect so. It's harder to terrorize a motivated crew."

"Not only that, you're showing the crew that officers can be people."

"You think so?"

She nodded and addressed her soup again. "Yes, and by being people, officers aren't scary."

"We're not? I always found officers to be very scary. Alys Giggone scared me silly."

Fredi got a funny half smile on her face. "Yes, well, she also got you into the academy."

"Point taken," I agreed and finished off the last of the baked pasta. "Did you ever meet Benjamin Maxwell?"

"Oh, yes. Do they still scare the greenies with the story that he's some kind of super spy and moves mechanically so he doesn't inadvertently kill anybody?"

I laughed. "Well, I don't know about still, but they did to me. Why? It's a pretty effective story."

"The true ones always are more effective," she said with a little smile.

"You mean...?" I found I couldn't finish the question.

"Oh, yes. Brilliant man. Kind, gentle, caring, and absolutely deadly. Somebody you need to have on your side."

I found myself staring and pulled my eyes back in.

"How do you know him?" I asked when I could get my tongue wrapped around a thought again.

"He was number seven," she said softly. There was a kind of dreamy smile on her face. She saw me looking at her and for the first time since I'd known her, she giggled. "What? You didn't have fun at the academy? Nobody there you'll look back on when you get to be my age and think 'more' about?"

She caught me with that and shocked a laugh out of me.

We sat there having coffee and watching the crew enjoy dinner. It was very nice.

"So, tell me? Why didn't you go for captain?" I asked as the coffee cups ran low.

"Why? Isn't cargo first important enough?" she asked with a twinkle in her eye. "I like being cargo first."

I shook my head. "No, it's not that. It's just..." I paused

trying to put my thoughts together. "You know I'm not a spacer, right?"

She nodded, holding her coffee cup in both hands, her elbows on the table and letting the warm moisture waft up and over her nose.

"Well, when I started noticing people around the orbitals and such, I always thought that when you look at a captain... you know they're a captain. You don't need to see a uniform, you can just tell."

She turned her head in my direction with a thoughtful frown. "Interesting, but how does that relate?"

"Well, I never met a captain who didn't look it—until I got here and met Captain Rossett. He's the least captainly person I think I've ever seen. Makes me wonder if there were a lot of people I thought were accountants and dentists who were really captains."

She laughed and said, "No, I think you're right. He's not got what they used to call command presence in any great amount."

"Yes, well. Remember that night when we had the problem with Penny. You headed down the passageway hell-bent-for-leather and I watched you go, thinking—clipper captain." I glanced at her and she was staring into space. "So, I wondered why you never... you know... went for captain..." My voice trailed off at the end.

Her eyes were totally unfocused and she was a million miles away for just a few heartbeats before she smiled at me. I mean really smiled at me. It was wonderful. She leaned closer and said, "I did."

The shock must have shown on my face because she gave me a little shushing expression.

"But—?" I started to ask.

A look from her quelled my voice but not my curiosity. "I sat for the test—even passed the interview. But I never wanted command. I felt I owed it to Alys to go as far as I could, but I like my little cargo world. I don't know that I actually have the—whatever it is—confidence, maybe."

She sipped her coffee thoughtfully and I could tell she was lost in thought again.

I turned back to my tray then, embarrassed that I'd made assumptions. Not sorry that I'd asked, but still a bit regretful.

From beside me she asked, "So, you thought I looked like a captain?"

I turned and looked into those deep green eyes. They were laughing.

"Yeah," I said and I felt my eyes laughing back. "Yeah, I did."

After lunch, I settled into the office with a cup of coffee and a small pile of cookies. Ulla joined me and worked on her able spacer exam questions.

About 1500 David Burnside stuck his head in the door. "This isn't your watch! Where's Arletta?" he growled.

"We traded," I said, looking up from the console. "She'll relieve me at midnight and take the midwatch with my section."

"Why?" he barked.

"Because otherwise I'd stand twenty-four stans straight and it only seemed fair."

Ulla was trying to crawl into her tablet.

"No, you little wise—" he stopped and seemed to notice Ulla for the first time. He took a deep breath. "Why have you swapped?"

"She had an all day appointment and couldn't get it changed to tomorrow."

"What kind of appointment?" he asked.

"I don't know. She didn't tell me."

He stood there for a few heartbeats trying to decide if I really did know but had decided against telling him. Instead, he turned on Ulla. "So, Ms. Nart?" he asked in a slimy voice. I knew the next bit was going to be ugly. "Is he trying to add you to his harem now?"

Ulla smiled most charmingly. "Oh no, sar," she said in a wispy little girl voice that she used to devastating effect.

Burnside snorted a kind of derisive what-do-you-expect snort.

Then she added, "I've been a member of Mr. Wang's harem since almost the beginning, sar." She turned and looked adoringly at me.

Burnside turned a bit red under the ears and said through clenched teeth—like he was trying not to explode, "I'm going ashore. I'll be back before my watch."

Ulla continued to gaze winningly at me.

"Okay, Ms. Nart. He's gone. You can knock off the act now."

In a voice that was definitely not her wispy little girl voice, she answered, "Who's acting?" She let a saucy little pause stretch out before adding a throaty, "Sar."

I looked at her and caught the glimmer in her eyes. "You've been associating with Ms. D'Heng, haven't you!"

"Yes, sar," she said promptly and proudly. "She's teaching me everything she knows."

I shuddered. "I fear for the integrity of the crew, Ms. Nart."

"This crew, sar?" she asked, as if taken aback by the very idea. "Integrity?"

"Point taken, Ms. Nart. Point taken," I said with a small laugh. "Now how are you coming on the able spacer exam?"

"Party pooper," she muttered into her tablet, but I saw her grin.

We settled down to wait for dinner to see how Mr. Vorhees would make out on his second attempt. So far there hadn't been much in the way of telltale aromas but it was still early.

At 1730 Arletta came back aboard. She stopped at the office and looked in. She looked tired but jubilant—as if she'd been wrestling all day but had emerged victorious at the final bell.

"Where's Ulla?" she asked with a smile.

"Getting coffee for Arnie. You look tired."

"I'm exhausted, but I need to tell somebody." she practically jittered with excitement. "First mate exam was today. I passed."

I felt my face splitting in a grin. "That's fantastic! Congratulations!"

"I'm gonna go grab a shower and get some sleep. I ate on the way back, but I need to lie down."

"We're under control here. Go. Tell me about it when you relieve me."

She practically skipped down the passageway, heading for her stateroom.

I was still smiling when Ulla came back. She looked at me suspiciously but didn't say anything.

We went to dinner and enjoyed a rich pork roast that had been crusted with a savory rub. I recognized some of the spices, but obviously Mr. Vorhees was experimenting on his own and to good effect. There was a nice chicken soup, flavored with sage and basil, and some lovely potatoes with parsley. Everything was delicious.

The rest of the evening passed without incident. Fredi and Mel came back from their dinner ashore around 2200, both looking very striking in tailored pantsuits—Mel in a deep cranberry and Fredi in a burnt orange. They were a bit giddy as they headed to their staterooms, but who was I to gainsay them. I was actually a little jealous. It had been a long, long time since I'd gone out with a wingman and nothing planned.

By the time 2345 rolled around, I was more than ready to get out of the office. We went through the watch change ritual pretty quickly. After the two messengers went off to bed and the mess deck as appropriate, we had a few ticks to talk.

"Long, nasty test. Hard chairs," she said with a grin, "but I did it."

"You're ready to move on up!" I said congratulating her.

"I wanna go celebrate. Burnside has the watch tomorrow. Ya wanna go out and party with me?"

"You and me?" I asked a little bit unnerved. "Sure!"

"Well, I was thinking of asking Fredi and Mel, too."

"Excellent choices. Where you wanna go?"

She shook her head. "I have no idea. I plan to spend some time looking up nice restaurants. Burnside relieves me at noon and then I can grab a few stans sleep before we go out at—say 1900?"

"Good plan. Now I need to get some sleep."

"Sleep well, Ishmael, and...thanks. Twelve and twelve is a sucky schedule, so thanks."

I shrugged it off and stifled a yawn with my arm. "You're welcome."

Somehow I got back to my stateroom and into my bunk. I don't remember getting out of my shipsuit even. All I remember is the cool sheets on my arms and legs and the soft pillow on my cheek. It had been a long, long day and I fell into a deep pool of sleep.

What is it about the sound of running water that sets up a sympathetic resonance with my bladder? The familiar pressure pushed me up from a cozy dream and over the threshold to consciousness. I heard the shower running in the head and realized that Arletta must have gotten off watch. The thought of her wet and slippery in the shower was deliciously agonizing and I hoped she wasn't going to be too long because that running water was interfering with my more pleasant mental muzziness.

She was quick, and in a matter of a few ticks I heard the door close on her side of the head. I grabbed the shower, while it was still warm, and in less than ten ticks I was in my civvies and heading for the lock. Other than the buying trip for Vorhees, I hadn't been off the ship since we left Diurnia and I was more than ready for a good walk about.

I headed toward the lift. The icy crispness of the dock air always felt good after being locked up aboard for weeks. Even the faint tang of hydraulic fluid and ozone smelt good. My warm jacket provided plenty of protection for the short time I was going to be passing through and it felt good to stretch my legs out after twelve weeks in a can.

When I got to the lift I had to make a choice. Food was my first order of business and I wanted breakfast. It had just gone 1230 and I still had about six stans before I needed to meet Arletta for her first mate celebration. I punched Oh-two and dropped down to the spacer areas. I was looking for something particular and I was pretty sure I knew where to find it.

It didn't matter what time you went to the Oh-two Deck or what orbital you were docked at, there was always something going on. I followed the passage to port and walked around the station letting my nose lead me. I didn't have to go too far before the aroma of coffee and bacon led me to a hole in the wall diner tucked between two bars. The sign on the door said, "Cackleberries."

The place was exactly what I was looking for: chromed, clean, and sporting red tinted table- and countertops. Round-bellied coffee pots lined up behind the counter and a pass-through gave access to the kitchen behind. There were a few people scattered at the tables and a half-dozen spacers lined up on the bar stools at the counter.

I threw a leg over an empty stool and snagged the menu from the small chrome holder at the back of the counter. The waitress came over and slid a heavy mug in front of me and held up one of the fat bellied pots with a look that asked the question. I nodded my answer and she poured expertly, leaving just a bit of room for milk and turned to slip the pot back onto a warmer behind her.

"Yanno whatcha want?" she asked with a practiced smile.

I scanned the menu and said, "Yeah. Three eggs over easy, potatoes, three rashers, and two slices of wheat toast."

She scribbled it onto her pad and slapped the order onto the pass-through before I'd even drawn my breath back.

"Be right up, hon," she said and went to warm the cups down the counter.

For as much as I loved Cookie's omelets back on the *Lois*, this breakfast was a tie to those of my childhood back on Neris. Every Sunday my mother and I would hit that place in Neris Port. She'd have blueberry pancakes, and I'd have sloppy eggs and bacon. Jo-Ann's Kitchen. That was the name.

The waitress startled me when she skidded the plate expertly, landing it right under my nose and providing a grin along with an expert splash to top my cup. I took a deep breath, grabbed a fork and lost myself in velvety yolk, crunchy bacon, perfectly browned potatoes, and buttery wheat toast. It was wonderful, and in what felt like only seconds, it was gone.

Looking down, I saw I had cleaned the plate to its glaze with just the faintest smear of egg across one side. There was still half a slab of toast so I leaned back and nibbled it slowly.

"Long run, huh?" the server asked with a grin.

I took a deep breath and said, "Yeah."

"Don't feel bad. Happens ten times a day here," she said with a wink. "You'd be surprised."

I sat there thinking about going for another round but decided that I'd let this one actually hit my stomach before I tossed more in behind it. The coffee was good and the toast was excellent. It didn't last very long and I drained my coffee cup as well. She handed me the tab, I added a hefty tip, and punched my thumb onto the pay button. "That was great," I told her. "I expect I'll be back."

She gave me a lopsided grin. "You do that, hon, and bring ya friends."

By the time I was up off the stool the dishes were gone and the counter cleaned.

I stepped out into the main passage and realized that the smell of bacon was stronger outside than in. I chuckled. Clever, but I couldn't help but think what that was doing to the port's scrubbers. On second thought, as I watched the press of bodies and took in the various aromas around me, maybe it wasn't such an additional load after all.

I let the swirl of people pull me along. It was a good time to check out the local stomping grounds. I didn't have anything in particular that I wanted to do, but when the time came that I did, it would be good to know what was where. Somewhere under me, I knew there were residence decks where the people who worked on the station found living quarters, along with transient hostels for crew caught between ships. Often those same people who worked on the station were indeed crew who had gotten caught between ships. On a confederated planet, you couldn't get deported for not having a job, but you could be left homeless and starving if you couldn't buy food or shelter. It was an interesting juxtaposition.

I'd made it almost all the way around the station by the time I found the pub, and it was predictably to the port of the lift while the main dance club was to starboard. I also located a couple of interesting shops that sold clothing, entertainment cubes, and food stuffs—not restaurants but more like grocery stores. That got me thinking about Cookie and Henri Roubaille, and I found that I missed my old life on the *Lois McKendrick* so badly that it took my breath away for just a moment.

I went into the pub—The Corner—and took a seat at the bar. The barkeep was an older man with a close cropped beard with a lot of gray in it, no hair at all on his pate, and a pair of startlingly green eyes in the middle. "What's yer pleasure, then?" he asked by way of welcome.

"Something in a light ale. Local if you have it, but I'm not fussy."

He grinned and pulled a short pint full of a golden ale and placed it on a coaster in front of me. "Try that, then, bucko, and tell me what you think."

I took a sip and it was just the ticket. I realized I'd been walking around the station for over a stan, and I was thirstier than I'd realized.

"Very nice!" I said.

"Local hops and malt. An everyday ale for midday whistle wetting. Long on flavor and short on kick."

I savored another sip and asked, "And what is this miracle of the brewer's art called? In case I'd like to order some more?"

He grinned. "We call that one 'Midday Whistle Wetter.'"

I blinked at him, trying to judge if he was having me on. He pointed to the chalked sign behind the bar and sure enough there was "Midday Whistle Wetter Ale" along with a "Wonder Wheat" and one named "Call It A Day Working Man's Porter."

The names drew a chuckle out of me almost despite myself. "Cute names," I said at last.

"Ah, well, too often people are tied up on the what when they're really lookin' at the when, don't cha know." He nodded at the sign. "There's a few snobby people want a particular kind of brew— Golden Malt Five Hops Dragon Piss or some such. But most folks come in for a pint because it's time for a brew—middle of the day, end of the day, sometimes just because. I make it easy for 'em by naming the beer after the occasion."

"It worked for me," I said giving the man his due.

"Works for most. Down here, if you come to my pub, you're usually looking for someplace quiet, off the ship, away from the crowd, and you drink a beer as rental on the stool." He shrugged as if it were all very obvious, and I suppose it was.

I settled down to think. I wasn't out of the woods in spite of the past few days of respite. I knew David Burnside wasn't going to go away, and I was relatively certain that he'd try something more dramatic than a punch in the gut. The ship was slipping out of his grip. His plaything had been taken away. The crew was acting more like a crew and less like a herd of wounded rabbits. With the food, if not up to Cookie's standards, at least better than it had been, there was going to be one more thing for David Burnside to blame on me. Sooner or later, I knew he was going to have to slap me down. I did not look forward to that at all.

The beer was a good sipping beer and the barkeep—his name tag read "Brian"—knew to stand back while a man was pondering in his beer. He offered a second when I got down to the bottom of my first, but by then I needed to get moving. I thumbed the tab and used the facilities before heading back out to the main passage. It was coming up on 1600 and I still had no idea about what to do when we got underway again.

My feet carried me idly around, closing the circle returning me to the lift. I stopped once and looked in a shop's grated and reinforced window. Inside were weapons—contact weapons: projectile throwers, blades—lots of blades—billy clubs, and coshes. I stood there looking at them for maybe three full ticks before realizing what I had been doing. I sighed and took a deep breath, closing my eyes. I couldn't believe they'd pushed me this far. I turned on my heel and walked away.

Here thar be dragons. And those dragons will bite you in the butt.

When the lift doors opened, I stepped out into a world I'd almost forgotten—the flea market. According to the chrono I still had almost a stan before they closed the doors on another day and I heard Pip's voice in my ears saying, "Better deals in the afternoon." I set out through the sea of booths, a bizarre bazaar of crap, craft, and kitsch.

Breakall was a corporate system. That limited the mix of goods available in the flea market to items that the planet could produce, but sometimes yielded unexpected treasures. It had been more than five stanyers since I'd helped organize the old McKendrick Mercantile Cooperative in order for the crew of the *Lois* to have a safe place to sell. I wondered how that was doing. It had been almost that long since I'd been in the flea myself. I didn't have cash to spare while I was at the academy and never even tried private trading on my summer cruises.

As I sauntered along the long rows of booths, nothing caught my eye. I kept thinking of my extra mass allotment and wondered how I could capitalize on it. Half the fun of private trading was the hunt for trade goods. "Low mass, high value," I mumbled to myself with a grin.

In what seemed like no time at all I heard the ping-ping-pong of the closing bell and joined the throng heading for the exit. On the one hand I felt mildly disappointed that I hadn't managed to find anything to buy, and on the other, I had enough on my plate without trying to play the trade game. Mostly, I missed Bev and wondered how she was doing on her family's ship.

"Hello, Mr. Wang!" A woman's voice speared me from my reverie and I turned to see Ulla Nart and Penny Davies walking up

239

beside me.

"Hello, Ms. Nart, Ms. Davies. Enjoying your day off?" There was just something about those two that made me want to grin. They wore jeans, pullover tops, sensible shoes, and each toted a small carryall. "Buy anything good?"

They looked at each other and giggled. "Well, we hope so, sar," Ulla said.

"Trade goods to take back to Diurnia," Penny added.

"It must be hard to find things on one system that would be in demand on the next. You cover the same ports all the time."

They shrugged in unison.

"Yes, sar," Ulla said. "But we have fun looking. And it's something to do."

"Big plans for tonight?" I asked. "It's last night in port and all."

"We've been talking about heading down to the club later for a little dancing, sar," Ulla said after a few heartbeats. The expression on her face said she might be doing more than a little dancing later.

Penny, on the other hand, didn't look all that excited about the prospect. Given that I wasn't sure her bruising had healed yet, I suspected that she might go along for the company, but wouldn't be staying out late.

"Well, you two have fun," I told them with a smile. "I'm off to have dinner with Ms. Novea."

"She likes you, you know, sar," Ulla said with that school girl "I know a secret" tone to her voice.

"I like her, too, Ms. Nart. She's a fine officer and an excellent astrogator." I hoped my tone gave them the hint.

"Yes, sar," she said simply, but her lips twitched in a little half smile of amusement and even Penny let a sly grin peek out.

At the lift, they took the ladder down while I stood in line for the next available car. They each gave me a little wave as they disappeared through the door. I just shook my head and chuckled. We really did have some very good crew on the *Billy.* As I stood there waiting, I saw two more of the crew walk by and head down the ladder—Herm Mosler and another of the engineering crew. I recognized the face, but couldn't remember his name. I sighed. At least he wasn't with Apones.

Back in my stateroom, I stripped out of my old green pea coat and jeans. They still fit well, in spite of the years, but my shoulders had filled out a bit since those days back in St. Cloud, and I knew I was going to have to retire that coat soon. Fitting well and fitting perfectly were miles apart, once you came to appreciate the difference. Henri Roubaille had spoiled me in that regard.

He'd also outfitted me with a wonderful charcoal jacket and slacks the last time I'd seen him before heading out to the academy. He'd cut that coat just a bit fuller and that one still fit perfectly even after all these stanyers. Moreover, it was—I had on good authority—devastating. I wondered how I could get additional decent clothing here. I had needed an introduction to even get an appointment at Chez Henri.

It was still almost two stans before we'd be gathering for dinner, so I put on my workout gear and headed for the gym. In spite of the long walk, or perhaps because of it, I found myself craving the quiet meditation of a good tai chi session.

One thing I hadn't anticipated in my planning was that I shared the head with Arletta. It was one thing to have last night in port while living in the berthing areas. There were plenty of sinks, mirrors, and multiple showers. It was quite another to have one facility to share between two people. When I got back from my workout, the shower was running, the chrono was ticking, and I was awash in sweat.

Chuckling, I toweled off as best I could and pulled out the charcoal jacket and slacks, brushing them down a bit and just generally laying things out so that when I got out of the shower, I'd be able to skin into my clothes and be ready to go. I stood there listening and realized she was singing softly to herself. A wordless tune I couldn't recognize but it sounded nice and I was oddly touched by the intimacy of it. While I was waiting, I dug out my kit and worked on cleaning up the odd nose hair using the big mirror on the closet door. Not a terribly glamorous task but it was the last night in port. With the shower still running after I finished that, I shrugged and clipped my fingernails for luck.

The shower cut off just then and in a couple of ticks she knocked on the door. "It's all yours," she said, and I heard her side latch shut.

I grabbed a fresh towel and my kit, then dove for the warm shower. It didn't take long to wash off the day's grime, and I was out and into my civvies in less than five ticks.

I had just finished adjusting the fall of my jacket, when I heard a soft tap on the stateroom door. Opening it, I found Fredi and Mel waiting for me. Mel was in a gorgeous cranberry blouse with a deep green jacket and slacks. Fredi was in a navy blue tunic and slacks. She wore a single gold broach on her left shoulder and looked very relaxed.

"Good evening, Ishmael," Fredi said with a warm smile. "Are you ready?"

I just grinned and stepped out into the passageway with them, closing the door to my stateroom behind me.

Mel gave me a rather frank once over and turned to Fredi to say, "For a boot third, he cleans up very nicely, don't you think?" There was a twinkle in her eye and an approving smile on her lips.

Fredi gave me one of her bird-like, head tilt examinations before replying, "I think he has promise."

We moved a couple of meters along the passageway and Fredi tapped on Arletta's door. We heard the unmistakable *thunk* of a trunk lid slamming shut and some indistinguishable scrambling before a moment of silence. The door opened and Arletta stood there, framed.

I was a little concerned that there might have been an oxygen imbalance because for just a bit, I had a very hard time breathing. She looked straight at me, and somewhere behind I heard Fredi and Mel murmur something that I couldn't make out over the rushing in my ears.

Finally, I managed to get a breath and said, "So, *that's* what a little black dress looks like."

Mel laughed out loud, and Fredi chuckled. Arletta just smiled and arched an eyebrow.

The dress was as black as the Deep Dark and even had some kind of sparkly texture to it so that very faint reflections of the overheads made it look like she wore stars. It clung and draped and floated freely in a variety of fascinating directions, and I wasn't even close to done admiring it before she stepped out of her stateroom, slung a wrap across her shoulders, and closed the door behind her.

"I'm starved," she announced. "Shall we go?"

Dinner was at a place on Ten Deck called Scotty's. It was one of those classy restaurants where the lights are low, the chairs comfy, and the food amazing. The company was clever and beautiful. I noticed several people—men and women alike—sizing me up and wondering what I was doing with a table full of gorgeous women. I just counted my blessings and hoped none of them objected to dragging me around with them.

It soon became apparent this wasn't the first time the three of them had been out together. Once away from the ship, there was an easy camaraderie among them that I recognized but could not yet share. Someday perhaps, but in the meantime it was pleasant just to be with them.

The salads were fresh and crunchy, the soups light and flavorful. We all ordered beef in one configuration or another and shared a gorgeous red wine, dry enough to complement the meal through all the courses. My steak was cooked to perfection and the others savored theirs as well. Coffee and a glazed dessert pudding topped the meal and left us pleasantly relaxed, full without feeling gorged. As a meal, it was probably one of the best I'd ever had. Masterfully created and presented.

It didn't hurt that I shared it with three brilliant women.

CHAPTER FORTY-ONE
BREAKALL ORBITAL: 2358-SEPTEMBER-12

The morning started okay. I woke up on my own, had nothing to do, and nowhere to go. I would have the duty at noon but that was still a few stans away. A glance at the chrono told me I'd missed breakfast, but with the meal from last night fresh in my mind, a little coffee would tide me over until lunch. Liberty was timed to end around 1300 but I suspected the mess deck would be pretty crowded for lunch. With most of us back aboard, Mr. Vorhees would be using the wardroom.

After a quick shower and fresh shipsuit, I headed toward the mess deck for some coffee and that's when everything started tumbling down. When I stepped onto the mess deck there was a sudden swiveling of grim faces. Not many for a midmorning with liberty running, but more than I would have expected. They looked at me as if they had been expecting somebody but I wasn't the one. They immediately turned back to whatever they had been doing, which wasn't much. I got my coffee and glanced into the galley where Mr. Vorhees was talking to Karen with the same grim expression. Karen was nodding and pushing a broom around in a small circle.

I took my coffee and headed for the office. Arletta had the watch, and I had a *very* bad feeling. Penny Davies should have had galley duty, not Karen. That was not a good sign.

When I rounded the corner and stepped into the office, Arletta looked up, worry furrowing her brow.

Ulla wasn't in tears, but she had been, judging from the color of her nose and the pile of tissues beside her. She looked up at me with hope, and I had no idea what I was supposed to do.

"Something's happened to Penny?" I asked.

"How'd you guess?" Arletta replied.

"Hunch. What do we know?"

"She's officially AWOL. She didn't come back from liberty this morning," Arletta said.

"Did she bolt?" I asked.

Thinking back over the voyage out, I couldn't say that I'd blame her.

Ulla sniffed loudly. "She headed back to the ship at 2200. I never should have left her."

Arletta shrugged and looked at me with an expression I couldn't quite fathom.

"There was this cute guy and we were dancing, but I had to get back to take the watch at midnight so we left a little early, you know?" she looked at me with those tortured, pink-rimmed eyes.

"Yeah, I know. Then what?"

"Penny said she didn't wanna hang out any more, so she was heading back to the ship. She had breakfast duty this morning. After the last couple of weeks, she's been... well, you know." Ulla took a tick to blow her nose on another tissue.

"When I got back, I just had time to grab a shipsuit and run up here to relieve Apones," she said holding back sobs. "I never looked around the berthing area, just grabbed a suit out of my locker and ran up here."

Ulla started sniffling into her tissue, so Arletta picked up the story. "When Ulla went to wake her for duty, her bunk hadn't been slept in, and the brow watch shows her checked out yesterday afternoon but she never came back in."

"Where do we stand?" I asked.

"Mel and Fredi have gone to the orbital security station. They're running sweeps."

"Where's the captain?" I asked, knowing the answer.

"He's due on the 1100 shuttle up from the planet. We notified him but he didn't change his schedule."

"Burnside?" I asked.

"At the Union Hall," she said with a bitter edge to her voice.

I arched an eyebrow. "Union Hall?"

"We sail this afternoon. He's not waiting."

She didn't need to spell it out any more fully.

Her tablet bipped and she stood up. "Betts says there's orbital security at the lock. Ulla, stay here. Ishmael?"

I nodded and followed right behind her. Betts had the lock open and the two uniformed orbital guards stood just inside the door when we bolted in.

"I'm Novea, the OD," Arletta said. "What can you tell us?"

The obvious senior looked at me and Betts before speaking.

"She's in medical. She's alive. Sweep team found her down on the Oh-eight Deck just around from the lift. We're reviewing video surveillance now." He bit off each sentence as if reading them from the report. For all I knew he was.

"Alive?" Arletta zeroed in on the pertinent fact.

"She was pretty badly beaten," the officer said again. "She's in the can now and the medicos are working. They've only just gotten her up from Oh-eight. One of your officers is with her." He consulted a tablet, "DeGrut?"

Arletta confirmed it with a nod.

Still looking at the tablet he said, "A Ms. Menas is reviewing video with the security team."

Arletta nodded. "Thank you, officers. At least we know what happened."

They nodded respectfully and turned to step back onto the dock. Just another day on the orbital, no doubt.

Betts had started cycling the lock mechanism but a shout from the dock had him reverse and open it back up.

David Burnside stepped over the coaming and into the ship. Behind him a young woman in a brand new DST shipsuit carried a suspiciously clean duffel.

"Oh, good," he said. "You're here. This is Mindy Jacobs. She's our new mess deck attendant. Ms. Novea, if you'd take Ms. Jacobs and get her signed in, we can proceed with readying to get underway."

"Welcome aboard, Ms. Jacobs," Arletta said as warmly as she could under the circumstances. "We're having a bit of a dust-up this morning, so please bear with us." She turned to Betts. "Mr. Betts, would you see that Ms. Jacobs gets mass allotment and systems record?"

"Aye, sar."

The Ms. Jacobs in question, a lovely girl of eighteen or nineteen stanyers, with lush brown hair and relatively impressive physical assets, reminded me of the phrase "calf to slaughter."

"Ishmael?" Arletta said. "I need to let the crew know. I'll go talk to Ulla if you'd make the announcement on the mess deck? And let Mr. Vorhees know he's not shorthanded?"

"Of course," I said.

I followed Arletta down the passageway into the ship. As we turned the corner she asked me, "Does it strike you as odd that he's already got a replacement?"

"Only from the perspective that he must have been pretty sure that Penny wouldn't be rejoining the ship."

"That was my thinking, too."

We split up at the office door and I only got a glimpse of Ulla Nart's hopeful, but tear smeared face before Arletta closed the door, and I headed for the mess deck.

When I got there, every head turned toward me and I just stood for a heartbeat. They all knew I had something to say. I saw it in their faces. Juliett and Charlotte were sitting with a couple of the engineering people. Apones and Mosler were at their usual table and the engineman I'd seen with Mosler outside the flea market was sitting with them.

"Ms. Davies has been found. She's getting medical treatment right now. She's too badly hurt to be rejoining the ship, but a replacement attendant is checking in now."

It was a brutal recitation, but there wasn't anything to be gained by beating around the bush. I saw Juliett and Charlotte bite their lips and reach out to hold a hand. Most of the crew had expressions of shock and dismay. Only Mosler and Apones didn't seem surprised, and the extra engineman—I suddenly remembered his name was Xiang—flashed a look at the two of them. He didn't look happy.

John Vorhees stepped out of the galley when I started speaking, and heard the whole thing. I walked up to him and we moved back into the galley. Karen was standing there, not looking much better than Ulla Nart in the swollen eyes and red nose department.

"Mr. Wang," he said. "Do they know...?"

I shook my head. "No, John. I'm sorry," I said. "They found her less than a stan ago. She's in the can up in medical and she's getting treatment. The officers said she'd been beaten and left on the Oh-eight Deck. They found her this morning on their lost-person sweep."

His eyes narrowed and he said, "They found her less than a stan ago, and we already have a replacement."

It wasn't a question.

"Yeah. Mr. Burnside went to the Union Hall himself to get us one."

"That was nice of him," he said with a growing hardness about his mouth and eyes. "And I'll assume that the said fortuitous replacement happens to be female, young, pretty, blonde, and fills out a shipsuit?"

"Close," I admitted. "Brunette."

"What are the odds, sar?"

"Astronomical," I replied.

He took a deep breath and I watched him calming himself by sheer strength of will.

"So," he said at last, just the one word.

"So," he repeated.

His eyes were focused elsewhere and his mind was racing, by the look of him.

"We need to have a little talk with our new lambie," he said softly, "and I'm afraid Ms. Cramer gets wardroom duty."

I clapped him on the shoulder. "Strength, John, we don't know. We have no proof. It looks bad, but we don't want to lower ourselves to their level."

Under my hand I felt the starch leach out of the man. He closed his eyes and struggled for control but eventually said, "Yes, sar. I know you're right, but—" he raised his eyes to mine—"she was my crew, sar."

"I know, John," I said with a sigh. "Believe me, I know."

There wasn't anything else to say, so I got out of his way and headed for the office.

CHAPTER FORTY-TWO
BREAKALL SYSTEM: 2358-SEPTEMBER-21

By the time we were nine days out of Breakall, things had reverted to what passed for normal on the *Billy*. The good news was that Mr. Vorhees took to his new spice locker with some amount of gusto. After being grateful for "warm and filling" for so long, I found it gratifying to look forward to something approaching "tasty" as well. The bad news was that the crew had been shocked back into fear. The afternoon study sessions had all but disappeared, and the condition of the ship slowly degraded. Burnside and first section continued to purposefully leave a mess on the bridge. So stupidly petty, it became something of a joke among the bridge watch. That was good. Otherwise it would have been demoralizing.

According to the standing orders, the mandatory ship's drills for gravity, hull integrity, life boat, and general quarters were scheduled for the day before the ratings tests. Knowing how long these drills took, I wasn't sure how we'd schedule all of them in a single day, and I had serious reservations about the utility of announcing them in advance. Every time I tried to bring it up with Burnside, he either ignored me or denigrated my concerns.

"We've been doing this a lot longer than you have, Mr. Wang. Watch and learn."

Burnside called me to the bridge at 1330. "Well, Mr. Wang, are you ready to learn how we do drills on a real ship?"

False camaraderie had been a hallmark of his behavior since getting underway from Breakall. Maybe he'd always been that way, but I only found it grating after the events there. I couldn't be sure.

"Pray, enlighten me, Mr. Burnside. I can't wait."

"What's the first drill, then, Ishmael?"

"Hull breach," I said.

He crossed to the ship's address system and punched the hull breach button. The warning klaxon was barely audible on the bridge and I wondered what it would be like down below. He then proceeded to read the required announcement for a hull breach drill from his tablet. As soon as he was done reading, he punched the button to shut off the klaxon.

"See?" he told me with a sneer. "How long did that take?"

I looked at him dumbfounded.

"How many people got into their protective gear?" I asked.

He looked at me and laughed.

Even Mallory snickered.

"You don't think we're going to waste good suits on that, do you?" he said when he'd gotten his humor under control. "I don't know if you're aware of this, Mr. Wang, but once you use a suit it has to be refreshed."

"Yes, actually, I am aware of that."

"Then you know that refreshing is expensive, and we have better uses for money than wasting it on stupid drills."

He crossed to the watch log and made a notation.

"There! Hull breach drill complete. What's next, Mr. Wang?"

He had me read out the drills to be done, and then he proceeded to ignore any and all practical applications of them. Within less than a stan, we'd run through all the quarterly drills required by the CPJCT. After each one he logged it as being completed.

When we got to the end, he dusted his hands and gave me his supercilious smile. "*That*, Mr. Wang, is how you do it on a real ship."

"*That*, Mr. Burnside, is how you kill people," I said.

Mallory looked startled at my outburst.

"What do you mean by that, Mr. Wang?" The tone in Burnside's voice made it perfectly clear that he knew exactly what I had meant.

I told him anyway. "I mean that by neglecting these drills, you are dooming the crew to die should we have an actual emergency. You've prevented them from getting the practice they need to be able to find, and get into their suits, in the case of a hull breach. If the day comes when we need to abandon ship, crew members will perish when they fail to get to the correct boat on the designated deck in time. By taking this attitude, you are behaving in a criminally negligent manner."

"Perhaps you'd like to take this up with the captain, Mr. Wang?"

"No, Mr. Burnside. I will take it on faith that since the captain has been sitting in the cabin all this time, listening to this travesty of quarterly drills, that he is involved in what can only be referred to as a criminal conspiracy to violate the rules and regulations under which we all hold our licenses. Taking me down to the cabin to have him assure me of such is unnecessary."

"Are you familiar with the term insubordination, Mr. Wang?" he asked with a wolfish grin.

"Yes, Mr. Burnside, I am. Insubordination occurs when a subordinate willfully and deliberately disobeys a legal order."

"And you do not consider this behavior insubordination, Mr. Wang?"

"No, Mr. Burnside. It would be insubordination to refuse to answer your questions fully and accurately. The simple fact that you do not like my answers does not constitute insubordination. Furthermore, my failing to point out this violation of the rules, regulations, and common practices associated with quarterly drills might be construed as dereliction of duty, which would make me liable to being charged for infractions more serious than a claim of insubordination."

Mallory took this all in. His eyes never left the helm display but I saw it in his face.

Burnside must have twigged that he had a witness present as well, because his expression lost some of its confidence.

"That will be all, Mr. Wang."

"Aye, aye, Mr. Burnside," I said and left the bridge.

I wondered if I'd survive to see Diurnia. A lot of accidents can happen in the Deep Dark. I put it out of my mind as best I could. There wasn't anything I could do until we got back to port. I'd probably already said too much, but the *Billy* was a catastrophe that was just waiting to happen—and already had happened to Penny Davies.

When I relieved Arletta for the midwatch that night I asked her, "Have the drills always been like that?"

"More or less. I think he was pushing the point a bit, just because you had made such a big deal out of it."

"He's a menace," I grumbled. "Treating drills like that is a dangerous practice."

"Ishmael," she said with a patient tone, "he's always been a menace. He was a menace before you came. He's still a menace. And unfortunately he's the first mate. There's not a whole lot you can do to him out here."

"True," I agreed. "Even a boot third knows that, but I can file a complaint when we get back to Diurnia."

She looked aghast. "You can't!"

"Why not? The logs are legal documents. He's certified the readiness and safety of the crew in them. And the CPJCT's specifications on drills are clear. You must have them every ninety days. You have to actually hold the drills!"

"Yes, I know," she said with a concerned look, "and you're right. His slapdash approach is dangerous."

She looked at me carefully to make sure she had my attention. "Do me a favor? Look up the pertinent chapter and verse in the CPJCT regulation? See what it says about drills?"

"You think he's right?" I asked.

"No, I think he's wrong, Ishmael," she said, "but I think he's legal. It's stupid but true. Check before you do anything rash, okay?" She held me in her eyes until I had to look away.

"Okay, I'll look it up on watch tonight."

She smiled. "Good man. And in that case, ship is on course and on target..."

I sat there with the Deep Dark all around after she had left. Juliett picked up on my mood, no doubt, because she had no comments for me. Even the redoubtable Ms. D'Heng had little to say. They were going over their last minute studying. The Deck and Steward Divisions would test first, then Engineering and Cargo the following day according to the published schedule.

There were no cargo handlers aboard so that part of the testing would be easy, but before I could deal with scheduling the rest, I needed to see if what Arletta had said was true.

It took the better part of a stan to excavate the pertinent appendix from the *Handbook*, a kind of a everything-you-need-to-know about being a spacer guide, but eventually I found it. The drill needed to consist of a presentation of the correct audible alarm or signal, followed by the prescribed text, and ending with "this is a drill." Rating and evaluation of performance during the drill was left to command discretion. The drill needed to be repeated every ninety days.

I read it three times in disbelief.

According to the CPJCT that travesty of crew safety had been perfectly legal.

I wondered if Burnside had known that at the time.

Two days later, when I relieved Arletta for the evening watch, I was dizzy with lack of sleep and giddy with the results of the ratings exams. Between the watches, the testing, and the overall success rate, I felt like I was making a real difference. Of the fourteen crew, nine did a double step by going up two levels instead of one, and the other five took a solid single step.

I was grinning when I came up the ladder and my only concern was staying awake until midnight when Burnside would relieve me. We now had a ship full of people who were qualified to move on to bigger and better things and I took some pleasure in my contribution to that. We were still twenty days from transition and another five weeks beyond that clawing back to Diurnia.

"Congratulations, Ishmael," Arletta said when she saw me coming. "I saw the results and they're impressive."

"Nothing I did," I told her. "The congratulations go to people like Mr. Betts here." I turned to him and said, "Congrats, Arnold. That was a great jump from able spacer to spec two ship handler."

"Thank you, sar," he said with a self-deprecating grin, "and begging your pardon, sar, but if it hadn't been for you believing in us, and showing us how to do it, none of us would have even tried. So thank *you*, sar."

Arnold looked shocked that he's said so much at once and even Arletta looked a bit taken aback.

I was flattered beyond all belief.

"Thank you, Mr. Betts," I said. "That means a great deal."

Juliett came up over the ladder and I grinned at her. "Another potential ship handler!"

She smiled at me.

"It's all in the wrist," she said.

She went to take her place by the helm and we got on with the business of changing the watch.

Arletta and Arnie Betts went below for dinner and I took a few ticks to check the log status. Things looked normal with no changes to course or speed for our watch. Nothing to do but to sit back and bask in the glow of a job well done.

I heard footsteps on the ladder and saw Ms. Jacobs bringing up my dinner tray. Even from across the bridge I could smell the delicate aromas of grilled fish in dill sauce and herbed rice. I was distracted by the smell and almost overlooked the floor show when Ms. Jacobs leaned down to place the tray on the console beside me.

"There you go, Mr. Wang," she said, leaning on the console longer than she had to in order to make sure I got the full effect. "Bon appetite."

She turned and sashayed back across the deck and down the ladder. Very slowly.

Juliett sniffed. Loudly.

"You have a comment, Ms. Jaxton?" I asked as I unlimbered the implements of ingestion and prepared for personal refueling operations.

"Me, sar?" she asked. "Comment about what, sar?"

"Oh, I don't know," I said, flaking off a bit of the pink fleshed fish. "Market conditions? Price of fuel? New mess mate?"

"Well, sar," she said, working up a head of steam slowly, "far be it from me to pass judgment on my shipmates, sar. I know we were all concerned that she might be the latest in a long line of prey and fall victim to certain members of the ships company who must remain unnamed."

"Indeed, Ms. Jaxton," I said, savoring the herbed rice and marveling at how far Mr. Vorhees had come in such a short time. "And you now believe that those concerns are unfounded?"

"Sar, that woman makes predatory take on all new meaning. If it wasn't for the fact that he'd enjoy it so much, I'd suggest we sic her on that certain member of the ship's company."

"My goodness, Ms. Jaxton, I'm glad you're not one to pass judgment."

"I know, sar. It could get out of hand."

Charlotte skipped up over the ladder and smoothly relieved Juliett for dinner.

"Thank you, Ms. D'Heng. We've been comparing notes about certain new members of the ship's company. Mr. Wang seems interested in how she's fitting in," Juliett said.

"Fitting in? Yes, sar. She's fitting in, and the general consensus among those who have reason to know is that she'll fit just about anything in, sar."

I'd learned some weeks back not to drink coffee while Charlotte D'Heng was speaking. As it was, I nearly choked on a bit of fish.

"Not a person we need to worry about becoming an unwilling victim, then, Ms. D'Heng?" I asked when I finally cleared my windpipe.

"No, sar," she said with a considering tone in her voice, "but I'd be leery about calling her a man-eater, sar."

"Really, Ms. D'Heng?" I should have known better, but she got me off center.

"Yes, sar. She'll likely eat anybody."

"Thank you for that clarification, Ms. D'Heng," I told her with what I considered heroic control. "And congratulations on making able spacer. Very nice job on the exam yesterday."

"Thank you, sar. The study sessions helped, and just knowing that we could jump grades like that made all the difference." She gave me a glance. "You're a nice guy, sar. Thanks."

"You're welcome, Ms. D'Heng," I said and I felt like I was blushing. "What other news can you share with me?"

"Well, sar, Ms. Cramer has inherited the attentions that were once lavished on Ms. Davies. She's ignoring those attentions, including the late night invitations to a certain stateroom."

"Good for her," I said with feeling.

"It helps that she got her able messmate rating, sar. We can expect her to leave the ship in Diurnia. She's always wanted to go to one of those passenger liners."

"I think we'll probably lose a lot of people, won't we?" I said, blatantly fishing.

"It's a long trip back, sar. That's going to depend a lot on what happens between here and there, I think."

"Like what?" I asked.

"Well, the food has gotten a lot better. The coffee, of course, improved almost as soon as you came aboard, sar."

"Those are things that have already happened, Ms. D'Heng."

"You're very sharp for an officer, sar."

"Thank you, Ms. D'Heng. I try hard to keep up."

"Those are things that make people think it doesn't have to be the way it's always been, sar, which gets them thinking about how things might get better."

"Do I want to know what things might get better?"

"Probably not, sar," she said.

"Well, given the success of the last round of testing, can we expect to see a little more participation in the afternoon sessions again?"

"Oh, that's very possible, sar. Not just for the studying but the fun of it. I don't know if you're aware sar, but those sessions were like a party, sort of."

"I hadn't noticed, Ms. D'Heng."

"Remind me to have Ms. Jaxton remind you to keep practicing, sar."

"Practicing, Ms. D'Heng?"

"Lying, sar. She assures me you're working on credibility. You still need work, sar."

"Thank you for your critique, Ms. D'Heng. It's always a breath of fresh air."

"You're quite welcome, sar," she said.

"Having the ship clean and the crew working together has helped, sar," she said after a moment. "We've had a bit of a shock with Ms. Davies and all. We know perfectly well who's responsible and we know none of us can ever prove it." She turned to look at me over her shoulder. "That sticks in the craw of a lot of people."

"Indeed it does, Ms. D'Heng," I said. "But we don't want to stoop that far. If we act like them, then we become them. I'm hoping for better."

"We all do, sar. But I'm willing to let a little of that pride go myself if it means we don't have another Penny Davies."

"Or Alice Stewart?" I added.

"Or Teresa Jaffee, and it's not just the blatant and obvious examples, sar. It's the everyday pick-pick-pick. It's everywhere, sar."

"Fish rots from the head," I murmured.

"What's that, sar?"

"Oh, an old saying, Ms. D'Heng. Sometimes I just talk to myself for no reason."

"I see, sar, and do you also answer, sar?"

I smiled. "Sometimes, Ms. D'Heng."

"I don't think you have to worry unless the answers surprise you, sar."

"Thank you, Ms. D'Heng. I think I've heard that before."

Juliett came back from dinner then, and we set into a quick clean up. In less than a stan, we had the bridge all shiny and clean again. Charlotte even ran the tray back to the galley and picked up three fresh coffees for us.

When she returned and we got ready to settle down she asked, "What should I study, sar?"

I shrugged. "What do you want to know about?"

"Astrogation," she said without any hesitation.

"Then try the spec three in astrogation."

"Why not spec two, sar?" she asked.

"Because you've never worked in astrogation and most of the concepts will be new and foreign. Try spec three and see how you do. If it seems too easy after a couple of weeks, trade up," I suggested.

"Logical, sar."

"I try, Ms. D'Heng."

When nothing happens, it's easy to begin to convince yourself that any suspicions you had held were all paranoid delusions. While the old syllogism about paranoia is undoubtedly valid, and they are all out to get you, the reality is that sometimes paranoia is just a state of mind. You see something. You jump to conclusions. It's self-defense.

We were still about ten days short of Diurnia, and it looked like we'd make it back without any further difficulties. Burnside found his attempts to woo Ms. Cramer ineffectual. I had it on good authority that remembering what happened to his last girlfriend made it easy to ignore his tablet bips. There had been no more assaults reported, and the Bumble Brothers had limited their hostility to a continual sneer punctuated with the odd glare for good measure. Mostly they were ignored when they weren't actively shunned.

We went through transition without any problems. The captain came out of the cabin for the half a stan that he needed to be on the bridge and then disappeared back down the ladder. For a mercy, he didn't call me down to strip my hide for anything. I rather expected to hear about how many of the crew had earned their ratings advances, but he didn't say a word.

My tablet continued to turn on intercom transducers as I moved around the ship. The audio logs were an amusing map of my day and week. I only hoped I hadn't said or done anything incriminating. The alarm that I'd placed on them had never been tripped. It was uncanny, although I suppose it made some sense considering that none of the crew had been aboard when the ship was commissioned.

"Did you hear about Xiang?" Charlotte's voice broke into my

reverie.

I looked up from the watch station and across the bridge. "No, what about Xiang, Ms. D'Heng?"

"Seems he broke his arm," she said.

Juliett was on the helm and she snickered.

"Unfortunate accident?"

She shrugged. "Alone in the gym and reportedly fell off the treadmill."

I raised an eyebrow in her direction. "Does that seem likely, Ms. D'Heng?"

"Absolutely, sar," she replied.

Footsteps on the ladder resolved into Mallory with Burnside not far behind. We relieved the watch and I went to bed very shortly after dinner. Normally I'd have run or done a couple sets of tai chi, but I was exhausted and only wanted to crawl into my bunk. I stripped out of my shipsuit and clambered in, pulling the covers over me and dropping into sleep like a rock into a pond.

I dreamt about a wolf and a fox playing tag in the woods and a falcon soaring in a crystal sky. A graceful heron stood on the edge of a pond and flashed to snatch a silvery fish. It wasn't a very clear or cogent dream but in the end a fierce owl with brilliant green eyes dived at my face, talons outstretched toward my eyes.

I woke with a start, sure that I'd heard something. I lay there for a few heartbeats trying to place the sound. I half expected it to be the bip-bip-beeee of the tablet alarm. I blinked my eyes open enough to see the chrono's glowing digits—0036. The sound didn't repeat so I sighed and snuggled back down into the bunk. I still had a few stans to sleep and I hoped the weird dream didn't start up again. I closed my eyes and started to slip back into the warm darkness, the after images of my stateroom playing against the back of my eyelids.

Just in time I recognized the shape of two people standing inside my door. Only their marginally darker shapes against the shadow of the door gave them away as the after images faded off the inside of my eyelids. I rolled off the bunk and onto the floor as the first fists slammed into the mattress where I'd been lying. Of course, that dropped me onto the feet of my attackers and with nowhere else to go, they fell on top of me in a heap when my weight and momentum caught them off guard. They were as tangled in themselves as they were in me, and that gave me a moment to wriggle out of the pig pile and scramble to the doorway. I flung open the door and slapped the light switch at the same time. The glaring overhead flared and cast a pool of light out into the dimmed passage. I turned to look over my shoulder and saw Apones and Mosler tangled in the narrow area beside my bunk, blinking from the sudden glare, and trying to find where I'd gone. Mosler had a hand up, rubbing the back of his head where he'd apparently found the edge of my desk as he'd fallen.

I was still marveling at the stupidity of trying to get me in my own stateroom, when my training kicked in and I heard movement behind me. I stepped to the side and a hard fist, backed up by a burly forearm, flashed past my face and crashed into the bulkhead. I heard the distinct sound of small bones snapping even over the thud of the blow into the wall and the subsequent wail of pain.

Burnside stood right beside me but he wasn't looking at me. The pain in the hand he'd driven against the wall was claiming the lion's share of his attention. He bit down on the noise and pulled his hand back to his chest, trying to protect it. Behind me I heard Mosler and Apones crawling out from under the desk and heading in my direction. They gained their feet and Apones had a look on his face that said several bad words without actually uttering a sound.

They rushed me, the pair of them. I thought for a heartbeat that they'd bind up in the narrow door, but Mosler hung back just enough to put his shoulder behind Apones and give him that little extra momentum. It was like watching a freight train coming straight at me. I knew it was gonna hurt like hell when they hit.

Tai chi is like that, though. The basic idea is that it's difficult for an opponent to hurt you if you don't stand still for the blow. I shifted my weight to my back leg and let my torso pivot around as the two burly crewmen exploded out of my stateroom. I felt Apones's lowered shoulder just slide across my upper body as I turned, the full mass and momentum of the two heavy bodies sailing by me and into the stationary figure of Burnside. They collided with his broken hand, driving it into his own sternum, before pushing him backward across the passageway where he slammed against the bulkhead hard enough to rattle the ship. I heard sounds from Fredi's and Mel's staterooms and, in the only conscious decision I'd made in the previous tick, I stepped back into my own stateroom and closed the door even before the tangle of groaning men slid to the deck.

All I heard outside was quiet curses and groans, and once, something that sounded like a slap.

My tablet bipped and I retrieved it from the shelf above my bunk.

It was a note from Mel. *You okay?* it asked.

I sent back, *So far.*

Anything I can do? came back once more.

Not tonight, I replied. *Let's talk tomorrow.*

I heard the commotion in the passageway getting sorted out and I braced myself against the door. They didn't try another run, and I heard them scuffling down toward Burnside's stateroom and the sound of a closing door. I let out the breath I'd been holding since stepping back into the room and seriously considered how I was going to secure the door against future attacks.

Burnside had the key codes to every door on the ship. I could change my code, but his access gave him the tools he needed to get in anytime he wanted. What I needed was a mechanical lock, or something to block the door. None of the furniture moved, everything was either bolted or hinged to the bulkheads. My eyes kept dancing from the desk to the chair to the bunk trying to figure out how to solve this problem.

I leaned up against my grav pallet and eyed the distance to the door, wondering if I could do something with the mattress from my bunk. I contemplated if there was a way to situate it so that the door would bind against the mattress if anybody came into my room. It seemed a bit of a stretch. I sighed when the answer came to me. There are days—and apparently nights—when I shouldn't be allowed out alone.

I leaned back, keyed the release on my grav pallet and maneuvered it out of the storage cubby. Sliding it over to block the door with a hundred kilograms of clothes and other artifacts, I made sure my toes were out of the way before I let the pallet settle to the deck. It wasn't flush against the frame, but instead would allow the door to open about two centimeters.

That looked about as secure as I could make it. The door wouldn't open through my trunk, and trying would make a racket.

Satisfied, I crawled back into my bunk and hoped I'd be able to get back to sleep.

I shouldn't have worried.

CHAPTER FORTY-FIVE
DIURNIA SYSTEM: 2358-NOVEMBER-7

My tablet woke me in time for watch and I felt surprisingly refreshed. Nothing like a little violence in the middle of the night to get your blood flowing. I headed for the shower, and the water felt good. I was grateful that I still had skin to feel it on. I did have one bruise on my hip although I couldn't remember where I got it, probably when I fell on the deck.

I got into a fresh shipsuit and eased the grav pallet back to the alcove. I locked it down and locked it closed. He may be able to get into the room, but he was going to have to work hard if he wanted my stuff. Somewhat gingerly, I cracked open the stateroom door and peeked out into the passage. There was one smear of something that could have been blood, down near the deck about where Mosler would have landed—face first, no doubt.

The coast seemed clear so I moved out, secured the door, and headed to the mess deck to get a cup of coffee to take to the bridge. I knew that Karen would be bringing coffee with breakfast, but that was almost a stan away and I wasn't about to wait.

When I got back to the bridge, I found all of second section gaping at me as I came up over the ladder. I checked my zippers ostentatiously and looked over my shoulder to see if there was anybody behind me. There wasn't. I was about ten ticks early to relieve the watch.

"Mr. Wang?" Arletta said, "A moment, if you please?" She nodded to the bridge wing.

"You're not gonna hit me, are you?" I asked with a small smile.

"I will if you don't tell me what happened last night, and I mean now, mister!" she said it fiercely and I was almost afraid.

It was quite a performance.

"Burnside sent the Bumble Brothers to rough me up last night," I said flatly with my back to the bridge. I wasn't sure how far the story had spread yet.

"Are you all right?" she asked, her brow furrowing in concern and her eyes scanning me for damage.

I shrugged and sipped my coffee. "I got a bruise on my hip, right about there," I said pointing to the approximate location.

She looked confused.

"I rolled off my bunk, and I think I hit their feet. Other than that, they never came close."

I gave her the quick outline, ending with using my grav pallet to block the door.

"They could have come through the head," she said.

"Yeah," I agreed, "but they had quite a lot to think about last night. David has a broken left hand, and probably a cracked rib or two. Those boys were traveling fast and the bulkhead is hard. One of them lost some blood from planting his nose, and it wouldn't surprise me to find out that at least one of them has a black eye. I'll talk to Mel today and see if there's some kind of deadbolt arrangement I can use on my side of the head. If they come through the door, that's one thing. But I'd like to prevent them from opening it first."

We stood there looking at each other.

"This is really messed up," she said.

"Ya think?"

"What can we do about it?" she asked.

"Relieve the watch so you can get breakfast, and let Mel know I'm okay. She heard the crashing and sent me a message on the tablet."

"Ishmael, we heard the clamor up here. I sent Ulla down to look, but by the time she got there, there was nothing to see."

"Well, that's a relief. The last thing they needed was a witness. I'm going to be interested to hear what story they come up with."

"Story for what?" Arletta asked.

"Well, David's going to show up for breakfast in a cast. It's going to be difficult to hide," I noted.

"You mean it? He broke his hand? That wasn't a figure of speech?"

"Well maybe only a few fingers, but yeah I think some of the small bones as well." I shrugged. "I could be wrong, but his fist was right beside my ear when it hit. It sounded nasty. The bulkheads are rather hard and somewhat unyielding. Mosler smashed the back of his head on my desk when he fell, and I suspect it was him that bloodied his nose when they bounced David off the bulkhead. You can see the blood on the plates just above the deck when you go down."

"What about Apones?" she asked.

"He was sandwiched between David and Mosler when the bulkhead stopped them. A lot will depend on how much cushion he got from David's body. For that matter, David may have a broken rib or two as well as the hand. It just won't be obvious."

Juliett came up the ladder then and I saw the relief in her face when she saw me standing there.

"Well, shall we do this thing we call watch?" I asked Arletta.

"The ship is on course and target. Loud noises in the passageway last night, but investigation turned up nothing significant. You may relieve the watch."

"You logged it?" I asked incredulously.

"What else could I do? I wasn't sure what was happening, but I know it happened less than a stan after I took the watch."

"I have the watch, Ms. Novea. Logged on 2358-November-7, at 0545 per standing order."

Juliett and Betts swapped places at the helm, and if she patted him on the butt in passing, I didn't see it, although I did approve. Mr. Betts went up a couple of notches in my estimation.

I sat down at the watch console and sipped coffee and reviewed the sparse notes that Arletta had posted. It wasn't very specific, but it did establish the time and place. I shrugged mentally.

Juliett was waiting patiently for me to finish my review but I could tell she was about ready to burst.

"Ms. Jaxton? Is everything all right?" I asked. "You seem a bit jumpy this morning."

"Very fine, sar, I was just concerned. There were stories..."

"Stories, Ms. Jaxton? I thought we'd established that gossip mongering was Ms. D'Heng's job?"

"Indeed we have, sar, and far be it from me to even try to step into her very capable shoes. Still, even amateurs hear things."

"Things, Ms. Jaxton? Could you be more specific? Is there going to be rain this afternoon? Should we man the bilge pumps?"

She chuckled. "Well, sar. Mr. Burnside is locked in the auto-doc. It won't let him out."

"Locked?" I asked.

"Yes, sar, apparently he had some kind of accident last night and when he went to sick bay and got into the auto-doc, it latched down and is still treating him."

"That seems extreme, Ms. Jaxton," I said. "Does anybody know what kind of damage he's being treated for?"

"According to Mr. Apones, he has a broken hand, three broken ribs, and a concussion."

"A concussion?" I couldn't help but ask, but as soon as I did, I knew how it happened. Those bulkheads are hard and with Apones and Mosler slamming into your chest, the whiplash would have been pretty painful.

"Yes, sar, apparently he bumped his head on something."

"That would follow," I agreed. I wondered if we'd be watch-and-watch for the ride into Diurnia. On the other hand, having nobody in the chair would probably improve the safety and security of the ship from what I'd seen of his watch standing habits.

"Is anybody saying how all this damage came about?" I asked after a few heartbeats.

"No, sar, although a few people thought they heard something just after the midwatch changed. Some kind of loud crash in officer country."

"Perhaps he fell out of bed," I suggested.

"Onto Apones and Mosler, sar?"

I blinked as I caught up. "Why? What's wrong with them?"

"Mosler has a broken nose, and Apones has a strained shoulder and a black eye."

"What a dangerous night it was," I said.

"Yes, sar, apparently so," she agreed.

"I'm glad I was safe in my stateroom and out of harm's way."

"Yes, sar, I am too." After a moment she added, "And, sar?"

"Yes, Ms. Jaxton?"

"Keep practicing, sar. You're getting better, but still not quite there."

"Thank you for the critique, Ms. Jaxton. I'll take it under advisement."

"Yes, sar. You're very welcome, sar," she said with a perfectly straight face and not even a hint of a giggle in her voice. It was masterful. Really.

A few ticks later, Ms. Cramer came up the ladder looking in my direction like she wasn't sure what she was going to see. It pleased me to see her look of relief.

"Here you go, sar," she said, walking up to the console and placing my dinner tray on the customary corner.

"Thank you, Ms. Cramer, it looks as delicious as ever."

She headed down over the ladder and must have passed Charlotte coming up.

"You two aren't mongering in my absence are you?" she asked brightly when she got to the bridge.

"Not at all, Ms. D'Heng," I assured her. "We were just comparing notes in preparation for your arrival."

I settled down to my breakfast while they traded the helm off and Juliett went below.

"So, what fresh news have you this morning, Ms. D'Heng?" I asked.

"Well, sar, there are rumors—and I stress that they are only rumors—that Mr. Burnside will be in the auto-doc for the rest of the day."

"The rest of the day? Isn't that rather extreme?"

"He took a blow to the chest, sar, that seems to have broken three ribs and cracked two others. You may be aware, sar, that lungs and heart are located behind the ribs?"

"I had heard something to that effect, yes, Ms. D'Heng, from relatively reliable sources."

"Yes, sar, I try not to put too much stock in unconfirmed reports, as you know," she assured me.

"Very good policy to have, Ms. D'Heng."

"Thank you, sar. Very nice of you to say so."

"Ms. D'Heng? We'll likely be in Diurnia in about nine days..." I prompted.

"Oh, yes, sar, well, the auto-doc has him latched in and sedated. It won't release him until it's stabilized his ribs and made sure he's not going to stab himself from the inside."

"And the concussion?"

"Oh, sar? Has that story made it up here already?" she turned to me, eyes narrowing suspiciously. "Are you certain you two weren't... you know... telling stories?"

"Well, the subject might have come up, but I assure you that it was inadvertent."

She looked unconvinced but proceeded. "Yes, he has a concussion and a rather large contusion on the back of his head, but that's a relatively minor issue."

"Relatively," I repeated.

"Compared to the ribs, yes, sar."

"I see. And in any of these rumors are there any suggestions as to what may have been the cause?" I asked.

"Oh, yes, sar. According to Mr. Apones, he tripped."

"Mr. Apones tripped?" I asked.

"No, sar, Mr. Burnside tripped."

"And fell on his... head?"

"Oh, no, sar," she smiled as if I were being quite funny. "On his side. That's how he broke his ribs."

"And the contusion on the back of his head? How did that occur?"

"Mr. Apones hasn't offered any explanation for that, sar."

"Has anyone else?" I asked.

"Well, there are rumors, sar."

"Yes, I'm sure," I said. "And his broken hand?"

"Mr. Apones has a broken hand, sar?"

"No, Mr. Burnside's broken hand."

She looked at me aghast, her eyes wide in surprise. "He has a broken hand?"

"It was just a rumor, Ms. D'Heng."

"You should be more careful, sar. There are a lot of amateurs around. They spread all kinds of tales."

"Thank you for that reminder, Ms. D'Heng. That will teach me to listen to amateurs," I assured her as graciously as I could.

She sniffed in dismissal. "I should hope so. Why there's one story making the rounds that Burnside let Apones and Mosler into your stateroom at about 0045 this morning, in order to pound some sense into you, and get you out of their way. But instead of pounding you senseless, you managed to give them the slip and got out into the passageway in your skivvies. When Burnside found you, he took a swing and broke his left hand on the bulkhead when you ducked, and then was steamrollered by his own thugs when you stepped out of their way. They slammed him across from your stateroom, which is how he got his ribcage smashed in and that nasty bonk on the back of the head."

I practically choked on my coffee and mentally kicked myself for drinking while Ms. D'Heng was speaking.

"Of course, that's just a rumor, sar. There isn't one shred of evidence to support it." She assured me.

"Rather a detailed rumor," I said.

"Oh, you know how people like to embroider stories, sar."

"And you're sure there's no evidence?" I asked, thinking I'd tripped her up.

"Quite sure, yes, sar. It's just a rumor."

"I see," I said quietly.

"Oh, sar?" she asked after a moment. "Did you know there was some kind of red smudge on the bulkhead across from your stateroom?"

"I think I saw something there this morning on my way to relieve the watch, yes," I said. "Why?"

"Oh, well, if you saw it why didn't you clean it up?" she asked crossly. "Aren't you always after us to keep the ship neat and clean?"

"I should have but I was in a hurry to get to the bridge."

"I understand, sar. It's okay," she said, her face crinkling into a smile. "I cleaned it."

Chapter Forty-six
Diurnia System: 2358-November-7

About 0945 Mel, followed by Arletta and Fredi, came onto the bridge. I gave Charlotte the nod and she discretely excused herself, while the rest of us gathered in the bridge wing.

Mel looked at me with an expression that was more curiosity than concern. "Well, you've probably heard we have a little problem."

"He's locked in the auto-doc?" I asked.

Fredi's grin was almost indecent. "Yes, and if I'm reading the diagnostic protocols correctly," she said, "he's going to be in there for a while until the quik-knit deals with his ribs."

"At least overnight, and then probably confined to bed rest until we get to Diurnia," Mel said.

She looked at me again with that "curious but I'm not going to ask" expression.

I shrugged. "Okay, so, what do we do?"

Mel made a sour face. "On a normal ship, the captain would take the watch."

"He's coming out of the cabin?" I asked surprised.

She shook her head. "I said on a normal ship. I reported Burnside's condition to the captain right after breakfast. That's why we're here."

I looked from face to face to face. "Arletta and I are going watch on watch?" I asked. Watch-on-watch was basically a two section rotation of twelve on and twelve off around the clock.

Fredi said, "I'm going to take over the first section."

I gaped at her. "So, is this something you've always wanted to do? Stand long deck watches with potentially violent crewmen?"

She smiled. "Oh, Steve Mallory isn't that bad, and he's the best

271

ship handler we have. Without Mosler and Burnside to back him up, I think we can count on Apones to toe the line."

"Where's Mosler?" I asked, not following the whole transaction yet.

"Mosler and Apones are confined to quarters except for meals and watch. That means Apones stays in deck berthing forward, and Mosler in engineering berthing aft. Never the twain shall meet, except on the mess deck and even then rarely," Mel said.

"When did that happen?" I asked.

"We're about to let them know. They're being held on suspicion of assaulting an officer," Mel said.

"Assaulting an officer?" I asked.

Arletta was in on it. I could tell because she was grinning, but I still hadn't caught up to the joke.

"But there's no proof they assaulted me," I said.

"Who said anything about you?" Fredi asked. "Poor David is in the auto-doc. And all Mr. Apones can tell us is he tripped? I'm sorry. That sounds very fishy to me."

Arletta's face took on an innocently agreeable look. "Me too. He and Mosler even have the marks and bruises to show that they were in some kind of scrap. Too darn coincidental if you ask me."

Mel shrugged. "And there we have it." She looked to me. "Are we clear?"

"Until *poor David* gets out of the auto-doc and starts raising a stink," I pointed out.

"You leave *poor David* to me," Mel said. "He can't admit what really happened because then he'll be in the soup. If he lets his stooges hang fire for a while, we'll drop the charges when we get to port in a few days."

I thought about it and realized that Mel had the right of it. She was senior officer present by virtue of being chief of engineering. She also had stanyers of experience, which helped her credibility. Until, and unless, the captain countermanded her orders, and so long as the first mate was disabled, she held operational command. They'd drilled the chain of command into us at the academy and the sense of it was indisputable.

"Okay," I said, "we're clear. Welcome to the deck watch, Fredi."

"Thank you, Ishmael. I think it will be quite fun for a few days. And, if I'm going to relieve you at midnight, I need to take care of a few things." She smiled all around and added, "If you'll excuse me?"

We all shrugged or nodded or both, and she picked her way delicately back off the bridge with a smile for Juliett along the way.

Mel turned to Arletta. "You've got the watch at noon?" she

asked pointedly.

"Oh, yes, I do," she said, taking the hint and following Fredi off the bridge.

Mel's curiosity boiled over. "What in the name of heaven happened last night?"

I felt like I should call Charlotte up to give the recap, but I gave Mel the highlights, finishing with, "And that crash you heard was Burnside being driven into the bulkhead by Apones and Mosler."

"No wonder he broke ribs. He's lucky to be alive," she said. She frowned a little looking at me, "And you didn't get a scratch?"

"I got a bruise on my hip when I rolled off the bunk," I said, pointing.

Her face took on an odd look for a moment. "No, don't show me," she said, with a short shake of her head. "They really did assault an officer. They hit him, drove him into the bulkhead, and broke his ribs. That's just icing on the cake!"

"How did you think he got beaten up?" I asked.

She grimaced a little. "Well," she said, dragging it out, "we knew he was after you."

I laughed in surprise. "You flatter me! There's no way I could hit him hard enough to break a rib."

"With friends like he has, you won't need to, but watch your step anyway, okay?"

"Yeah, I will. Thanks, Mel." I paused. "Oh, is there anything like a deadbolt or a door stop I can use so I can sleep without worrying that he's gonna turn the Bumble Brothers loose on me again? I need something to make sure the head door stays closed."

"You think they'd enter through Arletta's room and then through the head?"

"They did it before with Jaffee."

She looked at me for about three heartbeats before she said, "Lemme look into my bag of tricks. I'll get back to you."

"Thanks," I told her. "For everything."

She just winked and headed for the ladder.

Juliett and I settled down and Charlotte came up to the bridge around 1030 with fresh coffee.

"Big doing's?" I asked as she came up the ladder.

"Nothing you don't already know, sar. Apones and Mosler are taking it pretty well."

"Without a patron, they've gotta be feeling the breeze they're swinging in," Juliett said. "They'll bide their time until he's out of the auto-doc."

"What's the feeling on Ms. DeGrut taking over first section?"

Charlotte lifted one shoulder in a half shrug. "Most people think it should be the captain, but nobody expects he'll come out of the cabin until we set navigation stations."

"What's he doing in there?" I asked.

"We're not sure, sar," Charlotte admitted. "Nobody ever goes in or out, hardly."

I thought about Simon and Bayless and wondered why the rumor mill didn't know about them.

"Why? Do you know something, sar?" Charlotte asked sharply, watching my face carefully.

"I have no idea what he does in there. For all I know, he's writing poetry."

Juliett glanced at me out of the corner of her eye, but Charlotte nodded and sipped her coffee.

Arletta relieved me on time at 1145. "I have no idea how anybody else is taking it. David's still in the auto-doc, the Bumble Brothers are keeping their heads down." She followed it with a little shrug. "With Mel calling the shots, nobody's saying boo."

"Well in that case...the ship is on course and on target. No incidents or actions. Standing orders are unchanged. You may relieve the watch, Ms. Novea."

"I have the watch, Mr. Wang. Logged 2358-November-7, at 1145 in accordance with standing orders," she said with a grin.

I headed for my stateroom and a quick clean up before I went to the wardroom for lunch. Fredi and Mel were there and Ms. Cramer brought the food right in. She smiled shyly at me and I thought she looked a little more rested, a little less stressed than she had in a while. I wondered if Apones or Mosler had been harassing her.

"Any news on David?" I asked when Karen had gone.

Mel shrugged. "I looked in at the auto-doc just before I came down. It's showing that he'll be getting out in the morning. I suspect he'll be as weak as a kitten after this. He's going to be moving very slowly."

"What's to prevent him from just getting out of the auto-doc and making demands?" I asked.

"He can't," Fredi said. "Well no, he can, but he has no standing until the auto-doc clears him for duty. He'll have to report back to it until it says he can go to work, and even then, maybe longer."

I shrugged and finished my lunch. "He's not gonna be very happy, is he."

Mel snickered and Fredi actually laughed.

With just the three of us, lunch went pretty quickly. I needed a nap before I had to go back up to the bridge at six so I excused myself and went to my stateroom. On the inside of the door, I found that somebody had installed solid bolt locks on the inside of both my stateroom door, and the door to the head.

I threw the bolts on both doors, stripped to skivvies, and crawled into bed. It felt glorious, and even though I knew it was only for a little while, I thoroughly enjoyed it.

Chapter Forty-seven
Diurnia System: 2358-November-7

Fredi dispelled any reservations I may have had about her taking over First Section on that first midwatch. Around 2330 her slight, almost bird like, frail frame stepped delicately onto the bridge. She had her usual shy smile, but there was more to it. I can't put my finger on what it was, but something like a sense of "this is going to be fun" radiated from her.

And I believed it.

"Hello, Juliett. How are you tonight?" she asked on the way past the helm, pausing to listen.

"I'm fine, Ms. DeGrut. Ready for a little sleep, but very good, and you? Are you ready for the midwatch?"

"Oh, yes," Fredi replied with a gentle enthusiasm. "I think this is going to be ever so much more fun than riding herd on a tin can."

At that moment, I knew I was watching a pro.

Fredi continued onto the bridge and came over to the watch station. "Good evening, Ishmael," she said with a smile.

"Hi, Fredi. You seem pretty enthusiastic."

She gave a little half shrug. "One does what one must to chip in," she murmured. After a moment she added, "But yes, I'm looking forward to doing more than sitting around watching the ship go to hell."

She looked me in the eye when she said it, and I knew right then why Frederica DeGrut was number eight on the Alys Giggone's hit parade. It made me wonder why I was on it at all.

"Would you ask the delightful Ms. D'Heng to join us so we can relieve the watch on the bridge?" she asked me.

"Of course," I said and bipped Charlotte's tablet. "That's a great idea," I added while mentally kicking myself for not thinking of it on my own.

She smiled and sipped her coffee, her eyes roaming the bridge. She nodded to the locker door at the back. "Broom closet?" she asked.

"Yes, and there's a full maintenance cupboard just at the foot of the ladder below," I said.

"Excellent," she chirped. "Now, I've been over the standing orders for deck watch standers and this console looks standard. Is there anything I need to be on the lookout for? Things that are common knowledge but not in the book?"

"Well, we generally give the bridge a good cleaning on midwatch, but we've also been in the habit of giving it a quick wipe at the beginning of each watch."

She nodded. "Might make more sense to do it at the end of each watch," she suggested. "Leave it nice for the next section."

"Very true, but there was a problem..."

"Ah," she said, catching on immediately. "Somebody wasn't pulling his weight?"

"Just so."

"Well, that factor has been removed from the equation for the moment," she said. "We'll have to see what we can do, eh?"

Charlotte came up the ladder then with Mallory and Apones close behind. "Hail, hail, the gang's all here," Fredi said brightly. She set her coffee cup on the console with a glance at me, "One moment, Mr. Wang?"

I had no idea what she was about to say so I just said, "Of course, Ms. DeGrut."

Apones and Mallory had stopped at the top of the ladder. I knew they couldn't have been surprised by Fredi's presence on the bridge, but with both watches present, everything seemed a little out of kilter.

Fredi crossed to where they were standing and said, "First section, attention."

She didn't bark it in the approved drill instructor manner. It was more like a dog owner bringing a pair of puppies to heel. Mallory came to immediate attention and even Apones seemed surprised by his own compliance.

Fredi looked Mallory up and down, walking behind him as if appraising a particularly interesting horse. When she got to the front, she reached out one fine-boned hand and zipped a half open pocket on the side of his suit. Nodding to him with a smile, she moved to Apones. She frowned and tsked, walking around him the same way she had Mallory.

"As you were," she told them and crossed back to the watch

station. "Well, Mr. Wang, I'm ready if you are..." she said.

"The ship is on course and on target. No incidents or actions. Standing orders are unchanged. You may relieve the watch, Ms. DeGrut," I said smartly standing beside the station.

"First section has the watch, Mr. Wang. Logged 2358-November-7, at 2345 in accordance with long practice and standing orders," she said with a gleeful grin.

Mallory took Juliett's place at the helm and Apones started to turn and head down the ladder.

"A moment, Mr. Apones, if you please," Fredi called.

Apones froze like some cartoon character caught in mid-sneak.

Fredi arched one eyebrow in my direction as if to ask, "Why are you still on my bridge?"

I grinned and headed for the ladder, the rest of third watch in a file behind me. At the bottom of the ladder, we all stood there looking at each other in amazement for a moment before the two women headed on down the passageway. I stood there for a moment, reviewing the previous few ticks in my mind with equal parts awe and amusement, before heading down the passage toward my stateroom.

Behind me I heard Fredi bark, "Now! Mr. Apones."

I looked over my shoulder to see Apones belting down the bridge ladder and heading for berthing at a near trot. He spared one glowering look in my direction—a look marred by the black eye—but didn't linger.

Suppressing a chuckle, at least until he was out of earshot, I continued to my stateroom. Inside I threw the bolt, more to get into the habit than anything else. With Burnside locked in the auto-doc and Apones on a short leash, there didn't seem to be much threat on the ship.

I went into the head to do the needful and wash the day's grime off my face. It had been a long day, but I wasn't quite ready for sleep. The beginning of a twenty-four always seemed to have such potential but I always started it exhausted. I heard a quiet tap on Arletta's door and a mumbled, "Ya decent?"

"You should be sleeping," I said through the door, "but yeah. What's up?"

I heard a bolt slide on her side of the door and the latch released. She blinked into the bright light of the head as she opened it a crack. She was sitting on the side of her bunk in her ship tee and boxers looking tousled and thoroughly wonderful. I stuck my head back into the sink and splashed more cold water on my face.

"How's she doing?" Arletta asked.

"Great," I said, running a towel over my face. "I'm taking

notes."

"Really?" she asked with a grin. "About what?"

"Well, she started by having me call Charlotte up to the bridge so we could relieve the watch all together."

"Yeah," she said with a little yawn. "We talked about that at dinner."

"Then she had them stand at attention and inspected them before she'd relieve the watch."

Arletta blinked and chuckled. "And how did that go over?"

"Mallory had no problems, but I think she sent Apones down to change after the watch was relieved."

"He'll be standing his watch on the bridge," Arletta said. "Fredi likes that idea a lot."

"Oh, she also suggested that we should do our quick clean up at the end of the watch to leave it clean for the incoming one."

"What an idea!" she said with mock sarcasm.

"I thought so. She asked where all the cleaning gear was before I left. She's going to get First Watch to do their share, it seems."

"Nice," she nodded sleepily.

I took the hint and backed out to my stateroom. "Oh, did I hear you throw back a bolt to open the door?"

She grinned and took advantage of my leaving the space to step in herself. "Yeah. I saw Raymond doing the install on yours and asked if I could have a set too. Seems like overkill now."

"We're not out of the woods, but I know what you mean," I told her. I gave a little wave as I closed my side of the door. "G'night. See you at lunch tomorrow."

Stripping out of my shipsuit, I crawled into my bunk. I wasn't tired but there really wasn't anything I wanted to do—I glanced at the chrono on the bulkhead—0015. I snuggled myself down into the bunk, cuddling myself under the blanket and tried not to think about how good a warm and sleepy Arletta Novea looked in ship tee and boxers.

I woke in time to grab a quick shower before breakfast and when I got to the wardroom I found Mel and Ms. Cramer having a conversation that ended as I came through the door.

"Coffee, sar?" Ms. Cramer asked and poured a cup before placing the pot on the table. "It'll be just you two and Ms. DeGrut for breakfast, then?" she asked.

Mel shrugged. "I assume Ms. DeGrut will join us, yes. Mr. Burnside is a bit tied up, still."

Ms. Cramer grinned a bit at that. "Yes, sar. I'm aware." She gave a little nod—not quite a bow—and headed back through the pantry door. "I'll be back in a few ticks with your breakfast, sars," she called over her shoulder.

I took my seat as Mel took hers and we sipped coffee. "She seems chipper this morning," I noted.

"Yes, she does."

I raised a mental eyebrow at that and wondered what was going on, but didn't ask.

"How did Fredi do last night?" Mel asked.

"She did quite well, thank you, and she's here so you can ask her yourself," Fredi said with a grin as she swept through the door.

I reached to pour coffee for her and she smiled her "thank you" across the table at me.

Mel grinned at her. "You certainly look proud of yourself this morning."

"Why, thank you! I am," she replied, taking a sip of her own coffee and sighing in delight. "The bridge has been thoroughly cleaned. Mr. Apones will be reporting to duty in a clean shipsuit, and Mr. Mallory is really a very nice fellow. Quite a good time, even with Mr. Apones scowling at me across the bridge all night."

"What did you have him doing?" Mel asked. "Just sitting there?"

"Oh, no," Fredi said, "We cleaned the bridge. It was quite therapeutic."

Ms. Cramer brought our breakfasts then, with a bright smile and a flourish she set us each up with a delicious looking omelet with a side of bacon and some toast. She flitted in, did her job, and flitted out almost before we could say, "Thank you, Ms. Cramer."

Fredi raised her eyebrows in surprise and looking at Mel asked, "She's not usually so lively in the morning, is she?"

Mel shook her head. "Not as a rule."

"Is there a cause for this lively good humor this morning?" Fredi asked by way of making conversation as she buttered her toast.

Mel smirked. "Yes, actually there is."

Fredi glanced at me before looking back to Mel. "And you're not going to say what it is, are you."

Mel grinned and shook her head. "Not for me to comment. Let's just say, it's been a rough voyage for Ms. Cramer up to now."

Personally, I thought it had been a rough voyage for just about everybody, but I didn't say anything.

CHAPTER FORTY-EIGHT
DIURNIA ORBITAL: 2358-NOVEMBER-16

After all the excitement, the actual final approach and dock with Diurnia was pretty anticlimactic. David got out of the auto-doc after a full day in the can. He was still in a lot of pain and just stayed in the treatment booth for the better part of the following week. He never did get approved for active duty again before we docked. Ms. DeGrut handled the first mate chores for docking and did a bang up job of it.

Mel had placed a call to the orbital's med facility a couple of stans before we picked up the tugs, and two green-smocked medicos were waiting on the dock with the customs inspectors. The medicos had a kind of one-person grav pallet which they floated up to officer country. They grabbed a copy of the auto-doc's records and strapped David Burnside down on the transporter. By the time Fredi had the customs people happy, and the embargo locker secured, the medics were only waiting for the official say so to float him off the ship.

The captain did emerge from the cabin in time to take his seat during the navigation detail, but contributed no more to the process than he had on undocking. At least when he left the bridge, he didn't call me into the cabin. I wasn't sure if that was a good sign or not, but I suspected that he didn't want to be slowed down in his exit from the ship. According to D'Heng, he had the medical staff wait until he was clear before taking David for evaluation and treatment. At the speed he was moving, that wasn't a long wait, but it was still the principle of the thing. I know the senior officer has precedent for entering or leaving a vessel but to jump ahead of the ambulance, that was just low.

With both of them physically off the ship, that put Mel officially in charge and she set about organizing the rest of the crew. Liberty had been delayed while the confederation officials certified the embargo and Third Watch had the duty. Before we even got settled, Juliett bipped me on my tablet.

"Geoff Maloney is at the lock and wanting the OD."

I knew the name of course and forwarded the message to Mel as an FYI.

When I rounded the corner and headed for the lock, I honestly didn't know what to expect. I certainly wasn't expecting to see Harvey Blalock and his body guard, Kurt. I must have looked confused as I approached the brow. Juliett looked concerned and I saw her trying to figure out how to get the man-mountain out of the lock if things went wooly.

It all clicked for me when Kurt gave me one of his small smiles.

I stuck out my hand to his employer and said, "Mr. Maloney, I presume? Nice to see you again."

He had a pleasant enough smile and looked very much at ease while standing in the lock of one of his own ships. "Mr. Wang," he said. "I'm sorry I wasn't able to get to know you more on the way out from Newmar. Business, you know."

I turned to Kurt and gave an appropriately low bow. "Thank you for your lessons. They were very useful."

He actually smiled and returned the bow—still Teacher to Student—but at least not Master to Apprentice.

"How can I help you, Mr. Maloney?"

"Has any of the crew left the ship except for Rossett and Burnside?" he asked.

I looked to Juliett who replied, "No, sar. Liberty has not been declared and no personnel have left on ship's business."

"Very good," Maloney said. "Would you please close the lock and seal it, Mr. Wang? And then ask Ms. Menas to join us on the bridge?"

"Ms. Jaxton?" I said.

"Close and seal, aye, sar," she replied. She suited words to actions and the lock hummed shut with a *thunk*.

"One more thing, Ms. Jaxton..." I said.

"Sar?"

"Have you ever met Geoff Maloney, or seen a picture of him? Are you prepared to identify this gentleman as who he claims to be?" I asked.

"Sar?" she squeaked in alarm.

"Do you know if this man is Geoff Maloney, Ms. Jaxton? Have you ever met him before or seen him on the ship?" I asked again.

"No, sar. I have never met the owner. I cannot confirm that

this man is Geoff Maloney," she said.

"In that case, would you please contact home office and have them confirm the identity of these gentlemen, Ms. Jaxton?"

Juliett blanched, and I saw Kurt's lips twitch very slightly. Geoff Maloney on the other hand stared at me like I'd grown another head. "Mr. Wang? Are you insane?" he asked.

"Quite likely, sar. But until I can confirm who you are, I'd prefer not to let you loose in the ship or release you to the dock."

He started to say something but stopped, his mouth half open. "You're a strange man, Mr. Wang," he said finally.

"Thank you, sar," I told him with a small bow. "So I've been told."

Behind me I heard footsteps and Fredi stepped up beside me. "Hello, Geoff," she said with a smile. "Fancy meeting you here."

"Hello, Frederica," he answered with a cockeyed grin. "Your Mr. Wang here won't let me on my ship until I can verify my identity."

"Is that true, Ishmael?" she asked, turning those startlingly green eyes on me.

"Well, of course." I said. "The last time I met this gentleman he traveled under the name Harvey Blalock. I have never met the owner and simply require proof of his identity this time before I allow him access to the ship."

Kurt's lips twitched again and for that matter so did Fredi's.

"Thank you, Ishmael," she said, "that was rather fast thinking, but will you accept my personal assurances that this is, in fact, Geoff Maloney, owner of Diurnia Salvage and Transport and registered owner of the *William Tinker*?"

"Of course," I said. "Juliett, belay that last order."

"Aye, sar," she said with something akin to relief and disbelief on her face.

"Frederica?" Mr. Maloney asked. "Could we convene the officers on the bridge, please?"

"Of course, Geoff," she said graciously. "Ishmael, would you have Mel and Arletta meet us upstairs in five ticks?"

"My pleasure," I said and pulled out my tablet and flashed a quick message.

Fredi smiled at Juliett before turning to the guests. "Gentlemen, I believe you know the way?" she asked and extended a welcoming hand ushering them into the ship.

As they walked, Maloney leading the way with Kurt at his shoulder, Fredi turned to me with the strangest smile and just shook her head before following them into the ship.

When we got to the bridge, Mel and Arletta were already there. Fredi served as hostess and made the introductions. "Amelia Menas,

Chief Engineer, and senior officer present. This is the owner, Geoffrey Maloney."

Mel shook hands with him and murmured, "Pleased to meet
you, Mr. Maloney."

"Arletta Novea, Second Mate, Astrogation," she said holding a
hand to Arletta. "Mr. Maloney."

Arletta looked a little dazed. It's not every day one gets to meet
the owner of a shipping line.

"Thank you, all," Maloney said when the introductions were
done. "I'll keep this brief, because I know you have a crew that
would enjoy getting ashore. Your turnaround time is going to be a
bit delayed, so they'll have a day or two on the other end to make
up for not getting off the ship sooner," he said with a smile.

He appeared to understand the importance of liberty.

"As of this moment, with all of you as witnesses, I hereby relieve
Captain Leon Rossett of his duty as captain by my authority of the
owner of this vessel, pursuant to the rules and regulations set forth
under the Confederated Planets Joint Committee on Trade and in
accordance with the terms of his contract. In the absence of a commanding officer, I further hereby appoint Chief Engineer Amelia
Menas acting captain until such time as an individual holding appropriate Master's Certification can be hired. Until that time, this
ship may not get underway for any reason except those required
for maintenance of the ship or the station." Maloney stopped and
looked around at our faces. Mel looked stunned, Fredi looked—
well—like Fredi, and Arletta still had that dazed "I can't believe
I've met the owner" look.

Apparently satisfied by what he'd seen, he turned toward Mel
and continued. "Ms. Menas, as acting captain it is within your
purview to release First Mate David Burnside from his contract
and, as owner, I encourage you to do so." He paused, weighing his
words.

"Okay, folks, here's the deal," he said, abandoning the officialese.
"We know that Rossett is an idiot, and Burnside a criminal. He
ordered that poor woman to be beaten on Breakall Orbital. He
orchestrated attacks on at least three other crew, but what we know
and what we can prove in a court of law are two different things.
All we can do, and what you people have given me an opportunity
to do, is cashier a captain who should have been relieved long ago.
That, and get rid of the sadist that was pulling his strings. The
Tinker deserves better, and just walking up here from the lock, I'm
grateful for what you've accomplished."

He looked around the bridge at us.

"It's going to be hard to watch them 'get away with it' but this much I can promise you. Leon Rossett will lose his Master's Ticket for dereliction of duty and David Burnside will be blacklisted from here to Gretna and back. I can't pull his ticket, but I can sure as hell punch his clock," he said with a vicious grin.

"What I'm giving you is the *Tinker*. We need to find a captain and fill in some holes in the crew roster. I suspect we'll have a pretty good migration of hands off the ship between the change of command and the newly rated spacers you managed to train up out in the Deep Dark, so you'll have your work cut out for you, but you've worked a miracle here. I'm sure you're up to the rest."

He looked around once more.

"Any questions?" he asked.

There was a simultaneous and unanimous, "No, sar."

"Okay then, Ms. Menas, it's your baby for the moment. I'll try not to keep you in the hot seat any longer than necessary."

She smiled. "Thank you, Mr. Maloney. It'll be a good opportunity to clean house."

"You have my complete backing. If you need anything, call. I'll have my personal contact ID sent to your tablet."

She nodded her thanks.

"Mr. Wang, if you'd walk me back to the lock and ask your formidable Ms. Jaxton to let us go?"

Mel looked shocked, but Fredi just smiled that Fredi smile and her green eyes twinkled at me.

"Of course, Mr. Maloney. Right this way," I said, leading them down off the bridge.

When we got to the lock, I had Juliett open up, and I walked them to the dock.

"Mr. Wang, I wanted to thank you personally," Maloney said. "And apologize for setting you up."

"Sar?"

"I've been trying to get rid of Leon Rossett for the last five stanyers but contrary to popular belief, I can't just fire a captain because I don't like him. It's a so-called safeguard built into the CPJCT rules. The captain is the ultimate authority while underway. It's almost impossible for the owner to fire a captain for actions that happen in the Deep Dark except under some very specific circumstances. So long as the ship violates no safety regulations, turns a profit, and delivers goods on time, my hands are tied." He looked angry. "According to the law, he wasn't derelict until he didn't assume the watch when Burnside had been injured. That was enough for me to relieve him on a 'Conduct Unbefitting' charge. There isn't a skipper in the fleet, nor a bureaucrat in the Joint Committee, that would argue with me. It's slim, but it's legal, and I can finally nail his worthless hide to a bulkhead without my own lawyers turning blue from hypoxia."

"I'm not following what this has to do with me, sar."

He shook his head and grimaced. "The *Tinker* has had such a bad reputation that I was never able to get anybody with the combination of savvy, strength, and charisma to be able to break through to the crew." He paused as if considering how much to tell me but continued, "I was in Port Newmar for the biennial meeting for the Subcommittee on Rules and while I was there, I went to visit Bob Giggone. I told him what I was up against and asked for a recommendation from one of his new crop of third mates. I needed somebody who'd think on his feet, stand by his word, and do what was needed. I wanted somebody who wouldn't go in with an axe to grind or a chip on his shoulder, and who wouldn't be the next victim on the hit parade. Bob recommended you." Maloney smiled. "I have to give him credit for knowing his graduates."

"Thank you, sar," I said.

He grinned. "Yes, well, getting you to Diurnia in time to catch the *Tinker* was pretty easy. Bill Lochlan is a crackerjack skipper and he managed to get us in a couple days early so you'd have time to get settled. I arranged to move Ms. Jaffee out of your way, and then left the wheels to turn."

"And set me up as a stalking-goat," I said.

Kurt's mouth twitched in amusement.

Maloney had the decency to look embarrassed. "Yes, that too. It was an act of desperation." He paused and looked at me. "You gave me what I needed, Mr. Wang. I'm only sorry that we didn't get it before Ms. Davies was injured. I had no idea they'd go so far. In hindsight, I should have anticipated that, I suppose," he said with a regretful sigh. "She's made a full recovery, by the way. We've kept her on full pay and we'll take care of her expenses. Nothing can pay for the pain she's been through, but we can try to make things better for her going forward."

"I'll tell the others, sar," I said.

"I'll have my private contact ID sent to *your* tablet as well, Mr. Wang. I owe you for helping me get that ship back. Please let me know any way that I can help you."

"Thank you, sar. I only did what needed doing."

He chuckled at that. "Up to and including restraining the owner and his body guard until you could ascertain his identity."

"You wouldn't have thanked me for letting somebody steal the *Tinker*, sar."

Kurt almost snorted at that one, and Maloney barked a laugh. "A stanyer ago, perhaps I would have, Mr. Wang." He looked back at the ship and said, "But not now. You had better get on with things here. I think Ms. Jaxton is becoming concerned."

I smiled. "She's a bit protective, sar."

He chuckled and as he turned to go I thought of something.

"Mr. Maloney?" I called. "There is one thing."

He stopped and turned back to me. "Yes, Mr. Wang?"

"Can you get me an introduction to a good tailor here on Diurnia?"

CHAPTER FORTY-NINE
DIURNIA ORBITAL: 2358-NOVEMBER-26

Say what you will about how boring it was to be underway, being
docked for a week was enough to drive us crazy. The watches were
long and really dull. I felt sorry for the brow watch standers. Those
people got to sit in the drafty lock for twelve stans at a time and
watch nothing happen. They got relieved for meals and head breaks
and that was about it. It was a good chance to study, but deadly
dull after the eighth or ninth one.

Our time in port was not all dull.

The first excitement involved cleaning the cabin. There was pre-
cious little that Rossett had left that was personal. Mel appointed
a couple of enginemen to help Arletta and I pack and ship what little there was. Bayless and Simon certainly knew their way around
the place and I sensed a certain satisfaction in the way they *almost* folded Rossett's clothing and jammed it into the grav trunks.
Arletta and I pretended not to notice when they discovered the
video archive. The captain apparently liked to keep a record of his
"interviews," and it's possible a few items were damaged in transit.

We never did find out what the captain had been doing in there
for week after week. I did discover that he had a huge personal
archive of books. Most of them seemed to be romance novels written
by the same author—Lenora Rossetti. I copied his entire library
out of the ship's system and burned the archive onto a permanent
medium. That all went into the grav trunk too.

It didn't take long to clear the stuff out of the cabin, and when
the four of us were done and the trunks locked for transport, we
got Ulla to organize a cleaning party. Fredi took some interest in
this part of the activity and was soon up to her armpits in soapy
water with the rest of them.

Two days after that, Mr. Maloney was back to announce the appointment of Captain Frederica DeGrut. It was a surprise to most of the crew, but I was pleased beyond all measure. She was a marvel. I followed her around just to watch her work with the crew. If she'd been an invisible entity before, now she was a glowing star.

One of the big surprises for me was Apones. I figured that once Fredi was made captain, he would be gone. She did something to him, though. I don't know exactly what. It had started with that very first watch when she'd made him change his shipsuit. She never raised her voice to him again, as far as I ever heard. But while he may have been Burnside's man before, he was Fredi's now. He was universally polite, wore a clean shipsuit all the time, and bounced to Fredi's beck and call. We were all a little leery, but Fredi appeared serenely unconcerned.

"He's a good boy who fell in with the wrong crowd," she told me one day when I asked. "He just needs a strong hand and high expectations."

Of course, once there was a captain in place, things moved a little more expeditiously. Fredi promoted Arletta to the first mate position and there was another party to clean out Burnside's space. Not as big as the cabin, it was still the largest of the staterooms and had a private bath. They dumped the loose clothing and miscellaneous personal effects into a grav trunk it and trundled it off to the DST office for disposition. Then the cleaning crew applied copious amounts of soap, water, disinfectants, and other cleaners to every surface.

Fredi and Arletta moved into their respective spaces and their old ones were cleaned. For some reason, nobody felt the need to fumigate those. A simple sweep and swab had been sufficient.

While we were docked, some of the crew took advantage of their new ratings to find better jobs, but there weren't as many as I had expected. Mallory was one of the first to leave which left room for Betts or Jaxton to move up. Fredi asked them to decide which one would get the new job, and Betts bowed to Jaxton's seniority. I thought he'd leave the ship to find his own slot, but he didn't.

When the dust had settled, we lost about five or six people, but that made room for some of our newer ratings to actually move up to their new pay grades.

More problematic was finding a new second mate to replace Arletta. There was not a plethora of qualified seconds floating around Diurnia, but within a couple days, they found a skinny drink of water with shocking red hair, feet the size of shuttle craft, and a sense of humor that was, frankly, disturbing. He went by the unlikely name of Chauncey Schott. It was inevitable that his nickname was "Long."

Eventually we got the personnel issues resolved, the crew roster filled, and a cargo lined up. I could already feel the ship beginning to come to life. I stood on the bridge waiting for the last in port backups to finish when the captain came up the ladder and we stood together looking aft out into the Deep Dark.

"It's a lovely sight, isn't it, Ishmael?" she asked.

"I haven't grown tired of it yet, Captain," I told her with a satisfied smile. "When I first started I thought I might."

I saw her smile in the faint reflection of the glass. Seeing her standing there, eyes gleaming in the light of the displays, serene in the mantle of captain, she was magnificent. I felt honored to be in her company and slipped a small bundle from the pocket of my shipsuit and offered it to her.

She looked at the small cloth package in my open palm and then at me. "What's this?"

"I think this belongs to you, Captain. I've been carrying it for a long time."

"What is it?" she asked, curiosity lighting her face.

I held my hand up closer to her. "Open it and see."

She lifted it delicately and examined the string and wrappings in the lowered light, holding it up and turning it this way and that. She looked at me and said, "Thank you."

"You don't yet know what it is," I said in chuckling protest.

Her face crinkled in a smile and she pulled the string that loosed the knot. She carefully unrolled the soft fabric from around the small figure within. I heard her breath catch as the glinting lights from the display gleamed off the polished wood and reflected on the bit of shell at the heart.

In her hand, an owl sat perched on a stylized limb, the lambent glow around us showing the delicately carved feathering and the graceful curves of the head and back. The talons gripped the wood, each toe articulated to show the power in that wooden grasp.

"A whelkie?" she asked.

"Yes, Captain."

"I've heard of them," she said, wonder in her voice as she turned it this way, catching the light. "I thought they were a myth."

I held up my dolphin. "No myth, Captain," I said.

Her eyes widened slightly at the smooth, oiled wood of the dolphin, and she glanced into my own and back to the dolphin, then back to her owl. "How...?" she asked.

"Long story, but the *Lois* visited St. Cloud while I was with her. I got these on that trip along with some others. I intended them as trade goods, but I was never able to sell them."

"This is worth a fortune, Ishmael," she said blinking in realization of what she held in her hand. "I can't possibly—"

"Do you know the story of whelkies, Captain?" I asked her.

"Story?" she asked.

"Legend has it that the whelkie finds the person who needs it," I said.

"Then what does it do?"

I shrugged. "I don't know. It's a kind of totem, perhaps a spirit guide. The shaman carves the spirit of the animal out of the wood and places the shell to give it heart. The deeper the purple of the shell, the more powerful the spirit."

My words sounded odd in that technological space. Two people surrounded by the flickering fire of display monitors and console repeaters, we stood in the eternal night of space, in a bubble of air held by fragile metal, glass, and composite shell. I felt a moment of almost dizziness as I realized that while the planet seemed huge when compared to the ship, they weren't that much different in size when compared to the vastness of the Deep Dark.

Both just pin-pricks of life.

Both equally fragile.

"Why me?" she asked at last, breaking the silence that held us together.

"I don't know," I answered. I felt the smile tugging my lips. "It just seemed right to me."

She gazed at it for a moment, and then looked at me. "Thank you, Ishmael," she said at last.

"You're welcome, Captain."

We stood there on the bridge, the moment passing. Reality edged back into the world around us. She carefully rewrapped the whelkie and tied it up again, slipping it into a pocket of her shipsuit. I just held my dolphin, as I had so often before. The smooth wood felt warm from my touch.

"Why did you decide to go to the academy?" she asked after a couple of ticks.

I snorted. "Alys Giggone is a very persuasive woman."

She chuckled a little at that. "Yes, she is, but still... why?"

"We had a saying on the *Lois McKendrick*. We used to say 'Trust Lois'. Whenever things went wrong, or right, or east or west, and we didn't know what to do, we'd say 'Trust Lois' and everybody would do what needed to be done. And by doing so we always pulled through."

"So, you applied that principle to going to the academy?"

"Yes, Captain. A lot of people thought I should go. People I respected. People I loved. They thought it was something that would be good for me, and even if I couldn't see it, I needed to 'Trust Lois.' So, off I went to the academy."

She looked at me for several heartbeats, weighing me with her gaze.

"You're a dangerous man, Ishmael Wang." she said at last. "A very dangerous man."

The Golden Age of the Solar Clipper

Quarter Share

Half Share

Full Share

Double Share

Captains Share

Owners Share

South Coast

Tanyth Fairport Adventures

Ravenwood

Zypherias Call

Awards

2011 Parsec Award Winner for Best Speculative Fiction
(Long Form) for *Owners Share*

2010 Parsec Award Winner for Best Speculative Fiction
(Long Form) for *Captains Share*

2009 Podiobooks Founders Choice Award for Captains Share

2009 Parsec Award Finalist for Best Speculative Fiction
(Long Form) for *Double Share*

2008 Podiobooks Founders Choice Award for *Double Share*

2008 Parsec Award Finalist for Best Speculative Fiction
(Long Form) for *Full Share*

2008 Parsec Award Finalist for Best Speculative Fiction
(Long Form) for *South Coast*

Contact

Website: nathanlowell.com
Twitter: twitter.com/nlowell
Email: nathan.lowell@gmail.com

About The Author

Nathan Lowell first entered the literary world by podcasting his novels. The Golden Age of the Solar Clipper grew from his life-long fascination with space opera and his own experiences shipboard in the United States Coast Guard. Unlike most works which focus on a larger-than-life hero, Nathan centers on the people behind the scenes—ordinary men and women trying to make a living in the depths of interstellar space. In his novels, there are no bug-eyed monsters, or galactic space battles, instead he paints a richly vivid and realistic world where the hero uses hard work and his own innate talents to improve his station and the lives of those of his community.

Dr. Nathan Lowell holds a Ph.D. in Educational Technology with specializations in Distance Education and Instructional Design. He also holds an M.A. in Educational Technology and a BS in Business Administration. He grew up on the south coast of Maine and is strongly rooted in the maritime heritage of the sea-farer. He served in the USCG from 1970 to 1975, seeing duty aboard a cutter on hurricane patrol in the North Atlantic and at a communications station in Kodiak, Alaska. He currently lives on the plains east of the Rocky Mountains with his wife and two daughters.

25545009R00173

Made in the USA
San Bernardino, CA
03 November 2015